MAGICAL MIDLIFE ROGUE

Also by K.F. Breene

LEVELING UP
Magical Midlife Madness
Magical Midlife Dating
Magical Midlife Invasion
Magical Midlife Love
Magical Midlife Meeting
Magical Midlife Challenge
Magical Midlife Alliance
Magical Midlife Flowers
Magical Midlife Battle
Magical Midlife Awakening
Magical Midlife Rescue
Magical Midlife Rogue

DELICIOUSLY DARK FAIRYTALES
A Ruin of Roses
A Throne of Ruin
A Kingdom of Ruin
A Queen of Ruin
A Cage of Crimson
A Cage of Kingdoms

DEMIGODS OF SAN FRANCISCO
Sin & Chocolate
Sin & Magic
Sin & Salvation
Sin & Spirit
Sin & Lightning
Sin & Surrender

SHADOWBOUND FAE
Obsidian
Diamond Dust

DEMON DAYS VAMPIRE NIGHTS WORLD
Born in Fire
Raised in Fire
Fused in Fire
Natural Witch
Natural Mage
Natural Dual-Mage
Warrior Fae Trapped
Warrior Fae Princess
Revealed in Fire
Mentored in Fire
Battle with Fire

MAGICAL MIDLIFE ROGUE

BY K.F. BREENE

CHAPTER 1

JESSIE

"**A**RE YOU SURE this is wise?" Kingsley asked over the cell phone loudspeaker. The phone was sitting on a particle board coffee table in front of a faded green couch with suspicious brown stains.

Austin slouched in a faux leather chair with glued-on patches. He rubbed the stubble on his face and hunched over, his eyes losing focus as he considered the implications.

"Sure, what choice do we have?" Niamh asked. She leaned against a tobacco yellow wall that had probably started out white a few decades ago. This was the best room available in this ramshackle motel on the outskirts of nowhere. Only a few wayward truckers stopped along this route, servicing a collection of towns that people were born in and then moved away from. At least, that's what the thriving shifter population would have Dicks and Janes think.

This tiny town was the last stop before the paved country road turned into a gravel lane that led into the deep woods. Haunted woods, if the urban legends could be believed. And of course, they couldn't.

In actuality, the woods were a buffer between the Dick world and a shifter territory run by one of the most ruthless original alphas anyone had heard of, an alpha so volatile he was said to kill visitors who looked at him crosswise. He cut down travelers that darkened his doorstep unannounced and populated the alpha rumor mill with threats about what would happen to anyone who even *thought* about coming for his territory, now nearly a decade old.

"He's had positive fitness reports from anyone who has checked out his territory," Austin said, dropping his arms to his knees and leaning over. "His people seem happy. The territory has grown and appears to be thriving."

I stood by the window, looking out at the lush green foliage on the other side of the road. The dense canopy of trees shifted and swayed in the wind, charged with electric energy in dark gray skies. Despite the threatening late-April storm, the air hung hot and heavy in a way I wasn't used to.

"This place doesn't have tornados, right?" I murmured.

"Of course not, miss," Mr. Tom told me, handing me a cup of what I could only assume was instant coffee. The town didn't give us a lot of options. "Someone would've warned us if we were traveling into Doppler doom."

"The people checking out the validity and safety of his pack have not been alphas nor necessarily powerful," Kingsley said. "He is wary of other alphas."

"He's wary of other alphas that want to take over his pack and cash in on his hard work," Niamh said. "Austin Steele does not."

"What does that mean, about the fitness reports?" I asked, turning from the window and heading to the couch.

"Miss, no!" Mr. Tom hollered.

I started to sit down and froze. Austin's head snapped up in alarm.

"What is it?" Kingsley asked through the phone, his voice louder now. He must've been leaning closer. "What happened?"

"Don't you dare sit on that horror show of a couch without something under you!" Mr. Tom admonished, bringing me a blanket. "Have you no self-preservation? It looks like people have bled out on that fabric. You'd be lucky to only get a staph infection. People have likely gotten gangrene from less. With a couch like that, one open wound and you're a goner."

I rolled my eyes but waited for him to drape the blanket on the couch, then plopped down as he half-shoved me on top of it.

"Ye nearly made me spill me tea, ya donkey," Niamh groused.

"Now *you* I wouldn't mind sitting on that couch," he countered. "I'll even give you the wound to get you started."

A knock sounded at the door, and Mr. Tom spun across the room to admit Tristan and Broken Sue.

"Tristan." Mr. Tom brought himself up to his full height. "I regret to inform you that I do not have any decent coffee, only the instant dredge we were able to procure from the Quickie Mart at our last stop."

"That'll be fine, Mr. Tom, thanks," Tristan replied.

"We'd need to be knocking down a wall to fit in all this muscle, like," Niamh murmured. "*Jaysus*, mind yer elbows."

Broken Sue glared at her as he passed by, taking my spot by the window.

Tristan looked down at the empty cushion next to me on the couch. "Got another blanket?"

"There. See?" Mr. Tom brought one over. "*He* has sense."

"More than I can say for ye," Niamh told Mr. Tom.

"Fitness reports are the shifter way of ensuring a pack is doing things properly," Austin told me. "Pack standing in the shifter world is a little like the gargoyle world. Any alpha who wants a place with their peers will be concerned about the wellbeing of their people. A thriving pack should be a nice place to live, with prospering businesses, safety for children, education—everything a well-run town boasts. To prove their pack has these things, and that they are an upstanding alpha in the community, they will allow others in the shifter community to check in on them."

"And that person types out a report?" I asked in confusion.

Austin hesitated. "Not a report, as such, but…"

"Gossip," Niamh said. "They go and have a gawk, and then they tell everyone."

"Allowing people in to see the territory is also a way to show off," Kingsley said. "With established packs, like mine, we would invite other prominent alphas to visit. When they did, we'd pull out all the stops, taking them to our best establishments and showing off our worth in various ways to prove we have a thriving pack."

"It's to measure their willies," Niamh drawled.

"Yes, fantastic. Crass language in the morning." Mr. Tom sniffed. "Maybe we should go find a dive bar for you to reside in, some place you'd fit in a little better."

"I already found one," Niamh replied. "Doesn't open for another hour."

Austin ignored them. "It is also to ensure the alpha is providing a safe space for the people. Remember the alpha we had to tear down?"

He was referring to a month or so ago when we'd tried to get Kingsley's friends on board with the convocation, and they'd had us take out a sad excuse of a man who'd been terrorizing a town. We'd dealt with him and his cohorts in short order, freeing the town of their influence.

Austin nodded, seeing my acknowledgement. "An original alpha who wants to rise in the ranks allows people, or *invites* people, into his or her territory to prove all of that. Prove he has the safe space, prove his territory is growing, show it thriving, things like that."

"And this alpha did that," I surmised.

"Yes," Austin said. "In the beginning of his pack, he invited people in twice a year, allowing that person or persons free rein to walk around and talk to the residents. For the last few years, it's been once a year, but his territory is said to be growing. His people are happy. He is a madman."

I shook my head, thought about leaning back, and caught Mr. Tom's glare. Best not.

"If he was a madman, his people wouldn't be happy," I said. "Obviously he's just posturing and putting on a show. People thought *you* were unhinged, Austin, and that's only because they didn't know you."

Kingsley snorted.

"Do ye hear her, like?" Niamh asked no one in particular. "He's still unhinged, girl. You just don't care because he's a big oul teddy bear with you." She paused for a moment. "But listen, she's right. He brought people in twice as often in the beginning for checks and balances. He was making sure he was doing things the right way. Not because of alpha ballyhoo, but because he wanted to do right by his people. We can all agree there."

"Can we?" Tristan asked. "That seems like a leap—"

"And now that he is somewhat established, he doesn't need as much governing. He's confident. He's secure. But he is still opening up his territory for inspection. That seems like a level-headed sort of bloke who's interested in the wellbeing of his people, that does. Now…" Niamh sucked her teeth for a moment. "Not relaxing the way he is perceived…that's another thing. Not caring about fitting in…"

Her voice drifted off. She was thinking. Working things out. She did that a lot now.

"There is a reason he has only invited in lesser powered shifters," Kingsley said. "That speaks of insecurity."

"I beg to differ, alpha," Broken Sue said respectfully, turning from the window. "This is possibly the difference in being a successful generational alpha and being an original. I was technically an original alpha. I challenged into my old pack, and I had zero standing or experience. Zero training. The people of the pack welcomed me—wanted me there—and I had lineage connecting me. My biological father had been loved. Even still, I had a great many dick-swinging alphas come in and try to take over."

"Oh, joy, everyone has descended into crass language," Mr. Tom muttered. "Well...I guess it fits the establishment."

"The challenges grew less," Broken Sue went on, "but they did not stop. Not until we started having mage problems. That pack had a lot of experienced enforcers with a thorough knowledge of the territory. The enforcers were essentially generational pack members. They greatly helped me. If this alpha has started this pack, in a new setting, then he might be trying to cut down the amount of work for him and his enforcers, and the danger to his pack. There is always going to be someone bigger and stronger, someone that might tear the pack away from him and jeopardize the people in it. I've seen many examples of it."

Niamh nodded, her eyes slightly narrowed in thought. "It's nice to see ya using what's between yer ears once in a while, boyo. Yes, that is the missing piece. The danger. Sure, Austin Steele, ye know yerself the sort of danger that waltzes into a new territory. Ye saw a lot of it in the early years in O'Briens, and that wasn't even an established pack. Ye weren't tryin' to do feck-all with the place. It was just a bunch of derelict shifters mixed in with Dicks and Janes. Then, after ye made it into something, ye saw all sorts trying to cause a hassle. This alpha is tryin' to protect his people. He can do that best with the rumors and the posturing and whatever else." She nodded to herself. "He's a good sort. We want him on our side."

"I agree with Tristan, I feel like we're jumping to conclusions rather quickly here," Kingsley said slowly. "Regardless of his motivation, he *is* in fact opposed to strong shifters within his territory. There is always someone bigger and stronger, as you said, and Austin might very well be that person. In nearly a decade, this alpha has always attacked first and asked questions later."

"Then let him attack," Tristan growled.

"You might have one or two who are bigger and stronger," Kingsley countered, "but they'll have a whole pack ready to protect their own. I've heard they are vicious and effective. People don't leave that territory with a heavy dose of fear for nothing, and *they* were invited."

"We were invited," Niamh said.

"You were admitted passage with strict rules, including greatly reduced numbers for a meeting of this type."

"Admitted passage after another original alpha told him about us," Niamh fired back. "Terence in L.A. arranged this meeting, let's not forget."

Terence was the alpha we'd met when I had visited my family for Christmas. He'd found us in his cafe and met us at his offices. He hadn't been able to join our convocation, but he hadn't dismissed us, either. He'd connected us to his sister and brother, both generational alphas, whom we hoped to meet in the coming months, and he was doing everything in his power to open lines of communication with other packs of interest. He was helping the best he could, and we were very lucky for the happenstance meeting.

"Terence in L.A. made the connection possible," Kingsley said. "The *connection* possible. Austin arranged the meeting, and even though we now have many reputable alphas who agree that the rumors surrounding Austin and Jessie's convocation are true, a great many people still do not believe it. This alpha might not know the power that's on his doorstep, but even if he does, hearing about it is very different than what walks through the door. You will be a threat, Austin, and this alpha does not take kindly to threats."

Tristan opened his mouth, and Broken Sue turned a bit to speak, but Austin held up his hand. The room fell silent, and even Mr. Tom stilled.

"I will be seen as a threat, yes," Austin said. "So will the mages. Kingsley is right to be concerned. This is an incredibly dangerous situation with an alpha that barely plays by the rules. He talked to me directly on the phone, which is not usual in these situations, even for him. From what I've heard, at any rate. He will have no problem burying us in the woods if we step out of line. He made that abundantly clear."

Austin rubbed his chin with his thumb, troubled.

"But the facts are," he finally said, "we need him. *Him* specifically. Terence is not thoroughly admitted into the original alpha network because his family pack is generational. His territory is new, but his roots are not. He had seed money, and he has help. He's considered 'privileged' in those circles and his opinions discounted. And while Kingsley has been invaluable and the alphas we've recently met are firmly behind this endeavor, they are not enough to sway the more entrenched generational alphas. Those alphas simply do not want to budge. Not yet. I will need to provide more assurances. In the meantime, I need power. There is no one stronger than Drex of the Stonefang pack. No one. He holds great sway with the up-and-coming alphas, and if he is half as ruthless as everyone says, he'll help bolster our team. He is a cornerstone. We must try."

"Like I said, what choice do we have?" Niamh finished her cup of tea. "He's a good sort. I have a hunch. We just have to keep from making bags of the situation and ending up in an unmarked grave."

"Sage advice, as always," Mr. Tom muttered.

"Will you take Jessie?" Kingsley asked.

Everyone glanced at the phone before their gazes turned to me. I didn't comment, because Austin knew exactly where I stood on this topic. There was no way in hell he could leave me behind to "protect" me. I was co-leader and part of this team, but also, if he died, there would *be* no protection for me. To defeat Momar, it would take both of us and all our team besides. This only worked if we did it together. *All* of it, including walking into a highly dangerous situation, outnumbered, to meet a volatile alpha shifter.

"Yes," he said grudgingly. "It turns out, she's a lot more stubborn than anyone gives her credit for."

CHAPTER 2

Two days later, I stood with Dave and the basajaunak just outside the motel. A few of our vans and SUVs had doors or trunks open, waiting for the last of our luggage to be loaded in.

"We should be going with you," Dave told me, and the rest of the basajaunak nodded or grunted their agreement. "Something doesn't feel right about the trees in this wood. The mountain is unsettled, and it doesn't seem to be regarding that pack. Something is wrong here, Jessie. You shouldn't go without us."

"The alphas specifically said you guys had to stay behind."

Butterflies filled my stomach as I looked out at the trees. I knew what he felt, a strange sort of *wrongness* about the area, though I couldn't put my finger on why. Maybe it was simply nerves about what was to come, or maybe it was something else.

"They won't be able to see us if we go on foot," he

pushed.

"Any decent shifter would feel your presence, or smell you, and Austin suspects there are a few of them in this pack. We agreed to their terms, and so we need to fulfill our end of the bargain."

"But…" He shook his head and looked at the ground. "If you get into trouble, and we stay here, we'll be too far away to help."

"I think that's the point."

The butterflies turned ravenous. It wasn't just Austin that might cause this alpha to balk. Or Broken Sue, who would go, or even Tristan. Nessa and Sebastian, our resident mages, would be going as well. Our numbers were greatly reduced, but he was giving entry to some of our biggest power players, people who could do damage from a distance.

Why would the alpha allow the mages but not Dave? Austin couldn't figure it out. Hollace was allowed, but not Cyra. Niamh and Mr. Tom, but not Edgar.

Although, if the alpha had heard how weird Edgar was, that made sense.

Indigo had to stay behind, which also made sense. If he planned to take us down, he wouldn't want our healer with us, but Fred got an invite. She was a Jane and couldn't get a reading on this pack via technology, reaching the conclusion that they were off grid. Magical people were fine living disconnected? A die-hard tech nerd, Fred was flabbergasted, so I told her to stay behind. She wasn't needed and this was dangerous.

Apparently, Fred disagreed because a few minutes earlier, I'd noticed her sneaking into the back of a van, and she wasn't overly stealthy about it, either. I considered yanking her back out and decided why bother? Waste of time. Niamh would sneak her back in and do a much better job concealing it. Better to know where Fred was, I decided, and look out for her than not know and have her do something surprising and stupid at the worst possible time.

Jasper and Ulric had gotten a pass to go, but no other gargoyles. Six shifters would be allowed, chosen by Austin. Everyone else was told to remain at the motel in case the alpha had someone watching them to make sure they stayed put.

We hadn't seen a soul all morning, not even the cleaning staff. The front desk was unmanned, and the sidewalk outside was deserted. Not all that uncommon, but there were no cars on the highway.

"You have to admit, the situation is odd," Hollace said, walking over. He wore his cream suit from the alpha meeting with a red square tucked in the front pocket. We would mostly follow shifter protocol until things got dangerous.

"More than odd," I murmured, scanning the trees. "Where the hell is everyone? The town is tiny and there hasn't been much activity the last couple days, but there has been *some*. It seems suspicious that the day we leave you guys behind is the day everyone disappears." Sweat beaded on my forehead. "What if it isn't us who is in danger at all, but you guys?"

"We are in no danger," Dave growled.

"He has a point," Hollace said. "Those shifters wouldn't leave the basajaunak here with a phoenix and then try to take them out. They'd divide us up better than that."

I shook my head as the rear doors closed, and shifters took their positions next to the vehicles they'd be traveling in. They were waiting for my crew.

I took Dave's hand and looked into his eyes. "You be careful, do you hear me? Stay safe. Keep everyone safe."

The other basajaunak pushed in closer. Phil was wearing his kilt, a construction vest, and hardhat. He put a large hand on my shoulder.

"I can sneak in if you need me to," he said. "I can blend in."

He didn't seem to realize that more than his clothes made him stand out. Normal people weren't ten feet tall and had hair all over their body.

"Thank you, but you stay here, okay? Don't let anyone follow us. They might get picked off before they get to us."

"This is the least fair thing of all the unfair things," Cyra said, walking up. "Even if they attempted to kill everyone, I can't die. It's safer for everyone if I go along."

"Which is precisely why you didn't get on the approved list," Hollace told her. Grinning, he sauntered to the nearest van. He was rubbing it in. Cyra pouted as she watched him go.

Niamh waited beside a beat-up Jeep with scratches along the sides. It was a rental, in the lot right beside a moving truck and three clean and polished passenger vans. We hadn't bothered with insurance.

"Well," Niamh said by way of hello. She insisted this peculiar setup had been staged for dramatics. I sincerely hoped her "hunch" was right.

"Miss, watery dredge posing as coffee for the road?" Mr. Tom stopped beside me with a thermos. "I do not understand a town without a coffee shop, but then I also do not understand a town with three morgues and scarcely as many people."

I frowned, gazing at the deserted highway leading into town. I hadn't noticed the morgues. That did seem odd.

Austin strode over. He wore a tailored suit jacket and slacks, a dress shirt unbuttoned at the neck, and a pair of loafers without socks. He hadn't bothered with a tie, cufflinks, or any bells and whistles. He expected to shift and so was keeping up a minimum pretense. Not like I was that much better. I wore a pretty but expendable flowing dress with a stretchy belt around my waist and slip-on shoes. I could shed this in a moment or tear my way out of it.

"Jess." He wrapped his fingers firmly around my upper arms and looked down into my eyes. "Stay safe, do you hear me? If the worst happens, you fly out of there. You slam them with magic, and you fly. Do not take any chances."

I smoothed my hand down his hard chest and soaked in those beautiful cobalt eyes. They were filled with concern and love, and they sparkled with unspeakable violence. My accidental pulse of magic felt like a call to arms.

"We're going to be okay." I was good at assurances by now. I should be. I said them often enough. "It's going to work out, you'll see. We'll be fine."

I wished I believed it. I had a bad feeling we were about to find out what was plaguing this mountain.

Austin walked around to the driver's side door and climbed in. I followed suit.

"Undo that seatbelt, Jess," he told me. "You might need to get out in a hurry."

And I *would* get out in a hurry if he hit a stump and I was ejected from the moving vehicle.

I did as he said. Sometimes it was not easy to override my Jane training.

Austin started forward, leading the procession.

"I forgot to tell Edgar to stay out of trouble," I murmured, watching the trees rush past. "Or say goodbye to Indigo."

"I did." Sebastian reached around the seat to pat my arm. "Indigo was worried, and Edgar gave me an odd smile and possibly a wink."

"Possibly a wink?"

"One of his eyes randomly closed, which also happens. I think he might be physically falling apart. Is that possible?"

Anything was possible with that vampire.

"I haven't felt any presences." Austin directed the Jeep into the center of the road, which had narrowed to a single lane. "If they were watching us back there, they were doing it at a distance."

"The gargoyles didn't see anything," Tristan said. "Though it would be easy to hide from them. I kept them confined to the skies above the motel. How much do you think this pack knows about us?"

"More than enough if they really wanted to." Austin braced one hand on the wheel and the other on his thigh, his eyes scanning our surroundings.

"A lot of those are rumors, right?" I asked. "As far as they are concerned, I mean."

"Rumors that have been backed up by many trustworthy sources. I guess it depends on what he's willing to believe. The more they know, the better. We aren't trying to hide anything."

I nodded, sending out a spell to see if anything waited in the woods. Small animals so far, out in the distance. Birds and things in the brush.

"But like…why allow Niamh and Mr. Tom, but not Edgar?"

"Maybe he has something against vampires?" Tristan replied. "They can be incredibly deadly when in their prime. Unpredictable and without loyalty. They are always a wild card. This alpha might not know our vampire is half senile."

"More than half," Sebastian muttered.

"Why my gargoyle crew but not any others?" I pushed. "Why not the usual team of gargoyles we bring to match the shifters. You'd think they'd want to know their story."

Austin shook his head. "Maybe he doesn't think it matters."

I bit my lip. "Which would insinuate he doesn't care about our setup, and he wasn't planning to join up anyway."

"Right," Austin growled. "In which case, why allow us in? He can't possibly think I would leave my growing and prosperous pack for his. That math just doesn't work out."

"Curiosity?" I offered. "He invited Hollace. He'll get to see a mythical, spectacular being that isn't as dangerous as a phoenix."

"Or maybe he wants to pit himself against the biggest, baddest alpha out there," Tristan said in a low tone. "He's wants to see who's the king of the mountain."

"Bingo," Austin said.

I sent out another spell to detect anyone lurking in the trees as we passed.

"Are you getting anything, Jessie?" Sebastian asked.

"Small animals, mostly. And birds."

"Yeah."

The sky boiled with clouds, but no storm had come. No rain, either. The dense wood cut down on the available light. The air was heavy and humid and rich with the scent of damp earth, pine, and wildflowers. The edge of a felled tree jutted out into the lane, forcing Austin to slow to go around.

Nothing of note interrupted my spell. Still, my gargoyle started to churn. I held out my hand to stop Austin but didn't give the command. The urge to go airborne suddenly gnawed at me.

"What is it?" Austin asked, working the Jeep around the log.

Using my gargoyle's connections, I checked on the people we'd left behind. I sensed worry and frustration, but no cause for alarm. Those in the vehicles behind us were watchful and alert.

"I'm still getting nothing," Sebastian said.

I shook my head. Me, too. Except this gnawing need…

"Stop," I finally said.

"What've you got?" Austin asked as Tristan leaned forward.

Nothing, that's what I had. Absolutely nothing. Except…

I looked at the sky as the Jeep idled. My hand reached for the seatbelt release before I remembered I wasn't wearing one.

"I've still got nothing," Sebastian said.

I released a breath. I was jumping at shadows.

"Yeah, I—" Two shapes appeared within my spell.

"I got something," Sebastian barked. "Three—no five—eigh—"

"A team, coming in fast in shifter form," I said, throwing open my door. "Highly organized, flanking us. At a distance right now but closing in." I counted them as I readied more spells in my mind. The grisly ones popped up first, but I discounted them. No one tended to walk away from those, and this might not be as bad as it seemed. "Nearly twenty-five—no, thirty in shifter form surrounding us."

"I count forty," Sebastian said.

Yeah, I did now, too. Or near enough.

Austin peeled out of his clothes, as did Tristan. I glanced back. My team had exited their vehicles and were readying for the attack.

My connections fired with emotions. "Everyone is wondering if they should shift," I told Austin. "The gargoyles are asking if they should go airborne."

So was I.

"Hold," Austin said as the resident shifters slunk in, closing the circle around us.

I rattled off their positions. Their uniformity was damned impressive.

"I got three more," I said, feeling them enter the spell. "On the road in front of us. Human form, one a little in front of the others. The welcome party, I'd wager."

"Some welcome," Tristan murmured.

Austin placed himself in the middle of the road, feet planted and shoulders squared. He'd shift at a moment's notice.

I didn't stand with him. This was a shifter matter, and my presence would only make him unbalanced. He'd place my protection above diplomacy, and things would escalate quickly. Besides, it would be Tristan who fired me into the air if this got underway in a hurry.

A man walked toward us, a hunk of muscle, brawn in spades. He looked like he was carved from rock, but he moved like a swimmer, fluid and with ease. His white-blond hair was pulled back into a tight ponytail, and I clocked him in his late twenties. Hard to tell at this distance. He was a smidge taller than Austin's six-two and slightly less robust. His muscled arms swung from wide shoulders, swishing against the fabric of his purple muumuu.

Wide-eyed, I glanced at Tristan. He didn't return the look, so I turned to Sebastian.

"That *cannot* be a coincidence," Sebastian whispered. "That is something Elliot Graves would wear in this situation to taunt an enemy."

Yes, it was.

A man and a woman flanked Mr. Muumuu. They were dressed in pristine suits, sparkly jewelry, and expensive shoes, and they looked every bit the part of one of these meetups, except for the location. They scanned our gathered people—those they could see—but Mr. Muumuu only had eyes for Austin. The alpha's beast moved behind those gray eyes, the color of wet stone, and power pulsed from him like a second heartbeat.

From some unseen or unheard cue, those gathered around us started to close the circle.

"Their timing with the alpha is perfect and precise," I murmured to Austin in a low voice.

CHAPTER 3
AUSTIN

THE SHIFTERS SURROUNDED us, he could feel it. Alpha Ashvale had built a team with a healthy amount of power and a very loose hold on their aggression. These enforcers were used to violence and defending their territory, and they'd do so brutally.

Normally, that would be great news. Now, as they tightened around his people and his mate, it set his beast to thrumming for action.

"Alpha Steele, I presume," Ashvale said, his voice a rough growl. He was showing Austin respect by calling him alpha, but his beast sparkled in those slate gray eyes. This man was having a hard time controlling his wild side, a sort of rolling darkness Austin was all too familiar with. Austin had honed and sharpened his darkness to a fine point, and this alpha was still using it as a blunt tool.

He stopped ten feet away, probably closer than he

wanted to, but too far for this to be a meeting of equals. Drex Ashvale would not be able to stand in his beast's way. There was no doubt in Austin's mind that the end of this meeting would result in a challenge. Jess was about to get some practice as a referee.

"Yes," Austin said, his own darkness rising in expectation. "And you must be Alpha Ashvale, original alpha of the Stonefang pack."

Drex inclined his head. "You have every bit as much power as I have heard, but ten times more control. It's a testament to your stature."

Again, showing respect, alluding to Austin being an alpha worthy of high praise. Too bad their damned animals had to make things difficult.

He inclined his head in thanks. "I must confess, I haven't heard a tremendous amount about you. What I have heard seems to be in line with your greeting."

Drex didn't balk at the small dig. "On purpose, yes. I wanted to see what manner of alpha you were. How you would react." He paused for a moment. "We were setup to ambush you"—he turned and pointed farther up the road—"just over the berm there. You stopped early. How'd you know?"

Austin was silent for a beat, holding that weighted, aggressive, challenging stare.

"That is a question for my mate. Have a care how

you speak to her," Austin said, his voice laced with warning. "I have no control when it pertains to her."

A rush of rage filled his bearing. He would burn down the world if anyone were to harm her, and it was imperative this alpha knew that. Ashvale's people would not be safe if she were harmed. No one would.

Subtle movements flared along the alpha's body. His head inclined slightly, almost imperceptibly. *Respect.*

"Understood," Drex said. At least he had the same values where it concerned mates.

"Jess," Austin said.

He felt her hand slip into his as she moved to his side. She was giving him comfort, though she did not understand the root of the hostility. She likely never would. It wasn't how she or her beast worked, fighting those you hoped to align with. She did, however, understand a threat to her people, and he could feel her swirling hostility and knew that she had a firm hold on her magic.

"Hello," she said to Drex. Her tone was pleasant and light, accommodating, like this wasn't a standoff and she wasn't prepared to splatter his people across the dirt. The woman was perfect for her role as leader. "I'm Jessie Ironheart. You can call me Jessie. You are wearing the Ivy House uniform."

As though pulled by a string, Drex's bunched muscles smoothed, and his posture loosened, releasing his tension. Whatever issues his beast had with Austin, they did not extend to Jess.

"I am," he said, less gruffly. "I like to keep abreast of the goings-on in the magical community, and I saw a random comment about the absurdity of your training outfits. I wondered if it bothered you."

He paused for a reaction and was rewarded with an entire conversation in body language. First, Jess turned to give Sebastian a *look*, probably pertaining to the comment about Elliot Graves wearing something like that to get a rise out of her, and then she turned back in utter confusion.

"It's a cover-up," she said, crinkling her nose at him. "What are they looking for, a tux? Who wastes their time commenting on stuff like that?"

Drex's eyes started to glitter. "True. And honestly, now that I am wearing one, I find it quite airy and nice."

"That's what our phoenix says," she responded, displeased. "She could've told you herself, but you made her stay at the motel."

Drex's eyebrows pulled together marginally, and his lips tightened. *Wariness.*

"Yes," he said, his tone even. "Given how we planned to test Alpha Steele, I had concerns about the more dangerous members of your pack—or convocation, if that is more apt. I now realize we still allowed you too much power for what we planned. I confess, I didn't believe the rumors regarding your reputed might. Not when slimmed down and in comparison to mine, I mean. I've put together a solid team. A powerful team, filled with honed and trained fighters. No one has ever topped their combined power. I knew, with a phoenix, basajaunak, and battle-hardened fliers, you'd give me a run for my money. I didn't think, in my wildest dreams, this slimmed down version of your *crew* would cause me to fear for my people."

He paused, and for the first time, let his gaze slip beyond the line to the team with them.

"I didn't believe the shifter beta was a past alpha," he admitted. "People tend to inflate a beta's ability when they are above average. His name didn't register—I assume it has been changed and the past forgotten? But yes, there he is, with power nearly equaling my own." He shook his head. "And the gargoyle, larger than life, with his shadows and his subtle challenges that most people won't engage in. He can plainly see that I am not one of those people. I have a feeling I'll only get such a challenge in a dark alley when we can fight dirty and no one will know."

Drex was certainly well informed. He'd gone past the rumors and done some serious research. Austin wondered what Niamh made of that.

His gaze came back to Jess. "I'll be frank with you, Jessie, because you seem like an honest person, given you are advertising your every thought. My first inclination is to be humbled, but I'm inspired. More so because Alpha Steele doesn't boast about his incredible power or the might of his team. He doesn't flaunt it, or swagger, even as I stand here, waiting to engage. There is no ego in his posture or smug pride in his people. He, and they, are calm, rational ruthlessness. This *wasn't* rumored. Not by anyone. People are too busy being wary about his wildness to take in his stoic efficiency, and that is a real shame."

Austin inclined his head again, accepting that great compliment with the pride for which it was meant. "Given what I've heard of your madness, that is all anyone sees in you, as well."

Drex's gaze slid back to Austin. "I've cultivated that persona, but yes, that is all they see. And that's fine. It serves our purposes here. But should I leave the safe seclusion of these woods, I'll use you as inspiration—as a model, perhaps—of a more dignified way of making people nervous."

Austin nearly laughed. "High praise, though probably misguided."

"Credit where credit is due, and yeah, probably. Doing things the traditional way is boring, as you seem to know." He hesitated. "I must know, did you really best the phoenix? I know you have one, and legends say you must dominate them to earn their loyalty but…that is a little farfetched, no?"

"I did. I had no choice. Jess called in the phoenix with her magic, but she didn't yet have enough power to take one on. There was no one else. It was kill the phoenix or get taken down by her and my mate along with me. Since then, Jess has fought her own battle with the phoenix and bested her."

"Something I never want to do again," Jess said, her hand still tucked into Austin's. "Though now I have some very serious spells that might make it a bit easier. Maybe."

Drex nodded and his power started to rise. The challenge would come soon. There would be no avoiding it.

"Please, Jessie, how did you know about our ambush?" Drex asked. He wanted the challenge, but he wanted information more. This alpha was highly intelligent. "I haven't heard of that kind of magic."

Jess tilted her head at him and then glanced back at Sebastian again. She was probably wondering what kind of shifter knew enough about magic to catalog spells. Even Austin didn't know what was, and what was not, possible. He left that to Jess.

"I have a lot of power, as does my mage friend. We *do* have the magic to suss out hidden figures. Many powerful mages do—most, in fact, I'd wager. When I got closer, I would've known you were there."

"But you didn't get closer."

"No, because I am also a gargoyle, and sometimes…" She glanced back the way they'd come. "I don't know, I just get a feeling. There's no explanation. I'd thought I was jumping at shadows there for a moment."

Drex assessed her for a long moment. A grin played at his lips, the first break in his alpha persona since they'd met.

"Very honest, indeed," he said. "I'd heard gargoyles were expressive. You don't disappoint. You'll find my pack is, too, when we allow ourselves to be. Please, Jessie, call me Drex." His grin fell away. "Listen, there is a reason we haven't allowed strong shifters into our fold, why the people who enter these woods without permission disappear. There is a reason we're hidden away. And there are *two* reasons we admitted your faction, but before we discuss that, we should resolve the present issue."

"The overuse of eloquent linguistics in mundane conversations?" she said, probably without thinking.

His smile grew and faltered, and his gaze swung back to Austin. Drex's beast nearly jumped out of his skin, and wildness swirled in his eyes.

"My people might not be able to pull us apart," Drex said, glancing at Brochan and Tristan. Everyone discounted Jess, even people who had apparently done their homework. Then again, shifters discounted mages in general. It was why shifters were in this situation in the first place.

"Remember how we've practiced monitoring challenges?" Austin asked Jess, loud enough for Drex to hear.

"Wait..." She yanked his hand on impulse, her magic pulsing at her sudden confusion and unease. "What do you mean? I thought we were all getting along fine. He complimented you. You're not here for his pack or his people or to push your weight around. Can't we address this like we did with Kingsley and his friends?"

He turned to face her. Leaning down into her space, he offered her confidence and comfort. "This is a shifter thing. His beast won't back down until he is forced to. It's built into him. Neither will mine. Even if he could control it, and I could ignore it, our situation will always have the push and pull of our beasts until we handle this. You need to mitigate it. Remember what we've gone over? Remember what you did for Aurora's challenge?"

Her brows knitted together, and determination steeled her expression. "I hate this."

"I know. But you knew this would happen eventually. When you need to break us apart, do it. Do not give a warning, and do not try to coach either of us out of the darkness. You break it apart, hard and brutal, and start healing immediately, okay?"

The breath left her in a gush. "I really hate this."

"I know." He squeezed her upper arms as Tristan and Brochan stepped closer. He lowered his voice, for their ears only, as Drex conferred with his people. "I have more power, but he has a lot of access to his beast. He'll lean in hard and lose himself quickly, but I won't be far behind. It'll probably be a grisly battle. Jess, remember what we talked about. You need to let it go long enough for there to be a victor but not unto death. This one might be close, and it is going to take all your power to tear us apart. You need to allow enough time to do that. Remember?"

Her power started to pump, blanketing the wood and everyone in it. The resident shifters all stiffened and looked over. Jess didn't notice. Her focus was on Austin. She stepped back without a word and shifted into her gargoyle. If she needed to get physical while she applied her magic, she'd be hardier in that form.

Austin turned and exploded into his polar bear form.

CHAPTER 4
SEBASTIAN

"ANYONE NEED A beer?" Niamh called, bringing out the ugliest cooler he'd seen in a while. It was a vintage model from the seventies and showing its age. From all appearances, it had been kicked around for decades.

"What do I do?" Sebastian asked in sudden panic as Drex handed his muumuu to the man at his side. There was a burst of light and heat, and Drex shifted into the largest Kodiak bear Sebastian had ever seen, slightly shorter than Austin's polar bear but more muscled, similar to their natural counterparts. Austin would be taller when on his hindlegs, but not enough to make a difference. This beast would give Austin trouble.

Laying a hand on Sebastian's shoulder, Broken Sue stepped to his side. "Stay close to Jessie, if you can," he told Sebastian. "Follow her lead. If she has trouble separating them with magic, jump in and help but do what you can to prevent her from physically engaging in the fight."

"I'm not going to be sucked in and have to fight her after this, am I?" he asked, allowing Broken Sue to herd him closer to the circle being formed by the resident pack. They'd all shifted into human form, dwarfed by the two huge bears.

"No, this is between the alphas."

Well, that was good news, at least.

"I'm Vessa, the beta of the Stonefang pack," the woman wearing a sleek pantsuit and large diamond earrings said from the other side of the circle. "I, with the help of Dan"—she nodded to the man in the tailored suit—"usually shift to help end the fight, often with help from others. We've never overseen a fight of this magnitude, however, or with powerful magical workers waiting in the wings. We don't wish to cause alarm by shifting or give the impression that we're attacking, but we need to provide the protection our alpha is accustomed to."

"Shift, if you like," Broken Sue growled, "but Jessie will handle it."

He didn't offer any other information or give the other beta further notice, a huge slight in the mage world. Then again, Broken Sue never really cared about such things or spared the feelings of anyone outside his circle.

Vessa looked at Dan for a silent beat before they disrobed and shifted into their respective animals, a cheetah and a timber wolf. No one else from their pack returned to their animals. Broken Sue and Tristan stayed as they were.

"Hey," Nessa said, bounding up with a beer. She sported a gleaming smile. Nothing ever phased her, even two massive animals with a crapload of power about to rumble on a dirt road in the middle of ass-crack nowhere where Sebastian would somehow have to keep Jessie out of the fight.

He'd get sucked into it, he knew he would. He always seemed to, somehow, and then he'd scream in front of all these strangers as Austin Steele barreled down on him. It wouldn't be the first time, and he vividly remembered the last.

"Want one?" Nessa indicated the beer. "Niamh is passing them out like party favors. Too bad Edgar isn't here to wrap it in a doily."

Sebastian grabbed Nessa's arm and threaded through the widening circle after Broken Sue. Jessie stood just behind Austin in her gargoyle form, waves of shimmering pinky-purple light shedding from her rough skin. Her wings were delicately tucked against her back, and none of the resident shifters could seem to avoid looking at her for long.

Broken Sue stopped beside Tristan, slightly behind Jessie. Power pumped within the circle. The positions of the observers were set and now it was the alphas' show.

"Why don't we ever see any hippos?" he mused as Tristan stepped back, ushering Sebastian on. "Or, like…a rhino?"

"Not you." Tristan put out his hand to stop Nessa, gently moving her behind him. "Stay put," he told her in a commanding voice. "This is going to get vicious, and we might need to move in a hurry."

"And what, you're going to trip me so that you can get away?" she asked teasingly.

"No," he replied, looking back at the alphas. "I'm going to throw you in their way. If you're going to do a job, do it right."

She grinned, but amazingly, did as he said. Sebastian would've liked to do the same, but instead, Broken Sue ushered him closer to Jessie. Jessie looked back, nodding comfortingly. She was in the thick of it and still giving him encouragement. There was really no end to her courage.

Power throbbed from the alphas; Sebastian could feel it. They circled each other, slow and methodical. Drex lowered his head a fraction, then launched at Austin. Austin didn't close the gap right away, instead angling right as Drex reached him and quickly rose to his hind legs. Drex had the drop on Austin now but not the right position.

Austin pushed to his hind legs in a burst of speed and power, his arms outstretched to grapple. He tackled Drex and latched on with his claws, ripping at the Kodiak with teeth and incredible aggression. The Kodiak barely flinched, instead hunkering on his rump and rolling, taking Austin with him.

"Solid move," Broken Sue murmured.

Austin went with it, flopping onto the ground and using his claws to rip at the bear. The Kodiak followed suit, the two of them biting and tearing at the other. Blood spilled across the ground and matted in Austin's white fur, darkening the brown of the Kodiak, but neither showed signs of pain. However, they must've felt it because Jessie started shedding light and magic in increasing waves, though the pulses did not balloon out. It was so subtle, that if Sebastian hadn't been standing right next to her, he wouldn't have felt it.

Austin untangled from the other bear and lumbered backwards. Drex stood and lunged at him, trying to smother Austin to the ground again. Austin was ready for him, though. He darted forward, flinging his huge body at the Kodiak's feet, and barreled through. Drex lost his balance and fell. Before he could get back up, Austin had twisted and pushed back with his powerful hind feet. It was a move only the sleeker polar bear could do, and he used it to his advantage. He gouged the Kodiak, opening a weeping gash along his side and then his stomach.

Still Drex showed zero pain. He growled angrily and forced his way up, shoving Austin off. He ran at Austin like a linebacker and Austin met him. They crashed together with such force that Sebastian took a step back. Austin growled as Drex tore into his side, then latched his teeth on Austin's neck; Austin struggled to find purchase with the angle.

Broken Sue didn't move a muscle, watching in silence, but Tristan tensed. That didn't look good for Austin.

Fear rose in Sebastian. He glanced at Jessie, unmoving, and then back at the fight.

Austin flagged, panting. He was pushed back a step, and another, scratching and biting but not doing enough to beat the other bear back. His paws slipped from their purchase on the bloodied fur, too low now, leaving an opening.

The Kodiak was experienced enough to take it. He leaned in for the kill shot, his great maw exposing sharp canines, stained red. Austin hesitated, not jerking out of the way as he should. Drex latched onto Austin's jugular.

"Jesus, Jessie," Sebastian said, stepping closer to her. All that Kodiak had to do was rip his head side to side and he'd take out Austin's throat, killing the alpha. Given the force and growls and animalistic movements, the Kodiak wasn't using a human brain now. He was reacting as his bear. Kill or be killed. "Should I—"

Broken Sue's hand gripped Sebastian's shoulder, and Sebastian raised his hands to help, but suddenly, Austin surged up, slamming the Kodiak to his back. Austin's throat was still in the other alpha's mouth, but he didn't seem to care. He bunched his lower half, using that dexterity, and ripped with all four claws, raking across the Kodiak's soft, vulnerable stomach.

A wave of power so intense it stole Sebastian's breath gushed from Jessie. She half ran, half flew into the circle, her magic acting as a wedge between the bears, covering the Kodiak's stomach so Austin couldn't do any more damage. Drex's jaws still gripped Austin, but off to the side now. There was no longer any danger he would rip out Austin's throat. Holy crap, that must've been planned by Austin, somehow. The Kodiak still held on, weaker now, his jaws slackening and his eyes starting to glaze. He was at the brink of death.

Broken Sue shoved Sebastian into the circle. "Keep them out."

Sebastian stumbled. The cheetah and wolf were

running in to help their alpha, and Jessie had rammed into Austin's side, using magic and force to roll him off the Kodiak.

"Keep them out—"

But he didn't get a chance. When he took another step, he slammed into a magical dome, and the shifters on the other side hit the same blockade. Magic fizzed and sparked, issuing an electric shock. It was enough to make Sebastian jerk away, but the other shifters rammed into it, trying to force their way through, ignoring the pain. When he'd concocted the thing, he should've known shifters would need a more powerful version.

He worked on that now as Jessie stuck her hand into the Kodiak's jaws, trying to free Austin from his grasp. Still, he tried to hold on, even as he faltered.

Austin scrambled to his feet faster than any large animal had a right to and spun to go for Drex again. Jessie blocked him. Pushing outward with her hands, she hit Austin with a spell that singed his fur black in places. The great beast stood on his hind legs and roared, his size dwarfing the little gargoyle blocking him.

Despite his size and ferocity, she did not falter. Then she shifted, and it was Jessie standing there. "Ease out of it now," she said in a coaxing voice. Her magic wafted peace and serenity across the onlookers. "Ease out of it. It's over. Find your way back to me."

The Kodiak lay on the ground. His panting was incredibly shallow, and it looked for all the world like he was dying. His shifters redoubled their efforts to get to him.

"No!" She half turned and shoved back at them. "Don't touch him. He cannot be moved. He is on the brink. I'm stitching him back together and keeping him still. Leave him be so I can handle—"

Austin roared again, angry and lost to his animal.

"Broken Sue, explain to them," Jessie commanded, and he started around the magical dome to the other side of the circle. "Tristan, monitor everyone else. Keep everyone calm. The power and aggression in this circle is preventing Austin from releasing his beast."

Tristan headed off to the other shifters in the resident pack.

"Come back to me," Jessie cooed, stepping closer to Austin. "Ease out of it."

The great bear spread out his paws, like he was about to lunge forward and wrap her in a bear hug, before huffing and dropping down to all fours. His nose was nearly level with her face, larger than his natural counterpart. He opened his mouth, revealing crimson teeth.

"Stop that." She laid her hand atop his nose. "Relax. It's over. I'm tired and stressed. Shift back."

He closed his mouth, huffed at her again, his breath lifting her hair, and then shook his whole body. Drops of blood flew everywhere.

She stepped back, and so did he. Light and heat blazed, and the polar bear was replaced by a man. Blood oozed down his right side and across his chest. His neck dribbled red, and he had a huge gash in his leg. Even still, he stepped forward in a rush and wrapped her in his arms. His mouth came down onto hers, giving her a hard, deep, victorious kiss.

"That is so hot," Nessa murmured from behind him.

"Gross," Sebastian said, looking away. "He's all bloody."

The tab popped on another can of beer. "Yeah, I'd be fine with that. Where is that gorilla?"

"This is just about to go pear-shaped," Niamh said, and a moment later, the basajaunak burst through the trees, roaring.

CHAPTER 5

JESSIE

I YANKED AWAY from my mate in surprise. I was out of breath from that kiss, and my gargoyle was urging me to drag Austin into the trees to celebrate his victory with our bodies.

A dozen basajaunak ran toward the resident shifters, their hackles raised and their teeth bared. They were going for blood.

The shifters exploded into their animals without hesitation. Their readiness spoke well of them, but it was not conducive to calming things down.

"No, no, no!" I pulled back from Austin's body and pivoted, throwing out my hands. "No, no! Don't attack!"

Broken Sue and Tristan exploded into their animals. Thankfully, they were with the resident shifters. I threw up a wall as I ran, and Sebastian caught up to me and helped.

Tristan slammed into Dave, who tried to wrestle the gargoyle-monster out of the way. Phil batted at Broken Sue's gorilla, but his arm was grabbed, and he was spun around. I ran into the fray. My wall shoved back as two basajaunak ran into it and tried to break through.

I hit them with a stinging spell. "Knock it off, it's done!" I bellowed, my voice amplified. "Stand *down!*"

Ulric and Jasper dropped down in front of *Her*, whose name she had yet to make up on the sly, and somersaulted in the air. *Her* knocked them away, making a beeline for the resident beta, somehow knowing that shifter had the most power of those still standing.

"Good God," I ground out, pointing at Drex. "Someone make sure he isn't moved or bothered."

I hit another basajaun with a spell, then another, and planted myself in front of the resident shifters.

"Would you *stop?*" I yelled, blasting another basajaun and sending him flying backwards.

Slowly—much too slowly—the scene calmed down. Tristan flew just out of reach of Dave with his hands in the air, claws glistening. Broken Sue had his thick gorilla arms wrapped around Phil's middle to keep him from joining the fray, and Ulric and Jasper picked themselves out of the dirt.

I put my hands out to the sides, exasperated. "What

in the hell is going on, guys?"

The basajaunak all looked around at each other. It was Dave who spoke up.

"The vampire said you'd need him and started off toward you. You tasked me with making sure no one followed you, so I figured I'd better follow him and try to stop him."

"I followed him"—Phil pointed at Dave—"because that seemed like the right thing to do."

"I followed Phil—"

"Okay, okay." I held up my hands.

"And then we heard a battle through the trees," Dave went on. "You had our connections closed, which meant you didn't want us to know about it. We figured you needed us, because you always do that when the odds are tough and you're afraid we'll get hurt."

"You do," *Her* agreed. "It's a big flaw. We've thought for some time that you should work on it."

"Do you like this guy?" Indigo called. She was standing beside Niamh, who'd brought over a fold-out chair and her cooler and was currently watching the prone alpha. "Niamh says you like this guy, and you want him healed, but Austin Steele looks banged up, and I'd rather help him if I have a choice."

"Oh." Phil scratched his chest. "And we brought Indigo because…well, she asked."

"Does this mean I can come out now?" Fred called from the roof of a van down the way.

"Why?" I said to myself, wilting. And then, because there were certain things you really didn't want to lose sight of, I looked skyward. "Where's Cyra?"

Everyone looked around. Ripping open the connections, I took stock of the situation. I spotted her and pointed. She was going to their homestead, I'd bet.

"*Onnn* it," Tristan said through his gargoyle teeth before blasting skyward.

The gargoyles, at least, had kinda followed directions, as had most of the shifters.

"Yes, heal him, please," I told Indigo, shooing the basajaunak away from the resident shifters. "I'll work on Austin." To the basajaunak I said, "It was a challenge between Austin and the other alpha, which is normal, and the connections were closed so that you didn't *overreact and come here when you shouldn't.*"

"Ah." Dave nodded. "Well, if you didn't have that terrible habit of cutting our connections when you're in grave danger, we wouldn't have been confused."

"True," *Her* said.

I shook my head, motioning them away. "Give these people some space. They've probably had enough by now." I turned to the beta, who was still in her animal form. "I'm really very sorry. I'm the weak link in this leadership outfit. We work great together in battle, and they do what I say, but outside of that…" I flared my arms. "I mean, we can't even form a straight line. It is what it is."

None of them shifted into their human forms, and I didn't blame them.

"The line thing is embarrassing," Phil said. "I heard about that."

I pointed at all of them, my face stern. "Back off. Go hang out in the trees and wait for us to put this to rights."

They complied, and I turned to the resident alpha. Neither the beta nor their shifters tried to stop me. Then again, they probably didn't want to incite the basajaunak again.

Indigo sat cross-legged beside Drex, her hand on his shoulder. I knelt by his side.

His eyes fluttered open, tightened from pain.

"Hey," I said softly, using my bedside manner. "You're going to be okay. I left the pain because I don't want you moving around. You need to lie still for a while longer so your wounds and broken bone can properly stitch, but if you promise to do that, Indigo can make you feel okay while you heal."

His eyes focused on mine before roaming over my face and landing on my lips. "Alpha Steele is incredibly lucky to have found an angel like you."

I gave him a smile. People always let their guards down when they were hurting and grateful to be healed…until sense crept back in. "Stay still, okay?" I said. "Indigo is going to take over from here."

Austin was standing near the Jeep, straight and broad and hurting like hell. How he looked so composed when he could barely stand, I would never know.

"Here you go, miss." Mr. Tom met me at the Jeep and held out a purple cloth. A muumuu, obviously. He wore one currently, having shifted at some point to help out.

"Thanks, Mr. Tom. Can you grab some water?"

"Of course." He turned back for the vans.

After I slipped on the muumuu, I assessed Austin with my magic. Gashes and teeth marks and a broken pinky. He had blood all over, carving out the cut muscle and glistening in the low light where it was still flowing.

I set to healing immediately, not yet stopping his pain. I wanted him to get comfortable first.

"Here we go." Mr. Tom laid a blanket beside the road on a tuft of grass before setting a water bottle on top of it. "Just what you need, miss, a little rest and some water to quench your thirst. Why don't you have a break while the other pack composes themselves."

Behind Austin's back, he made an arc with his hand

before pointing. "That is really for him," he mouthed, only it came out in a whisper, and he wasn't fooling anyone.

"Thanks, Mr. Tom." I put my hand on Austin's arm to direct him that way.

"Protocol says I should stay standing if I am able," Austin grunted.

"Protocol doesn't trump your mate asking you to please sit on the blanket with me while I rest for a moment. I've done a lot of magic, and I'm tired. I could use your company."

He issued a little smile before acquiescing. "If it pleases milady."

I let him painfully situate himself before sitting down next to him and slipping my hand in his. My touch helped him heal faster, and it also gave him a pass for lounging.

"I couldn't have stopped the fight any sooner, right?" I asked, looking at everyone else. The basajaunak were all lounging in the trees, mostly out of sight and content. The other pack was still clustered together in their animal forms, closer now to their alpha. The beta was watching over him. He lay as he had, his eyes closed. Tristan had flown back to the other gargoyles. Cyra was with him, and the rest of my crew were idle, waiting, except for Edgar, who was randomly wandering around in the woods for some reason.

"No," Austin replied, leaning a little harder into me.

He turned his head for a kiss, and I met his lips, falling in and losing myself for a moment. He pulled back and grunted. The pain was getting to him. I eased it a little, but just enough to make him comfortable. He clearly needed a reminder that he was a long way from being healed.

"You did perfectly. Exactly as we needed and better than anyone else could've." He smiled at me and then let his gaze roam toward the others. "That was a hard fight."

"The hardest ever?"

He huffed out a laugh and then winced. "It was just one guy. A tough guy, with a powerful beast, but still just one guy. A shifter guy, at that. The toughest ever might be Cyra…or it might be one of those hunting parties back in the day. Cyra certainly hurt worse." He took a deep breath. "No, Drex wasn't the hardest, by far. I wondered if he could take Brochan or Tristan, but now I don't think he could. He has the potential to be exceptional, but it hasn't yet been realized. He lacks experience. Hiding up here, for whatever reason, has stunted him. He's been out of the game for a while, and it shows. I didn't need to take so much damage, but I wanted to see his range. His kill shots. He had some good moves, but he couldn't tell when I was baiting him. Still, he's a damn powerful shifter with an inspiring drive to keep going at all costs, and his people showed courage in the face of half a dozen charging basajaunak."

"Yeah, I noticed you didn't bother running to help with that," I teased.

"I didn't want to be dragged behind one of them like Brochan." He laughed. "I wish I'd gotten a picture of that."

"So, you were testing him, baiting him, and then you nearly killed him to prove a point? Because I very nearly didn't get there in time. I don't think you realize how close it came."

"Yeah. That." Austin rubbed his thumb across the bottom of his lip. "I baited him, and he reacted a little better than I expected. He got too close to my jugular and…"

"The beast took over."

"The beast dragged me all the way in and swallowed me whole." He dropped his hand again. Love soaked through the bonds, and he looked at me with reverence in his eyes. "And only one person in the world can stand in front of me and use mere words to bring me back to the surface. To bring me back to her."

"Well…a spell that covered half of you in burns and

some words, sure."

He gave me a cute lopsided grin and shrugged before wincing.

"You know," he said thoughtfully, "Cyra might've been the hardest fight, certainly one-on-one, but she wasn't the most pain I've ever felt. That honor goes to the spell that closed off the cave where you met Dave. Do you remember? It burned off an entire layer of skin. Not blacking out was a miracle. I still have nightmares sometimes."

I did remember, and I *had* blacked out. I'd been out for a day or two while he'd gotten up and kept going. His pain tolerance was legendary, and the fact that it came from a hard life before this choked me up. Still, he was here now. It had all led to this. I said as much.

"Yes, and I'd do it all again to be sitting beside you right now, taking in this somewhat decent day in a desolate part of North Carolina while Edgar hides in the foliage staring at everyone."

"What?" I looked around and saw Edgar. He was standing in the middle of a bush with the leaves of a tree branch framing his upper half, doing just as Austin had said—staring at everyone, his gaze unblinking. It was incredibly creepy. "It must be a joke. There are levels to weirdness and that one just doesn't exist."

"He's created an entirely different plane of weirdness," Austin agreed.

"And for some reason, Drex thought he was as dangerous as Cyra." I shook my head slowly. "Joke is on him."

"Joke is on all of us."

CHAPTER 6
JESSIE

AN HOUR LATER, Indigo gave the all-clear to move Drex to his bed. His wounds had mostly healed, and there was no danger of them ripping open if he took it easy. He'd protested when she'd refused to let him walk until she'd released the binding, letting him feel the pain, and then he'd yielded to the stretcher.

Vessa, the beta, approached, wearing her suit and jewelry and a wary expression.

"Alphas," she said. Austin stood, and I joined him. "As you know, Alpha Ashvale will be detained for some time further. He would like to speak with you, however. We invite you and your pa—convocation to stay with us. All of them, the gargoyles and ba—" Her voice caught, and she cleared her throat. "Excuse me. The basajaunak, your remaining shifters. Everyone. We mean you no harm, and we believe you will honor your word and present no harm to our pack."

Her words ended in a pregnant pause.

"Listen, I'm really sorry about that basajaunak thing," I said. "They think of us as family, and they can get a little extreme when they believe their family is in trouble. But they're good now. They know to stay calm. They're lovely, honest, and nice to have at BBQs. Shifters, especially, generally love them—"

Austin touched the small of my back. Humor colored the bonds. I was babbling, and he thought it was funny.

My teeth clicked shut.

She cleared her throat again. "We'll have a cook-out this evening in your honor, and tomorrow, if Alpha Ashvale is well, we can go over some details he'd like you to know. However, we also understand if you'd rather stay at the motel."

"You have accommodation here for all of us?" Austin asked. "The basajaunak will likely prefer to stay outdoors, but we have a large party." He glanced around at the remote location.

"Yes, we have room," Vessa said. Again, with the pregnant pause.

I fidgeted. I didn't know what was expected, and I couldn't read her well enough to fill in the gaps. This was getting awkward.

"Forgive me," Vessa said, letting me off the hook.

"We are extending a lot of trust here, and ask, above all, for peace. Whatever surprises you find in our territory, they are benign. There is no danger to you, but we ask that you give Drex a chance to explain. After what we witnessed this morning, we are assured that our well-being is solely in your hands. We ask that you keep that in mind."

"I am in-*trigued*," Fred said from behind us in her scratchy voice. She'd sneaked closer without me realizing it.

I glanced back. She was sitting in the backseat of the Jeep with her phone in hand. Our eyes met, and she reddened.

"Niamh said I might as well come along," she said, "and that you wouldn't be mad about it, and even if you were, you'd get over it. And then all the Big Feet—Big Foots?" Her flush deepened. "Sorry, I'm not supposed to call them that even though that whole thing blew my *mind*! Anyway, they showed up, and now we're all welcome, so I figure I'm good, right? Except in the woods. I'll get lost in the woods almost immediately. Please don't leave me in there. I will definitely die."

I raised a brow at Austin.

"I heard her sneaking closer before I felt her," he explained. "I figured you'd find out eventually."

I gave Vessa a smile of apology that rode a sigh. "If

you can handle the oddness of my people, sure, we'd love to stay."

Vessa nodded and strode away, pausing to exchange a few words with Dan before walking on. According to Tristan, who'd checked in earlier, they had vehicles stashed half a mile up, and their town was a few miles beyond that.

"Tristan," I called as I folded the blanket.

"How dare you!" Mr. Tom admonished me, wrestling the blanket away. "You are the mistress of Ivy House and the co-leader of an important and prestigious convocation. You do not pick up a dirty blanket and fold it like some sort of washer woman."

"Yes, Mistress Ivy House?" Tristan said with a devilish smirk as he drew near.

I stared after Mr. Tom. "What does he have against washer women? Also, what decade does he think this is?"

"He's still looking for his golden ticket to the chocolate factory," Tristan supplied. "At least he won't be like Grampa Joe, who is bedridden, letting someone work and cook and clean for him, until he gets a chance to go to a coveted factory. Suddenly then he's the picture of health."

I narrowed my eyes at him. "I feel like you took that movie a little too personally."

"He cheated Charlie's mom out of that trip, and that woman was doing all the work! To hell with Grampa Joe," he groused.

"Agree." Nessa lifted a fist as she jogged by. "Good for nuthin'…"

"Okay, well, Grampa Joe aside"—I wiped my forehead free of perspiration, the humidity pretty intense—"get in the air and summon the gargoyles and shifters. We're all invited to spend the night."

"Aye, aye, mistress." He stripped off his muumuu and turned.

I shook my head. "Not him, too," I drew out.

Dan, their lead enforcer, was waiting to lead us to town in his beat-up Bronco, and we fell in line. Exiting the woods, we entered a small, thriving community that was vastly different from the depressing town at the bottom of the mountain. This settlement boasted cute walkways and cobblestone roads that wound through shops and cafes and little eateries.

Outside the main hub, modest houses dotted both sides of the street. Kids ran and played with abandon, and watchful residents slowed as our progression passed.

"They're wary of strangers," Austin remarked, earning a grunt of agreement from Broken Sue. "I'm wondering about these secrets of his."

Roads intersected and spiderwebbed, evidence of the town's growth and the builders' planning. About a mile in, we turned into a small cul-de-sac backed by the woods. The houses here, though smaller than some we'd passed, were cute and boasted flowers, porches, and rocking chairs.

"Remind me to tell Niamh that she is not allowed to throw rocks at people," I said, and then held up a finger. "Or start bar fights, assuming this place has a bar."

"If it doesn't, she'll probably take a trip down to the dive bar in the dead down," Austin replied.

That was probably true. It wouldn't take long with wings.

"I don't want to go," Sebastian quipped. "If she decides to go bar hoping, let me know so I can hide."

I grinned. He'd accompanied her on a mage-finding mission near Kingsley's territory. He'd been badgered and hadn't forgotten it. She no doubt remembered it, too, and would probably try to bring him along for sport.

Dan stopped and climbed from the SUV.

"Alphas," he said, striding up to the Jeep. "You have the option of taking a house here with your people, or we have a larger establishment nearer downtown. We don't have the wealth you're used to, but the furnishings are in good taste."

"Here is great, thank you," Austin said respectfully.

Dan nodded. "You are welcome to dine in any establishment downtown, the alpha's treat. If you would rather cook something yourself, you can find everything you need in one of the shops downtown. The alpha's treat, of course. You'll find the information for tonight in the houses. Please call the number listed with any questions."

We said goodbye to him and settled into one of the houses, along with Nessa and Sebastian, as we had in Kingsley's territory. No one here had expressed any animosity toward the mages, but it was better to err on the side of caution.

Mr. Tom was not amused.

"I call bottom!" Nessa shouted, checking out the bedroom. There were only two, and one had a bunkbed.

"You always call bottom, and I always let you, and then I *always* fall out of the top bunk," Sebastian groaned, lugging in his suitcase.

"Yes." Nessa appeared at the end of the hall. "And I *always* laugh."

He frowned at her but didn't complain, dragging his suitcase that way.

"Yes, sir, we all know you like your independence," Mr. Tom told Austin, who was handling his own luggage and mine, "but you are still healing. You really do need to focus a little more on the important things. Moonlighting as a bellboy is not one of them. This is beyond the pale."

Nessa stopped in the hallway and pointed at Austin. "I am famished. Are you well enough for me to spank you in a cooking competition or shall I just make you the best dish you've ever tasted in your life?"

Austin smirked, and then laughed, stopping to put down the bags.

"Finally." Mr. Tom scoffed at him before collecting the bags and starting down the hall, grumbling to himself.

"I'm plenty fine to whip up something," Austin said, "as long as it is Jess's favorite. She's pulling double duty with healing right now."

"It's fine." I waved it away, but yes, I was tired. I needed a little relaxation time.

"You're on!" Nessa paused and then switched her point to me. "What is your favorite?"

CHAPTER 7
SEBASTIAN

AUSTIN PARALLEL PARKED on the cutest street in the history of the world. Sebastian loved the pop of color from the flower boxes and the hanging vines in the shop entryways. The cobblestones were so clean the street looked like a movie set, and there was not one piece of trash on the slightly raised wooden walkways. It was clear these people put a lot of care and diligence, not to mention pride, into their town.

The grocery store sign jutted out from a red awning, the letters glowing faintly in the dim noon sun.

"I wish it would storm or not, you know?" Nessa said, climbing out of the Jeep and peering at the sky. "It's gloomy."

"Yeah." Austin closed his door after he'd stepped out. "We should really put the top back on the Jeep. I wonder if there is a way for the gargoyles to fly it in."

He wasn't totally healed, but Jessie had given him

the go-ahead to trek into town and buy some things for their lunch. He didn't want to leave his ingredient picking to Nessa. Jessie could, and was, continuing to heal him from a distance. Tristan had offered to stay behind with her, freeing up Broken Sue to follow Niamh and make sure she didn't get into any trouble. Broken Sue would have his work cut out for him on that score.

"Are we making the dish how we think it's best," Austin asked, "or getting the exact same ingredients and going from there?"

Nessa twisted her lips to the side. "How we think it's best. Should I bake something, too? She might need some chocolate after today. Tristan would like that, too."

"Since when do you care what Tristan would like?" Sebastian asked innocently.

He didn't miss her slight flush as she shrugged. "He's fun to taunt and chocolate makes taunting him easy."

Sebastian smirked. She was finding a fun and intoxicating game in that gargoyle-monster, but more importantly, all the teasing and taunting and forced proximity was starting to break down her shields, little by little. She was letting her cracks show, and Tristan was paying attention. Maybe he'd finally be the one to get her to let down her guard and trust. Sebastian sincerely hoped so. High time she was taken care of for once, by someone who would know how, someone who could protect her better than Sebastian had ever been able to. Someone who would guard her heart as well as her person.

Lost in his reverie, it took him a moment to recognize the crawling sensation. A watcher, and not one that evoked a primal response, like a powerful shifter or gargoyle. This one was the result of intense focus—someone assessing or analyzing him. It was a feeling he'd grown incredibly used to whenever he'd played the Elliot Graves role. It was a mage.

A flash of adrenaline heightened his senses, but he didn't look around. Muscle memory kicked in, not as Elliot Graves, but as a guy who didn't want to be mistaken for his other persona. He hunched and ran his fingers through his hair. His clothes were already creased and mussed, so he put his watch hand into his pocket as he followed Nessa and Austin down the wooden walkway.

Nessa picked up on the change in him immediately.

"Where?" she asked out of the side of her mouth, and then she started laughing to detract from the seriousness of the situation. She didn't have any makeup on, thankfully. Her clothes were wrinkled, almost frumpy, and her hair was in a ponytail. She wasn't dressed like the Captain right now.

"Somewhere to the right," he replied, barely moving his lips.

Austin picked up on the situation and tensed, then shook it off, controlling his bearing like Sebastian and Nessa.

"Oh, Austin." Nessa put her hand on his elbow and steered him past the grocery store to a little cooking and appliance shop beyond. "Have you seen one of these?" She pointed, stopping at the window. "I've been meaning to get one of these pots—wait, is it this one?"

Sebastian hunched even more and assumed an attitude of boredom, glancing to the right. He spotted the woman immediately. She was standing on the walkway on the other side of the street, and she'd stopped dead, facing him, her body stiff. Frizzy brown hair framed her round face, and thick, black-rimmed glasses sat atop her small nose. She wore a flowing black top tucked into a brownish-paisley skirt and lacking any sort of style.

It was her hands that caught his attention. She held them in front of her *just so*, out and bent, ready to do magic.

As he watched from under his lashes, the pad of her pointer finger reflexively grazed her bare wrist. She wasn't wearing a watch at present, but she was used to one. Or had been, at any rate. She was currently feeling its absence, which meant he reminded her of it.

"What is it?" Nessa asked as she leaned closer to the glass, hand still on Austin's elbow.

He shuffled a little closer to her and kept his voice low, pretending to be absorbed by the window display.

"A mage," he murmured, leaning against the wall and facing Nessa. You did not turn your back on a mage you didn't know. Hell, if you had any sense, you didn't turn your back on a mage you *did* know. That was a fast way to get killed.

"Why the hell is a mage here?" Nessa said in a calm voice, but Sebastian knew she was already thinking of ways to fight back and escape. They'd been in this situation more than a time or two, except not with friendlies. Not with shifters and gargoyles and Jessie.

"I don't know," he replied as she straightened again.

"This would explain why Drex wondered about a particular spell earlier," Austin murmured, turning for the grocery store.

"Yeah," Sebastian said, remembering that comment.

"Why wouldn't they tell us outright, given our history?" Nessa asked, taking his cue and heading that way.

Sebastian used their movement as a distraction to get a good look at the woman. Would he recognize her? He knew all the big players, especially those in the

Guild, and especially anyone dangerous.

They made eye contact, and she tensed.

"Take cover—" he began as she shot a spell straight for him.

He dove to the side, already erecting a shield. He shot a spell back, but she was already on the move, dodging behind a parked car. Crap, she was quick.

"Don't hurt her," Austin said, yanking him off the sidewalk by the scruff of his neck and dragging him toward a parked car on their side.

"But she fired magic at us," Sebastian said, poking his head around one end of the car.

He could just make her out. She was on the other side of the street, framed by the window of the car she'd taken cover behind. She popped up and lifted her hands to throw another spell at them over the roof of the car.

"She *keeps* firing magic at us," Sebastian said, erecting a magical barrier to catch the spell and determine its power.

Before she could fire the spell, however, a gargoyle rushed up behind her and caught her wrists in the air, forcing them down by her sides. Dangerous move—a mage of Sebastian's caliber could still do magic like that, but the gargoyle clearly didn't care.

Another gargoyle rushed to the first ones aid. The woman screamed and thrashed, trying to free herself, but gargoyles had tough hides, and she didn't have the power to stop them.

"Okay, we're good." Breathing heavily, Sebastian rose from behind the car.

Another blast of magic shot at them from the right, down the street.

"What in the hell, man?" Sebastian hollered, spinning to return fire.

Except Austin shoved him before he could release the spell, and Sebastian's spell went wide, hitting the wall, and sending him tumbling into the unforgiving metal of the car.

A swarm of insects turned into Edgar right behind a gangly man with a bad comb-over. The man still had his arms up, ready to do another spell. Edgar grabbed him by the shoulders and clamped his teeth onto Comb-Over's neck. A gargoyle in human form came running. He'd clearly seen the commotion but had been stationed farther down.

He wouldn't be needed. The serum in Edgar's bite worked quickly, putting Comb-Over to sleep. Edgar dropped him to the ground.

The sound of heavy wings drowned out the yelling and screaming from the town's residents. The town's shifters turned into animals and two people jogged into the street, their hands raised to do magic.

A surge of magic rolled down the street, a warning that stung but was not terribly painful. The thunder of wings grew louder, and Tristan descended, carrying Jessie in gargoyle form.

Flexing her claws, she sent another heavy blast of magic at the shifters running toward them, and they bent.

A plethora of gargoyles flew from all directions, joining Tristan and hovering about ten feet above the street.

Larger animals ran in now, these in perfect synchrony. They formed a half circle on either side of the street before slowing and finally stopping, blocking Jessie's people in and their people out.

That was, until the basajaunak joined the party.

"Oh, crap." Sebastian scurried toward the wall and ducked down. He did not plan to handle this. He was quickly joined by Nessa.

"Whoa, whoa, whoa." Austin stalked into the street and put out his hands. The resident shifters scattered to the sides of the street. Unlike earlier that day, this time they did not plan to stand their ground. They'd let Jessie and Austin handle it.

"Wise," Nessa said, clearly thinking along the same lines.

Tristan let go of Jessie, and she flew to the ground

before shifting into her human form.

"Stop, stop, stop." She flung out magic to slow the rampaging basajaunak before they reached the local shifters. "We're not supposed to kill. I felt all the conflicting emotions. What's going on?"

CHAPTER 8

JESSIE

I T TOOK AUSTIN very little time to relay the details, mostly because there weren't many. He didn't seem worried that we were in danger and given the one mage held by the gargoyles had relaxed, and the others hadn't engaged, I assumed he was right.

"She attacked first?" I looked over at Sebastian as he entered the street.

"Yes," he replied. "She spied me soon after we got here, watched us for a while, and when I fully looked up at her, she attacked. Then the other guy attacked before Edgar bit him."

I vibrated with anger. What the hell? Not only did they have mages—surprise, indeed—but those mages attacked us?

We kindly ask that you give Drex a chance to explain, Vessa had said. *After what we witnessed this morning, we are assured that our well-being is solely in your hands. We ask that you keep that in mind.*

"Power level?" I asked as car tires squealed at the end of the street.

"I can't be sure, but it appears not enough to do magic without using her hands," he answered.

Smoke curled up as a red sedan slid around the corner. Everyone turned and braced as it sped toward us. The basajaunak's hair puffed out and then they stepped forward until I held out my hand to stop them.

"And the guy down the street?" I asked, watching the car while simultaneously readying to cast and dive, if necessary, because I wasn't nearly powerful enough to explode a car off the street.

"Didn't seem strong. The two mages that ran out to help didn't have the poise and arrogance of top tier mages. I'm not sure we need to be worried, but I also know next to nothing about them other than a snap judgment."

"They didn't attack and run, though," I mused. The car started to slow at twenty feet away. Austin put his hand on my shoulder, probably getting ready to hustle me out of the way. "They kept attacking. Their friends came to attack."

"Yeah," Sebastian replied. "They aren't cowards, but then, they might not have known they were out-gunned."

I shook my head in frustration as the driver door flew open and Vessa got out of the vehicle. She visibly slowed as she took in the scene, pausing on the woman being held by the gargoyles and then her people huddling to the sides, having run from the basajaunak.

I didn't give her a chance to speak. "You thought it was somehow a good idea *not* to tell us that you had mages in this town?" I walked closer, and Austin kept pace with me. "Drex knew a lot about us, and so I assume he knew we've had some run-ins with mages. And yet you thought springing them on us, having them *attack* us, was the best idea?"

"He wanted to explain *why* the mages are here," she replied, stopping in front of us. "He thought he'd be able to do that after the challenge. He hadn't realized he'd be incapacitated to this degree." She shook her head, her gaze direct and apologetic. "I don't know why they attacked. Please, give me a moment to find out what is going on. They're skittish, these mages. They've had run-ins of their own. Drex will explain when he's able."

I put out my hand to keep her put. "You need to understand something. Your people are *incredibly* lucky Austin was here to stop Sebastian from killing that woman and the guy down the street. Austin was acting in good faith with your alpha and had the presence of mind to read the scene. If it had been anyone else, including me, you might have *several* dead townspeople right now, not just a couple mages. Keeping us in the dark is about the stupidest thing you can possibly do. You have no idea how incredibly dangerous we really are."

I lowered my hand but kept my stare levelled on hers. I'd *love* to ring her bell right now, all their bells. I was tired and out of patience and energy. What sort of absolute moron would start a fight with us? Had they not heard about the basajaunak?

I gestured at the gargoyles holding the woman, while simultaneously daring the beta to challenge my authority. "Bring that mage over here. Let's settle this right now."

She dropped her gaze from mine in submission, a gesture that would probably make a shifter feel power-ful, but I was just annoyed.

The woman's brown eyes were wide with fear, and her gaze was rooted on Sebastian. As she neared us, her gaze flicked to Nessa, then back to Sebastian. Trem-bling, she tried to shrink away from Sebastian.

"Why'd you attack?" I asked without preamble.

Her gaze swung to me and darted back to Sebastian. "Do you know who that is? He might look disheveled and dorky now, but that's all an act! You've got a snake in your bed. That is Elliot Graves, and the moment you turn around, he'll kill you."

"Ah." The breath gushed out of me.

She struggled in the gargoyle's hold.

"I will not go quietly!" she gritted out. "I will die before I work for him *or* them, but that doesn't mean I'm going to tell you anything. I will not succumb to whatever it is you plan to do to me."

I put my hands on my hips, glancing at Sebastian with raised eyebrows.

He shrugged. "I don't remember her face. Maybe a name would help?"

"Is she correct?" Vessa asked, her gaze wary. We were giving her a lot of nightmares with our visit.

I couldn't admit who Sebastian was, not in front of all these people. Some, no doubt, filming this whole interaction on their phones through the shop windows. And even if the service up here was lousy, that didn't mean they wouldn't spread the word. It wasn't time to tell the world that Elliot Graves and the Captain were our mysterious mage helpers, even though Momar probably knew already. He hadn't told the mage community at large, so Niamh said we shouldn't either. Not yet.

The problem was, I was bad at lying, especially to shifters. Anyway, I suspected they already knew the answer, considering Sebastian had essentially spoken on Elliot Graves's behalf.

I sighed. "Look, I guess we've all got some secrets we need to chat about. *If you stop attacking us* you won't be in any danger. Otherwise, I'll let the basajaunak loose."

Vessa's expression smoothed to hide her emotion. "Understood."

"We'll be keeping to ourselves this evening," Austin said in a hard tone. "We can postpone the dinner until tomorrow or not at all. I think it's best for all involved if we keep to our own devices. We might have one or two of ours in town, but they'll know to keep their heads down, and they won't be mages. If they experience any trouble, they'll handle it brutally. You're warned."

"Yes, alpha," Vessa said crisply. "I apologize for this lapse in etiquette."

Austin put his hand on my shoulder, steering me away. "Nessa and I still need to get groceries and now organize dinner for everyone tonight. I want to give some orders, as well. Why don't you go back to the house with Tristan, and I'll meet you there shortly."

I glanced around the street and then the sky, getting an idea of numbers. Austin would be fine. If something happened, he wouldn't need my help. This town didn't have the sort of fighting prowess they thought they did, at least not compared to us.

I nodded and shifted back into my gargoyle, fatigue dragging at me. All the fighting, healing, stress, and shifting was wearing me down. Staying in tonight and relaxing was a dream come true.

✦ ✦ ✦

AUSTIN

"Tristan," Austin called, then waited for the gargoyle to drop lower in the sky. Jessie paused when he spoke. "Take Sebastian with you."

Sebastian nodded in understanding and walked away from Nessa, putting up his hands like a child. Tristan swooped down and grabbed him, flying a little too closely to Nessa and dusting her with the upswing of his wing.

She jerked back and wiped at her face. "Really?" she said in irritation. "Keep it up and I won't make you any brownies."

He blasted into the sky, trailing Sebastian's scream behind him.

"C'mon," Austin told Nessa, not sparing another moment for that beta. She probably did not look forward to relaying all this to her alpha. One thing Austin understood, however, was the frustration of wild cards. He had a great many in his setup, and clearly this alpha did, too.

"How did you know those mages weren't dangerous?" Nessa asked as they walked back to the grocery store.

He slowed to allow her to enter first. "The woman was practically screeching with fear as she cast her spells."

"Her body language?"

"Yes. She clearly thought she had no other choice and didn't think much of her odds. If the beta hadn't requested we stand down and acknowledged that we had the upper-hand power-wise, I would've let Sebastian handle it. As it was…"

"And the other mage?"

"I caught sight of Edgar loitering near a flowerpot down the way. By the time Sebastian was readying magic, Edgar was nearly to the mage. I figured he'd handle it. I did not know how, and really hoped it wouldn't be fatal, but there wasn't much I could do at that point."

"Huh." She grabbed a small shopping cart. "That was a lot of very fast deduction followed by excellent decision-making."

"And that is why I am an alpha."

"It seems so." She led the way, starting at the aisle to the far right. The other patrons made themselves scarce, leaving the way clear.

She collected a few ingredients, her mood obviously pensive, and he followed in silence. Halfway through the store, she took out her phone and looked at the screen.

"Zero service," she murmured, slipping it back into her pocket. She chewed on her lip. "There are not a lot of high-profile female mages."

"Oh?" He pointed at a box of brownie mix and raised an eyebrow.

Her expression soured. "How dare you," she said, mimicking Mr. Tom. "I do not make things from a box. What do you take me for? Oh! We should get some good coffee. Mr. Tom brought his French press."

They turned toward the next aisle.

"I should say there *weren't* a lot of high-profile female mages," she amended. "In the Guild there still aren't. Much like the Dick world, where there aren't nearly as many female CEOs and VPs and all that, the Guild tends to elevate men. There is a lot of misogyny." She chewed her lip again and put a couple more items into the cart. "The females that do get elevated tend to be tough and great at their trade."

"Their trade?"

"Yeah. If a mage is lower powered, they still have options. They can excel in certain types of magic. If

Sebastian was a lower powered mage, for example, he could still get placement in engineering new spells and potions. He's a genius at it. I could get placement at the admin level, organizing teams for extractions or attacks or whatever else."

"What does that have to do with high profile female mages?"

She glanced around. "Let's finish up."

He nodded without comment and did just that, grabbing enough for a few meals, including something for breakfast tomorrow. If they needed more, someone could be sent to grab it. He did not sense any danger in this place, not at all. Despite the mage attack, this felt like a sleepy town. A forgotten town. The residents seemed fragile, almost, like they'd had a hard time of it and could finally take a peaceful breath. It was in the way they carried themselves before and after they spotted strangers in their midst.

O'Briens had felt like this in the beginning of his time there, right after he'd made his stand and backed up his claims to provide safety for those who needed it. Drex had created a force of fighters to secure this place, and he was doing so ruthlessly, like Austin had.

"Alpha Ashvale would be happy to pick up the tab," the store clerk said after scanning all the items.

"Give him my thanks," Austin replied.

"And I'm sure someone could deliver food from the restaurants in town, if you like. The fried chicken here is the best you'll have."

"I thank you." Austin inclined his head and wheeled the cart out.

It wasn't until they were underway that Nessa continued. "The Guild still doesn't make a habit of elevating female mages, but Momar does. He used a lot of them at Kingsley's, and he did so marvelously. Did you notice she said she wouldn't work for him *or* them?"

"Momar or the Guild," he surmised.

"Who else. Momar tries to poach only the most valuable players, and she doesn't have enough magic to be desired by the big dogs in the Guild, so she must have some other trait that makes her valuable. Very valuable if she's this worried about it. She seemed afraid she'd be dragged back and forced to work."

Austin didn't bother asking if they really did that. From what he knew of each of those organizations, they'd do that and worse. Much worse.

"And she knows Elliot Graves," he said, driving through downtown and finding two bars. Both were welcoming, but one was a littler rougher than the other, with a lone smoker outside. That's where they'd find Niamh.

He looked for a parking spot.

"She does," Nessa drew out, her eyes far away. She wasn't just good at organizing; she was incredibly intelligent and great at problem solving. "She knows him even though *I'd* hardly know him when he's looking like this. He is only ever Sebastian when he's with family. In a professional setting, he is always Elliot Graves. *Always.* That includes dress, hair, posture, everything."

"She didn't know him at first. She suspected, but she wasn't sure. She was trying to figure it out."

"She suspected. That's more than anyone else in the mage world would have, not in this setting." She shook her head and looked out at nothing, back to chewing her lip.

"Momar found you guys, and he has people in the Guild. He must know your connection to us. Niamh is sure he does, even if he doesn't advertise it. Is she still working for them? Or maybe was until a month or so ago?"

She shook her head slowly. "With her hair like that? Her clothes? No watch? Nah. She's been away from that long enough to shake off the training." She switched, chewing her nail this time.

A car was leaving a spot. He waited and then took it, two spaces down from the bar. He turned off the Jeep and sat for a moment.

"I'm going to have a quick chat with Niamh," he said. "She's good at information gathering. I honestly don't think anything will happen to you if you stay in the car, nor do I think people will steal our groceries, but it doesn't hurt to be cautious. I'd rather leave you here to guard the groceries than have to guard you inside."

She spit out a laugh.

"I'm really hungry," he said, allowing a grin. "I figure they'll take you and forget about our groceries. I can then just send Edgar or Tristan or someone to get you."

She laughed harder. "Send the basajaunak. They'd be delighted."

"Yeah, true." He sobered. "Do you want to come in with me?"

Her smile was soft this time and her eyes grateful. "Jessie is a lucky woman to have a guy like you around. People probably don't tell you that enough since they're intimidated by you. Thank you, but no, I'm sure I'll be fine. If anything happens, I'll yell, and gargoyles will pop out from the walls and basajaunak will fill the street and Edgar will spring out of a bush… I'm covered."

He nodded and opened the door, leaving the keys in the ignition. "There is a gargoyle right in front of the Jeep, against the wall."

She huffed. "Figures. Blending into stone and walls—that must be handy."

"It is, especially when the magical world at large doesn't seem to know they can."

She quickly turned pensive again and he made his way into the bar. Niamh sat at the far side where she could see most of the inhabitants. Brochan sat behind her at a low table in the corner, his presence and power warning everyone away.

He'd always taken a similar position in Austin's bar in the early days. Now, it was rare he didn't sit with one of Jessie's crew, or a gargoyle, or Niamh herself. He was starting to find his footing in a new life. Maybe it *was* time to adopt the name Sue and leave that wayward, lost, broken persona behind.

He stood as Austin made his way down. The patrons stiffened as Austin passed.

"Well, how 'r ya now?" Niamh asked in greeting. "Get everything sorted?"

He paused, narrowing his eyes at her slightly. "What'd you hear?"

"Ah, sure, same ol' pandemonium with our crew, so it is. We show up, scare the holy trinity out of everyone, and people start jumping at shadows. Can't hardly blame them. Especially when some pasts don't want to stay in the past."

She paused to get her point across but was incredibly blasé. If he didn't know her better, he'd miss the subtexts. She knew about the mousy mage attacking, and either already knew the woman's past, or planned to get it.

"Sure, this place is a safe haven," she continued. "Ye know something about that, so ya do. I told them all about the anxious wee sorts we had back in the day. Still do. I ignore their bellyaching—ye have'ta or it'll drive ya mad—but I know what it's like. Anyway, sounds like you've got it all sorted. I didn't bother me arse to help. They have a strong setup here, sure they do, but nothing like we have. There was no point in me rushin'."

"Jessie communicated through our link," Brochan murmured. "I checked it out, but I wasn't needed so I returned here. I assume you guys calmed down the basajaunak."

Austin couldn't help himself. "Without getting dragged behind one of them, yeah."

Niamh spit out a laugh.

Brochan's eyes glittered. "Don't expect I'll live that one down."

"Probably not, no. Why are they so riled up, did they say?"

Niamh's eyes turned sharp, and her body tensed. *Shut up!*

"Ye know them, like," Niamh drawled, picking up her glass. "They thought yis were battlin' without them earlier today, and now they are chomping at the bit. Once they wander around the woods a bit and relax, they'll be grand."

He nodded, reading Brochan's body language, a movement so subtle he barely caught the meaning. He doubted anyone here, or many at all, could pick it up. *She's got it under control.*

"I'm telling everyone to lay low," he told them. "We'll postpone the dinner until tomorrow night and eat in tonight. I'm going to keep the mages secure, but you're welcome to stay out. I'd like to remind you that you are a guest here. Be on your best behavior. That said, I have warned the beta that you will not hesitate to defend yourself should you need to. And you'll do so violently."

"It'll be grand," Niamh said. "I'll probably have a wee bite downtown and see yis for dinner."

In other words, she'd gather more intel and meet everyone later to tell them what she learned.

CHAPTER 9

NESSA

"**D**ON'T PUT YOURSELF out too much," Austin said as Nessa grabbed a smaller bag from the back of the Jeep and headed toward the house.

She grinned, then started chuckling. When the scary alpha let himself relax, he was a funny and great pal. She'd told him that Jessie was lucky to have found him, and that was incredibly true, but he was just as lucky to have found her. They brought out the best in each other, and their crew polished it to a high shine.

"Yeah, you know, hard day 'n all," she shot back over her shoulder. "Sitting on the sidelines with a beer while you fought nearly to the death was taxing. I need a break."

She heard him laughing as she climbed the three steps onto the porch and grasped the doorknob. The door opened quietly, and she stepped inside. She'd barely crossed the threshold when a large shape rushed toward her.

She squeaked in alarm and jumped, flinging up her hands to ward off an attack.

"Whoops." Tristan bent and grabbed the shopping bag before it could hit the floor. "Did I scare you, little monster?" He straightened with a smug grin. "I thought we were beyond that?"

She let out a slow, shaky breath. Glaring at him, she snatched the bag back and stalked into the house with her nose in the air. Tristan's dark chuckle followed her into the kitchen.

"Hey." Jessie looked up from the high table, a make-shift island. "Any news?"

Nessa set the bag down on the counter before opening the little broom closet near the hall and pulling out a fold-up wagon. She'd found it earlier when she'd cased the place. "No—"

"Let me." Sebastian hurried to help her with the wagon. "What are we doing with this?"

"We have a lot of groceries."

"Oh." He hefted it and headed toward the front door. Austin stepped inside, carrying three bags in his huge arms.

"Hey!" Fred came from down the hall, the sound of a toilet flushing behind her. Her green and pink hair was spiked with gel, standing up at all angles. She wore a green and pink pant suit, the fashion choices some-what matching Ulric's usual blue and pink. She flashed a toothy grin. "Good to see you! I have—"

She stopped at the door and turned, standing in the way of Tristan coming in with three bags of groceries.

"Oh. Hello. What've you got there?" She stood on her tiptoes to peer into the bags. "Chores? I'll help!"

She shouldered past him and hurried down the steps.

Tristan's brow furrowed in confused humor. "That woman couldn't fit in better if she tried," he said, pausing inside. "And I really hope she doesn't try."

Nessa laughed as she passed him, reaching out to run her fingers along the underside of his suede-soft wings. He tensed before shivering, his eyes sparking lust.

"Are those wings sensitive, Mr. Monster?" she taunted.

Most gargoyles didn't feel anything particularly ex-citing when their wings were touched, whether in human form or gargoyle. The wings were somewhat smooth to the feel, like leather, but apparently affected them no differently than if someone ran fingertips over their ankle.

Not so with Tristan. His mysterious heritage had affected his wings differently. Touching them gave him an almost arousing sensation, a pleasure not as strong as his genitals, but certainly lust inducing.

He turned to watch her, his eyes bright with desire. She was playing with fire, she knew that, but sometimes it was fun to dance in the flames.

"There are steps here," Sebastian said as he and Fred finished loading grocery bags into the wagon. "And we have a lot more people than just the two of us. It probably would've been easier to let everyone help."

"We *are* letting everyone help." Nessa grabbed the wagon's handle, and Fred grabbed two more bags from the back of the Jeep. "Austin can grab the last three bags, and you can help me lift the wagon onto the porch."

"Here, I can take that," Austin said, pulling the wagon toward the porch.

Tristan met him there, lifting the wagon by himself. He carried the whole thing into the house, turning sideways to get it through the door.

Austin met her at the back of the Jeep and grabbed the three remaining bags.

"In the end," he said, "you ended up doing almost nothing. Great work."

"I supervised." She brushed her hands as though to rid them of loose dirt. "Work smarter, not harder."

He chuckled and she checked the Jeep to make sure

they'd gotten everything.

"Many hands make light work," Fred said with one bag, now heading towards the house.

Sebastian took Nessa's hand as they followed the others.

"I'm happy here," he said. "We might be besieged with mages tomorrow after word gets out that I am here, but I still wouldn't regret being here with them. I won't leave them again, despite what might come."

His words sapped her humor. It was her job to make sure that didn't happen.

✦ ✦ ✦

JESSIE

AUSTIN SET THE bags of groceries on the counter as Tristan unloaded the wagon.

"I feel like I should be helping," I said wistfully. I'd tried, but Austin wouldn't have it. "I sit around doing nothing while Mr. Tom runs the kitchen, but he's not worth arguing with."

"Neither are Austin and Natasha, trust me." Tristan winked at me. "Do you guys need help squaring this away, or will I be in the way?"

"In the way," Nessa quipped. "This kitchen is much too small for this many enormous guys."

"There are two of us," Austin replied.

"Exactly. Get out." She started shoving at him. Tristan was already vacating. "I think better when my hands are busy. I'll let you back in when everything is organized."

"Idle hands are a devil's playground," Fred murmured from her seat beside me. Tilting her head, she squinted. "I'm not sure if that's the right saying." She shrugged. "Anyway, Nessa—am I to call you Nessa or Natasha? Natasha is a very pretty name, and it fits you very well when Tristan No-Last-Name says it, but not so much when *I* say it. It's almost like hearing a balloon deflating."

Nessa laughed. "Nessa is fine. What are you, the name guru?"

Fred looked down at a pile of technical items she'd purchased from the shops downtown. The shop owners had tried to stop her from paying, and she'd literally thown cash at their faces before running out the door.

"I don't like owing people," she'd said.

She grabbed an item from the pile and ripped into it. "I changed my own name, but I can't go around changing everyone else's names to suit me, you know? Not to their faces, anyway. Except you guys all agree with the practice of changing names to fit the person, mostly, and now it's a fun little brain teaser. Which name goes best? It's something I never considered until now."

She set the item she'd unwrapped on the table and ripped into another one.

"What have you got there?" Nessa asked, barely stopping to look.

Austin and Tristan stood against the wall and Sebastian took the third of four chairs around the small table, leaning back to let Fred have all the surface area.

"Huh?" Fred looked up, her brows raised, then at the items around her. "Oh, this is to build a satellite link. As far as I can tell, these people are trying to cut visitors off from the grid." She shook her head adamantly before going back to unpacking. "I might unplug one day but today is not that day. The thought gives me hives."

Austin crossed his arms. "Just visitors?"

"Well, definitely visitors, at any rate," she replied. "There's no Wi-fi or service up here, just TV dishes and satellite." She looked around at them. "They don't always look like actual dishes." Back to her task. "That's how the people here are getting internet so they can research and keep up with the magical world." She chuckled. "Who would've thought I would be working for and talking about a magical world. A *magical* world!" She paused to give them a toothy grin. "Look ma, I'm in the magical world!"

"Focus, please," Nessa said jovially.

Fred nodded and returned to her task. "They've cleared away all the trees and have a view of the sky. These guest houses have TV dishes, but TV dishes only receive broadcasts. I can't rig them to work for internet. But look it-here, they have all I need—*more* than I need—in their shops. They asked if I'd need help installing it and reached to make an appointment. Which is odd, right? If they wanted guests to have internet, wouldn't they make these houses internet ready?"

"The townspeople are operating on a different wavelength than the governing body, I think," Austin said. "Than maybe the mages."

Fred bobbed her upper body, her version of an enthusiastic nod. "That makes sense. They're very nice, most of the townspeople. Friendly and smiley and everything. But then you guys got attacked, so there's something wrong there, obviously."

"How long will it take you?" Nessa asked her.

"Oh, not long. I've done this plenty. The hardest part is setting up the satellite." Without looking up, she touched a square package about the size of a standard piece of paper, flat, and only about five inches or so thick. "Then I'll use the picture you took of the mage, saunter my way into the ones and zeroes of the world, and find out who our mysterious friend is."

"It's a race against Niamh's version of fact-finding," Tristan said, crossing his arms over his chest like Austin.

Fred held up a finger. "*Au contraire, mon frère*. She is getting the word-of-mouth contingent. The little anecdotes about this mage's past. The items of note that might not be strictly factual, but photos taken with an ever-changing lens and stored as rumors. I will get the hard data. Places of employment, fitness reports, moving dates or maybe disappearing dates, things like that. Then I'll do my own little social reconnaissance. What her co-workers thought of her, her hobbies, friends, enemies, whatever. Together we'll construct an overall picture of this lady. We'll know her better than her friends probably do. Assuming she has any."

"She didn't point you out as the Captain." Sebastian turned in his chair to look at Nessa. "That's telling. She recognized me, even like this, but not you."

"I thought of that, yeah." Nessa folded a bag neatly and put it on a pile of others. She started emptying the next, putting everything onto the counters in groups. Once done, she did the next until there was no room, and then she started moving items into the fridge or various cupboards. "We don't have enough room for all of this."

"We can distribute what doesn't fit into the other houses," Austin replied.

She gave him a blank look, and then comically frowned. "Withholding information like that from your loyal subjects is not how you work smarter instead of harder, Mr. Alpha King." She sighed and looked around the kitchen. "I have to start over."

Austin smirked and Tristan started chuckling.

"Yeah, ha-ha." Nessa pulled items out of the cupboards and put them back into groupings. "Let's make Nessa do one job twice."

"Well, really, it's only one job done one-and-a-half times," Tristan replied.

"Don't bring semantics into this," she groused.

"I bet she's seen me before." Sebastian's eyes held a faraway expression. "In person." He drummed his fingers against the tabletop. "I bet she has worked for the Guild in some capacity. They would have pictures up of me in all forms. They brought me in to torture. They'd have an image of me at my absolute worst."

Fred looked up at him with wide eyes. "Does Niamh know that?"

Sebastian's eyebrows furrowed. "Yes?"

"He didn't mean that as a question," Nessa said, emptying the fridge. "The question is only why are you asking?"

"Ah." Fred bobbed her upper body with an affirmative. "I was about to ask." She went back to her task. "Because Niamh is very good at getting revenge, and she goes about it in such a calculated way that it is neither scary nor horrifying. Eventually I'm sure reality will slap me in the face, but by then, maybe I won't care."

I toggled my hand, a mere spectator in this conversation so far. I needed some caffeine or a snack or something to get back some energy.

"When you find out what these people are capable of," I said, "you certainly won't care as much as you might think. But I'm still not comfortable with half the things we've been doing lately."

"You're softer than me," Fred said without preamble. "With more morals. I think that bodes well for my mental health, don't you?"

How was I still the most squeamish one in this group when we had a Jane that *hadn't* acclimated to a violent animal like mine? It defied logic.

"Okay." Nessa got everyone's attention. She studied the heaps of food on all available surfaces. "Let's get this food distributed. Boys, you'll be the runners. Here we go."

Sebastian hadn't looked away from Fred. "Niamh is going to help me get revenge, yes. So are you. So is Jessie and Austin. By tearing down that organization, and Momar's with it, that is all the revenge I need. Putting up a better organization in its place, one fair for all magical people, *that's* how I heal."

"And also," Nessa said, "everyone who laid a hand on him, and who ordered it done, are already very dead in the most painful way we could imagine."

"Well, yeah, and that," Sebastian murmured.

CHAPTER 10

JESSIE

ONCE THE EXTRA food was delivered to the other houses, raising interest in what we were having, Nessa and Austin started collaborating on a meal that would take much too long for my level of hungry.

"Seriously, I can't wait," I said, holding my growling stomach. "Lasagna takes a long time, especially with Austin making pasta from scratch, and I am starving."

"Excuse me!" Nessa gave me a hoity expression. "I will also make pasta from scratch. You could've picked another dish to be your favorite since there is no way this is it."

Austin smirked at me. "This is Jess trying to be fair to our competition while also knowing we can make large batches and feed others."

"How is she being fair?" Sebastian asked.

"Because she thinks lasagna is *fine*," Austin said. "She neither loves nor hates it. For that reason, I've never made it for her. Tristan, before you help Fred, can you run down and ask Mr. Tom to make us some sandwiches to tide us over? He'll be all too pleased. Also, tell him that we're making enough lasagna to act as a side for dinner tonight. I'll get some steaks and tri-tip marinating, but if he could start working on some salads and prime some potatoes and things like that, that would greatly help."

I smiled at Austin. "See? Now this is perfect. He gets to help without being a nuisance, you guys get your challenge, everyone gets to participate in the voting, and we get lunch rather than all passing out waiting for your perfection to manifest into cheesy goodness."

"*Voila!*" Fred said without looking up, and kissed the tips of her fingers.

"Nessa, you can use that oven." Austin pointed at it. "It won't fit all four of our lasagnas. That's what we're doing, right? Two each?"

"Yep," she replied.

"Feel free to set the temperature. I'll use the oven in one of the other houses."

"Cool." Nessa stepped back from her carefully organized ingredients for a moment. "Let's do this."

After Tristan had delivered the message to Mr. Tom, Fred said, "Tristan, you're tall. C'mere and help me." She grabbed the satellite portion of the setup and motioned him toward the front door.

Sebastian moved seats so that he could face the kitchen, and we settled in to watch them work.

✧ ✧ ✧

TRISTAN

"THAT'LL DO, THANKS." Fred gave Tristan a thumbs up while looking at the satellite, a mostly flat, rectangular device they'd attached to a long pole. He'd had to work that pole into the hard packed earth, driving it down deep enough that any wind that kicked up wouldn't knock it down.

They'd only need it for a short while. They couldn't stay here long—they still had to get to the Nikken cairn to meet that new leader. Then Austin had a few smaller but influential packs he wanted to hit before he tackled one of the larger, prestigious, long-established packs whose alpha dominated the collective brain of the shifters. That alpha likely wouldn't agree to work under Austin's tutelage, but that meeting and the probable standoff between the two would go a long way to showcase Austin's power and organization. It was necessary to finally put the rumors to rest.

It was time for Austin Steele to flex, and Tristan could not wait to see the reactions he got, or for them to pick on Jessie. She would rock their world.

Tristan nodded and held out his hand for his shirt. Mr. Tom should've been here with sandwiches by now. He was starving.

"Oh. Yeah." Fred handed over the garment, sparing a quick glance at his torso. "I'd be really afraid to meet you in a dark alley."

He grinned. "For many reasons."

She formed a duckbill with her mouth, nodding, as she looked at the sky. "I hope we don't have a hurricane or a tornado or whatever passes for terrible weather in this part of the world."

"For many reasons," he repeated, turning for the backdoor.

Sebastian jumped up when Tristan entered the kitchen. "Here, you can have my seat."

"No, it's fine, I'll—"

"You'll want to watch her at work." Sebastian dragged another of the chairs away toward the wall and sat down. "Besides, maybe showing off for you will give her an edge."

Natasha glanced at him in annoyance, saw Tristan, and did a double take, freezing with her knife poised over a half-chopped onion. Her gaze roamed his gleaming chest, slick with sweat, and her energy spiked. Frenzied pulses of light danced between them, reaching for him as desire filled her eyes, daring him to come closer. Daring herself to will it.

"Or maybe I'll be a distraction," he said with a smirk. Dropping his shirt onto the table, he headed for the bathroom. "I'll just clean up and allow you to get back to it, shall I, little angel?"

She jerked as though slapped, and now her energy turned tumultuous, churning and rolling. It washed across him, thick and heady. Needy, almost. She liked the teasing, even if she wouldn't admit it. He remembered that she'd liked being manhandled by him, as well, relinquishing control and delighting in his dominance. It hadn't been the right time to explore it. It still wasn't. She was edging closer to the cliff, taunting herself with the games, daring herself to give in, but she wasn't quite ready to jump. She still feared no one would be there to catch her.

He didn't mind waiting. The fun was in the chase.

He winked at her before he was out of sight. Her scowl made him laugh.

After cleaning up, he passed through the hall in time to see Mr. Tom come through the door carrying a large brown paper bag.

"Need help?" Tristan asked, putting a hand on the doorframe.

Mr. Tom eyed him. "With what, getting dressed?"

He didn't wait for an answer, hurrying toward Jessie and leaving Tristan to close the door.

"And here we are," Mr. Tom said as he stopped at the table. "I apologize for the delay, miss, but half the food you bought was already eaten by the time I got Austin Steele's message, and I had to send Ulric to the store to get more lunchmeat. You'd think we hadn't fed any of those people in the last year. Well, anyway, I made you plenty to tide you over while the culinary contest drags on."

He threaded between Austin and Natasha to grab some plates.

"Thank you, Mr. Tom," Jessie gushed, reaching into the bag to grab one of the brown wrapped bundles.

"Now, miss, you don't know which one that is." Mr. Tom pulled the sandwich away from her. "This is ham." He set it down before looking into the bag. "I also have oven roasted turkey, salami—"

Jessie grabbed the sandwich again and tore into it. "I don't care what it is as long as it is edible."

"And that is what you get for entertaining these silly cook-offs when I am perfectly capable of managing."

Mr. Tom pulled out two other sandwiches and Tristan put out his hand for one.

"Which would you like," Mr. Tom said, looking at the one in his right hand. "This is—"

"I don't care." Tristan reached a little closer.

Mr. Tom sniffed before shoving both toward him. "One wonders why I put all my blood, sweat and tears into making these edible delights, only to have you inhale them without tasting a thing."

"If it tastes like blood, sweat and tears, that's probably for the best," Sebastian mumbled, taking the sandwich Tristan handed over.

"Alpha?" Tristan asked.

"Two," he answered.

Tristan grinned and delivered two sandwiches.

"Lovely Natasha?" He paused behind her and was rewarded with her little shiver and her energy blanketing him in swirling desire.

"A little more space, and an amazing edible delight in the form of a salami sandwich."

"You want salami between your buns?" he teased, not moving. Her energy throbbed and she lightly swayed, her back nearly touching him, before regaining herself.

"Yes, hilarious, I'm sure all of our sides are splitting." Mr. Tom stepped around Tristan and deposited a sandwich on the counter. "Thank goodness I don't have to deal with terrible jokes when I am in the kitchen."

"You are a terrible joke," Sebastian blurted, and then flinched. "Sorry, Niamh's been in my head a lot lately, and that's the sort of thing she would've said."

"Very amusing," Mr. Tom replied, and it was clear that it was not. He pulled glasses from the cabinet and the lemonade and iced tea from the fridge. "I'll just leave these sandwiches here and go work on the salads and side dishes for tonight. Call me if you need anything, miss."

"Thank you, Mr. Tom." Jessie gave him a grateful smile. "This sandwich is amazing."

"Of course it is." He poured her iced tea before heading for the door. "I don't have to waste time competing in order to feed people."

"Why is Niamh in your head a lot lately?" Tristan asked as he took a seat at the table and unwrapped his sandwich.

"This situation is reminding me of our efforts outside of Kingsley's territory and how often she yelled at me."

Tristan put his fist in front of his mouth as he laughed. "She was playing a part more than actually yelling at you."

"She was doing both," he grumbled, slouching in his chair, and Tristan laughed harder.

Natasha dropped the diced onions into a hot pan. Steam curled up and kissed her beautiful face. She flicked her wrist in a practiced movement, sending the onions folding over each other again and again. Her breasts pushed against her tight white top, jiggling as she worked. She set the pan down to let them cook before twisting out of Austin's way and over to her carefully organized cheese section.

"This for me?" She looked at Austin and lightly touched the edge of a glossy yellow bowl.

Tristan wanted her to look at him, instead. He wanted her focus and to lose himself in those sparkling greenish-hazel eyes. To watch her cook something in nothing but an apron or maybe a G-string.

"Yeah. I have one over there." Austin jerked his head at the edge of the counter he was working on.

She grabbed it and elegantly spun. Her energy swirled around her in an exotic dance, beauty in motion, showing her happiness, the joy and companionship she was finding with everyone sharing the moment, even him.

She measured out the ricotta cheese before gliding the few steps to the stove to once again flip her onions. She added in diced garlic and then she was spinning away again, back to her cheese. She cracked an egg on the side of the bowl and opened the shell with one hand. She poured dried parsley in her cupped palm before dashing it into the bowl, followed by the parmesan cheese, that she poured and apparently measured by sight alone.

"It's almost erotic, isn't it?" Jessie murmured, leaning toward him. "Watching him—or her, in your case—cook?"

Tristan had forgotten to eat his sandwich. To chew, even, mesmerized as he was by his little deathwatch angel creating a culinary delight for her chosen and beloved family. His heart warmed.

"Very," he murmured.

"You missed the pasta making." Jessie leaned away again and took a sip of her drink. "I highly recommend watching the pasta making. I watch the muscles. You'd watch a similar part of the body."

Yes, he would and imagine the salty taste of her skin as he licked a taut nipple before sucking the peak into his mouth.

Natasha practically danced around Austin as he stepped away from the stove, his onions on. She added in the meat and then took to it with gusto, breaking it up to cook. Tristan ate his lunch without tasting it—without even looking at it—focused as he was on her.

"Got it." Fred finally came into the kitchen with her computer. She jerked to a stop, seeing the table. "He got here with the sandwiches, and no one told me?"

"You were right behind us in the living room." Jessie frowned at her. "This house is tiny. You must've heard us. What would yelling at you have changed?"

"Say the name," she said, taking the remaining chair and setting down her laptop. She peered into the bag. "What do we got?"

"We should've called her in." Sebastian balled up his trash. "Asking for the types of sandwiches would've made Mr. Tom happy."

"I think that is turkey," Tristan said, though he really had no idea. They all looked exactly the same. Mr. Tom hadn't even scribbled a letter on them.

"Sweet." Fred nodded, making more room for her lunch and her laptop.

Tristan took the rest of the sandwiches and put them into the fridge, eyeing Natasha's muscular butt as she finished browning the meat.

"Natasha, can I help you so that you can eat?" he asked, pouring her a lemonade and then one for himself.

"Umm…" She glanced at the glass being set on the counter. "Could you unwrap the sandwich, maybe?"

"Of course." He did as she said before taking the can of crushed tomatoes from her grip. "I'll open the cans. Eat something."

She opened her mouth to argue.

"Eat," he said in a deep, commanding voice.

Her fingers relaxed, and she gave him the can. A

wave of goosebumps coated her flesh. Her gorgeous eyes dilated with desire and her energy sucked at him, coaxing him with what she wanted. Prodding him to take control.

His groin tightened as he reached with a free hand for the sandwich. The kitchen and everyone in it dropped away as he brought the sandwich to her lips. He wasn't a shifter, who found feeding their mates erotic, and gargoyles didn't typically have a culture around food, but all the same, he felt a jolt of pure erotism as her teeth sank into the bread, and she took a bite.

Mate, the moment whispered. Her energy tugged at him harder. It would've been impossible to refuse her unspoken order, not that he'd ever try. He waited for her to swallow and then he bent and grazed his lips across hers before settling them firmly. She moaned, barely heard, and then her energy was coaxing him away again, wanting him to back off.

"Check that meat," he murmured against her lips, and then he pulled back and turned to grab the can opener. She wouldn't struggle to get her bearings if she had something to do, allowing the hum of their mutual desire to linger, to live inside her until she couldn't be without it.

He didn't spare her a glance as he opened the various cans she had set out. When he got back to the table, she had eaten half the sandwich and was adding various herbs and spices to the cooking mixture.

"Okay!" Fred took a gulp of lemonade and wiped her mouth with the back of her hand. She crumpled up the paper that had held the sandwich. "I've found our mage. I have more digging to do, but I have a name, an occupation, and how much she is worth if someone brings her in."

Sebastian's chair creaked as he leaned forward in surprise. "She's got a price on her head?"

"Do they do that often?" Jessie asked.

"Very rarely," Natasha answered. "Anyone worthy of a price on their head holds a coveted position. They are pampered and treated well and paid handsomely. They usually don't want to leave."

"Who is it?" Sebastian asked.

"Tilda Grange," Fred supplied. "Former head potions engineer for the Mages Guild with a five-million-dollar price on her head."

"No way," Sebastian said on a release of breath. "*Tilda?*"

Natasha spun around. "That was Tilda Grange? You've *got* to be kidding. I thought she was dead!"

"So did I," Sebastian replied.

"The official standing is that she is presumed dead,"

Fred said, "but her files suggest the Guild doesn't believe that. They are hunting for her. I need to do more research, but she's got a few flags in her file, and they have the location where three employees have disappeared while searching for her."

Fred looked up at Jessie, and there were shadows in her eyes.

"Here," Jessie said.

Fred nodded. "This general area. She was tracked to a small town about forty miles away. This was after she left the Guild—without permission, I am assuming, though that is not evident in her file. I have to do more digging. After that town, she disappeared. Mages have been deployed to look. Some have returned. Those coming to this lonely mountain have not."

"The lonely mountain dominated by a shifter pack," Austin said as he turned.

"Yes." Fred pointed at her screen. "That is noted in her file—not the pack or alpha name or anything, just that there is a shifter pack in this area. Two people came looking and didn't return. The third was sent as a test." She made a face. "He passed said test by also not returning. They are wondering if this pack killed her as well and are in process of sending in a team to get answers."

"They won't stop until they know for a fact," Sebastian said. "And the only information you need to look up is why she left. I know all about her and her work. She is an absolute genius. Low in spell casting power, but that woman can dream up potions I never would've thought of. I've heard, anyway. She's a legend. I cannot *believe* she is alive! And *here!*"

"But you didn't recognize her?" Jessie asked.

"No. I've seen her from a distance, and that was in her work attire. Guild members are expected to dress well. Her appearance now, compared to then, is as different as Elliot Graves and…" He looked down at himself.

"But she recognized you," Jessie pushed.

"And not Nessa," he replied. "I was being dragged to and from torture sessions. They used me as a fear tactic for some Guild departments and, while they'd usually spare someone in a position as high as hers from the displeasure of seeing a torture subject, she had to work with the grunts. She dreams up the potions, but without the power, she has to instruct others how to materialize them. She would've seen me looking worse for wear, much like I am now. She clearly remembers."

"Why'd she try to attack you?" Tristan asked.

Sebastian made a face. "Because she thinks Elliot Graves would make an example of her. He'd drag her into the public eye and viciously kill one of the Guild's precious workers."

"And would he?" Jessie asked.

It was Natasha who answered. "Depends on why she left. She helped the Guild orchestrate some atrocities. She's complicit in their crimes. If she had no choice because they wouldn't let her leave, that's one thing. But doing it of your own free will?" She tisked. "An example would need to be made to show magical people that we will not stand for it."

"If you were to try that here," Austin said, "it seems Drex and his pack will try to stand in the way."

"In the way of us," Sebastian said, "and in the way of the Guild when they invariably break in and get what they came for. This pack clearly doesn't understand the hell they are inviting to their doorstep."

CHAPTER 11

JESSIE

THE EVENING PASSED uneventfully, with a big cookout in the backyard and the taste test between the lasagnas. Sadly, for Austin and Nessa, both dishes were incredibly delicious, and people were so blinded by their tastebuds, they forgot which one they'd sampled in their hurry to get seconds.

I had to admit they were both incredible. I had a long history with lasagna. It's the thing I made when someone needed dinners during a trauma recovery of some kind. It was a good potluck dish, or something that created a lot of leftovers and kept me from cooking for a few days. My lasagna, however, was mediocre at best, something to stave off hunger. I should've known Austin would create something exceptional. He always did, and I now knew Nessa was talented in the kitchen, too. It was obvious she loved cooking. If Austin were ever detained and Mr. Tom wasn't around, I'd invite myself over to Nessa's house for dinner.

I was finding all sorts of ways to keep from cooking.

Nessa had also made brownies, but they didn't make it to the cookout. We each had one, and Tristan ate the rest. I had no idea how he kept his figure with the amount of chocolate he consumed. Jealousy might not become us, but it didn't stop me from feeling it.

I stood in the kitchen as Mr. Tom tidied up after breakfast. He hadn't waited to be invited over this morning. Instead, he'd stolen the front door key the night before and had let himself in before I'd gotten up. My pant suit had been pressed—by him—and my shoes shined. Also, by him.

I wasn't wearing either.

Niamh had come over last night with a lot of rumors and speculation. The townspeople were wary about the mages but appreciated the quiet peacefulness of the community. They weren't prone to raising a fuss. That is, until the mages randomly attacked visitors. Vistors the townspeople quite liked—Niamh was on her best behavior.

Those rumors, though, told in whispers, were nothing compared to what Sebastian and Nessa knew about Tilda. That mage had some serious explaining to do, starting with why she was endangering a pack and ending with why Drex was letting her.

And so, I wore my muumuu. If Drex tried to stand in my way of mage business, there'd be a battle.

"Ready?" Austin entered the kitchen wearing rip away sports sweats, a T-shirt, and flip-flops. He was dressing down in anticipation of shifting, but it was still a meeting with another alpha, and he apparently drew the line at a muumuu.

Sebastian walked in wearing a suit, an extravagant, sparkly watch inlaid with way too many diamonds, his hair slicked back, and all the swagger of a rich, powerful mage at the top of the hierarchy. In other words, he was going as the grim reaper, Elliot Graves himself. He had his own statement to make, and he had not taken kindly to Tilda impassively watching him as he was dragged to and from the torture chamber all those years ago. She hadn't shown one hint of remorse or sadness or any emotion at all, and he held a grudge.

Nessa followed him, her heels clicking against the floor. She was wearing a cream silk romper, a chunky necklace of red beads, and her own flashy and extravagant watch. The Captain was on duty.

She pointed at her flowy and fashionable clothes. "She'll know this means I want to show off the blood I extract from my victim. Her, in this case."

Her bubbly attitude heavily contrasted with her words and, quite frankly, made them that much more terrifying.

I swallowed. "What happened to you not wanting to get your hands dirty?"

"This is a family matter. She wronged my brother, and that I can't stand for. Besides"—she shrugged nonchalantly—"this is war, and mages are violent. So are shifters. And gargoyles. I think maybe I needed a little perspective."

"You needed the freedom to choose," Austin said, checking his phone. "We all get a choice, and then we go hard. We don't do things by halves in this team. You're no different. Let's get going. Everyone is ready."

Nessa gave me a glittering smile, squeezed my hand, and practically bounded after Austin as he headed for the door. Her mannerisms seemed usual from all the time I'd known her, but somehow they also seemed wholly different. She almost looked…lighter, somehow. Graceful and carefree. Joyous. I couldn't put my finger on why, or even if that was true, because maybe it was just me being better at reading body language, but regardless, I was happy she was happy, as cliche as that sounded.

Everyone loaded into the vehicles. Austin held my door for me before climbing into the driver's side of the Jeep. This time, Tristan and Broken Sue sat behind us. We'd lead the procession.

"I anticipate an interesting meeting," Tristan murmured as we got underway. Fred gave us a thumbs up from the porch of the house she was staying in. She'd remain behind in case things got dicey.

"To say the least," Austin said, following the directions to Drex's house.

"Drex better have a damn good explanation for why he has those mages harbored here," I said. "If he doesn't, we don't want his support for the convocation. We can't bring on a guy who willingly hides and protects the deviants of the mage world, the same people we are trying to root out."

"Agree," Austin said as we turned into a wide street.

A large house flanked either side, leading to an even bigger house at the very end.

"The beta, the lead enforcer, and Drex," I guessed. "These are large residences."

"That's usual," Austin told me as he stopped in front of the house, parking in the middle of the street. "Look at my brother's pack. His house is massive. You didn't see it, but his beta's house is, too. A show of wealth is usual in a shifter pack. If the leaders are prosperous, it means the town is prosperous. The way we set things up, one can't happen without the other."

"Except Broken Sue has a moderate house," I argued, "and your house in the woods is gorgeous but not extravagant."

"I wasn't looking to establish a pack when I built that, and Brochan didn't plan to join one. Now, it isn't a pack at all."

"Ivy House puts every rich alpha to absolute shame," Broken Sue said as he pushed open his door. "No one can compete with it. We don't need to be fancy, we simply have to point to Ivy House and call it a day, especially now that Naomi has remodeled the interior."

Austin started out of the Jeep and paused, turning back to me, his features knotted in thought. His gaze delved into mine, as though trying to poke through into my brain and get insight into whatever had entered his head.

"What?" I asked.

He watched me a little longer and then glanced at the alpha's residence again. In silence, he climbed from the Jeep, leaving me to wonder what he was thinking.

Sebastian and Nessa didn't file in with the Ivy House crew, standing to one side instead, posh, poised, and sophisticatedly unimpressed. It was their call to arms, and they were ready for battle.

My stomach fluttered as I motioned my crew in line. I could feel the basajaunak hovering around the large house, probably blending into the trees and ready to sprint to our aid at a moment's notice.

"They seem awfully keyed up this trip," I said.

"Who?" Cyra asked, swinging her arms in boredom.

"The basajaunak. I get rushing into a fight, but they usually relax after they've accepted an all-clear."

"They think the mountain is unsettled," Niamh said, for once without a cooler or even a libation. "Nature or the trees or whatever is not happy. They get a bad feeling from this place."

Right. We'd talked about that, and then all the other issues with this trip had taken precedence, including the discovery that mages were coming here to look for Tilda. That needed to be addressed with Drex today. We didn't know when those mages might come through. Their force wouldn't be anything we couldn't handle, but we had a full travel schedule—we wouldn't always be here. If those mages came in without us, Drex's pack wouldn't have a prayer. We had some things to figure out, and the first was whether we'd help them at all.

Two lines of town shifters filed down the street in orderly rows. As they neared us, they spread out and formed a semi-circle, closing us in.

The door opened behind us, and I turned to find Drex's shifters filing out of the house in loose garments. Dan came out and went right, and Vessa went left, heading up the crisp lines.

Drex exited last, as was usual for these types of meetings. He took the focal point in the middle, the door open behind him, a purple muumuu covering his body. This time it wasn't to see my reaction. His stern face and flashing eyes said he was ready for battle, and that muumuu would be torn off at a moment's notice.

"Alphas, we meet—"Drex cut off.

More shifters entered the street now. Ours. Austin had prepared for hostility, and our people had been watching. They came in four lines before stopping in formation to block Drex's shifters. Basajaunak stepped out of the trees, all around us. Gargoyles lowered in the sky.

Drex's expression turned to granite. "Alphas, we meet again."

"Under similar circumstances, it seems," Austin replied.

"So it seems. Forgive my tardiness. And my extra personnel. You've created an unsafe environment for some of our residents, and so I had to fortify my defenses."

My jaw went slack, and I struggled for words. *We* created an unsafe environment? We hadn't staged an attack in the middle of town or created an ambush in the trees and then kept a bunch of secrets.

Austin laid his hand on my back, ready to take the

lead. That was probably wise, given that my anger level had just shot sky-high.

"Which of your residents feels threatened?" Austin asked.

Drex paused for a moment. "The mages. They are in the house. I'd hoped to clear the air about yesterday, but it seems Mirelda was correct. That was—is—Elliot Graves, and he has brought the Captain."

"Mirelda?" Austin asked.

"The mage you met yesterday. You must understand my position, Alpha Steele, having started a similar situation yourself. I have provided a safe haven for these people. I gave my word, and I will provide that service until my dying breath, which I realize might come very soon. I would not have invited you here had I known the risks you would pose. This is the first time I took a chance, and it turned out to be the wrong decision. I'll lay down my life to try and make that right. It's my job as an alpha."

I put my hands on my hips. That sounded incredibly sincere. Shifters. When would they yank their heads out of the sand and stop being so naive? He was woefully unprepared for the likes of the Guild.

"Mirelda is actually Tilda Grange, correct?" Austin asked. "I want to make sure we're talking about the same person."

Drex hesitated, his gaze flicking to Sebastian.

"Our mages didn't recognize her," Austin said. "One of them took a picture of her yesterday and our technical person looked her up. Tilda is well known in the mage community. About as well-known as Elliot Graves, or so I'm given to understand. What our mages didn't know, however, was that Tilda is still alive. They also didn't know about the five-million-dollar price on her head, or that the Guild was hunting her. They certainly didn't know, and maybe you don't either, that the Guild has narrowed down the search to one rural mountain where their operatives keep disappearing."

More than one shifter adjusted their positions, showing their unease. It was clear they did not know that.

Austin continued. "You are correct in that I will, and have, laid down my life to protect those in my territory. I will not, however, protect those who have spent most of their lives helping a corrupt organization do unspeakable things to innocent people. I certainly will not endanger an entire territory for such a person. Ignoring one bad apple can ruin an entire crop, and in this case, that apple will get you all killed."

Drex stared at Austin for a long, silent moment. "And yet, you have the notorious Elliot Graves in your employ."

"Elliot Graves has killed a great many, that is true. As have I. As has Jess. None of them were innocent, however. This is war, and he chose a side long before we joined his cause. *We* joined *his* cause. He is and has been working to tear down the organization that Tilda helped to thrive. An organization that tortured him and many others for money or power or their potions. That kills and steals and rules the magical community with violence and illegal activity, and an organization who helps Momar, someone who wishes to eradicate the entire shifter population.

"Elliot Graves and the Captain helped us protect my brother's pack from Momar. *They* were the secret mage weapons on our side. Without them, I'd be dead, and my family and friends with me. Tell me, has Tilda warned you that the mages will siege this small pack, kill you all, and take her back? That's what the enormous price on her head means. It's how mages in general and the Guild, specifically, operate."

Drex dropped his stoic demeanor. "I didn't know about the price on her head, not that it matters," he said with a sigh. "She mentioned that the Guild was after her. That it was a corrupt organization seeking to use her. I've built my pack to be top-heavy with fighters. We're ready for them."

I grimaced. The fighters on the porch were certainly

tough and capable. Kingsley's top crust wasn't even as good. The ones gathered in the street, however, were less so, and there weren't nearly enough of them to do what he was suggesting. They'd be overrun in a blink. Less.

"My god, woman, must you be so expressive *all* the time?" Drex asked with gritted teeth, shaking his head a little. His thread of humor cut through the tension.

Austin held up his hand. "I think it's time we sit down for that chat. As you've clearly read in my mate's demeanor, you don't have nearly enough information, or power, for what you're attempting. I also doubt you know the half of what Tilda has done. Less, probably. The people of this town have no idea. None. Niamh sampled the waters. I doubt they'd be so keen to have her here if they did. Neither do you know how mage society works. It's best you face the facts if you want to save your pack from a terrible fate."

"Keep the mages at your house until we ask for them," Drex murmured to Vessa. "Take them out the side door and transport them through the woods. And keep the mages away from each other for now."

"They'll run," she replied. "You know they will."

Drex glanced at the tree line where the basajaunak waited. "They won't get far. I think it's important for them to have their say. We do not persecute here without first hearing both sides. I also think Alpha Steele is right. I've been operating with half the truth and a lack of knowledge about what we face. It's time I rectify both."

The mages were clearly one of his secrets. Hopefully, the others wouldn't be as devastating.

CHAPTER 12

JESSIE

D REX'S EXPRESSION WAS grim. "Alphas. Please, let's go to the back garden. It's beautiful and your people can watch from the trees or sky to ensure there aren't any more surprises."

I looked over at Tristan. "If those mages run, you bring them back and deliver them directly into the hands of Sebastian and Nessa." I switched my focus to them. "If that happens, don't hurt them. Don't even speak to them. They'll be judged, and I want to be there for it."

They nodded, and I waited for Austin to take the lead. He did, and Drex stepped off the porch, leading us around the side of the house along a beautifully cultivated path with vibrant flowers, lush green bushes, and most importantly, a design to it all. Edgar needed to study this layout, not that it mattered with those horrible gnomes running around.

"Edgar needs to get rid of the blasted gnomes," I murmured, slipping my hand into Austin's. It felt like a lovely place for a lazy Sunday stroll. The sun peaked out of the clouds above.

"What's that?" Drex half turned to glance back. He was showing us his back, a sign of trust. He was putting himself at our mercy.

"I was just admiring your yard and wishing our vampire gardener would take some notes."

"He's welcome to come through here any time."

"If you knew him better, you wouldn't extend that invite. Besides, it doesn't really matter. We have this terrible gnome infestation. They'd ruin all the beauty by chasing us with whatever sharp objects they happened to grab."

He glanced back again, this time a smile stretching across his face. His slate gray eyes danced with humor. "I didn't know gnomes were sentient beings."

"Ignorance is bliss, trust me. I wish *I* didn't know. Don't even ask about the army of dolls. You'll never sleep again."

He laughed as we reached a strip of green grass lined on either side with chest-high plants. Fragrant flowers bloomed in different colors. The path led to a garden conservatory with a black metal frame and panes of glass. Plants and bushes and flowers pressed in on the right and left of the structure, and as we got closer I spied a collection of couches and chairs within, positioned in a circle over a patterned beige rug.

"The refreshments will be brought out shortly." Drex reached the door and slid it open before stepping to the side and glancing at Austin. Something passed between the two of them before Drex focused on me. "Ladies first."

I inclined my head in thanks. If there were any surprises, it would be easy to blast my way out of this place or blast someone on the other side of the glass.

At the back of the structure were vibrant flowers and another grassy path, this one shorter and opening onto a lovely lawn set for croquet. Beyond that was a large pool featuring a rock wall and a slide winding down to the water.

"Oh, man." I threaded through the couches to survey the amazing yard. "This is fantastic. Why can't Edgar do something like this with the backyard?"

"I think Mimi is working on a plan to revamp Ivy House's grounds," Austin said. Fabric and springs softly groaned as he took a seat. "You should take a picture or two to show her what you like about this. I'm sure she'd take it into consideration."

I reached for my phone and belatedly remembered I didn't have it. "Rats," I murmured.

"I host a lot of parties." Drex stood by a chair, waiting for me. Austin had taken one of the loveseats. "In the summer, at least. The winter up here isn't as nice."

I sank down at Austin's side, leaning in when he put his arm around me.

"So." Drex took his seat and crossed an ankle over his knee. "If it's acceptable, I'll be expressive in this meeting so that Jessie can understand any body language I might use."

Austin inclined his head.

"Before we start, I'd like to humbly apologize for yesterday. Mir—" He caught himself. "Tilda was told that mages were coming. She hadn't expressed any concern. I didn't anticipate her reaction. I'm sorry."

"The basajaunak showed up without invitation and charged you," I said. "We have that to answer for, and the others showed up uninvited, too. Let's just call it even."

His smile was faint. "I'm grateful your people showed up, unasked. Indigo, especially. She put in a lot of effort. It is well appreciated. I didn't expect to be so thoroughly dominated."

"There's a reason I'm considered feral," Austin said. "I made my brother's territory nervous. Always have, as a matter of fact. I'd thought that was partially my activities in my youth, but it's just my nature."

Drex shook his head. "Wild is one thing. I have that in spades. Power is another, and I have plenty. No, you are an experienced and adept fighter. You're not the best because you were born with a lot of power, you're the best because you've earned it through your trials and your motivation to improve."

"You're very free with your compliments," Austin said guardedly, though I felt the pride worming through the bonds.

Drex laughed. "The compliments are not political, I assure you. I'm not trying to kiss ass. It's simply credit where credit is due. I've heard the same rumors everyone else has, and once again, the most important facets of you weren't mentioned. It's easy to chalk up someone's prowess to things they were born with. Even your wildness is a more comfortable explanation for your talent and skill to those who don't possess either, like some of the higher standing generational alphas. But I'm not jealous of it, I'm inspired. I plan to tell others what I've seen, so I thought I'd start with you. Besides..." He shrugged with a devilish grin. "Ladies always like to hear their mates complimented for being big strong men."

Austin huffed, smiling. "Thank you, then. I *do* have a lot of experience. Some of it from my youth is not pleasant. Some of it is a badge of honor."

"I understand completely, including about youth." He pulled his ankle from his knee and dropped it back to the ground. "Speaking of, that's part of my explanation. There is a reason we haven't accepted strong alpha shifters in here, both before and after the mages. I was born to a single mom in a pack where the alpha didn't believe in mates or monogamy, but he *did* believe in procreating. I had twelve half-brothers and sisters, none of them with the same mother. Seven of those got his animal, me included, but nine were alpha material. Three were as powerful as him, or more so, also me included. Alpha Steele, I'm sure you know how that worked out."

"Please, call me Austin. What number were you by age?"

A hollow chuckle escaped him. "Second to last. The alpha—who never acted as any sort of father to any of his kids, and certainly never trained us how to lead—held his position until I was ten. By then, he'd realized his mistake. He'd created a mob of alphas that wanted his title or at least to prove their dominance over him. The fighting was intense. The oldest of his children went after him first. He failed, but the next didn't. She took over the pack, but by then, the rest were ready to test themselves. Soon, it was war. They killed the enforcers for backing the alpha, or the alpha killed them if they didn't. No one policed the pack, and so random fights broke out everywhere. Prosperity dwindled, since everyone was worried about power and not the people. Safety eroded. I got challenged as a normal part of my day—people trying to test their mettle against one of the alpha's brood. I found my beast in a hurry, and I let it take me away as often as I needed to. I could see my mom's desperation. Even I knew time was running out. Then, at twelve, when I was heavily growing in power, the three remaining siblings noticed me."

A wave of nervous shivers washed over me.

"I had more power than any of my siblings at that age," Drex went on. "Not by much, I guess, but enough that the rest of the siblings knew I needed to be taken out before I properly came of age. My mother was saving money to take me away, but it became clear that she wouldn't get the chance. My siblings didn't plan to let me leave alive."

Dan entered the conservatory with a tray of drinks and nibbles. Drex didn't wait for him to set them down and leave before continuing. His focus was rooted to Austin.

"It was Alpha Barazza that saved me. Us," he said, and another wave of shivers washed over me. "Kingsley Barazza. I was in a very bad place. I knew I would die and worried about what would happen to my mother. I had seen friends torn apart, been close to death more times than I could count… I will *never* forget the day that tiger came crashing into the territory with his perfectly synchronized pack and went straight for the first alpha he saw. He didn't stop to ask questions or even pause. He laid into that alpha with a ferocity that gave me hope. The other two alphas attacked with their band of supporters, but he never balked. He never backed down. He waged a bloody war that day, against powerful shifters, but it was his determination, leadership, and motivation that saw him through and saved us all."

Dan left us, leaving the door open, as he'd found it. Drex was not worried about people overhearing his story. He wasn't ashamed of his past, which was reassuring. Hopefully, it meant he had made peace with it.

"The first reason I allowed you in, Austin, is because I owe your brother my life. My mother's life, probably. Her happiness, certainly. Alpha Barazza tried to help the pack reestablish, but the damage done prior to his arrival had been too great. We didn't have enough people to cobble together something that would stave off rogue alphas looking for an easy setup. And so, Alpha Barazza gave money to anyone who needed it and offered his pack as a place to live should they want it. That stuck with me. His willingness to help others any way he could stuck with me, and I vowed that I would lead a pack in his image. That I would follow his lead and always provide a safe space for those who needed it."

Austin had taken my hand. His thumb lightly traced over my skin. "I know something of the debt you feel. It's funny, but I essentially did the same sort of setup as you, although I was much less noble about it."

"I don't know about that." A smile ghosted Drex's lips. "Your brother believes in you. You are trying to succeed where he has failed, and I want to help you do that. I want to help him. I just don't know if I am able." He reached for a glass of sparkling water.

"Did you go back with Kingsley?" Austin asked.

"No. My mother took us to her cousin's pack. It had always been the plan, and with help from Alpha Barazza, she was able to get us there and get us settled. And that was fine…for a while."

"But you had too much power."

"Yes, and soon I was too good at this shifter business." He faintly smiled again. "That pack alpha never challenged me, and I didn't plan on challenging him for the pack. I know the result when a pack is taken by force, and I didn't want that. He didn't believe me. After three years, he handed me my hat. This time, my mother didn't go with me, at my request. It was time to establish a new pack."

"At fifteen?"

"One month shy of sixteen." He shrugged. "I felt a lot older than my years at that point. I'd had to grow up fast. But first, I learned what it is like for a high-powered rogue."

Austin snorted. "I know something of that, too. So does my beta. No one rolls out the welcome mat."

"No. But strangely, people followed me. I honestly have no idea why. I didn't promote or ask or have much of a plan, but people kept following me until I established a small pack down the way."

He pointed in an arbitrary direction that I assumed was the town we'd stayed in.

"In the town of three morgues?" I asked.

Drex laughed, a hearty, joyous sound. "Those came later. That town is the first line of defense—mental warfare. It unnerves people. They're already spooked by the time they get to me."

Niamh had been right, and now I was thankful she'd been taking notes.

His smile slipped. "We had the hobby alphas come knocking first. They saw a teenager and thought he was easy pickin's. I was sport. They had no idea how I'd grown up. Many of them didn't walk away after the challenge. I made a statement. But it was exhausting and took time and effort when I needed to focus on establishing the pack, not to mention I *was* young and hadn't grown into my full power. I worried someone would inevitably come through that I couldn't handle. So, I moved the pack into this area to give us a little peace while we set things up."

"And did it?" Austin asked.

"Yes. Hobby alphas are lazy. They either didn't want to come all the way up here or didn't put much effort into fighting me when they did."

"But you still allowed in shifters to check the status of the pack."

"Of course." Drex frowned at him, not thinking much of the question. It's a reaction I would've given. "Above all, I want my people happy and prosperous. This was always about providing a good life for a pack."

"You still didn't let in powerful shifters."

Drex tensed. "No, for two reasons. One was that this town grew quickly, peacefully, and became prosperous despite the remote location. We've had a lot of wealthy shifters move in for one reason or another, and they give heavily into the community. Allow in delegations, and now, instead of hobby alphas, you have more established alphas wanting to take their shot. At a certain point, I had no worries about holding my own, but I remembered how Alpha Barazza had led his enforcers. An organized alpha and his or her enforcers would tear me down and change the way of life for these people. I couldn't have that. So, I created a madman type persona and played it up for the shifters checking the pack's status. I displayed my power and beat the drum, as it were, and the rumors spread. More serious and powerful shifters came, curious about the pack. I met one and all in the woods, and after they were dominated, accepted them into the pack. That's how I started building my might. We train constantly. We stay honed. They've told friends, and the pack continues to grow. It's a nice place to live, honestly. Quiet and friendly. It's a tight community where everyone helps everyone else. We usually don't have any problems. But then, the reason for not allowing in powerful shifters changed…"

CHAPTER 13
AUSTIN

J ESS TENSED AT his side. Goosebumps spread across her bare arms. "The mages," she surmised.

Drex put down his drink and leaned back, suddenly wary. "The mages," he confirmed. "Now we reach the second reason I allowed you in. You have experience with mages. You are advocating creating an organization that *includes* them. I thought you'd be open to mages in a pack. Many shifters aren't. I wasn't aware how ignorant I am about their magical culture. I'm not sure what I'm dealing with. They were utterly truthful in their representation of their plight. Mages aren't subtle in their movements, like Jessie. But…it sounds like I'm only getting a slice of the reality?"

"Tip of the iceberg." Jess nodded slowly. "But who knows. Maybe they did see the error of the Guild's way, have wanted to leave for some time, but haven't been able to. I guess the Guild doesn't like losing some people, and so they make sure those people don't or can't leave. Maybe these mages *were* scared Sebastian planned to kill them or take them in or whatever. I don't know. We need to hear their stories with people who know more about the situation than we do. Our mages can help there."

Drex faintly smiled. "You're the good cop, I see."

She shrugged. "Not always, but I do like to give people the benefit of the doubt. My gargoyle, however…" She trailed away.

"How'd they come to be here?" Austin asked.

"Two years ago, our sentries were doing a random sweep and found the mages five miles from here, half dead. They were starved, terrified, and desperate. Usually, when we find Dicks and Janes, lost for whatever reason, we give them money and return them to town. They find their way. These mages had nowhere to go. They were being pursued by the Mages Guild. They would have been killed or worse if they were found, and had no plan."

"Did they warn you that you'd be in danger?" Jess asked, crossing one leg over the other with wary patience.

"They said the Guild was hunting them. That implied the danger. I took them in, anyway."

"Hmm," Jess said noncommittally.

"And these mages of yours?" he asked her. "They have a bad reputation. I knew the name Elliot Graves without needing to look it up. Then, seeing him… He has a lot of swagger, and apparently, even more power. Forgive me, but those combined attributes don't inspire a lot of trust."

A burst of frustrated power filled the room. "Sorry," she said in response. "On the surface, no, they probably don't. But I know them well."

"And what made you decide to give Elliot Graves a shot?"

"I decided to give Sebastian a shot, a weird mage who nerds-out with magic. Elliot Graves is his persona for the mage world, and I was just about to kill him when I realized who he really was."

She gave him the gist, explaining how Sebastian came to be in their lives, their hiccups and learning curves, and what they were now.

"I don't know Elenor," she said.

"Who?" Drex asked.

"Do you mean Tilda?" Austin asked.

Jess screwed up her face in irritation. "Tilda, I meant. I don't know *Tilda*. But I know Sebastian and Nessa. I know them beyond their personas, beyond their walls and barriers. I've seen their worst, and I've heard their sins. Niamh has recently *created* some of those sins." At his confused look, she waved that away. "I am the mostly broken moral compass of this crew, but I do not put innocent people in danger, Drew—"

"Drex," Austin helped. He'd never seen her so wound up.

She screwed up her face again. "*Drex!* Craps-sakes, I'm turning into Edgar. It's just…" She looked away, her eyes becoming distant.

"You good?" Austin asked. A shiver worked down his spine. She'd been like this on the way here before Drex's attack had a chance to come.

She glanced up through the glass ceiling, taking in the clouds. "Yeah. I just feel strangely…expectant. I'm probably reacting to confronting those mages. Anyway, *Drex*, I do not needlessly kill. I have the same mission as you and Austin—to protect those who cannot protect themselves. To create a safe space. And those mages are not—"

She blinked rapidly before turning to stare at the pool area. Then she angled her face skyward again. Her emotions started to churn.

"Should we send out people?" Austin asked, scooting to the edge of the couch.

"A few of the basajaunak connections just lit up with emotion," she murmured, standing. She walked to the glass door leading out toward the pool, currently shut, and looked out. "I feel like I need to get sky bound."

Her gargoyle was acting as a warning system, like on the way into the territory. Maybe her beast detected the same off-ness about this mountain that the basajaunak had. Whatever the reason, he wouldn't ignore it.

He stood up even as Dave came running across the lawn, trampling the flowers in his haste. Jess froze, watching him, and suddenly her gargoyle connections glittered in his mind's eye. She was connecting them all as a unit. That meant battle.

"Let's go." He motioned Drex on.

"We're being attacked," Jess ground out, hurrying for the door.

"What?" Drex shot up.

"Follow her lead," Austin commanded, hurrying after. "She has a way to connect her people. She'll know what's happening better than anyone."

✧   ✧   ✧

JESSIE

THOSE MAGES MUST'VE gone dark before the extraction. That's why Fred hadn't seen anything about it online. We'd walked right into an ambush.

The timing made this situation incredibly suspicious. So, too, did the reaction of the basajaunak. They'd known something was *off*, but not what. That shouldn't have been the case.

We'd have to dissect it later.

Dave tore through the bushes. I could feel the other basajaunak moving through the trees on our flanks, heading for the front of the house. They'd meet us there to discuss. Only one stayed behind. *Her*, the basandere in charge of the Ivy House woods. She could read the pulse of the trees better than anyone.

I didn't bother asking Dave for information, not when one of us would have to repeat it.

At the front of the house, Broken Sue and Tristan were standing together, waiting for me to reach them. The shifters that had been farther out in the street had pushed in to join the other pack. The town's shifters had let them, though they were clearly wary about the situation.

"What've we got?" Tristan asked, ready to rip off his muumuu.

"Fifty people," Dave said as we stopped in front of them. "All coming up the south side." He pointed for my benefit. "Half are coming up first in organized lines. They step through the wood lightly and don't disturb the trees too much. The rest tramp through and rub against trunks. All are on two feet, and none seem like shifters or gargoyles. *Her* is positive."

"Mercenaries and mages," Sebastian said, jogging over. "They'll be looking to acquire Tilda, but they won't want to expend the effort and danger in looking. They'll grab shifters to question and kill the rest."

"*Question* means torture the information out of," I told Drex. "How many will they grab?" I asked Sebastian.

"Doesn't matter," Austin replied. "They won't get that chance." He yanked off his sweats. "This is known protocol when mages attack. We can handle it. Sebastian, what do you surmise will be the power scale of this crew?"

"This is textbook Guild protocol when confronted with a dangerous force," he said.

"When confronted with shifters in general," Broken Sue growled, stripping.

"Exactly," Sebastian said. "It's a blunt approach and I'd bet solely the Guild. Not Momar."

"No," Niamh said from not far off, her eyes distant. "It's the timing that's Momar. And managing to hide fifty people from the basajaunak until the actual attack."

A chill ran through me, and Sebastian's face lost its color. Niamh had surmised the same thing I had.

"Nothing for it," she said. "Proceed as normal. We don't have time for anything else."

"Proceeding as normal," Sebastian said, re-taking control, "the numbers in the attack are for the shifters because Tilda doesn't pose any real threat magically. Ordinarily in this situation, they'd have mediocre mages. They won't use higher powered mages in case something goes wrong. Jessie and I can distract them easily, take out a bunch, and the shifters can handle the rest. Mercenaries will be similar to what we've dealt with in the past: magical guns, organization, unused to shifter power, and certainly not used to fliers. In a *normal* situation, we'd be able to handle this."

Niamh nodded. "Momar wouldn't send in anything better. He'd know we'd kill them. He's lost too much power to us already. He's looking for something else here. Some other information crucial to his plans and he's sacrificing Guild personnel to do it. Nothing new there. We'll have to figure out what he's after later." She swore under her breath. "This lad is starting to get on my nerves. He's dancing around in the shadows, watching us fumble. That needs to end, like."

We needed time to devote to unraveling the spider's web, as Fred liked to think of him.

"A problem for another day," I said, power thrumming. "We need to take care of this now."

Sebastian handed his jacket to Tristan and continued to undress.

"Then what are we waiting for?" Drex asked, ripping off his muumuu.

"Kill as many mercenaries as you need to." Nessa stripped down to her underwear. She must've brought a change of clothes. "*Do not* kill them all. Wound them, leave them, and let them limp back to where they came from. They need to see the carnage and tell their friends. We need mercenaries to stop taking jobs against shifters."

"Yeah, agree." Sebastian pushed down his pants. They'd both brought a change of clothes.

"As far as the mages—"

"Capture them all." Niamh finally headed our way. "Don't kill any of them, mercenaries included, if ye can help it. Some of them need to fill us in on Tilda. They'll talk easier than she will. The rest..." A crease formed between her brows. "I'll figure out when I have a moment to think."

"Okay, we know what we're doing." I grabbed the back of Austin's neck and yanked him down for a kiss. "Be safe. I'll be right above you."

"Likewise. Guard my heart."

I smiled, knowing his heart was me.

"Tristan." I pulled off my muumuu and tossed it to the ground as Sebastian grabbed his stuff from Tristan and ran for the vehicle he'd come in wearing only boxers. Nessa had already headed that way. "We get to officially see if my training has taken root, huh? Let's hope I learned something."

"Yeah," he said, standing ready. "Don't screw up."

I laughed, the thrill of battle beating through me. Time to earn my keep.

"Leave your people here," Austin told Drex. "We've got this. They'd just get in the way and possibly get killed. If you want to come along to see how we handle mages and to see what mages can do, you'll need to follow orders from me and my beta."

"Understood," Drex said.

"Keep those mages in that house," I told Drex. "Do not let them out. If they run, it might be into the hands of the enemy. Right now, they have a fighting chance of explaining their situation. If the Guild gets them, they'll have no hope of salvation."

He nodded. "Got it."

Edgar had already taken off, always with Nessa in battles. Everyone else stood ready, muumuus on the ground and anticipation sparkling in their eyes.

"You heard what Niamh said," I told them. "No killing." I pointed directly at Cyra before I swung my finger to Dave. "Did you hear that?"

Through *Her's* connection, I could feel the mercenaries getting closer. The mages were behind them.

They weren't moving fast, so they must be walking. Two others, these on four legs, were running for all they were worth toward the town. Sentries, probably, coming to alert Drex.

"Heavily maim, but *no killing*," I told my people.

Dave's brow sank low. "It must've been them loitering in the woods, planning their violence, that made the mountain uneasy. The mountain asks that we exterminate—"

"No killing," I interrupted. "The mountain will get plenty of blood. It'll be fine with that." Probably. It was a mountain, since when did they give orders?

"How about burning off a limb?" Cyra asked hopefully.

"Just don't kill," I reiterated. "Or start a forest fire. I don't want to spend a bunch of energy sucking away your flames."

The number of times I had to repeat stuff like that.

I shifted and took to the sky. Tristan was right behind me, blasting up faster and grabbing me as he went. Cyra shot up, following the others, except for Hollace, who needed more space before he shifted into his mighty Thunderbird form. Thunder rolled as he rose into the sky, which was thankfully still overcast. The mercenaries walking up the last bit of the hill to the shifter town wouldn't think anything of it.

A large gargoyle grabbed a newly clothed Sebastian, our weird mage wearing black sweats and runners. It was time for him to fight in a way Elliot Graves never could.

If Tristan guided the gargoyles with wing movements, the sound would reverberate down the mountain, so I sent the command to prepare for battle through our connection, and the gargoyles wasted no time. My crew fit into their positions.

Our people below had all shifted and fallen into their own formation, Austin was in the lead with Broken Sue coming up behind. Despite his issue with dominance when he'd first met Austin, Drex had no trouble falling back, a huge bear fitting into the other shifters as they started forward at a fast pace. The basajaunak briefly flanked them, before disappearing into the trees.

I sent directives to push them faster, instructing them to remain invisible and slip past the mercenaries so they could then crowd around the mages. When we struck, they would, too.

We kept pace with the shifters, flying above the trees. More thunder rolled around us. I could feel the location of the enemy advancing; not far now. They moved steadily, no doubt their magical blaster guns drawn. The more expensive of those guns could rip through magical defenses and then flesh and bone. However, these mages didn't expect much in the way of a magical defense. They would be worried about the shifters, so I doubted the blasters they carried would be high-tech. Hopefully, they wouldn't be a problem for us.

Hopefully being the operative word. You just never knew with mages, especially with the unknowns of this attack.

The trees blurred as Tristan put on a burst of speed. The mercenaries should be just ahead.

Anticipation hit me. The basajaunak had sighted something. They didn't slow, splitting instead to curve around what I surmised was the enemy. I pointed in that direction and Tristan veered right.

He started to dive. *Here we go.*

My heart picked up pace. I couldn't just flap around on my own this time. I had a team and a flight plan to navigate. My wingman would be trying to lead and anticipate me at the same time. This was real-life training and getting it wrong could mean death.

With a deep breath I wiggled, and he let me go. I dove, magic at the ready. I could feel Sebastian's ride diving with me. Near the top of the trees, I saw the first mercenary. He sensed something and slowed, looking to his right and left, but not up.

They hadn't been told what they'd face. Otherwise

up was the first place they'd look.

I hammered down with a wide spell, and Sebastian did the same. One mercenary screamed and another splatted against a tree. Crap. That was supposed to be a low energy version of one of the grisly spells. I'd meant to scratch him to hell, not explode his middle. Hopefully, Cyra hadn't seen that. She'd take it as a green light to go nuts.

I angled right as a gargoyle team of four flew over me. I picked up the pace to match their speed and covered them with a spell. A jet of yellow shot through the trees, hit my spell, adding to my energy, and then filtered through my connections to the generic magical defenses I applied to the shifters. It was by far the best magical discovery in one of the Ivy House books.

I fired a different altered spell, and a black line slashed across a mercenary's head. He gave a bloodcurdling scream, his head tore in two, and he fell.

Dang it! I'd *greatly* reduced that spell, but the result was every bit as dangerous as the original. Clearly, these spells wouldn't be tamed.

Blasts came fast now. I had to pull up and focus on defense. Tristan caught me and flew me toward the mages. We'd done enough to distract the mercenaries. Their guns wouldn't be able to bleed through my protective magical defenses on the shifters. Austin knew how to handle them.

The mages had stopped. In a moment I saw them, hands out and at the ready. They weren't looking up, either. They must not have been able to see the mercenaries through the trees.

I squirmed and Tristan released me again. Sebastian pulled up next to me, and I met his eyes. I gave a slight nod, and his gargoyle transport dropped lower with me to the treetops. I hammered spells as fast as I could, mundane ones that *should* hurt like hell but not kill, but the tree cover was thick, and I couldn't see well enough to hit the targets.

I angled my wings, dropping to get a better view, and my wing hit a branch. Pain lanced through my back. A mage looked up and saw me, a look of horror crossing his face, and then fear. He fired a spell at me, shouting something I didn't understand, and I threw up a shield. My other wing caught in the branches as another spell came in. I tried to clear myself, but my angle stopped me.

I heard a thrum, and large hands grabbed me and yanked me upward. Tristan tucked my wings in and pulled me in close. I knew a moment of abject terror, instantly transported to a time when Nathanial had done the same thing.

"*Nooo*," I said, my fear rising.

"Ea-ssy," Tristan said through a mouth full of fangs. "Eeaa-sy."

He wrapped his wings around me and dropped, crashing through the leaves and branches. He then spread his wings with a *snap*. Thunder rolled above us, and lightning crackled. The trees were too dense for many of our team to get in easily. In our haste, we hadn't thought of this contingent.

I covered us in a defensive layer as spells came in hard. Mages stepped from behind trees long enough to shoot jets of magic at us and then hid again. If they'd been any stronger, I wouldn't have been able to withstand their fire. As it was, the sheer magnitude of magic in close range was frying my defensive spell.

Tristan landed, hustling us out of the way on foot. Another gargoyle dropped out of the sky. He unfurled his wings, revealing Sebastian, who was firing spells.

I pushed away from Tristan and fired. Tristan and the other gargoyle slipped behind the trees and ran at the closest mages. Roaring, the basajaunak exploded from the trees. One snatched up a mage and then another, bashing them against a tree, while a basandere tossed yet another mage through the canopy like a rag doll.

"Don't kill!" I shouted, but I was in my gargoyle form and it came out garbled.

Mages took off running. Some panicked and ran in the wrong direction, straight toward the shifters. Others hid in the trees, cowering away from the basajaunak hunting them.

More roars and snarls. I felt Austin drawing near. A mage screamed, and then another, and I saw jets of spells and sensed pain from three different people.

I tried to hurry, but I wasn't as fast in my gargoyle form. The dense canopy blocked me in, and my wings weren't strong enough to push through. I doubted any of the gargoyles could push through. We were stuck on the ground.

"Jessie, here," Sebastian called.

Two mages were firing at him. I added to the protective spell covering him as a mage went flying above my head, slammed into some branches, and fell. A basajaunak was on him immediately, knocking the mage out with a hard punch.

As I reached Sebastian, a spell hit his defensive barrier, and I returned fire without thinking, accidentally releasing another one of the stronger spells. A spray of blood said it wasn't a maiming blow.

"Crap," I muttered as Sebastian's eyes widened. He clearly hadn't seen that spell before. "Sorry," I tried to say, but the words came out in a mess of syllables.

Shifters filled the space. They were better suited for

such terrain. It was why working with both groups made us ten times more effective. A huge Kodiak burst through the trees. Drex saw the mage and charged him with a snarl.

He wasn't part of my gargoyle's connections, though, and I didn't have a defensive spell on him.

"Wait!" I tried to shout, bursting into my human form and closing the distance between us. The mage fired twice in quick succession, his eyes round with terror when he saw the charging bear. A wet stain spread across his crotch, and I expected him to freeze. He didn't, though he would wish he had.

His first spell hit Drex with a loud sizzle. Drex flinched but didn't stop, and my defensive spell covered him before the second spell could hit. That spell bounced off, back toward the mage. It sprayed him, the ground, the tree next to him and a bush with magical acid. Well…globs of magical acid, more like. The tree trunk started to sizzle, as did the dirt, and the bush…and the mage.

He screamed and looked down as the globs of magic burned his clothes away.

"Oh, no," I said, wracking my brain for the counter spell. I was sure I'd learned it…

The mage's shrieks grew louder as the spell blistered his skin and spread. I hadn't known it would do that.

Drex stopped, transfixed by the writhing, screaming mage.

The mage patted himself to stop the burn, spreading the magic to his hands, something else I hadn't known would happen.

"Crap." I shoved at Drex's big shoulder to get him to move out of the way. "I think I can fix this."

"What the hell is that spell?" Sebastian asked, stopping beside me. "Jesus, Jessie, that kinda thing was outlawed in the dark ages."

"Ha ha, very funny."

"I'm not sure I'm kidding?" He sounded confused, as though he were trying to remember history.

"Like mages outlaw anything. It's fine, though. There's a counter-spell." I tried what I thought would do it.

The mage screamed in anguish as a gaping hole opened in his belly.

"Ah, man." I breathed heavily and thought about throwing up. "That wasn't the counter-spell."

"Oh, we get to kill?" Dave asked from somewhere behind me.

"No!" I put out a finger and looked around. "No, killing. This was an accident!"

Someone screamed before quickly cutting off.

"That was an accident," one of the basandere called.

I sighed. This hadn't gone as planned, and it was mostly my fault. Cyra would never let me live this down, especially because she was stuck above the tree line and couldn't participate. At least she'd followed directions and hadn't set fire to the trees.

"Right, okay. Well…" I put my hands on my hips and listened. Silence. We'd gotten through the enemy.

Austin stood off to one side. Only a few of our people were hurt and none of them badly. This hadn't been a powerful force, and they'd also been unprepared. Niamh had been right. We'd now have to figure out what information Momar had been after.

"Fine," I said. "There's still a bunch alive, so I call that a win. It'll be good enough."

Someone tsked, and Nessa walked up. Her hair was messy, and she held bloody knives. "Jessie, Jessie, Jessie," she said with a grin. "Niamh is going to be so mad at you."

"Should I make art out of him?" Edgar asked with a toothy grin. "It always sends some sort of message."

The big Kodiak was staring at me. Even the bear face looked shocked.

I held out my hands. "We're not all perfect, okay? Sometimes my spell work is a little…"

"Volatile?" Nessa guessed.

"Horrific?" Sebastian said.

"Surprising," I finished. "Sometimes it is surprising and doesn't react how I expect. They were the enemy. They had it coming. Anyway, let's head back."

Someone grunted in pain—Phil—followed by a loud scream.

"That was an accident," Phil yelled. "Kinda."

I bowed in defeat. I couldn't even yell at him. I'd started it.

CHAPTER 14

JESSIE

THE AFTERNOON WANED as I sat in a lawn chair in Drex's lovely backyard. The water lapped at the sides of the pool and a glass of sparkling wine sat on my right, untouched. Mr. Tom had thought the wine would improve my spirits.

A shape in my peripheral vision caught my notice—Drex, walking along the stone path that led from the back door. The watery sunlight highlighted the plains of his narrow face. He carried a glass of sparkling wine.

"Jessie," he said by way of hello, and took another of the lawn chairs.

"Hey. How are things going?"

He'd wanted to be in on the "fact finding" chats, as I liked to think of them, sitting in with Sebastian, Nessa, Niamh, and Tristan as they questioned the enemy mages. He'd wanted to know how mages typically operated, and he'd also wanted to hear firsthand about who he was harboring.

"Not well." He took a slow sip of his wine before placing it on the table beside him. "I threw up."

"Ah."

"I notice you didn't ask me to elaborate."

"No. I've been in on those things. Mine probably went a lot more chaotically."

He took a deep breath. "The person who sent them applied some sort of spell to keep them from talking. One guy bled out through—Never mind, I'll spare you the details. Suffice it to say, the spell killed him, and it wasn't pretty. Sebastian figured out a work around, and the others started babbling pretty quickly when they realized it would keep them from dying."

That was interesting. Niamh clearly wanted them alive to use them in some way. Or maybe they were ready to swap sides. We needed eyes and ears in the mage world.

"Sebastian filled me in on the sorts of practices the Guild engages in," Drex said, "and the mages we captured told us stories about the things Tilda's team had created. What they've done." He shivered. "I had no idea the mages operated like that. It's not right."

"And believe me, there are worse stories you *haven't* heard."

He grunted in acknowledgment.

He was quiet for a while, and I went back to listening to the water lap against the side of the pool. A fountain wouldn't go amiss somewhere out here. I'd remember that when I talked to Mimi about the backyard.

"You were right," he finally said, his face somber.

"I always am." I smiled and squinted at the sun. "About what specifically?"

"Many things." He let that linger for a moment. "I spoke with your mages. They seemed like completely different people than the two I saw outside my house, in their suits and silk and diamonds."

"That was their mage gear. You really don't want to be dressed like that in a battle."

"No. And they did battle. They changed their clothes and their personas, and they met a charge not intended for them. Actually, intended to capture someone they clearly do not like."

I laughed. "I get what you're saying, but they are in ten times more danger from the Guild than Tilda. A hundred times."

He took another sip. "I asked them why they did it. I asked them separately, and neither of them hesitated. They did it because of you and your crew. You're family to them, and they protect their family at all costs. Their inclination in case of an attack is to slip out the backdoor, or the equivalent, but for you, they marched directly into battle. Apparently, even though it's always terrifying, they always have."

An unexpected wave of emotion overcame me, and my eyes glazed over.

A tear slipped out, and I wiped it away. "They have. And they are."

He watched me steadily now. "It's refreshing how expressive you are. I know exactly where you stand, and it's a heartfelt place. An honest place. You've earned their trust and, though they don't think they deserve it, they've earned yours. You've created the sort of pack I've been striving for."

"It sounds like it's the sort of pack you've achieved."

He shrugged and looked away again. "Not quite. I feel like I'm flailing. I'm making everything up as I go. Book learning only gets you so far."

I nodded, because boy didn't I know it. My early days with Edgar reading magical books wearing a helmet surfaced. Sebastian had changed my learning curve dramatically.

"The next thing you were right about," he said, "was your frustration with me about mages." He held up a hand. "I'm not as good as Austin or...Broken Sue? Is that his name?"

"For the moment. I think it's in the process of

changing again."

He tilted his head in confusion. He needed to spend a little time with Fred.

"I'm not as good as they are when it comes to reading—or hiding—body movements, but I'm decent. Not that I need to be with you. You were frustrated, and I get it now." He laughed humorlessly. "My force would've taken heavy losses from that attack today. That's if we came out on top at all, and I'm not sure we would've. Austin's people made it look so easy. I was young, but I remember Alpha Barazza's force vividly." He shook his head. "Alpha Steele is better. Sharper. *Harder* in battle. Perfectly synchronized. The timing, the way they sliced through the enemy, the overall direction… It looked like anyone could beat those mages and mercenaries, but I'm not so naive as to think that is true. I've tried for a battle unit. He's created a battle unit. You both have."

"I connect us all," I said. "We're a unit, yes, with a lot of experience. It didn't always look so organized, trust me. This was a low-powered assault with a limited enemy. They weren't prepared for us."

"Austin mentioned that, too." He held his drink, his eyes on the water. "Those were low-powered mages and yet I had to be healed from that magical spell."

"You didn't really, we just helped things along. If it

had been a proper battle, you would've been left to heal in agony while we saw to the dying."

He gave a crack of laughter. "Don't break it to me gently or anything."

I shrugged. It was hard to remember being on his side of things, when this was all new. After Kingsley's, smaller skirmishes were wastes of time.

"Then there is what you can do." He grimaced.

"Okay, well…" I held up a finger. "There aren't many mages as powerful as I am. Sebastian is nearly my equal. He's ingenious, but I have spellbooks that are supposedly taboo these days." I thought about what Sebastian said. "If Momar got ahold of them, I suspect he'd be giddy."

"Dangerous books, then."

"They are in a very safe place, trust me. A magical house isn't something people escape from."

His head thumped back against the lounge. "I thought I was well-read but today has thrown me."

"You'll get used to it, unless Edgar comes and talks to you. You don't get used to that. Run. Don't cross that bridge until you are forced."

He chuckled and ran his hand down his face. "To borrow a phrase from my grandma, what a trip."

I frowned at him. "How old are you again?"

He didn't seem to hear. "If we hand over Tilda and

the others to the Guild, Sebastian said the Guild would probably leave us alone and we could stay hidden on this mountain and be fine."

"Except you won't turn them over, and you won't kill them. That's not your style."

"No, it isn't. I'm not at the stage where I kill in tepid blood."

"*Tepid* blood, huh?" I laughed.

"But that's not the point," he continued. "We would *probably* be fine. The Guild, or Momar, *probably* wouldn't hold a grudge and wipe us out for spite."

"There are no assurances when it comes to those groups."

He fell silent again, and I let time pass. An emotion came through the Ivy House link from Niamh: impatience. I wondered who was annoying her. Everyone else seemed fine.

"But what about people that aren't hidden away on a rural mountain?" he said quietly. "What about people who don't have you to rush in at the last minute and save them from themselves? What if the Guild *does* hold a grudge or Momar wants a little sport? What then?"

We both knew the answer to that. That's why Austin and I were here, asking for help with the convocation, after all.

"I'd planned to hear you guys out," Drex said. "If

you were in any way decent, I'd planned to join the convocation and help you sway others. I know my voice is loud in the original alpha sphere. People tend to listen when I speak, probably because I don't speak often." Once again he paused. "But I see now how shallow my support would've been. I see what is needed—what Alpha Kingsley envisioned and what you two are building. Sitting here in a peaceful town on my mountain is, at best, a waste of my skill and power. At worst, it is lethal to this pack."

"What will you do?"

He took a deep breath. "Join the fight. Not just the convocation, but the actual fight. The next time I go against mages, my pack will be better prepared. It's time to move again, this time for good. It's time to establish myself in a busier place and join the shifter world in a meaningful way."

"No more madman persona?"

He quirked an eyebrow. "I didn't say that." He grinned. "Lord help any shifter who tries to take this pack from me." He downed the rest of his sparkling wine. "Come on. Niamh requested I grab you. They want to talk to Tilda now."

Ah. Now Niamh's impatience made sense.

"Should I be dreading this?" I grabbed my glass and stood with him. He stepped out of the way for me to go first.

"I don't know, and because I don't know, *I* am dreading it."

Fair.

Tilda sat in a chair in the middle of Drex's living room. The coffee table and couches had all been pushed to the walls to allow more space. Niamh sat in one of the chairs in the corner and Sebastian and Nessa stood to either side of Tilda. They'd donned their Elliot Graves and the Captain attire, and both were splattered with crimson. They were very good at mental warfare. Broken Sue and Aurora were against the walls, one at the front of Tilda and one at the back, probably watching for body language. Austin sat on the couch to the side.

"Did ya get lost or what?" Niamh demanded when we entered.

"Nah." Drex took my glass. "I took a page out of your book and poured myself a drink."

Niamh's brow lowered, but amusement lit her eyes. "Sure, ye need a cooler. Do two things at once, like."

"Okay, Jessie." Nessa bounded over, her ponytail bobbing. "Everyone in this room knows the sordid history of Miss Tilda here. You know a little, and that is plenty. You don't need to hear the rest. Just trust us that it is bad."

"Yup." I took a seat next to Austin. He draped his

arm over my shoulders.

"We also know when and how she left the Guild," Nessa said. "Basically, she poisoned a bunch of people and snuck out."

Tilda lifted her chin slightly and pursed her lips. She didn't feel badly about those deeds, not that I would, either.

"Why'd she take people with her?" I asked.

Nessa paused before looking at Sebastian. "I didn't even think to ask that, did you?"

"Yes. Usually Guild employees, especially those of higher status, think it is everyone for themselves. I wondered what they had that she needed."

Now Tilda's eyes narrowed, not liking that comment. We wouldn't even need Broken Sue or Aurora in here. Even I could read this mage's body language.

"Okay, we'll get to that in a while." Nessa bit her nail as she moved to stand directly in front of Tilda, who was not tied down. Her hands were free. She could use magic if she was quick enough, and Sebastian was making a statement that she wasn't. "Tilda, my darling, are we going to do this the easy way or the hard way?"

Drex came back in, his glass filled. He'd correctly surmised that I didn't want one. He sat down on the couch opposite Austin and me where he had a full view of the room and the front door beyond. He'd be a spectator, trusting in our mages to handle things.

"Just so everyone here knows what you are," Tilda said, "what is the hard way?"

Nessa laughed, swishing her stained cream romper. "They know exactly what we are, Tilda. They helped us with your past work associates, though you probably didn't know them. The Guild members were in the extraction department and much lower in the hierarchy than you. I know how the Guild likes to keep up the status quo."

Her lips thinned.

Nessa lifted her eyebrows. "Aren't you going to ask what the easy way is?"

"I'm not an idiot," Tilda spat. "I know how these things work."

"Because you've participated in these things," Sebastian said, using a knife to clean dirt out from under one of his nails. "We know. I guess it isn't just what *we* are, is it, Tilda?"

"Well…it is," Nessa said. The two of them were always amazing at playing off each other in these things. "*We*, as in *all* of us, her included."

"Oh, yes, right." Sebastian ticked the air in Tilda's direction with the knife. "By your definition, Tilda, we are all scum."

"I didn't have a choice," she replied angrily. "I created and administered the potions, or I was punished."

"Ah." Sebastian ticked the air again. "But you did have a choice. You either created and administered the potions, or you got punished. Tortured, if we want to put a name on it. I know this because *I* had a choice once. Pay an exorbitant amount of money for the privilege of being let go or continue to get tortured. Given that you saw me dragged to and from that room, I don't have to tell you which one I chose."

Her jaw clenched. She didn't respond.

"So, what's it going to be?" Nessa asked.

Tilda rolled her eyes. "I have nothing to hide. I told Alpha the truth."

"And now you can tell *us* the truth." Sebastian smiled pleasantly, a predator sighted in on its prey.

Tilda huffed out a breath. I could see her body trembling. "Look, I know"—she grit her teeth, apparently deciding not to start there—"I started in the Guild when I was eighteen. I had talent with potions but not a lot of power. The Guild was where you could earn some real money, so I started there near the bottom, and learned all I could so that I could advance. All I saw was that ladder, I'll admit it. I learned the culture, fell in step and stole, lied, and bought myself better and better potion recipes. Better know-how."

"By breaking into other people's labs?" Nessa asked,

walking around Tilda.

"Yes."

"By killing anyone that got in your way?"

Tilda's jaw clenched. Her eyes flicked to Drex and away again. "Yes. That's the way it was done."

"I realize that," Sebastian said. "I killed a—"

"No, you didn't," Nessa cut in. "You don't need to take the rap for me anymore, remember? *I* killed the mage that broke into your lab. I killed him from behind as he was about to deliver a killing blow to you."

"Right," Sebastian replied. "He was a powerful mage and a Guild favorite. It didn't matter that we killed him in self-defense, or that he was trespassing. We were held accountable. Well, *I* was. I took the blame because I knew they wouldn't kill me. I have too much power to waste. They would've easily killed Nessa. I was tortured for that death, and then I was tortured because I wouldn't pay to be released. Hell, maybe I was also tortured for shits and giggles. Honestly, it's hard to tell with the Guild."

"True," Nessa agreed. "Continue, Tilda."

If she cared or felt remorse on behalf of the Guild for any of that, she didn't show it.

"I learned. I advanced and got higher and higher positions, more money, and respect. I advanced faster than any potions engineer ever had. It was a badge of honor for me. I got invited to all the important dinners and parties."

"And what, pray tell, went wrong?" Nessa quirked her eyebrow. "What brought Humpty Dumpty tumbling off the wall?"

Tilda picked at her nail. "It wasn't any one thing, at first. It was a lot of little things. I checked into some of the people they took to those rooms—"

"To torture," Nessa quipped. "Which some might think is more than a *little* thing, but sure."

Tilda cleared her throat. "Some of those people had killed top mages when they shouldn't have, but others hadn't done anything wrong. They hadn't paid for the Guild's protection, even though the Guild never really provided protection. Or they offended someone. Or they had information the Guild wanted, even if it was somewhat arbitrary. Things like that. I heard of some political maneuvering that wasn't…entirely above board."

"It's got to be bad for you to be squeamish about it." Sebastian put his hand on his hip. "I'm very intrigued. But we'll get to the Guild's secrets later. We don't want to take up Jessie's precious time."

I swallowed and burrowed a little harder into Austin. Drex glanced at me and then away. If he was uncomfortable, he wasn't showing it. Not to me, anyway.

"About this time, a new power started infiltrating the Guild. It was subtle. Whispers here, information exchanged there, late hours by some of the higher-level staff, fancy new cars and watches people couldn't afford on their Guild salary. No one was talking. After a while, I was approached by someone claiming to be a representative of a powerful new mage on the scene—Momar."

Goosebumps covered my arms.

"We had conversations about duties and money. About loyalty and keeping secrets. I never met the man himself nor anyone else who worked for him. Just that one contact. He didn't tell me who else was employed, or if they were all working double-time for the Guild and Momar both. I tried to bring it up to a few people who'd seen a larger cash flow and then learned why you stayed in your lane where it concerns Momar."

"Lemme guess…" Sebastian bent a little to catch her eye. "The 'punishments' you didn't want to earn with the Guild. You got your ass handed to you."

"They nearly killed me," she spat. "They broke me up so badly, I was out of work for a month. The Guild didn't ask any questions. I didn't have to give any excuses. I didn't even call in—they'd already known I was out of commission. I was a privileged employee, and they did nothing." She swallowed. "That scared me.

I started paying more attention to things then. I mean, if the Guild would let that happen, what else would they allow? I saw all the shadow deals and the filthy things that started going on. The double-crossings, the quiet killing…" She took a deep breath. "The potions they started asking for were worse than anything I'd devised so far. Vile things. The Guild seemed like it was getting more ruthless, less civilized. I knew I had to get out. I couldn't work for them anymore. I was afraid to work for Momar. I didn't know who was on whose side, or if it was all one side, or what, I just knew I needed to leave—"

"Just so everyone in the cheap seats are caught up…" Sebastian put up a finger. "Let me break that down for you. She got treated like so many innocent people and people in low positions, and that scared her. She'd thought she was *special*. She'd thought she was above all that, and then she realized she wasn't."

"Quite a sobering realization," Nessa said.

"Indeed," Sebastian replied. "So, then she *started* to notice the normal operating procedure of the company she'd been working for and helping all this time. She took off the blinders and lo and behold, she was surrounded by monsters."

"She *was* a monster," Nessa said.

"I don't think that's the realization she actually

came to." Sebastian twisted his mouth to the side. "Which is a pity. It would've helped me like her a little."

"Not me." Nessa shrugged.

"She didn't leave because she sobered up to the horrors of the Guild." An edge crept into Sebastian's voice. "She left because she realized she was not immune from the horror, and she didn't want to be subjected to it."

"They didn't used to be so filthy," Tilda ground out. "It's Momar. He's infiltrated the Guild, and he's rotting it from the inside-out. He's gutting it of its valuable mages and tearing down the rest. No one is safe."

Nessa took a deep breath. "Once an egocentric mage, always an egocentric mage. Stay while the getting is good and get out when it turns."

Sebastian's eyes were hard and haunted as he stood in front of Tilda. "I have followed the actions of the Guild for a long time and trust me. It has *always* been rotten. Now it just has someone smarter and more cunning at the helm. But you are correct in one thing— no one is safe, least of all you."

He meandered out of the way and Nessa took his place, like a well-oiled machine.

"But why, pray tell, did you bring your flunkies with you?" She snapped, making Tilda jump. "Wait, I have a guess. You needed them to get you out, right?"

Tilda narrowed her eyes at Nessa. Her fingers

twitched. She was itching to blast Nessa with a spell.

"The answer is yes," Broken Sue said, his arms crossed over his chest.

"I'm sure the whole room could read that," Aurora murmured.

"Why'd they go with you, though?" Nessa scratched her chin. "Why would they risk their lives and livelihoods for you?"

"They're low in the hierarchy." Sebastian was standing behind Tilda now. "They already knew they didn't have any protection, were probably treated badly on the regular, and that Momar wouldn't want them. I'm sure they saw the writing on the wall. If Momar took over, they'd be expendable, and expendable in the Guild is not pleasant. A candied word or two from Tilda and *voila*. Time for a prison break."

"Also yes," Broken Sue said after a beat.

Nessa nodded in thought. "And they didn't turn her in and collect the rewards because they'd be killed for helping her escape. If she gets caught and they're with her, they'll be killed for the same reason. Any way you slice it, their lives are forfeit. Might as well live in this nowhere town with a bunch of animals than go back to the hell that was their life."

Drex tensed. Broken Sue tightened his arms over his chest and Aurora caught my eye, nodding subtly. Nessa was right. These people had been walking all over Drex's good intentions. Telling the truth, my ass.

"Well, here we are," Nessa said cheerfully, smiling down at Tilda. "You're just as rotten as the Guild. Thank you for reaffirming my world view."

"The question is, what do we do with her?" Sebastian asked.

Drex's whole body screamed *uncomfortable*. He'd given his word, and even though Tilda had taken advantage of that, and honor meant nothing to her or her people, he'd built his pack based on his principles. To go back on that word, even when it was justified, would make him no better than the enemies he fought to protect his pack against. He was not equipped to handle the messy reality of dealing with the Guild.

"She doesn't deserve our leniency," I said, taking control, "but she can be useful. This is what I propose— Tilda, are you listening? You'd better be, because there are worse things than a broken body. I have the power to break your mind. I'd rather not, but you helped drag me into this war, and so I will battle you the way mages dictate I battle." I paused to let that sink in. "I propose that Tilda answers every question Nessa, Sebastian, and Niamh can dream up. Easy way or hard way, there is a lot of knowledge in that noodle, Tilda, and we need it. We will take down the Guild and Momar with it, which will help you. It would behoove you to be open with them."

"Behoove. Nice word choice." Nessa gave me a thumbs up.

"Once they are satisfied," I continued, "Elliot Graves and the Captain will stage a murder. They'll send out footage of your extravagant death and taunt the Guild with it. Fred will then create a new alias for you, we'll give you seed money and ship you to a place where you can disappear. You can get a job with Janes and live in peace. Or whatever you want to do. Your cohorts will be shipped to other locations. None of you will know where the other is, and if any of you find each other or try to go back to the Guild or even *fart* in our direction, I will allow Niamh, Tristan, and Edgar to make a shrine out of you after your very real death. Does that sound good to everyone?"

Drex's muscles slowly relaxed, and he gave me the briefest of nods. *I can live with that.* Then a wink. *Thanks.*

"I couldn't think of a better plan meself," Niamh said with a nod, and I knew that was only because she'd read the same thing in Drex that I did. Otherwise, she'd call me a bleeding heart or something and "accidentally" kill those mages before wasting money on setting them up elsewhere. I was not fooled.

Sebastian held up a finger. "I request that you keep her here for a bit so that I can ransack her house and take her potions notes." He turned to her. "You did bring your journals with you, I assume? Very few mages leave without their best work."

Tilda didn't answer.

"Yes, she did," Broken Sue replied on her behalf.

"Go ahead," Drex said. "It sounds like that's all stolen knowledge anyway. It doesn't belong to her any more than it will belong to you. Might as well make use of it." His gaze swung my way, and he inclined his head. "Thank you for honoring my position and creating a solution that will absolve me of my duty to protect her and her people."

"Ye need to stomp on those rose-colored glasses, boyo," Niamh murmured.

If he planned to join the fight and get his hands dirty, that would happen soon enough. We might as well let him have his hero-complex just a little longer.

"Right so." Niamh pushed to standing. "That was fruitful. I'm hungry. Let's go see what that *bollocks* Mr. Tom has made for a late lunch."

CHAPTER 15
AUSTIN

FOUR FIRES GLOWED merrily within a large park just off the downtown strip. Smoke wafted from BBQs and people laughed and chatted. At every break in the cloud cover, a blanket of stars glimmered jovially.

This was their fifth evening in Drex's pack and the fourth cook-out he'd organized for Austin and Jess's people. Most of the pack was in attendance, providing food and smiles, drinks and a good time. The atmosphere was calm and relaxed in a way Austin could barely remember. Most of these people had a comfortable life without experiencing a hint of danger and it showed. Drex had provided exactly what he'd set out to, a safe haven where people could be free to live in peace.

Even as he was thinking it, Drex wandered over with a glass of something bubbly.

"Alpha," Drex said by way of greeting.

Austin inclined his head in hello. Jess was across the

way, chatting with Ulric and Jasper while Edgar stood to the side, wearing a strange smile while seemingly looking at nothing. Austin wasn't sure if he was trying to fit into the merriment or if his brain had randomly stopped while he was laughing at a joke.

"How goes it with the mages?" Drex asked, managing to hide his wariness at the thought. Mostly.

Niamh, Sebastian and Nessa had been working with the mages around the clock to gather information about the Guild and Momar. Brochan and Aurora and Tristan all took turns helping out, the first two reading body language when the mages tried to hide information, and Tristan lending his nightmare magic to loosen lips when the mages got stubborn. For the most part, though, the mages answered the questions willingly, knowing their only hope was in helping the convocation take down the Guild. Their fates were less than certain. Had been, since before they'd walked out of the Guild's doors.

"They're staging the murders now," Austin said, his hands in his pockets. "They'll film it and post it to message boards and what not. It's all politics at this point. They got the information they were after."

Drex took a sip of his drink. "To be brutally honest, none of this sits right with me."

"It didn't with me in the beginning, either. I was

viewing them through a strictly shifter lens. I've since learned more about the different magical cultures and some things aren't a problem anymore. Like breaking into someone's place and stealing their spells. That's usual in the mage world. They expect it and prepare for it. It's like the gargoyles staging a mock battle to steal that cairn's possessions."

"They do what?"

Austin chuckled and filled Drex in on the gargoyle raids.

"Huh. Whatever passes the time, I guess." Drex's eyebrows pulled together, but his movements suggested lightheartedness. He was a man eager to learn and with an open mind. That would serve him well. It certainly had helped Austin.

"Another thing mages do, apparently, is take trophies when they kill an enemy. Like a very rare and expensive sports car."

"That right?"

"Yup. Sebastian and Nessa acquired one from a mage that helped plan the attack on my brother," Austin said. "They sent Kingsley the car. It took a little convincing to get him to take it, because mage antics don't sit right with him, either, but he's coming around. Hard not to when you're staring at a piece of automotive beauty and your passion is collecting cars."

Drex laughed, a deep, hearty sound. A few people looked his way, smiling. "I can see how that would be persuasive, especially when it belonged to someone like that."

"The thing to remember is, we're currently dealing with the drudgery of mages. We're dealing with the worst of the worst. They're the ones in charge, and because of that, the honest mages—the ones who *don't* want to engage in this sort of behavior—try to stay out of the way. They try not to get caught in the crossfire, or make too many waves, because if they do, they'll be killed or punished. You heard Tilda. We've spoken to other mages who are doing everything in their power not to be noticed. They want change, and they want peace and a fair governing body, but they are sorely outnumbered, and so they are quiet."

"You're planning to seek out those mages and collect them up?" Drex asked.

"Yes. If we have any shot at winning this thing, we need mages on our side. We need more magic."

"But first you are after the shifters," he stated.

"The shifters, more gargoyles, more basajaunak..." It was overwhelming to think of how much effort they'd already put into this and how much further they still had to go. Would they have what it took to reach the end? "After we leave here we're going to meet a new cairn leader. We're hoping to get his support, and if we do, we're hopeful more will join up."

Drex took a sip and let silence filter in for a moment. Someone shrieked with laughter near one of the fires. An older man offered Jess a hotdog, reaching out to her as though offering her a bite.

A flash of rage boiled through Austin before he could tamp it down. His arms tensed but he resisted ripping his hands out of his pockets and running over there to make a show of possession. Hell, he wanted to beat the guy's face in.

He trusted Jess to handle it, and she did. She shook her head and stepped back, lifting her hand in a stop motion. He could tell she was politely declining. Wave after wave of love and support rose through their bonds, reassuring him. Helping him clear the red tinging his vision.

Jasper put his hand out to keep the man away. Two of their shifters and a couple of Drex's enforcers quickly drifted closer. Wrapping his arm around the man's shoulders, Ulric grabbed the hotdog with his free hand, took a bite, laughed, and led him toward one of the fires, diffusing the situation.

"I apologize for Clark," Drex said, his voice tight. It took Austin a moment to realize the other alpha was tense, ready for action. He'd seen what had happened.

"He came to us from a life with Dicks to *find his roots*. A midlife crisis, I think. His dad was a shifter but took off when he was young. He wants to live amongst shifters but doesn't seem to want to learn the culture. He's created a few problems because of it but he's harmless. We've let a lot go where it concerns him."

Austin sucked in a deep breath through his nose before letting it out again. He tried to will calm and release the need to go to Jess and wrap his arm around her shoulders.

"I have a tricky past," he said, "where that sort of behavior would mark him as a dead man. I try very hard not to be that guy."

"I thank you for that." Drex took a deep breath, too. He would've tried to diffuse the situation to save his pack member but obviously knew many alphas would kill anyone stuck in the way. Austin had the power to do so. "You have unbelievable control. I have only loved once, and it was in my youth, but I wouldn't have been able to stop myself from handling that in a very violent way."

"Something mages and gargoyles would think was barbaric and ridiculous."

Drex huffed. "I guess it is a little bit." He tilted his head. "It's probably a good thing I didn't allow shifter delegations in here. Clark flirts with any pretty woman he sees. He'd probably be dead now if I operated this pack like a usual shifter pack."

"Very likely."

Silence passed between them for a moment. Jess glanced his way, her body language suggesting she wanted to close the distance between them. She glanced at Drex and hesitated, then turned away to give them a moment to talk.

As if on cue, Drex said, "There's something I wanted to talk with you about." He paused and Austin waited. "I will join your convocation, if the offer still stands. I've already contacted a few of my closer friends about you and Jessie, and about your people. I've told them about the mages and what went down here. One of them asked if it was a setup."

Austin huffed, making Drex nod.

"I hadn't even thought about the prospect, to be honest," Drex said. "The notion is ludicrous to anyone who witnessed what went down, but it is quite a coincidence."

"It is. And we're thinking it *was* engineered, in a way, we just don't know why. Niamh is working on it."

"By Momar."

"That's the thought."

"They want to meet you, and I think that is wise. I've validated all the rumors, plus given my own insights, but they want to see for themselves. You were firmly established as something of a myth, mostly unbelievable. Now the winds are changing as more people validate the rumors. The myth is becoming a legend, and your mate is playing a part. They want to see for themselves, and I have a feeling their excitement to be part of something bigger will ripple through the community. It would be good for what you're trying to do."

But to stay even a few more days would delay a visit to the new cairn leader who'd taken over Nikken. They'd already been here two days longer than expected.

Drex was right, though. If he could garner some excitement, and these other packs spread that around, he could secure the support of powerful original alphas. That *would* go a long way to furthering the cause, not to mention they'd provide some muscle. They'd also be easier to direct, with their openminded approach and good work ethic, attributes needed to start a new prosperous pack.

He'd ask Tristan how bad it would look if they were late for the cairn meeting. If Austin could make it work, he would.

"I'll let you think about it," Drex said, good at reading cues and flowing with them. "I plan to move this pack into a more open and magically engaged area. The rural mountain has done its job. It's time to step out into the open."

"What about the people who don't want to go with you?"

"Leave no one behind." He nodded and *respect* colored his posture. "You and your brother have a lot of the same characteristics when it comes to leading a pack."

"He taught me even when he should've tossed me out."

"It shows, and I mean that in the best way." He finished his drink. "Vessa has agreed to stay and step into the alpha role. We'll have a plan in place for them to go out the backdoor, as the mages say, if danger comes. Most will move with me, though, I think. For whatever reason, and I do not know why, people tend to follow me."

"It's because you do your best to keep your promises. Your word is your oath, and your oath is genuine. People trust that."

"I try." He nodded in thanks. Sometimes people needed to hear the validation. He'd recently learned that himself. "I plan to move out in your direction. The way I see it, you're the target. You're the hub. You might need help and need it fast. I'll give you plenty of space, obviously, assuming your territory will continue to grow, as hopefully will mine, but my goal is to mobilize quickly and provide backup at a moment's notice. I've decided to join the fight, and I want to be in the action."

"Another pack close by would be welcomed, but you should know that my territory is not even remotely as laidback as this place. These people won't even tolerate me wandering around amongst them. I'm on the outskirts to give them a little peace."

Drex grinned. "You've got a certain presence about you. They probably sense your wildness and raw ruthlessness, and it messes with their *chi*."

"Yet they are totally fine with the basajaunak, for some reason." Austin shook his head in bewilderment. They even chatted to Edgar. How was Austin the problem here?

"Apparently, the mountain has calmed down," Drex said, "and the basajaunak with it. That's what my enforcer said, as though that would make sense to me. Spoiler alert, it didn't. But the basajaunak really are pleasant to be around. Jessie had mentioned that, but I didn't believe it. You just…aren't, clearly."

"Clearly," Austin said dryly, and Drex laughed.

"Anyway," Drex said, "I'll connect with you down the line, asking for advice on where to settle. I know time is against us, so I'll aim to move quickly. This isn't the first time I've picked up and moved on, as you know. I'm surprisingly adept at it now."

"I'll help in any way I can."

Drex tipped his glass upside down, emptying the last few drops onto the ground. "I hear you're headed to gargoyles near the Cascades. I thought I'd mention this to you, as well." He looped his fingers around the stem of his glass and let it hang. "I've heard of a powerful rogue up in Washington state. I don't have a lot of information on him. A friend of mine had a chance encounter and passed it on. He's a former alpha, I guess, with no interest in continuing that role. He's tried to find a place to settle, but as you can imagine, no shifter packs will take him. Even Dick and Jane towns are a problem for him, I guess. They treat him like an escaped convict or something." He shrugged. "I don't know. Being constantly watched or run out of town is no way to live. Now he's squatting in a forest on his own. I feel bad for the guy."

Jess's patience gave out. She excused herself from talking to a local and started Austin's way.

"My friend sympathized with him, too," Drex continued, "but this rogue's power is substantial. If he decided he might like to head up a pack again, or even if he caused trouble, he'd be a problem."

Jess smiled up at Austin as she reached him, not

even sparing a glance for Drex.

Austin bent down to kiss her. "Hey, baby."

"Hey." She slid a hand around Austin's waist and pressed into his side. "What's going on? You guys look very pensive over here."

Austin draped an arm around her and held her firmly, finally able to exert his possessive behavior to show this territory who his mate belonged to. And who he did.

He quickly told Jess what Drex had said so far.

"The rogue's power is possibly more than mine," Drex said after Austin had finished. "I'd like to offer him a place here, but my beast would get in the way. This rogue apparently doesn't want anything to do with challenges or dominance, but I wouldn't be able to let it go. You've seen that. Given your power, your setup, and your incredible control, I thought I'd let you know in case you wanted to step in."

"Obviously, we'll step in," Jess said, her free hand resting on Austin's chest. "We should at least extend the offer. Right, Austin?"

He nodded. "I'd planned to check in with some rogues anyway. He'll be a good practice run. We've got place for him if he wants the option. We just need to fit in the visit."

"Good. It's not easy being alpha material without

wanting alpha responsibilities," Drex said.

Austin knew that from experience, even in a Dick town, as Drex had said.

Drex stepped away and hesitated. "A word of caution. My friend said this rogue had cagey eyes and seemed jumpy. He wasn't threatened by my friend, and so he didn't attack. With someone of your caliber, though…" He shrugged. "I'm just guessing, but we do rash things when we think we're cornered, and someone like you might be triggering. He might attack before he knows why you're there, and he's mighty. Watch yourself."

CHAPTER 16
TRISTAN

TWO DAYS LATER, Tristan slowed the Jeep as he noticed Fred in the middle of the road. She was walking toward the houses they were all staying in at the end of the cul-de-sac. She had a flowery reusable shopping bag looped around her shoulder, but it didn't seem to have much in it.

He pulled up beside her and matched her speed. "Need a ride?"

She glanced over like she hadn't heard the Jeep approaching. "Oh, hey," she said, recognition lighting her expression. She kept walking. "How goes it?"

"Good. Need a ride?"

"No. I'm just going…" She pointed at the houses at the end of the street. "I'm almost there. Thanks, though. Nice day, huh?"

He glanced up at the partly cloudy sky. The heat seemed to boost the humidity to almost unbearable proportions. He wasn't used to it. Fred clearly had no problems.

"Doing a little shopping?" he asked with a grin.

"Nah." She looked at the bag. "I was wandering around downtown for a little exercise and this nice lady in the flower shop insisted I take this bag to hold my computer. I've found it is very hard to argue with these people. They're extremely pushy in their kindness, you know? They don't take no for an answer. I like it as much as I hate it, I think. I mean…I *like* it, I'm not Satan, but it also kinda weighs on you, you know? Now I feel like I owe her something because I took her bag."

He chuckled. There was something so fun and refreshing in her eccentricities. He found no end of amusement in her.

"You should buy one of her flowers," I suggested.

"I can't! I can't run fast enough to get away after paying for things. Yesterday, I bought a burrito and tried to pay and got that push back I was talking about. So, I smiled and nodded and laid the money on the counter. The man pushed it back, so I tried to explain that I'm not really part of this pack thing, that I'm a Jane, and so I would rather pay for it. I pushed it toward him, he pushed it back. I slid it at him again, and he tried to push it back, but I'd already turned around and started running. Well." She stopped and faced Tristan angrily. "He ran after me, right out of the store, caught me down the street, smiled at me and curled my fingers around the money. Then he patted me on the back and asked if I needed a hand carrying anything. *That man is eighty years old!*" she hollered. "How can I feel good about myself when I can't pay for things, I can't be as nice as they are, and I can't even outrun an octogenarian!"

She shook her head and started walking again.

"When are we leaving, anyway?" she asked. "I can't stand the niceness."

"Maybe you *are* Satan."

"Yeah, maybe," she muttered. "What a thing to find out about yourself, right? I like the rude, surly Irishwoman better than salt of the earth, heartfelt, lovely people."

He laughed. "Well, it's a good thing you are employed by the former, then. The alphas have the meeting with the original alphas in an hour. If that goes well, we can leave as early as tomorrow, I think. Maybe the next day depending on transportation."

"And if it doesn't go well?"

"Then there will probably be challenges and Jessie and Indigo will probably want to hang around and make sure no one dies. But we shouldn't have to stay too much longer."

Fred nodded and trudged on. He figured that was his cue to leave her alone. She and Niamh had had their heads down a lot lately, working closely with Sebastian and Natasha on the information they'd gathered from Tilda and the other mages. They were a solid team, but they were still way behind Momar. They had a lot to figure out about his operations, motivations, and goals before they could start going after him directly.

He parked the Jeep and then let himself into the alphas' house. Mr. Tom bustled by holding a stack of folded laundry. He didn't pay Tristan any attention.

Jessie sat at the table wearing a flowing pink dress and no shoes. Shifters dressed like that when attending a meeting where there might be an unexpected challenge or an attack. It let them get out of their clothes and into their animal as quickly as possible. She held a steaming mug of coffee, and her shoulders were tight with anxiety.

"You okay?" Tristan asked, dropping the Jeep keys onto the table.

She gave him a half-smile. "Yeah." She didn't elaborate, which meant she had multiple things on her mind.

He pulled out a chair and took a seat across from her. "What's going on?"

She studied him a moment, eyes narrowed, as if trying to decide whether to burden him with her issues.

"Wait." He held up a finger, then rose and crossed the kitchen to a pile of papers Fred kept there for safekeeping. At the bottom was the little kid's diary Mr. Tom had started for Jessie.

He slid it out and grabbed a pen from the junk drawer that was heavily organized. Clearly, no one lived in this house long enough to accrue the sort of junk that should live in that drawer.

Jessie snorted when she saw what he'd grabbed.

Back in the chair, he twisted the key in the metallic lock and popped it open. On a blank page, he positioned himself and prepared to write.

"Okay, fire away." He held up his finger again, his expression utterly serious. "Don't pepper in your hopes and dreams. It is my duty to make those up for you."

She blurted out a laugh, easing a little tension. Then she sighed, breaking down. He had learned that she rarely asked for help when she needed it.

Still, she hesitated, a crease forming between her brows. Her thoughts must've been jumbled.

"Start with the first issue," he instructed.

"These alphas we're about to meet—" She took a deep breath. "Drex warned us they're rough and tumble. They are all powerful, and they've all had to fight off attacks from other shifters trying to take their territory. They might be compelled to challenge."

"Austin can handle them. Even if there are multiple attacks, he can handle them. He's primed and ready for it. He's in his element. And you've shown that you're adept at breaking it up. You've both got this."

"I know, and I've mostly made peace with that…but Drex is wondering if they might also challenge me."

"Ah." Tristan tapped his pen against the diary. That would be a great entry. His goal was to fill this little journal and give it to her so she could laugh at it. "And you're worried you'll go too hard?"

She swallowed and then shrugged. "I can do some very serious damage now. You saw that skirmish with the mercenary and mage attack. That was me trying to *maim*."

He hadn't seen her get challenged in an official capacity, but he'd heard about it. She'd been so incredibly vicious, apparently, and theatrical in her violence, that no one had ever challenged her again.

"Maybe just stick to the old spells," he offered. "That's easy enough, isn't it? I do think it will help this convocation to show what you can really do. They are probably only thinking of challenging you because Drex told them what he saw with those mages. You need to be a part of Austin's urban legend. You need to show them what you bring to the table, but also how terrifying mages are."

She took another deep breath. "That's true."

"And it is a shifter challenge. For all they poo-poo how mages do things, they bake a lot of killing into their culture. If they challenge, that means that they know they could die. You won't be at fault for killing them." He shrugged. "They took the risk, and they have to accept the results. Austin had to harden himself to the mage culture. You'll have to harden yourself to shifter culture."

She put her elbows on the table and slumped over them. "Yeah."

He gave her a moment to ponder that. "What else?"

"I had a bad dream about going after that rogue last night. Like maybe he was more powerful than Austin and I didn't get there in time."

Tristan pursed his lips in thought, deciding the best way to counteract that one. Her gargoyle had been giving her some great warnings of things to come on this trip. That was likely because of the connections she had with the basajaunak, but maybe not. Maybe it was another facet of her magic rising to the surface. She was probably worried the dream had been a premonition. He didn't want to ask, though, in case she hadn't thought of that.

So instead, he went for reassurance.

"Austin fought and killed a phoenix. He's more

than just powerful. He's got a strong will and unstoppable motivation. Even if this shifter is stronger—even if he is better in every respect—Austin is a hard man to kill. Before this shifter could manage, you'd feel Austin's pain or hear him, and you'd show up to play hero. Austin would hang on until you did. You two are a team. Ain't no shifter strong enough to tear you two apart."

She smiled at him gratefully. "Yeah," she said softly.

"Next?" He made a *keep it moving* gesture. "I need to write down all these thoughts and dreams before we go."

She put out her hands expressively, her eyebrows raised. "We're three days late in meeting Evan from Nikken." She tugged her ponytail in frustration.

Austin walked in wearing a white, button-down shirt with the sleeves rolled up to his forearms. The top few buttons were undone, showing his chest. His slacks had the top button undone. He also didn't wear shoes. This wasn't like the meeting that Kingsley arranged. He wasn't trying to show his control and decorum. For this meeting, he was ready to rumble.

Shivers washed over Tristan. He sincerely hoped one of their betas wanted to play, as well. Tristan never got challenged at these things despite his not-very-subtle taunting.

"I realize he said it was fine when I called him to explain, but I'd wanted to make a good impression. Being late is not it. And we're not even sure if we can get out of here tomorrow. Mr. Tom is having some problems with the transportation since we missed our initial reservation."

Austin stopped behind her and ran his hands up her arms to her shoulders. He kneaded slowly, further draining away her tension.

"Actually, that's why I'm here early," Tristan said. "Gerard sent his own connection request to Evan. Patty called to let me know. Sorry, I should've led with that."

"So, he's going to take our slot or something?" Jessie asked in confusion.

Tristan shook his head. "Apparently, Gerard has kept tabs on you since he helped us with the battle at Kingsley's. You gave them a taste of what they were meant for, being a battle species, and he doesn't want to be left out of the next fight. I think he cares about that more than joining the convocation." Tristan chuckled. "Anyway, when he heard you'd sent Evan a connection request, he sent one of his own. Obviously, there is no way Evan would turn Gerard down, since Gerard is one of the other three top cairns. Gerard needs a week or so to get there, and Evan needs to prepare for another leader, so we have a little buffer."

"Oh." The breath gushed out of Jessie followed by a relieved smile. "That's great news! For meeting the cairns, at least." She leaned her head back against Austin and looked up at him. "What does that mean for your plans?"

He gazed at her for a quiet moment, drinking her in, Tristan knew. He ran his thumb along the edge of her jaw and his eyes softened. Her smile turned serene. He didn't need words to make his love for her known. Tristan needed to take notes.

"I'm good," he finally said. "I'll make it work. Rather than hang around here, though, maybe we can swing by and check out that rogue. It's not all that far away from our destination. I'm curious about him, not to mention I feel sorry for him."

Her brows pinched together, but she didn't comment.

He bent to kiss her forehead, a comforting gesture. "No one is going to take me down, baby, I promise. Not in"—he glanced at the oven clock—"half an hour, and not when I meet that rogue. I got this."

Tristan had the utmost faith that Austin did. When Austin was the one being challenged, anyway. He wondered how Austin would handle it when an alpha challenged Jessie, something that might happen very soon. He couldn't imagine the big man would take it lightly.

Then again, in the world of shifters, he also didn't have much choice. And if she wanted to lead, neither did she.

CHAPTER 17

AUSTIN

H E KNEW OF every single alpha at this meeting. He'd sought out Drex specifically because he had the ear of these shifters. They were tough, they were vicious, and they clawed their way toward prosperity. They were the muscle—the packs that could pivot on a dime and were used to hard times. None of these men and women had been handed anything. They'd all started with nothing, unlike Austin himself. Unlike Jess.

They also wanted Austin to prove himself, and they'd be hard judges.

Fine. He'd show them the side of him that he tried to keep buttoned up when in the presence of generational alphas with their trust funds and their sprawling, largely peaceful packs. He'd show them what had earned him the bad reputation while also showing them how he would overcome it. He wouldn't have guessed this just two days ago, but going into this meeting and expecting violence, he was in his element. He didn't have to hide who he was, the wildness that lurked within. He could display the way he came to have a pack and how he'd keep it moving forward without hesitation. He'd show them how he could protect them all.

By the time Austin arrived, orderly lines of hard-eyed shifters waited outside of Drex's house, and at the head of each waited an alpha, he or she facing the inlet of the street. As before, Drex stood on his porch, his upper tiered enforcers spread out on either side. Just like at the meetup with Kingsley, these packs wanted to see Austin's arsenal.

Austin parked the Jeep at the curb His people followed suit. He got out first and crossed in front of the vehicle, stopping at Jess's door. He opened it and waited for her to get out before taking her hand. He showered her with his full attention and kissed the inside of her wrist, a show of devotion for his mate and co-leader.

It was also a warning.

These alphas should know the rules of a meeting like this, but that didn't mean they always followed them. If they broke code and endangered her in any way, he'd kill them without hesitation or remorse. Now they knew.

Her wariness crept through the bonds. She read his mood and sensed the danger.

"Treat this as you have past meetups," he said as he walked her to the center of the street. "As you did Kingsley's. If anything kicks off, react however you need to, okay?"

"Okay."

"Don't worry about me. I'll handle whatever comes."

"Okay."

"I love you."

She squeezed his hand. "I love you, too."

His people separated into their lines, gargoyles on one side and shifters on the other. Shadows curled around Tristan's large frame, and Brochan walked with his shoulders rolled forward, as though headed toward a brawl. Their lines created a V, in the middle of which flocked Jess's crew. Surprisingly, however, they didn't form a loose hoard like at the last meetup. This time, they walked in a mostly straight line until everyone as a group stopped, and then they jostled into a few uneven rows. Indigo didn't even trip.

"Alpha Steele." Drex inclined his head in greeting. To Jessie, he allowed a tiny smile before putting out his hands. "No muumuu? I wore mine."

She returned his smile, albeit nervously. "I confess, I didn't know it was an option. While we're talking about dress code, I don't think flip-flops would go amiss."

Drex glanced at her feet. "Then how would we pretend we're so tough by walking on the rocky ground?" He looked around at the other alphas. "Let me make introductions."

He gave the alpha's names, the age of their packs, and their various locations. He also mentioned what they'd started with—very little—and what their townships were like now. For each one, Jess showed how impressed she was with the growth and nodded with each point.

"And this is Jessie Ironheart and Austin Steele, original alphas of the Dusky Ridge Convocation. The convocation is nearly a year old, incredibly new, but already the size of three towns and growing. They reside in the Sierra foothills, where I will look into moving my pack. I must confess, however, I don't have the details of what they started with."

Except he did, knowing that Austin had inherited a fortune from his generational family. He was allowing Austin to define his wealth. Or maybe wondering if Austin would make light of it to better fit in.

He had nothing to hide, and he'd never fit in. He'd made peace with that after visiting Kingsley's territory following the long time away.

"I showed up in O'Briens with a large inheritance and no desire to use it," he said, getting that out there right off the bat. "I started a business, a bar, and used the proceeds to buy some land and build a home. It wasn't until I decided to officially take the title of alpha and build up my territory in a hurry, that I dug my hand into my deep pockets."

"Why did you need to build a territory in a hurry?" Rhea asked, a woman on the shorter side with dark skin and deep brown, piercing eyes. She'd started with debt and now had the most prosperous territory of this group. She seemed like a helluva businesswoman.

"Because Jess took the magic of Ivy House and needed a strong force to protect her," he replied. "She's been a target since day one. I decided I would be the castle guarding her keep."

All eyes turned to Jess.

"And you, Alpha Ironheart?" Drex said.

"Oh." She seemed surprised that they should care. "I was a Jane who'd just gotten divorced and didn't want to live with my parents. I thought I was getting a job as a caretaker of an old house. Instead, I became magical, took a blood oath to tie me to the house and its magic, and got an absolute shitload of money. Just a ridiculous amount of money, along with a whole lot of danger that might kill me before I can enjoy it. I don't know anything about running a territory or creating businesses from scratch because I'm too busy learning this tidal wave of magic and putting together an army that Austin and I need to co-lead to stay alive. I'm going from battle to battle, challenge to challenge, fight to fight while desperately trying to shake some sense into shifters who are too scared or stupid or both to realize the very real danger you are all in. While also trying to find the mages who are very aware of the danger *they* are in and so are trying to hide in plain sight so they won't be killed by the incredibly cunning and powerful mage organization that is threatening the entire magical world. I know we have to prove ourselves, and theoretically that makes sense, but honestly, this feels like just handing Momar a bunch of time that he will wisely use to create a plan to kill me when I least expect it. Sebastian and I are currently the only thing keeping him from systematically killing all the shifters, and he knows it. Without magical power, you're all dead. Don't bother trying to organize, there's no point. So, every moment I spend meeting alphas is a moment I'm *not* meeting mages that can help me magically stand up to Momar's people."

The torrent of words cut off, her eyes widened, and she clicked her mouth shut. Her body language did the equivalent of finding a hole and crawling inside. Her stress and anxiety with their whole situation had finally boiled over and honestly, there couldn't have been a better time. There could be no doubt that she was genuine, as well.

Edgar tsked. "Jessie," he whispered, "that is not how we make friends."

"I do not love that I agree with that vampire," Ulric murmured.

"Truth," Jasper quietly responded.

"Well, then." Fenric, a barrel of a man with a straggly red beard stepped out of his pack's line. "Not that any of us doubted Drex, but if we did, we can plainly see Alpha Steele has the power we've heard of and a certain something else to go with it. I understand now why he makes people nervous. The beta with the power of an alpha checks out, too. The massive gargoyle, the basajaun, all that power there in the middle."

"Which are the mages?" Barek asked, in his early thirties with a wiry body. Despite the almost slender frame, Austin had heard this guy was serious trouble in a fight.

Jess turned and pointed. Sebastian and Nessa stepped out.

"I'm not magically powerful," Nessa said. "My uses are more in-line with espionage and strategy."

"I'm powerful," Sebastian said without emphasis.

"You're Elliot Graves, is that right?" Rhea asked.

"Correct, though that is a secret that Momar almost

certainly knows but is not sharing in the magical world. We're not sure why."

"And why aren't you sharing it?" Drex asked.

It was Niamh that spoke up. "Because they are the bad cops, and we are the good cops. They will attract the mages that don't mind breaking the rules and getting their hands dirty, and we will attract the opposite. We'll reveal our joint venture when it will do the most good, and hopefully before Momar does. I just need to figure out why Momar is keeping it to himself still. He's a cunning one. I can't quite get a handle on him yet."

Drex asked Jessie to introduce her people. When she'd finished, they asked if they could get a demonstration of Cyra and Hollace. Their expressions didn't change when the great thunderbird rolled his sonic boom across the sky and then zapped down lightning down the street.

Cyra didn't play things so safely.

The phoenix swooped down toward them and opened her beak. A thin stream of fire burned a line into the concrete, tracking straight for Fenric.

Two feet away, Jess stepped forward, her hands out, and looked up. "Take it easy," she called up at Cyra.

The fire continued, not slowing. Fenric's eyes tightened marginally. His fingers spasmed, the only indication of his wariness. Still the fire burned a black line toward him. A foot away now. His loose clothes and face glowed from the fire. Sweat broke out on his brow. He took a step back, giving himself more space. The fire kept coming. If she was playing chicken, she'd just won. Clearly, she wasn't playing.

"Damn it, Cyra." Jess went active, shoving her hands forward.

A torrent of wind raced upwards. Halfway to Cyra, wind turned to water and spread out. An angry hiss issued from the stream of fire as the water hit it. Steam so thick it looked like fog enveloped Cyra as the water washed over her.

"Wow, Jessie," Sebastian said. "How'd you devise that?"

"On accident. I found a better way to do"—Jess sent up another spell—"elemental magic. It's easier to control this way."

The spell exploded by Cyra's side. The turbulence of the air rolled her before Jessie sent up a slash of magic to slice into her wing. Cyra chirped, her signal for giving in. She haphazardly flapped her way to the ground before shifting back into her human form.

Jess flared her hands in irritation. "What are you doing? They weren't looking to get their faces blasted off, they just wanted to see what a legendary phoenix could do."

Cyra looked at the gash in her right arm and grinned. "They wanted proof of our power, right? I figured blasting off a toe would be good proof."

Hollace landed farther down the street and walked up.

"Did you see how easily she backed me down this time, Hollace?" Cyra asked him. "Work smarter, not harder. Don't I always say that?"

"No. Everyone else always says that and you nod," he replied.

"Yeah, same thing."

"I thought that was great proof," Indigo said. Stepping forward, she placed a hand on Cyra's back to start healing her. "They obviously wanted a show. A missing toe would've done it."

Jess gave the alphas an apologetic shrug. "We train for battle, not for show and tell. Sometimes, they go overboard."

Fenric stepped back into his place. He was still sweating heavily, but he had his body back under control.

Expectation filled the air. They wanted more. They got their theatrics, and now they wanted this done the shifter way. To lead them, one would need to dominate the strongest of them. That was Drex, but they hadn't been here for that challenge. They'd need to stand witness to another.

This time, Austin wouldn't test or bait. This time, Austin would put them down hard and fast.

Finally, Derrick stepped forward, a jaguar. He had strength and power, but his best advantages were in stealth. He was fast and ruthless, Austin had heard. It was an odd choice for the challenge.

Derrick looked straight at Jess.

Cold trickled down Austin's spine. Drex had mentioned this might be a possibility, but Austin had discounted it. Jess could shift, but she wasn't a shifter. She wasn't of the culture. Yes, she could certainly be challenged because she was co-leader, but he hadn't thought any high-level shifters would bother, just as they didn't tend to challenge Tristan or the other gargoyles.

His blood felt like it was turning to ice as Derrick walked into the middle of the gathered shifters, his gaze rooted to hers. His challenge was clear. He'd go after Austin's mate. He'd hurt her, nearly try to kill her.

Ice turned to an inferno as his beast rose up. Red throbbed in his vision, yanking at him to become action. To rush forward and rip that shifter apart for daring to challenge Austin's prize. His heart. The darkness swirled and sucked at him, trying to pull him under.

"Hey, it's okay." Jess's soft voice cut through the haze. Her hand touched his chest, over his heart. Her other hand flattened against his jaw, gentle. "It's okay. We knew this day would come eventually, right? I need to prove my worth or whatever. They have every right to challenge me."

The idea of a male challenging his mate ate at him. It smacked of encroaching on his territory. It wasn't an unfair fight—well, actually it was because Jess could kill him easily—but it felt like it for some reason.

"Deep breath," Jess whispered, taking her time with him. She would clearly make Derrick wait all day if she had to. "I got this. Kinda. I mean, I'm very nervous that I'll accidentally do something terrible, like explode his head or something, but I'll be okay. You can step in if something goes wrong. I watched you, and now you'll watch me."

He cradled her face in his palms. "Do not let him hurt you. Don't let him even touch you. Defend yourself, okay? Don't take damage to prove a point. Don't take any damage at all."

"Okay." Her fingers wrapped around his wrists. "I'll be fine."

He let go a breath and kissed her soundly. "I hate this," he murmured, echoing what she'd said when Drex had challenged him.

She smiled, realizing it. "I know."

He let her go and stood his ground, not shadowing her toward Derrick as he really wanted to.

She stopped ten feet from Derrick, probably because that's the distance Drex had given Austin the other day. Her nervousness was plain as she fidgeted.

"I just want to give you a moment to think this through," she told the shifter, worry seeping into her voice. "I do magic, and I am very powerful. I have trained solely for battle, and I've trained hard. I do not need to shift to kill you, and accidently killing you is a very real possibility because I am still learning. This is a very dangerous challenge for you. You'll be dead before anyone realizes I did a killing spell, including me. I won't be able to heal you from some of the stuff I do, *and I do them on accident*. I can't stress that enough. I'll be desperately trying to do the safer spells, but if I get nervous…" She shrugged. "Curtains. Do you really want to go through with this?"

Drex had a lopsided smile on his face. One of the other alphas, Selene, a stocky woman, allowed a hint of confusion in her expression. They likely didn't know what mages could really do, and this probably seemed absurd to them. Jess was one hundred percent correct in warning him, though, especially after what she'd done in that battle. She hadn't had Sebastian to practice with for a handful of months, and it showed. They needed to carve out more time for her magical training. It affirmed the change in plans he was thinking of.

"He's showing you that he will proceed," Brochan said, and Austin forgot about Jess not being able to read the subtler body mechanics of shifters, a necessary trait when leading in animal form.

Jess bowed in defeated resignation. "Fine," she grumbled. She stripped off her dress. "Sebastian, can you think of any way you can help if I go too hard?"

"Not unless I keep up a shield for him, and that defeats the purpose. They need to see what Momar and his people—what you and I—are capable of."

Austin couldn't agree more.

"Fine," she repeated grumpily.

"I notice you didn't give your phoenix all these theatrics," Derrick said in smug indifference. He thought Jess was full of shit. It showed in his tone and every line in his body.

"Yeah, because she comes back from the dead, genius," Jess said without missing a beat.

Brochan grunted, a laugh for him. Drex's smile couldn't get any bigger.

"This is a terrible idea," Sebastian said, pushing forward and walking around Austin.

"What are you doing?" Austin asked as Jess shifted

into her gargoyle form.

"He's going to rile her up, and then she is going to hammer him. I can't be the only one who sees that. When she does, I'll try to put a wall or something between them to filter some of those spells. It's the best I can do." He lowered his voice to a murmur. "She better not challenge me after this. I hate when she does that."

"Welcome to the bloody circus," Niamh said from somewhere in the back.

"Yes, we realize you present yourself with the utmost decorum in any situation," Mr. Tom told her. "Your cooler says it all."

Austin held up his hand to quiet them as Jess took to the sky, shedding her magical light. The alphas' eyes glittered even if they didn't show any other reaction. She was a beautiful sight to behold.

Derrick shed his loose clothing and shifted into his panther, sleek and graceful and way outmatched. No doubt he had experience with fliers, having run across them over the years, but not like Jess. Fliers had to swoop in to attack. She didn't.

Derrick prowled around the ground, looking up at her, waiting patiently.

"Shheeed," Jess called down.

"What?" Sebastian asked.

"Shh-eee-lll-ddd," she enunciated.

"Shield," Tristan said. "Shield him."

The panther tensed, flicking his tail.

"He doesn't want it," Brochan called up.

"She didn't ask," Tristan said before she could attempt more words. "Strong as you can, Sebastian. The gargoyle has emerged. Time to make an example."

CHAPTER 18
AUSTIN

TRISTAN WAS CORRECTLY reading the situation.

Jess lowered until she was just beyond jumping distance and then let loose. She slammed down a spell. It hit the panther and knocked him flat. She hit him with another, and another, firing them as fast as she ever had in battle. She was practicing.

How had he ever felt fear on her behalf?

The panther cried out as slashes opened on his skin, red cutting through the black. He fought through it, pushing through the tumult and the pain.

"How do we know that mage is really shielding him?" Fenric asked, but one look at Sebastian was all he needed.

Sebastian's face had gone red with exertion. Sweat dripped down his temples. His whole body was tense with determination, and his hands were moving quickly.

The magic changed. Now flares of color erupted against the panther. It coated the furry body in places, outlining the magic surrounding him. Ask and you shall receive.

"How are you keeping up the strength for all these spells?" Sebastian called to her. "They're too powerful for a battle. You don't need all this to kill. It's a waste of your energy. You need to go for less energy spells to keep up your endurance. I barely lasted through the battle at Kingsley's, and I was being very mindful about my energy."

Jess didn't relent, smashing down more spells, clearly trying to go faster.

"She practices at this level until exertion, and then she moves on to the less powerful spells until she can barely stand," Tristan told him. "She's been training like that since you left specifically *for* a battle like Kingsley's. She is purposefully working on her endurance with the more powerful spells, and she's found plenty of those in the Ivy House books. Hence, her worry about accidentally killing this dude. Good practice, though. We haven't had anyone to shield us, so she hasn't been able to practice on a person."

The panther growled, still attempting to stand. He'd only gotten as far as his belly. His head was low, and he was fighting against the tide of pain. Burn marks appeared in places, more cuts, lumps of flesh taken out.

"This isn't a challenge," Barek said, his eyes tight and his body tense with wariness. "This is too one-sided for a challenge, even if that mage wasn't doing anything at all to help. Derrick is just enduring it. He's not fighting back."

"He *can't* fight back," Drex said, his smile gone. "That's the point I was trying to make."

The magic stopped, and the damage on the panther started to heal over.

"She's healing him," Austin said, so they would know what was happening. "That is not a mage trait, that is a trait exclusive to a female gargoyle, who is a sorceress. She's more powerful, she can connect with her people through battle bonds, and she can heal."

"Among other things," Tristan murmured.

Sebastian was breathing heavily but didn't step back. He watched Jess closely as she did a circle around the panther and then slowly lowered to the ground.

"Apparently, I need to work on my endurance, as well," Sebastian said. "She doesn't even look winded."

The moment Jess landed, the panther lunged. Austin stepped forward in a rush, but Tristan and Brochan grabbed him, holding him in place.

"Let her handle it," Tristan said under his breath. "She doesn't need our help. That panther does."

"Not ours," Brochan said. "Sebastian's."

The panther hit a magical wall. A great buzzing echoed against the house. The panther howled in pain and flew backwards from the force of the magic.

Jess shifted into her human form. Where before her expression held worry and unease, now she was stoic and calm, watching him with calculating eyes. The gargoyle had emerged and with it, her battle sense.

The panther rose again and stalked toward her slowly, sizing her up.

"A mage wouldn't wait around for a shifter to engage," she said, her eyes hard as she surveyed him. "A mage would be firing or running, and I am losing patience."

Her hands thrust forward. The panther jumped and burst through a sudden wall of magic. Flame covered his fur. She calmly got out of the way as he landed and started to roll. She sapped the magic away, now on the other side of him. He turned and ran at her, snarling, lips pulled away from long white teeth.

Jess didn't move this time. She held her position and started hammering him. The first spell hit, and he endured. Then the second, the third—she blasted him until he was cowering on the concrete, shaking with the onslaught, unable to fight through the magic. The most powerful shifters might be able to, handling the pain, but he wasn't one of them. Or maybe he just didn't have the experience of enduring something like this. He didn't have experience with mages.

"He's done." Sebastian jogged forward and threw his own spell, hitting her square in the chest.

She shuffled backward and bent, her hand coming up to palm her solar plexus. "Ouch." When she straightened, her eyes were alight.

"Damn it," Sebastian mumbled.

"Derrick, stand down," Drex called as the panther struggled to right himself. He'd lost. There was no point in continuing with this.

Jess zinged another spell Sebastian's way. "Use your strongest shield. I'm going to up the power."

"I hate when you do this," Sebastian said, firing faster than Jess could. She'd done a lot of practice, but he had decades of experience and was at the top of his class. "I'm going to do the same, though apparently I won't last as long."

"He missed training with her." Nessa wandered closer. "He might be grumbling, but he loves this. We haven't had much training time since we've been back. Not in any real way. He missed teaching her magic and watching her blossom."

It showed in his little smile as he dueled with her, hitting her with a spell, and then spinning away from her answering magic.

"I've found that if you create a moving target," Sebastian told her, "classically trained mages get caught up. It messes up their spell work."

Jess didn't bother moving, instead using the time to gather a stronger spell and blasting him with it.

"Okay, well…" Sebastian grunted, flinching at the onslaught. "Obviously, you are not one of them."

"I've never practiced on a stationary target," she said, walking a little closer and hitting him with another spell. He answered with one of his own, forcing her to step back and shake her head in pain. "Ouch. That was a good one."

"Yeah. Lower on power but should hurt like hell."

"It does."

"You're a liar, though." He walked to the side and hit her with two spells to her one. "Austin stood there and took it when you were learning, remember that? You tore him all up, and he just readied for the next. Or like, got off the ground and climbed back to standing to take the next one. I'll never forget that. I thought you two were joking when you were about to unleash that one spell on him. Remember?"

"Vaguely." Jess grunted. Her face was screwed up in pain and annoyance. "Say *uncle*."

"What—crap." Sebastian's hands started moving

faster as Jess's new spells hit him. "Jesus, Jessie. What—*shit*."

Jessie walked toward him, her eyes sparkling with viciousness, her gargoyle peeking through. The pain had triggered the darkness, and she was letting it consume her.

"Get ready," Austin said to Tristan and Brochan. "Tristan, shift. Sometimes, it's easier than others to pull her out of it. Take Sebastian out of here if she gets to be too much."

Sebastian had stopped talking, his expression determined once more. His face once again turned red. He walked left and right, taking her spells and then throwing them back. She walked straight at him, like an animal cornering its prey. Blood seeped down her skin from a dozen or so wounds, but she didn't let it slow her. Sebastian's clothes were ripped and charred and sticky with blood in places.

"Damn it, what are these spells?" Sebastian muttered to himself. "Think it through. *Think it through...*"

His knees started to buckle. Still, she bore down on him. His breath came fast.

"Uncle," Sebastian said, staggering backwards. "Uncle!"

"Take him out," Austin barked.

Tristan snapped his wings and hop-stepped forward, snatching Sebastian out of harm's way as Jessie hit him with a spell. A sheet of skin ripped from Tristan's arm where it wrapped around Sebastian. He growled with the pain but didn't recoil. Blood immediately started running down his arm. He bent and then rocketed into the sky, his wings jetting him high in a blink.

"Hey." Austin took Sebastian's place with his arms out in surrender. "Back down now. Come back to me. The challenge—both challenges—are over."

Jess stopped, her eyes flickering with uncertainty, lost in the viciousness of her gargoyle, and then they cleared.

She took a deep breath. "I'm tired," she finally said as Nessa bounded over with her pink dress. "Indigo, Tristan is going to need healing. He gets surly when he's hurt."

"I don't mind putting my hands on that gargoyle," Indigo replied from somewhere in the back of their people.

"Uh, Jessie?" Drex still stood on his porch, a grin peeking through his expression. "You've got a rogue vampire on the loose."

Two tense shifters on the porch made a show of staying perfectly still. Standing too close to their backs, as though trying to push into their line, Edgar waited with that strange simpering smile. As Austin watched him, one eye blinked before the other.

She sighed. "Edgar, go into the backyard and check out Drex's flowers, would you? I love his layout. I'd love something like that for Ivy House."

"Oh. That sounds like the perfect use of my time." He stepped through the line of shifters, bumping them out of the way. "Everything is going smoothly up here, in case you were wondering."

"She wasn't," Niamh drawled. "Is it just me, or has he gotten worse?"

"You both have," Mr. Tom intoned.

Jess slipped on her dress as Tristan landed with Sebastian. Indigo stepped forward immediately, waiting long enough for Tristan to shift back into his human form, then pushed in close and put both hands on his chest. She smiled up at him in silent laughter. It was clear she was joking about how much she enjoyed their proximity, and just as clear he didn't care either way. That spell had obviously hurt something awful.

Austin put his arm around Jess's shoulders and walked them to the front of their crew again. He faced the other alphas and their people, letting his posture ask if anyone else wanted to step up.

"I do so love to say, 'I told you so'," Drex said, grinning.

And just like that, all the alphas relaxed.

"I feel like a sacrificial lamb," Derrick said, huffing with a smile. "If she wasn't so intense, I'd be embarrassed. I didn't do much more than pavement surf."

"You let her hit you with those spells?" Rhea asked Austin.

"That gargoyle took one," Selene said.

"She didn't have all her power when she was practicing on me." Austin squeezed Jess a little closer. She'd shown incredibly well, and she'd been in no danger, but he still hated that she'd had to endure the challenge. It was one thing when gargoyles went after her, being of her people, but for some reason, it really unsettled him when alpha shifters did. "But they were still grisly. We didn't have much choice. Not if she wanted to get better."

"It would blow your mind what he endured to help her." Sebastian shook his head. "Though I don't feel much better at the moment. Jessie, do you have the energy to heal me?"

"'Course." She leaned her head against Austin, utterly spent. She didn't have the energy, but she wouldn't admit it.

"I'm in." Fenric grunted. "I want *in* the convocation. I want to be part of this legend in the making."

"Me, too." Selene nodded. "I'm all the way in."

"In," Derrick said. "But I don't ever want to challenge her again."

"I'm in," Barek said.

A little hollow of silence descended as everyone waited for Rhea.

"I'm in," she finally said. "Now I understand that speech Alpha Ironheart gave. She is wasting her time traveling to meet shifters. I agree. We can obviously take mages physically, but what does that matter if we can't get close enough to make use of our strength and power?"

"Alpha Steele's power is a gut-punch, though," Derrick said. "His team of shifters and gargoyles and everyone in between is eye-opening. Stories and rumors, even if you believe them, don't do this show of strength justice. I'd pay admission to see that phoenix, alone. She had ol' Fenny crapping his pants."

"Yes, she did." Fenric tightened his lips and bent his head forward. "I doubt you would've stayed in place so long."

Austin couldn't believe how loose these alphas were in front of their people, and especially strangers. They were carrying on more like gargoyles than shifters. It was clear they were also good friends. Austin had heard Drex had their ears, but he hadn't realized they were so close. That was fortunate.

"We have some problem solving to do. That is"—Drex appealed to Austin and Jess—"if you'll allow us to help?"

Austin scooped Jess up into his arms and hugged her close. "Absolutely. We've been granted an extra couple days by a gargoyle cairn. Let me take my mate home so she can heal and recover, and then I'll meet back."

"Here, I better be in on that meeting." Niamh raised a finger. "After seeing these bunch of lummoxes, I've got some ideas."

"Is that a challenge or a salutation?" Derrick looked between the other alphas. "I can't tell."

"I wouldn't bother me arse to challenge ya," Niamh replied. "I'd have to chase ya around the street trying to get ye on yer feet. Waste of time."

Drex burst out laughing and turned to open the door. "Austin, just walk in when you return from securing your mate. Jessie, we'll see you when you're ready."

CHAPTER 19
JESSIE

"THIS IS A show of weakness." I let my head thunk against Austin's shoulder. I'd hammered that shifter and then Sebastian with a lot of high-powered spells. They always required a lot of energy, but it was good practice. "I shouldn't be carried home when my challenger is only limping into a house."

"One challenger is limping, and that one had a mage protecting him from you." Austin set her into the Jeep gently. "The other challenger is being helped to the car by Nessa, and Tristan, who got in the way, is carrying Indigo like a toddler on his hip so that she can still touch him to heal him. I'd say you're fine to be looked after by your less than concerned mate."

"Less than concerned?" I quirked an eyebrow at him.

"I'm not concerned that they'll think you're weak, but if they do, and try to make something of it, you'll have me standing in the way. You've proved your worth. If they press, I will get to prove mine, and I'll do so viciously."

My heart swelled. I angled my head up for a kiss and he moved in slowly, cupping my face in his hands and touching his lips to mine.

"You were spectacular," he murmured before deepening the kiss.

A wave of lightheadedness overcame me. I gripped his shoulders as my head got woozy.

"Let's get you home." He buckled me in. "Stop healing Sebastian. He can be tired for now. You've overdone it."

I shouldn't have, because I'd gone that hard in practice before. Then again, this was a much higher elevation. That probably had something to do with it. Also, I was defending against spells from Sebastian this time. Usually, I was just doing spells towards trees.

The Jeep started, and I closed my eyes. As it rolled forward, I heard Austin say, "She doesn't have enough energy. Is it dire?"

He must've been talking to Sebastian, who then responded, "Sorry, I didn't realize."

"It's fine," I said, more quietly than I'd meant to.

"They just need a nap and some food," Nessa called. "We're good."

The wind of the moving vehicle felt good against my heated cheeks.

"That shifter hadn't a hope of standing up to me," I said, eyes still closed. "When in gargoyle form, they'd be sitting ducks. When on the ground, they'd have to sneak up on me or come at me with numbers. The first wave of those numbers would die before they were able to bring me down."

"And now they know."

"Yeah." I heaved a sigh. "We already did, but it's been a while since I've made it that clear."

"But you're forgetting the garhettes. I've gotten reports that a great many are squeezing their way into our territory. We need to start stockpiling weapons that they can use to level the playing field until we get more mages. Those blaster guns work at a distance. Throwing knifes, axes… Hell, *spears*, I don't know. They're as fierce as the males but not so hardheaded. They'll be easier to train, and they'll want to prove themselves, one and all. We need to use them."

"True. I heard they showed well at Kingsley's."

"They did, and not just on the battlefield. They are also incredible for community and morale. We had to adjust to the gargoyles, but I think the garhettes will fit in easily."

I nodded as the Jeep slowed to a stop, and the engine cut off.

"C'mon, let's get you inside."

I didn't bother trying to get out, just sat there and waited for him to open my door, unbuckle me, and lift me into his arms. Wrapping my arms around his neck, I snuggled in close.

"Food or nap first?" he asked.

"Maybe a protein shake and then a nap. Later, I'll want a victory bang where you do most of the work."

He laughed quietly. "Already in the plans, love."

"You need to bulk up," Sebastian said on the right, "so you can carry me like he's carrying her."

"Yeah, I'll get right on that," Nessa replied.

Austin opened the door and carried me into our bedroom, where he laid me on our bed.

"Clothes on or off?" he asked. "Covers or no covers?"

"Just as I am is fine. I'll be good in a while. Just need to give my body a chance to rest."

"You need fuel. I'll go make you a protein shake."

"Thank you. I love you."

He kissed my forehead before making his way out.

✧　✧　✧

NESSA

"I'LL BE NICE and let you nap in my bed, so you don't have to climb up to the top bunk." Nessa pushed the front door open and marshalled Sabby through.

"I need food."

"And I will make you food just as soon as I can stop babying you."

"Just the table is fine for now," Sebastian said, pointing toward the kitchen. "My brain is whirling. She's gone after me with that level of power before. In the caves, remember?"

Austin paused in front of them. "Need help?"

"Nah, I've got it." She gave him a salute. He nodded and went into the kitchen.

"No, I don't remember," Nessa told Sebastian, guiding him after Austin. "I was ineffectively hiding from a large gorilla and then being carried down to you like a sack of potatoes."

"Oh, yeah, right." Sebastian slouched against the edge of the table. "Crap, I'm tired." She helped him climb into the seat, and he slumped forward, arms out on the surface. "Well, she's always had more brute strength than me. She hammered me and hammered me until she eventually incapacitated me. And then she let me live."

Nessa nodded as she stopped behind Austin. He was bent over, grabbing things out of the fridge. She would've offered to make something for Jessie and let him get back to his alpha meeting, but she knew it would be a waste of time. This shifter liked to take care of his mate, and cooking was his love language. He not only wanted the duty, but he also loved providing her something she so obviously cherished.

Nessa's heart glowed for them. Theirs was such a perfect, reciprocal love. It was probably that, more than anything else, that kept peeling back Nessa's reservations and letting her dare to hope there was someone out there who would treat her so well and with such devotion. Someone she could fully trust and open up to. Someone who wouldn't judge her for her past and that would make her feel safe within that intimacy. She'd never thought anyone out there could forgive her multitude of wrongs, but now…

"What are you making?" she asked Austin.

He put some spinach on the counter before straightening up. "Protein smoothie. Lady's request. You?"

"A big omelet. It's his favorite after he's done too much magic."

Austin grunted in acknowledgement before moving away. "Any surprises in making it?"

"*Maybe.*" She gave him a hoity one-shouldered shrug, lifting her nose into the air. "Not like I'll tell you."

He huffed with a grin and began prepping his ingredients.

She smiled, looking over at Sebastian for him to keep talking.

"Well, so she's always had brute strength," Sebastian said. "I can manage for a while, but eventually—in close range, at least—her spells overcome me and would eventually kill me. But they don't drain me as much because it's basically blocking and casting, blocking and casting. Her new spells, however, are not only powerful, but also incredibly complex. The blocking is not as simple, and her defenses aren't as straightforward. It takes more energy to counteract one of her spells now. It's exhausting. And…" He propped up onto an elbow. "The complexity of her spells is odd. Not like I'm used to. Like *any* mages are used to, I'd wager."

"It's those Ivy House books," Nessa said, pulling out a cutting board. "They're from a time lost."

"Yeah." Sebastian's voice drifted away, obviously thinking that through.

Nessa chopped the ham and then pulled over a bell pepper. The red of that reminded her of Tristan and the wound he'd taken in getting Sebastian to safety. He hadn't balked or even flinched. He certainly hadn't backed away. He took the pain and pulled Sebastian to safety without a moment's hesitation.

He deserved a really chocolatey dessert.

"You should've seen the spells she did in that battle the other day," Sebastian said, laying back down on the table. "They were hardcore. Like, I haven't seen spells that *grisly* ever. Mages can be horrible, but they don't dream up spells like that."

"They would if they could, I bet," Nessa said, taking the seeds out of the tomato. "The Guild would throw money at her for those spells."

"Yeah," Sebastian said again. "I'd wondered if they were outlawed. I mean, Nessa, they were *that* bad. Death on delivery. Boom! But according to her, mages don't outlaw stuff, and she's right."

"Maybe not now." Nessa sliced up the tomato. "But the Guild and mages as a whole weren't always this corrupt and vicious. They weren't always the bad guys. There have been times throughout history when they've regulated magic for the safety of the user."

"Yeah," Sebastian repeated.

Austin pulsed the blender before wiping his hands on a kitchen towel and dragging his phone from his pocket. He tapped it a few times before giving it to Sebastian.

"I thought Niamh would've shown you this," he said, heading back to the blender. "She's had her hands full, though. That's a video from an onlooker at a pack we aided. It was right before we went to help you, actually. That day, Jess was trying out some of her Ivy House spells."

Sebastian tapped the screen to play it. The sound had been turned off so Nessa couldn't glean what was going on. That was, until Sebastian started reacting.

"Good God," he whispered, his eyebrows pulling together. He leaned away from the phone, then leaned back in. "Holy hell." He squinted an eye, his face screwing up in horrified humor. "Jesus…*phew*." He flinched. "This is way worse than the other day. This is like a spoof horror movie or something."

He put the phone in front of him before picking it up to watch it again. This time he'd analyze. Then he'd alter. Then he'd likely make something even deadlier but more effective in some way, reducing energy or hitting more people or who knew what.

"You definitely do not see spells like this anymore," he murmured, stopping the playback for a moment and tilting his head in thought. "We've seen a decline in overall magical power through the ages. Meeting Jessie and learning about the books in Ivy House has made me realize this. Jessie is the most powerful mage—or sorceress, whatever—in the world. That we know of, obviously. I'm a close second, and then that team of twins Momar has is more powerful than me, maybe Jessie, when they work together. In general, on average, we don't see brute strength like Jessie, anymore. And Tamara Ivy might've lost some power when transferring her magic to the house. I can't do the higher-level spells Jessie can do. But to create actual books with those types of spells in them, they would've had many people who could."

Austin poured his concoction into a glass. "There could be any number of reasons why the power level dwindled through the generations. Maybe it happened because of mage in-fighting—the powerful killing each other in political maneuvering or power plays. Not to mention the fact that the mages we've met haven't been family-oriented people. They seek money and power and don't spend their time procreating. Not the powerful mages, anyway."

Sebastian flared his eyebrows to concede those points. Nessa had to say, the family dynamic aspect was certainly true. Mage culture was more independent, each mage working toward riches and power and not so much toward building communities. Not in the traditional sense, at any rate. Obviously, some mages did settle down and have families, but the more powerful mages tended to pursue their interests, rather than family. At least in this day and age. There was no saying what it was like in the past.

"Anyway, it doesn't really matter," Nessa said. "However it happened, very few people can use those Ivy House books."

"Momar does happen to have a couple that probably could, though." Sebastian sighed and laid his upper body down on the table again. "The moment they see what Jessie can do, they'll want to know how. They'll want those books."

"Ivy House is a strong deterrent," Austin said as he headed out of the kitchen with Jessie's shake.

"Yes, but I was able to get people on those grounds undetected."

There was a scuff in the hallway as Austin abruptly stopped.

"I did the research, and I figured it out," Sebastian said. "I devised a potion to hide from Ivy House. Momar has a few ingenious mages who made that thing at Kingsley's. Ivy House isn't impenetrable, Austin. It would be a mistake to assume it is. But even if they can't get in to steal those books, if they see what is *possible*, they have an opportunity to devise something similar. The question is, are they good enough? And after seeing what they did at Kingsley's, I think the answer is probably yes, they are. This battle we're fighting might get a lot harder before the end. We'll want to be prepared."

"Which means we'll want to pour through those books," Nessa surmised.

"Pour through them and weed out our competition."

They needed to focus on the mages, rather than on touring the packs. They couldn't study if they were constantly on the go. Austin and Jessie might have to split up to see this through, something that had probably occurred to everyone earlier when Jessie had made that speech, and later when that alpha had agreed with her.

Austin would not like that one bit.

CHAPTER 20
AUSTIN

THE JEEP MOTOR died, leaving Austin in silence as he sat outside of Drex's house. A million thoughts rolled through his head, all lining up with what he'd already vaguely decided. It was a plan half-formed and with a million risks, but they didn't have any more time or another choice, not anymore. That had become glaringly obvious. Now, he needed details.

He left the keys in the ignition and climbed from the Jeep. Jess was at the house napping and Sebastian wouldn't be long in following suit. Nessa, after making Sebastian something to eat, had decided to stick around and start baking. This trip was winding down.

He let himself into the house as instructed and heard a murmuring of voices at the end of the hallway. The alphas were sitting around the large table in the dining room with pitchers of water and lemonade amid snacks. Two of the alphas had opted for a beer.

They fell silent when he entered the room, all eyes on him. They'd need to get a shifter's version of pleasantries out of the way before they started planning. He hoped to hell they had some good ideas or he'd be making things up as he went, something that was bound to fail.

"Alpha." Drex stood in greeting, and the rest rose respectfully.

Austin stopped from showing his surprise. They were treating him like *their* alpha.

"Greetings," he said, because 'hi' seemed too informal, and then he felt like a social outcast with such a lame salutation. The Ivy House crew was rubbing off on him.

He tried again as he sat down. "How goes it?"

The rest sat with him except for Drex.

"Lemonade?" Drex indicated the spread before him. "Beer?"

"Beer would be great, thanks."

Drex nodded and moved off toward the kitchen.

"Did Niamh not stick around?" Austin asked, cluing in through the Ivy House bonds to locate her whereabouts.

"She went to check on the vampire," Derrick said. "Drex said the vampire was welcome to look around and she called him a damned fool." Derrick grinned.

"Are all pucas that surly?"

"I have no idea but based on what she's said about her family, I think they are."

The others chuckled quietly.

Drex popped the top on a can of ale before pouring it into a glass and setting them both in front of Austin. He moved to take his seat again.

"I was telling them a little of your battle setup," Drex started. The environment around the table was relaxed and laid back, not at all like the cultivated showmanship that went on with generational alphas. These people knew what they were about, could size the others up, and felt no need to talk a big game or show strong. Their confidence was built brick by brick, not manufactured through family and training. Austin didn't really fit in, as he had the training and the ties, but he still felt so much more at home here than he did in those other meetings.

"You have a lot of balls in the air, it sounds like," Rhea said, taking a sip of her beer. "A lot of pieces and moving parts that you didn't grow up learning how to manage."

He toggled his hand at that. "The gargoyles aren't so different from the shifters, once you get over the stubbornness and cultural differences. They appreciate strong leadership and an organized structure. And remember, I'm not doing all the heavy lifting. My betas, Tristan and Brochan, handle a lot of the details. Tristan takes what I do on the ground and alters it for the air. Brochan handles a lot of alpha duties that I can't get to."

"And Jessie's crew?" Drex asked.

"Are managed by Jess." Austin took a sip of his beer. "I have no idea how, and if I tried, it would blow up in my face. She has a way of dealing with them, and it works. They are messy and chatty and incapable of the sort of structure shifters present to the world, but…it works."

Drex drummed his fingers on the table, his eyes narrowed as he surveyed Austin. "You are not at all like the generational alphas I've met."

"No," Fenric said in a grunt. "Not even a little bit."

"I was trained like one," Austin said. "I was taught by my mom and then my brother and guided by my grandmother. I have all the privilege a generational alpha does, including the large bankroll."

"True." Rhea studied him, too. "But that's where it ends."

"I told them about the rental vehicles I had stocked for your crew." Drex stilled his fingers but continued to assess. "You never complained about that Jeep."

"I thought the options were odd, but they worked. And that Jeep…" He shrugged. "I have a similar one back home. It's nearly as beat up." He allowed a smile, thawing to match the others. "Make no mistake, when it comes to flaunting my assets, I am well able."

"You've lived without means, even if you had the safety net," Selene said.

Because Austin hadn't thought he'd deserved that money. It was inheritance, so he'd kept it, but he'd always intended to give it back to Kingsley's family, the rightful alpha. Austin hadn't risen to his potential, and so he didn't think he deserved the boons that came with it.

It was only now, when his intention was to provide for Jess and make his territory and therefore fortune grow, that he felt comfortable spending it. Investing it. He still hoped to return it someday to Aurora or Mac, whoever needed it more, so that they could start their lives independently.

"I had my reasons," he said simply.

They didn't press.

"You aren't as rigid as a generational alpha, either," Derrick said. "I think we were all surprised by that."

Drex spread out his hands. "Jessie's speech clued us in to how much you are trying to get accomplished in a dwindling time frame. It's a huge undertaking that would normally take years. More than that, it would take negotiations with some of the more powerful alphas, meetings and platitudes, shows of power—and that's just shifters. We're all *in*, you know that. Now we are trying to fill in the gaps of what we've heard and what is right in front of us. I hope you don't mind."

Austin put up his hand in a "go for it" gesture before answering Derrick. "I used to be just as rigid as you would expect. When meeting my brother and his friends, I put on that hat. But gargoyles have a very loose culture. They joke and tease and make fun. Basajaunak as well, in certain ways, if you follow their somewhat odd rules. Jess is a past Jane, and she is incapable of hiding—"

"Anything," Drex cut in with a smile. "She is incapable of hiding even a stray thought. Sometimes that is refreshing. Sometimes it really isn't."

Austin grinned and relaxed a little more. "We tried to teach her but…it was thought by most that she's better as she is. She doesn't lie and doesn't hide truths. She's an open book, and she's new to all this. It's better people see that she's worried about killing them, rather than it coming as a surprise."

"That freaked me out, I'm going to be honest." Derrick blurted out a laugh. "At first I thought she was full of it, but once I realized she wasn't, I would've backed down if it wouldn't've made me a coward."

"And now you don't care if you're called a coward,"

Selene teased. "You'll back all the way down and right out the door."

"Truth." Derrick laughed harder.

"Then Jess's crew is…" Austin shook his head. "They don't make sense in the best of times. They are so incredibly odd you wonder if you're dreaming. So, to integrate all these different characters into one territory, it took—takes, I guess—patience and a very open mind. I am working the shifters to be a little looser in mannerisms and a little less volatile. I'm compromising with the gargoyles to reduce some of the brash stubbornness and taunting. The basajaunak…kinda just do what they want. Jess deals with them. They'll attack me where they'll excuse her."

The alphas all around the table nodded solemnly.

"You overcame a lot in your youth, is that correct?" Selene asked.

Austin tightened in unease. "I created more conflict than I overcame. My brother is an incredible alpha. He nurtures the good in people, even when those people don't deserve it. He gave me a second chance. That time around, I knew better than to squander it."

Selene looked at Barek, who gave the briefest of nods.

"Shows some big balls to admit you were the problem," Fenric said, and it was probably the explanation for the previous silent exchange. That had been a test. They'd wondered if Austin would play victim or make light of the things he'd done. They wondered if he'd fess up. His answer would define the sort of man he was and let them know if he could be trusted at his word.

A few years ago, he might've answered differently or refused to answer at all. He'd been carrying around a lot of guilt and shame, and he wouldn't want to expose the monster he'd been.

Now, however, he had a woman who loved him despite all his faults. She knew about his past, knew his darkness and the things he wasn't proud of, and loved him anyway. She'd helped mend what was broken between him and his brother, and what was broken in himself, so that now he could look these people in the eyes and admit his faults. He could own his past grievances knowing he was doing something to make up for them.

"It seems like we've heard all about your life," Fenric said. "I hate drama. I don't care about rumors, and yet I've heard much more about you than I care to admit. Now I'm realizing that people were eager to believe the bad and disregard the good as nothing more than tall tales." His voice reduced to a murmur. "It's bullshit."

"There's only a few that are pushing the tall tale angle at this point, though." Selene pushed her wheat-colored hair over her shoulder. "And they're just worried about the power aspect. They have more power than Kingsley and worry they won't have more power than the little brother."

Drex barked a laugh. "They've been fed with a silver spoon all their lives. They didn't have to fight for anything. Sure, maybe they got challenged a time or two, but they've never known what it is to be against insurmountable odds and decide you'll go down fighting rather than give in. Until they know that, they don't have a prayer against Austin Steele."

"O' course they don't." Niamh walked in with a beer and sat down at the table. "And that is why they are going to do everything in their power to avoid a challenge. Now. Are we finished with the pleasantry nonsense? I need to get this sorted quick-like. There's a lovely bartender downtown I'm on the verge of cracking. He is going to yell at me. I can feel it. This is a great test of my skills, like. If I can get under his skin, I can do anything."

"We have a bet on," Fenric told Austin. "I know that bartender. Too damn cheerful. No one can ruin his day."

Selene rolled her eyes. "It is a wonder that you two are even trying."

CHAPTER 21

NESSA

S EBASTIAN SNORED SOFTLY on the couch in the living room. Jessie was comfortable in her room, sound asleep. Nessa left a glass of water near each of them before picking up the dessert and stepping out the door.

Tristan's residence was two houses down. The clouds had mostly cleared away, leaving the sun to beat down on the neighborhood. Gargoyles flew overhead, patrolling in their formations. Members of the convocation wandered the street, coming or going. With Austin meeting the alphas by himself and Jessie indisposed, the rest of their people had time off.

"Ah, Nessa, there you are." Mr. Tom came out of the house she was passing with a full grocery bag in one hand and a bundle of what looked like blankets under the other arm. He looked at the cloth-covered plate in her hands. "What are you doing?"

"I'm just taking this to Tristan—"

"Yes, fine. The miss is sleeping, I trust?"

"Yes, she's—"

"Fantastic. I just have to pop in to Ulric and then I will take over watching her. She shouldn't be alone. She might need something and have to fend for herself." He walked into the street to cut across to Ulric's residence up the way.

It was as though he'd forgotten that Jessie had been a wife and mother, raising a son and a man-child for nearly twenty years. She could look after herself if need be.

Then again, if you didn't have to why bother?

Nessa hurried on her way. The dessert was best warm and soon it wouldn't be. She let herself into the residence and heard someone chatting in the living room. She popped her head around the corner and found two gargoyles she didn't know well. She couldn't remember their names.

They looked up with raised eyebrows.

"Hey," she said. "I'm going to check in on Tristan."

They both nodded. As she walked away, she heard, "Lucky bastard."

Nessa laughed silently. Nice to be noticed.

It occurred to her that she didn't know which room was Tristan's.

She paused at the end of the hallway. The house was

the same layout as hers, with two bedrooms and a similar kitchen and living room. Given he had clout in the convocation, he'd probably get the big room.

She peeked in the bunkbed room as she passed and found it empty. That must mean she was correct. That, or he wasn't here.

The door to the big room was closed. She thought about knocking, but that guy had no qualms about peering in her windows to make sure she was accounted for. He didn't deserve privacy.

She pushed the door open quietly. His large form lay on the bed on his back with his wings mostly beneath him. His arms were bent at the elbows and his hands rested on his bare stomach. The white sheet bunched low at his hips.

Even though his eyes were closed, he said, "Natasha," in his deep, whiskey voice.

Shivers crawled across her skin. He always seemed to know when she was near, even before she'd known she could use energy to influence others. Even before she knew that was even possible with magic.

She stepped into the room and closed the door behind her. "Hey." He still didn't open his eyes. "I made you some dessert to say thanks. Or to appreciate a job well done. Or just to be nice, if you're feeling prickly and won't accept the other two reasons."

"Any and all reasons are good enough if I get to eat the dessert. Is it chocolate?"

"Yes, can you smell it?"

"No. Hopeful."

She smiled and closed the small distance to the side of the bed, looking down on that handsome face, with his almost severe cheekbones and arching black brows. Raven stubble lined his jaw, and his dark hair fanned across the pillow in a loose curl. If the man wasn't so wicked, he'd make angels sing. As it was, he probably made the devil nervous.

"How do you feel?" she asked. Given his eyes were still closed, she let her gaze roam freely over that fantastic body, his pecs perfectly defined and leading down into his eight pack. An ebony happy trail led from his navel to the sheet.

"My arm hurts like hell but I'm down to a dull throb, so it'll be fine. Are you getting a good look?"

How the hell did he know? It was inhuman the way he could read her, even when he couldn't see her energy. Even when no one else seemed to pay attention to her at all.

"Yes. You're a work of art, like all the sculptures you always look at in the art room at Ivy House. Or don't you still spend time appreciating those?"

"Every spare moment I get, yes. I love art, as you

know from the first time we met."

"When you thought I was an otherworldly being, yes, I remember. What happened to Indigo? I thought she was healing you."

"She healed me enough to stop the bleeding and lessen the pain. That's good enough. I'm not in the mood for people. Pain is better than annoyance. And you *are* an otherworldly being. A beautiful sprite who enchants and entrances everyone she meets. Men can't help but flock to your siren's call even though they might follow you to their demise. They'll love the journey and count themselves lucky they were able to take it."

"Is that what you're doing, following me to your demise?"

"Maybe I am, but I won't turn back now. If you should lead me to my doom, it'll be a treasured ending."

She inched closer, her shins bumping the mattress. He sounded genuine, no teasing or taunting. No playing games. So...sweet, even though he was essentially saying she'd be the death of him. Of any man. That should strike her as odd, or worse, horrible. But instead, her heart warmed. When he said it, it didn't seem like a bad thing, and she didn't feel like such a terrible person.

Her breath released slowly as she drank in the sight of him. His beauty. His form in repose.

"Well, anyway," she said, ready to depart.

"I hope you're not planning to leave without letting me taste that dessert."

She hesitated. "Don't you want a little peace?"

"Yes. Desperately. But right now, I'll settle for some of that dessert. What is it?"

She frowned in confusion. "A chocolate lava cake. I put a square of ganache in the middle to make it more decadent. If you're not in the mood for people I can grab a fork and set you up. You don't need to humor me by eating it in my presence."

"Did you not hear what I just said? You are not *people*. You are an ethereal being sent here to torment me. Please, grab a fork. I'll push up a bit."

She crinkled her nose and grinned. She liked this strange new facet of his personality, liked the job of tormenter almost as much as she liked it when he held her throat and whispered threats in her ear.

That surely couldn't be normal. But then, what in her life had ever been normal? Besides, he liked those things, too. She wasn't the only odd one.

Butterflies filled her belly. "Okay." She set the dish on the end table and bounded out to get a fork and something to drink.

With a fork tucked in her back pocket, she carried a glass of milk in one hand and a water in the other. She didn't know which he'd prefer. Maybe both.

He'd scooted up in the bed to eat. Lines of pain still creased his face, and his hurt arm was tucked close to his side. He still hadn't opened his eyes.

"Here." She set down the drinks and moved in to fix his pillows. She used one arm to slide under his wide shoulders before lifting and adjusting. "Better?"

He let out a breath he'd obviously been holding against the pain. "Yes, thank you."

"You couldn't handle a little more annoyance to get some much-needed healing?"

His breathing was deep and slow, managing the pain. "Indigo is a very sweet person, and I'm sure she has a great sense of humor, but when I am in pain, I want everyone to shut the hell up and leave me alone. I didn't want to hurt her feelings and have her hold a grudge against me. She might try to kill me next time, rather than healing me, so I figured it was better for me to suffer in silence. When Jessie wakes up, she'll feel this and heal me from a distance. I much prefer that approach. Please don't tell Niamh any of this. She has been searching for things that rile me up and she'd have a field day with this one."

Nessa laughed and pulled out the fork. "Your secret is safe with me." She pulled the cloth away from the lava cake, hesitating when he didn't open his eyes or reach for the plate. "Uhhm, you did want some, right?"

He opened his mouth expectantly, and an array of sparks danced up her middle.

"Oh," she said, blinking at the fork in her hand, then the plate, then his opened mouth. "Okay."

She sat on the edge of the bed, mindful not to crush his wing. The fork slid past the cake portion and through the soft, dense middle.

"Dang," she murmured, hesitating.

"What?"

"You're supposed to serve this when it's warm so that the chocolate inside oozes out. It's gotten cold now, and the middle has firmed up."

"Will it still taste good?"

"Yes, it—"

"Then I don't care."

She smiled at his eagerness and finished cutting a piece. His lips parted again, and she gently rubbed the fork against his bottom lip, so he'd open a little wider. He complied and she delicately slipped the bite into his mouth.

Those lush lips closed over the metal tines. She watched them with a strange fervor, foreign in its intensity, as she pulled the fork free. He chewed for a moment, then groaned softly, his jaw movement pausing. He was savoring the flavor.

"That is incredible, Natasha," he finally said, swallowing. "Unbelievable. You should challenge Austin with *that*. You'd win, hands down. Nothing can compare."

She smiled with pride and cut out another bite.

"Larger," he said.

"What?"

"You're going to do the same size bite you just did, right?" He paused. "Make it bigger. I want more in my mouth at one time."

Her stomach flipped over, and her core wound up tightly. He wasn't trying to be sexual, but her body clearly didn't know that.

Struggling to level out her suddenly accelerated breathing, she did as he said. Her focus once again turned razor sharp as she watched his lips skim along the chocolate-covered metal. His groan this time was indulgent. Intoxicating, almost. He savored the flavor before opening his mouth for more.

She complied, leaning closer, this time running the fork along his bottom lip before giving him the bite. His lips continued to stay closed. He ate it as he had, and then his tongue came out to run along his lip, cleaning away the chocolate.

Great god almighty, he was so incredibly sexy. *This* was so incredibly sexy, feeding him a dessert she'd made while he let her take and keep all the control. She'd realized before that she liked when he took the dominant lead, and she still did, but this was highly sensual, as well. It was its own kind of thrill. Which was a strange realization because she'd often taken the lead with men. She usually called the shots and chose the pace, but it had never felt like this, so electric.

Maybe because those other men hadn't been so mysterious and insanely dangerous. It was almost like Tristan was allowing her to play, and at any moment he could snap and take back the reins. She was being a naughty little mouse while the cat was indisposed.

The fork scraped against the porcelain. She fed him the last bite, smearing a little of the chocolate across his bottom lip. He swallowed but didn't lick it clean.

She leaned forward before she knew what she was doing and ran her tongue across his lip, lifting away the chocolate.

Before she could swallow it, he whispered, "Don't take my dessert. Give it back."

Her stomach dropped away, and she kissed him, feeling his mouth open. Her tongue tangled with his. She tilted her head, and their lips slotted together like a puzzle piece. Their surroundings slipped sideways as their mouths moved in perfect synchronicity, slow and relentless.

Her fingers uncurled, and the fork clattered against the plate. She sucked in a breath and backed off, grabbing the dish and the fork.

"Is there anything left on the plate?" he asked without opening his eyes. It felt like he was giving her permission to do anything she liked.

She put the fork on the nightstand before dragging her finger through the smears of chocolate and crumbs left on the plate. Her heart quickened, not knowing how far she planned to take this. Not wanting to be impeded by reason or reality.

His lips were only slightly parted, and she grazed them with the tip of her finger. He opened, and she pushed her finger deeper into his mouth. His lips closed over her digit, and he sucked, swirling the tip with his tongue. His groan sounded tortured.

She felt her heartbeat deep in her core, pounding. Her finger was wet when it slid out, like she was between her thighs. She replaced her finger with her mouth as her hand touched down on that fabulous expanse of muscle on his chest. Then down, she couldn't stop herself if she tried. She ached for him. Couldn't stand not touching him.

His mouth consumed hers, greedy and insistent. Her palm flattened against his lower stomach, and his muscles contracted, and his breathing sped up. Lower still, needing to feel him. Her searching fingers slid under the sheet where she found his hard length.

The breath whooshed out of him as she stroked down to the base, feeling that smooth skin. Then back up, holding firmly. Her thumb ran over the tip, and she knew it wouldn't be good enough.

She pulled back from his lips, and he followed her, rising from the pillow so as not to break the connection. He winced though and had to stop, lowering back down. Yes, she was in control. This big, strong gargoyle was at her mercy.

It would take too long to kiss down that chest. She'd have to do that another time, licking between the muscles and teasing his nipples. She was certain he'd let her, assuming she didn't come to her senses and run away from this vicious monster like she probably should. Instead, she shifted her position and ripped away the sheet covering him. His breath hitched when she once against took hold of him, but this time it was her tongue running along his tip.

She licked across and around before sucking him in deep. He was large—larger than she'd experienced before—and she struggled to get him as deep as she wanted. To compensate, she worked her hand up and down in time with her mouth. She pushed her other hand under the waist of her pants and down between her thighs. Her finger circled as her mouth took him in, feeling the pleasure with him.

His groan matched her own and she took him a little deeper. Pushed past gagging to go deeper still. Ran circles with her finger faster and gyrated her hips, shaking the bed. If it was hurting him, he didn't say.

His breathing sped up, his hips jerking in time with her efforts. Her body tightened and she felt his doing the same. She was right there now, chasing her climax. On the edge.

He grunted in pleasure, and she exploded, moaning. He filled her mouth, shaking with his release. She took it all down and then slowed, backing off to give a last couple licks, smirking when he shivered with sensitivity.

When she moved to get up, he reached out, finding her wrist and then sliding his hand down to hers.

"Stay," he whispered. "Stay with me."

"Why won't you open your eyes? Did something happen to them?"

He took a long moment to answer. "No. I desperately hoped you would visit while figuring you probably wouldn't think of it. When you did, I didn't want you to see how grateful I was. You tend to run when things get emotionally charged or mushy. And then I didn't want your visit to end…for many reasons. I still don't. Stay with me."

Her heart melted. "I'm just going to get a warm washcloth to clean up. I'll be right back, I promise."

He let go of her hand, letting his own hand drop onto the bed. She came back and did as she said before tossing the washcloth into the hamper in the corner. Sitting on the bed again, she gently traced the stubble on his jaw.

"Lay with me." He put out his good arm, creating room between that and his body.

When she'd needed him, he'd stayed with her, protecting her against her nightmares. Even though he probably didn't need her in the same way right now, she'd return the favor.

She slid off her shoes and then her pants, because they weren't comfortable to sleep in, before slipping in next to his big, warm body. She tucked his wing between them before stroking the soft texture. He shivered again.

With a smile, she pulled the sheet up and settled her head into the hollow between his shoulder and neck. His arm curled around her protectively, pulling her in tightly.

What she'd just done would probably make things complicated. It would certainly blur the lines between friend and foe and lover.

Then again, he'd kissed her in front of Austin and

Jessie and Sebastian, and no one had said a word. He certainly hadn't or even acknowledged that it had happened. Neither had she, come to think of it.

They were two people good at "no strings attached". It was basically part of their life plan. This was just another example, she was sure. Soon they'd be thrown into yet another tense situation. Par for the course with her life and now Jessie's, and life would trundle on as it always did.

She was having a hard time deciding if that was welcomed.

CHAPTER 22

JESSIE

"RIGHT, OKAY." I clapped, because I felt great. Better than great. I felt like I had things under control.

Austin had come up with some sort of plan with the alphas that would apparently change his entire schedule and the way he went about meeting the rest of the important alphas. What was the plan? No idea. Niamh said I didn't need to "bother me arse" about it. Fine.

I'd had to heal Tristan, who'd apparently been in pain the entire time I took a three-hour nap, because he didn't want Indigo sharing space in his bedroom. The guy had suffered in silence, and no one had woken me to help him. I felt super guilty about it, mostly because I'd caused the wound, and when I was about to go apologize, Niamh told me I shouldn't "bother me arse."

Fine.

Now, a day later and arriving via plane, train, and

automobile—not quite but whatever—we were about to enter a dense forest. It was the domain of a powerful, emotionally scarred and dangerous shifter rogue, one that neither shifters nor Dicks would allow in their towns or cities. Apparently, his very presence screamed *unhinged, approach with caution!*

In the interest of time, we would stalk this dangerous character as the afternoon waned and threatened to turn into night. Long shadows pooled in dense pockets between the trees, creating many places to hide. Once we found him, we'd likely be attacked, and then we'd attempt a meeting to issue an invitation to O'Briens.

Did we have any sort of plan? No, we did not. When asked if maybe we should? Niamh assured me that we wouldn't "bother our arses".

That didn't even make sense in the situation! This was tomfoolery to attempt without a plan.

But fine. If I was going to live in ignorance, I'd do so with a wonderful disposition, like all the people of Drex's town.

This disposition annoyed Niamh to no end.

"Shall I go first, then?" I smiled big and threw everyone a thumbs up as they climbed from the various passenger vans Mr. Tom was able to procure at the magical air strip posing as an airport. We hadn't had anything to comfortably put the basajaunak in, and so they were making their way to us on foot. They'd been happy about it, actually. They loved the feel of the woods and mountains of the Cascades.

The rogue was said to be about halfway up one of the mountains. What mountain? I had no idea. I'd stopped asking questions when Niamh was in hearing range at that point.

"Hang on, babe." Austin shut his door and looked around at everyone assembled before taking in the trees around them. "Tristan."

Tristan stepped up. He wore a purple muumuu and a hard expression on his face. He was ready for battle.

"The trees are dense. You guys won't be much good to us, and I don't want him to hear your wings and think there is some sort of manhunt on the way. Stay here at the cars. If we need you in a hurry, Jess will send a magical pulse."

Tristan nodded and fell back.

"Brochan." Austin waited for his beta to fill Tristan's spot. "Take all the wolves and other pack hunters. Spread out. You will be seeking and reporting. Don't make contact or get too close. Stick to the trees and stay out of sight if possible. Once you have something, send a pulse through Jess's connection."

Brochan nodded and moved away.

"Sebastian, Nessa, Edgar." The three stepped up,

Nessa and Sebastian in black pants and shirts, and Edgar in a muumuu. "Sebastian, you'll be with Jess and me. I'll be making contact with him or getting in the way of him attacking someone else. You will help Jess try to tear us apart as peacefully as possible. Detain him if possible. Another of the alphas at Drex's said he'd heard this guy has some serious power. Possibly on par with my own. He might challenge, but we are not treating it as a challenge. Tear us apart as quickly as possible. Do you understand?"

This was ruining my upbeat disposition. Niamh would probably be glad.

"Yes," I said as tension built.

"I really hope I don't resort to my old ways and use you as a shield," Sebastian told me. I laughed even though he was probably serious.

"Nessa and Edgar." Austin waited, his intense alpha gaze beating into the vampire until Edgar stopped smiling. "You guys are good at being in the right place at the right time. Stay together. Have a look around. If you think you might've spotted him, *do not engage.* Keep your distance. Edgar, you'll need to let us know since Nessa doesn't have a connection. Also, make sure no harm comes to her."

"Eyes, captain," Edgar responded, his hands clasped behind his back. He must've heard Tristan say "aye, aye,

Captain" and misinterpreted.

Austin didn't acknowledge. He'd learned to let Edgar go his own way and hope the Ivy House crew handled it.

He stepped back to address the group. "The point here is to offer help to a guy who's been shunned by his own community because of his power. The goal is to offer him a home that will accept him and peace if he wants it. A job if he needs it. Or to leave him alone if he'd prefer it. We're trying to meet him on his terms, so let's keep that in mind if things get a little hairy. We're the intruders here."

"Shouldn't we wait for the basajaunak?" I asked Austin quietly. "They'll be able to easily figure out exactly where he is."

"They are also prone to aggression, and I'd like to try and keep this situation calm. I'd like to avoid a fight if we can."

I nodded because that made perfect sense.

Broken Sue and his team shifted to their animal forms and took off into the trees. Fog drifted between the large, ancient trunks, quickly enveloping them. We followed, Austin in the lead. He stepped silently and avoided any reaching branches or brushing against the leaves. I tried my best to mimic him, avoiding what he did and watching where I put my feet.

Edgar waved as he took a deer trail to the right. Nessa followed him, her knives in their sheaths but her hands ready to grab them if needed.

Sebastian pushed in closer to me, his feet shuffling along the tiny deer trail laden with leaves and twigs and patches of grass.

The scent of damp earth and pine perfumed the cool air. Wildflowers bloomed in little patches of light, often giving way to ferns and cushions of thick moss that thankfully seemed to swallow sound. Sebastian wasn't as good as me at keeping quiet, and I was a long way from shifter material.

Onward we walked. The mist now almost seemed to cling to the trees, a curtain hiding the pooling shadows behind. Bird song echoed in the distance but fell silent as we passed through. Every way I looked, it all seemed the same, a tableau of green and brown and muted colors. I really hoped someone had brought a compass, because I'd get lost in this place almost immediately. Fred hadn't even gotten out of the car. She'd taken one look at the trees around her and asked if she could stay put and lock the doors. She probably had the right idea.

About twenty minutes in and the first of my connections flared to life.

"Austin." I pointed off to the right, though he hadn't looked back at me. He'd be able to feel it himself as I fed it along.

Another connection flared, and then one more, three people in about the same vicinity. They spread out into a large arch and slowed, slinking through the trees so they wouldn't be noticed. It occurred to me that the side they left open was likely upwind.

"Jess." Sebastian's tone was subdued but wary. "Are you monitoring your surroundings?"

He meant magically, something I always forgot about in these situations. I used eyes and ears like a Jane instead of magic like a female gargoyle.

I sent out the spell, felt the feedback, and grabbed the back of Austin's shirt in alarm bordering on blind panic.

✦   ✦   ✦

JOHN

THE USUAL SCREECH of the Mountain Jay abruptly fell silent. John hesitated, looping the blue yarn and threading it through. The little crochet whale was really coming along. Very cute, this thing. The kit he'd found at the store was probably meant for kids but was a nice way to pass the time. He could send it to one of his nieces when he'd finished.

The Jay didn't regain its voice, a sound like a frog

dying in a murky pond. Or so he'd always thought. Bird chatter took on a different personality when you really listened to them all. Some were pretty and some needed a tune up. Or to move out of his neighborhood and find someone else to disturb.

He glanced up as a familiar feeling started to encroach on his awareness. He took note of his surroundings and leaned hard into his intuition. He didn't feel any specific presences, so his watchers weren't checking in, but something else existed in these wilds that didn't belong. That hadn't been here before.

A wave of goosebumps covered his skin as he delicately balled up his little whale work-in-progress. There was no point in rushing. If the presence hadn't come crashing through the trees already, it wasn't likely to. It was stalking him, whatever it was, like a hunter. Treating him as prey.

He wanted to laugh as a trickle of adrenaline wormed into his bloodstream. He'd been many things in his life, and continued to evolve, but no matter how relaxed he allowed himself to be these days, there was one thing he would *never* become: prey. This creature— or creatures—would learn that the hard way before they met their untimely demise.

He tucked the arts-and-crafts into the little bag it came in before straightening from the worn-in seat on the naturally felled log. He stepped lightly around his camp, practiced in avoiding making noise but now being careful. The feeling sank down into his middle before solidifying in his gut.

Whatever was out there was hanging around, growing in danger. That probably meant more of them, covering more ground. Spreading out around him, probably, but not upwind. They had experience and they were likely here for a specific purpose. Him, obviously. No one else would be so stupid as to invade these woods. Not with what lurked within them. Except him, of course, but that was out of necessity. He'd had to fight for the right to be here.

The pressure around him continued to build. No sound filtered through the dense forest. He didn't catch even a thread of a scent.

He stripped out of his clothes to make shifting easy and took a trail toward one of the presences he sensed was out there. As he moved, everything moved with him—the presence in front of him, as well as the feeling of others to the sides. They perfectly kept their distance, synchronized with each other and flitting through the trees like ghosts. Wolves, probably. They were good at this sort of thing.

These wolves, however, were expertly trained and very well led. This wasn't a glory seeker situation. This smacked of an established alpha.

So be it. He'd taken down a great many of those.

The pressure continued to build. More must've joined. They'd sighted their target and were collecting their force.

And then the pressure turned into a throbbing drumbeat, a serious warning of a battle imminent. There was some serious power in these woods, he could feel it with the sixth sense that had kept him alive thus far.

He continued to move, not shifting yet. He was better at this internalized warning system in his human form. It had the most practice. He'd shift when he was ready to kill.

The drumbeat anchored in his gut, a fight or flight reflex.

He didn't run. Hadn't, ever. He wouldn't start now.

Still his lurkers hid from sight. They tracked him, operating around the outskirts of an invisible bubble. They were *very* well trained and clearly experienced. Someone had called in the best to finally get rid of him.

A scent caught him. He snapped his head in that direction, fully upwind and not one of his watchers. This one was foreign to him, and he was being obvious, making his presence known. His people might sneak, but he did not plan to.

Was this a trap?

He moved in that direction carefully. As he did, the bubble moved with him, changing formation. The lurkers ran ahead of him, circling until he could scent them all, in behind the first.

Not a trap, then. The intruder wanted a face-to-face.

Would these alphas ever just focus on their own territory and build their profile the old-fashioned way? They were exhausting.

He sped up now, feeling all the danger in that direction. Up ahead, light glowed around a few of the trees. Beyond was a little clearing and a beautiful waterfall. He traveled that path often.

He did so now, head high, wanting a look at the challenger before he shifted and made a bloody mess of them all.

The second he stepped through the trees, though, he looked straight into the eyes of death itself. He could've been looking at a mirror with all the wild, ruthless scars sparkling on the surface.

He did not hesitate, knowing action might give him the edge. He shifted in a heartbeat and burst forward.

CHAPTER 23

JESSIE

AN ENORMOUS LION burst out of the trees straight at Austin. Standing to one side, I flinched in surprise, and then I was running at him, magic at the ready.

"Crap, Jessie wait!" Sebastian ran after me.

Austin shifted into his huge polar bear form, tearing his clothes. Broken Sue ran toward him, having stayed back. I was already closer.

I created a blistering wall of magic between the two large shifters as the lion leapt, front paws out and claws gleaming in the sunlight. His mouth was open in a snarl, his long canines protruding from his gums.

Austin didn't advance. He held his ground, braced and ready for defense only.

The lion slammed against a magically electrified wall, like the one I'd used in Drex's territory, only stronger. Flares of magical light and sparks spit into the sky. The lion's fur singed and blackened, and he crashed to the ground.

In a moment he was up again, scratching at the wall, handling the pain. He shoved the wall forward, eroding my magical spell. This dude was *powerful*. Only Austin had ever been able to make this much headway.

Realizing he wouldn't get through, the lion stepped back and prepared to go around.

"Should I help block him in?" Sebastian yelled.

"Yes, hurry." I threw out another spell, this one not as painful but just as strong. Sebastian helped, strengthening my spells and closing in around the lion.

The lion rammed into the side and then clawed at the pink sheen in front of him. He turned the other way and found the same thing. At the back, he stopped and let out a frustrated, mighty roar.

Gargoyles flew in above us, having clearly felt our emotions through the connections and coming to help. They stopped above the clearing in an organized pattern, looking down.

The lion slowed before walking in a circle around his magical cage. Austin shifted back into his human form and Broken Sue pushed back to give him space, keeping his gorilla form.

Those golden feline eyes fastened upon Austin as the beast halted in front of my mate. He didn't shift back. Just waited patiently, likely for an opening to get out and lay waste to everyone around him or die trying. His posturing was very easy to read.

Austin put up his hands as I walked to his side. Sebastian fell in behind us with Broken Sue.

"I'm not here to challenge you," Austin said calmly. "I'm not here to harm you. The magic around you is to give us a chance to talk. I want to offer you a place to stay in our territory, no strings attached."

The lion lunged against the magical wall in front of him, then tried another spot and another. Pacing the magical cage, he took in everyone around him. That fierce golden gaze met mine, and it felt like my skin was flayed away while I was dropped onto a giant scale.

Again, the lion roared, a deep sound that reverberated through the trees. His tail flicked, possibly in annoyance, before he once again honed in on Austin.

"Take the magic down, Jess," Austin told me.

I looked at him incredulously. "Are you serious? He's still pissed off."

"It's okay. Take it down."

I shook my head at the lion, my mouth turned down in frustrated unease. I lifted my eyebrows, still incredulous, and debated not listening to Austin. I could take *this* one down and then put up an invisible one instead, just in case. It wouldn't be as strong, but it would give us a little buffer if this beast lunged, which he very much looked like he wanted to do.

"We can read your every thought, Jessie," Broken Sue said. He'd clearly changed back into his human form. The shifters around us were doing the same.

"Bring down the gargoyles and have them shift," Austin told me.

"I think this is madness," I muttered, hesitating there, too. My worry got the better of me, and I addressed the lion. "This is my world"—I pointed at Austin—"and I will not tolerate a threat to him. If you try to harm him, I will kill you before you can reach him. Gruesomely, I might add. It'll be gross. We're here to help you. We don't want trouble. Don't make me hurt you."

Now the lion was staring at me, the force of his gaze incredibly unsettling. It was hard to keep looking him in the eye. My instincts said to apologize and lower my gaze.

Threat delivered but unsure if it was properly received, I took a deep breath and sent a pulse to the gargoyles to bring them to the ground. That done, after another pause, I tore down the spells containing the lion. I was happy we were going to a cairn next because I was getting tired of all this shifter hostility and posturing.

"There," I said, releasing a breath. I debated whether to keep my hands raised in case I needed to quickly fire a spell.

The lion didn't move. His gaze was rooted on me now. Austin kept silent, apparently letting the lion assess. The ball was in his court.

Feet hit the ground as the gargoyles landed, and I heard the sound of boulders, which meant they'd shifted.

The lion backed up. There was a bright flare of light and a wave of heat, and a man stood where the lion had been. He straightened from a crouch. He was about ten years older than Austin and me, pushing fifty, with salt and pepper black hair. Scars marked his chiseled body. He was slightly leaner than Austin, probably from a lack of food, but just as in-shape. He was probably six feet tall, maybe a smidge taller. Hard hazel eyes assessed us from an incredibly striking face. Age had not stolen any of this man's beauty.

He didn't speak for a minute, and everyone in the clearing silently waited for someone to speak first. I glanced at Austin, figuring it wasn't me but making sure just in case.

"Since when do shifters work with mages?" the man finally said.

"Since I mated a female gargoyle and she pulled

mages into our territory," Austin answered.

"That would explain the gargoyles, then. There's a cairn not terribly far away."

"Yes, we're on the way there. We heard about a powerful rogue that couldn't find a place to settle, as is often the case with people like you. Like me. I was one myself, once. I finally settled in a Dick town."

"I tried that," the man said ruefully. "I got tired of fighting for the privilege."

"I didn't," Austin stated simply. "Your sisters said you were dead."

I looked at Austin in confusion. I didn't realize he knew who this guy was.

"Exiled," the man said without emotion. "What do you want?"

"Nothing." Austin lifted his hands. "I came to offer you a place to settle, if you'd like. A community where you won't be bothered. If you didn't take anything from your former pack, we can help you get started."

"I have no interest in challenging into a pack."

"We don't run a pack, firstly, and second, you don't need to. We still have some Dicks and Janes in the territory, as well as all manner of creatures. Gargoyles and shifters, as you see here, a couple mages and hopefully more, some legendary creatures, and anything that shows up besides. We are a mix of magical types, and only those interested in joining the convocation challenge in. Everyone else lives and works and minds their own business. I'd ask only that you follow the territory rules and keep things peaceful. Other than that, your life is your own."

"Convocation?"

Austin briefly and simply described what that was and why. He went over why he took the alpha title and how we ended up here. When he was done, he said, "Our territory is dangerous, I won't say it isn't. It'll probably get worse. But you'd be among those our convocation would protect."

"And if I decide I want to join the pack down the road and help do the protecting?"

"Then you would challenge in, like everyone else. You'd work your way up the shifter portion of the convocation."

"And if I decide I want to be an alpha again?" The man's face was emotionless. "If I decide I want to take over?"

A warning shiver trickled down my back, but I tried to keep my wariness from showing on my face or through my body.

Austin matched his tone. "You couldn't get out of the magical box my mate devised. Do you really want to try a forceful takeover and test her magic?" He paused for a moment. "But I'd be happy to take that challenge. Now or down the road, doesn't matter to me. You already know the outcome."

For the first time, the man reacted. He slightly narrowed his eyes, as though thinking that through.

"But you don't need that challenge to define where I sit in your hierarchy?" he asked.

"No."

Before I'd met Drex, I wouldn't have understood what that meant. Now, though, I realized Drex could never have a powerful shifter like this in his pack. He'd need to challenge, even if the guy just wanted to live amongst them and not officially join the pack. If Drex didn't win, he wouldn't be able to stomach the shifter hanging around. He'd always worry the shifter would forcibly take the pack.

The other alphas had probably had the same reservations. They'd wanted to help him but didn't want to risk it. They worried he would do exactly what he just said, not really believing he had no interest. Worried he might change his mind.

I believed him, though. If he'd wanted to take over a pack, he would've, rather than living out here by himself. He'd chosen this solitary life to try and find some peace in a world that couldn't believe he wanted it. I didn't know him or anything about his past, but that seemed obvious.

Compassion finally broke down my wariness. "We're not like shifter packs." I took Austin's hand. "Or gargoyle cairns. Or anything else, really. We only have this convocation to try and help magical people." I let my tension bleed away. "Austin created a safe haven before he ever planned to be an alpha. I'm helping him extend that to the rest of the shifters, and hopefully, down the line, mages. Come on, let's get a fire or something and some food, and sit down and have a chat."

His gaze shifted to me, and he was once again silent. "I've never heard of a female gargoyle," he said finally.

"I got the magic from a house. Seriously, a fire and some food. It's chilly here. I'm not used to it after being in suffocating humidity for the past week. Or at least a sweatshirt."

His eyebrow ticked up. He hadn't been expecting that.

"Who are you?" he asked Austin, clearly not ready to trust us and let down his guard.

"Austin Steele. Formally Austin Barazza of the Gossamer Falls generational pack line."

The man's eyes widened in evident surprise. "The youngest Barazza boy?"

"Yes."

The man's eyebrows lifted. "That explains the power. I heard you had a very healthy dose. The wildness, too. The rumors didn't do you justice."

"I'm hearing that a lot lately."

The man grunted. "You made something of yourself, huh? No one thought you would amount to anything after you…left the pack."

"Slunk away in disgrace, you mean?" Austin replied sardonically. I leaned into Austin comfortingly. Also, he was warm. He let go of my hand and put it around my shoulders. "I wouldn't have, not in any real way. The gossiping alphas would've been right. But then I met my mate and…" He shrugged. "Things change. We have food we can grill up. We can tell you the whole story, if you want."

The man assessed me for a while longer. "Fine. There's just one thing. I'm not the only danger in these woods. You're trespassing, and the watchers have shown up to check it out. They don't have a strong compulsion towards forgiveness."

CHAPTER 24

JESSIE

BASAJAUNAK EXPLODED FROM the trees. They ran at us, growling, their hair bristling. To my surprise, the man stepped forward with his hand out to stop them.

"They didn't know," he said loudly. "They are here for me—"

He cut off as the basajaunak slowed, relaxing into grins, their focus on Sebastian, who had jogged a few steps away. Dave stepped out from within them.

"I told you!" he said, devolving into laughter. "*Did you see his face?* He always does that, even when he knows we're around."

We'd met a band of basajaunak on our way to this clearing, hiding in the trees and watching us. It had taken no time at all to explain that we didn't know this was their territory and that some of their distant kin were part of our team, and they were on their way. It was easy after that to gain admittance to the area. Dave had declared me and our crew family, and that included even distant kin.

I tsked. "Dave, stop terrifying Sebastian."

"I can't seem to get over how scary they are," Sebastian said in a shaky voice.

Half the basajaunak broke down laughing. The man stared at us as though we'd grown another set of heads.

"You have basajaunak in your…what'd you call it?" he asked.

"Convocation, and yes," Austin said.

He shook his head in disbelief. "I had to fight for the right to stay here. They decided I was too dangerous to keep trying to kick out."

"That and we felt a little sorry for you," one of the resident basajaunak said. "Come on. We have started preparing for a feast. I want to hear about *Him* that has followed his star, and the stick builders who are now part of our family."

The man snorted, putting his hands on his hips. To Austin he said, "I'm not agreeing to go with you, but I must say, I am curious about this story."

✧　✧　✧

JOHN

MULTIPLE FIRES BLAZED within the darkness. The ground had been cleared of forest life, leaving a heavily trod-on dirt floor. Austin Barazza's—no, it was Steele now—people had hunted, and their game roasted on spits over the fires. The basajaunak had provided root vegetables, seeds, berries, and other natural bounties that could be found in the wilderness.

While all that had been collected and prepared, John had sat quietly and listened to Austin and Jessie's incredible story. A Jane that inherited magic from a house? A phoenix and thunderbird on board? Basajaunak as kin? If he hadn't been sitting amongst those creatures, had it all verified time and again, and read the obvious truth within the Jane's body language, he wouldn't have believed it. Then again, he also wouldn't have believed the power and might of Austin himself.

The alpha network, something John had never had any time for, apparently didn't believe much of this. John could understand why. They wouldn't want to come around, either. Austin said as much. To admit to the power amassed here, the alphas would realize they didn't have enough to keep their perch at the top. It was an uphill battle Austin faced.

It didn't seem to faze him. The cause was noble, if

that part of their story could be believed. John wasn't sure he did believe it or if he even cared. It all sounded like an awful big hassle.

A warning blared within him. Something was skulking up behind.

He'd moved away from the others after the story, wanting to sit on his own and reflect for a while.

"That's a dangerous place to be without a very good reason," he said, a growl lacing his words.

The presence kept coming but veered slightly to angle to John's side. An old creature stepped in line with him, facing front but looking his way. He had a long face and loose jowls with blindingly white teeth. As John watched, the canines elongated.

"Vampire?" John asked, not seeing much of a threat.

"Tigress?" the vampire replied. He wore a strange little smile, like they shared a joke and he'd just told a punchline.

Was John the punchline?

He turned back. He decided he didn't much care if he was.

The vampire took a sidestep closer. "I visited your camp. Pretty lonely. Do you get any callers?"

John's brows pinched together. "What?"

The vampire nodded like that had been an acceptable answer. "Yes, I thought as much. You'd be much happier with us. The Irish woman says so. She'd tell you herself, but she's busy drinking the poisonous brew. They'll regret offering it to her. She'll drink them dry. Phil knows—but don't call him Phil. That's a secret." Placing a long, spindly finger to his lips, he said, "Shhhh."

John was starting to feel mildly uncomfortable, not an easy feat. He'd mostly given up caring what people thought of him, what they said, how they acted—if someone wasn't a direct threat, he ignored them. Something told him that wouldn't be wise with this creature. He was a vampire, after all. They could be wily and unpredictable, and in this one's case, fairly creepy and somewhat *off*. It was probably the age. This one seemed old as dirt.

"I happened to notice your crochet kit," the vampire said. He sidestepped closer still. "A little blue creature. I didn't notice any doilies. You know, the doily is the Picasso of the crochet world. I'm working on creating the perfect one. My skill has backslid in recent months, what with the demands of hiker-killing flowers, but I won't give up! One day I will master that doily, and then..." The creature's smile grew. He held his hands near his chest, his long fingers dangling like some sort of vaudeville villain. "Colors!"

For the first time in maybe his entire life, John felt

like picking up the rock he currently sat upon and scooting it away in wariness. There was a time for fighting, and a time to maybe slink away. This might be the latter.

A large shifter cut across the merriment. The gorilla, with alpha power and energy, and a beta title. It was one of many things in this "convocation" that John had a hard time reconciling.

"Oh, here comes the chief of four-leaf clover finding." The vampire watched the shifter come closer. "He has an eagle eye. I can't seem to top him. It's like he's been doing it all his life."

The shifter hit the vampire with a hard stare, full of all that lethal power and energy. His body flared, a warning to get lost.

The vampire didn't seem to notice.

"Broken Sue," the vampire said pleasantly. "Or, as he's known around the campfire, Suspicious Susan."

The shifter's frame tensed for just a moment, the equivalent of him rolling his eyes.

"Edgar, you're needed by the alphas," the shifter told the vampire.

"What joy it is to be needed. I just hope she doesn't ask about the stray gnome I saw peeking out of the ferns on the way here. If I was a guessing man, I would say it has murderous tendencies. But I'm not a man, so I shouldn't guess." One of his eyes closed. It didn't seem like a wink, but might've been? John wasn't sure.

He very nearly moved his rock this time.

The vampire loped off.

"Don't mind him," the shifter said. "He's part of the Ivy House crew. They're all a little eccentric. He's very old. Vampires tend to get a little unbalanced when they are that old, I guess."

That wasn't a good enough explanation for that creature.

The shifter put out his hand for a handshake, and John rose to take it.

"Sue," the shifter said.

"That's actually your name?" John blurted. He wasn't usually so frank, but that vampire had rattled him somehow. "Sorry. John. You probably know me as Yazanth Golden Fang. It's not a name I use, anymore. That I really want to hear, anymore."

Sue shook John's hand. "Did you choose a new surname to go with it?"

"Smith. John Smith. About as boring as you can get."

Sue grunted before taking a seat on the ground next to the rock. "Yes, I've heard of you. I've had a few names, as well. Lately, it was Brochan. Then Broken Sue because of a mage meeting and a changed identity.

Now…Sue, I suppose. Not sure where the vampire got 'suspicious' from, but I've found it's better not to ask. He might tell you."

John smirked. Across the fire, the Jane—Jessie—laughed in delight. She touched Austin's knee, who smiled along with her, his arm around her shoulders possessively. He'd found a much different woman than the one in his youth, it seemed. This one, or maybe age and experience and wisdom, had smoothed out all his rough edges.

"I thought you might want to know how I came to be in this convocation," Sue said. "We share similarities though we aren't the same."

He described how he came to be alpha, taking the pack by force from the shifter who'd taken the pack from his biological father, a father who hadn't raised him. How he'd leaned on those around him for training, and how he'd gotten on his feet, then lost it all at the hands of mages.

"And you willingly work alongside mages?" John asked.

Sue didn't answer for a time. "Not all mages are the same, just like not all shifters are. Not all alphas are. Truth be told, I don't much like the underhanded culture, but I've made peace with the people themselves. We have an opportunity to effect change and stop what happened to my pack, at least partially. It's worth pushing past the knee-jerk reaction relating to my past."

John nodded at that. It would be hard to follow the example, but he saw the merit in doing it.

"I was a rogue for a while," Sue went on. "I'm sure you can guess how that went."

"I don't have to guess. I can tell you from experience."

"Exactly. I'd heard about Austin Steele, someone who was supposed to have power in spades. Someone who might not fear me as much as other alphas. I was done wandering. I was at the end of my journey and didn't much care what came next. I declared myself to him when I arrived at his territory and then went my own way. I hung around, adrift. Purposeless."

John looked over at Sue, noticing the small details of the other man as he spoke and reacted. His pack had trained him well, but he also had natural talent, like John. Like Austin. "And he let you?"

"Yes. He didn't have people watching me. He didn't check in. He didn't try to intimidate me. He had zero fear I'd take his pack from him, just like he has zero fear you will try. You have more power than me, and obviously much more experience than both of us, if all the stories I've heard are true, but that doesn't matter to him. He killed a phoenix to keep Jessie safe. He'll tear you down, too, if he must."

It was hard to believe he'd killed a phoenix, but John had heard it from the phoenix's own mouth.

You already know the outcome. Of a fight between Austin and John, Austin had meant.

Yes, he did. John nearly had as much power. He did have more experience. He had the same level of ruthlessness and the same access to his beast, if he had to guess, but John's first instinct when he'd looked at Austin had been correct: he'd been looking death right in the eye. That alpha would not lose. He was fighting for more than himself, a cause greater than his worth, and because of that, he would not allow John to best him. His assurance was so ironclad, it was fact.

John had never run into someone like him. Not ever. John had never met someone he couldn't take down. And he realized that he liked it. It took a load off, honestly. He didn't have the weight of being the biggest and toughest in the room resting on his shoulders. He wasn't the target for once. He could just *be*.

Instead of saying all that, he grunted.

"Did you know him when he was in his brother's pack?" John asked.

"No. I did go back with him recently. He was apparently a terror, but even if he wasn't, he wouldn't have fit in there. He doesn't fit in now."

Like John didn't fit in with the pack he'd helped protect. That he'd saved. Not anymore. His past had changed him, and not for the better. He'd been right to leave like he did. Austin must've been the same, though for different reasons.

There were a lot of parallels between his and Austin's paths. Even his and Sue's.

"What about the Jane? Jessie."

"If you keep calling her a Jane, her people are going to take offense, and you'll find yourself with a knife in your ribs when you least expect it. Take the warning."

It wasn't delivered as a threat, just more facts. More assurances.

"Her people are loyal, then," he surmised.

"All of us are loyal, yes. The entire convocation is. She's a giver. She's a protector. And she's up against some tough odds."

She sacrificed herself for them. There wasn't much more to say, really. She also seemed very lovely and open. Smart, as well. Pliant but stern. He could see her being a good leader and a great balance for Austin.

"What's the pack like?" he asked. "Austin seemed confident that I wouldn't be bothered, but alphas only tend to know a fraction of what goes on in their territories."

"It's a new territory that has a lot of might within it.

Normally, sure, people would want to see what you were made of, but we are under constant threat and we're always training. We always have new people challenging in. We're always changing and perfecting because we're growing at an insane rate. No one has time to bicker and fight. No one bothered me, and I was there early, when it was still chaos. Now it's a machine. Not to mention, Jessie will vouch for you. She'll probably take you under her wing, and that's a big *back off* sign to the others. If you want a place to live your life, that is it. It's a nice community if you can stand all the various creatures."

John let out his breath silently. The troubled Barazza boy, who hadn't even been able to help himself, was now here to help out a notorious alpha that no one wanted darkening their doorsteps. It was poetic, in a way. They'd both been heavily featured in the rumors, John for being the meanest, baddest of them all, the king of the hill, and Austin for being a downward spiral. They'd been on the opposite ends of the spectrum. Still were, except now Austin was climbing up onto the throne while John had tumbled from grace. Was apparently rumored to be dead.

He huffed out a laugh, shaking his head. These people seemed expressive, and John had gotten used to being more open to almost fit in with Dicks and Janes.

"This sounds too good to be true," he finally said.

Sue pushed up to standing. "That's just because you've been living a half-life for the last handful of years. On the surface, it's a town, like any other. Dig a little deeper and you realize it's a harbor for strays. An outcast put it on the map, and a magical house and its Jane stands in the middle. The strength of the territory is in its ability to bring all the misfits together. I recommend visiting, if nothing else."

He walked off without waiting for a reply. He was trying to help, like the alphas. He'd gotten a hand, and he was reaching back to help someone else.

Being in a pack again, even a weird one by a different name, made him nervous. Memories of his trials as an alpha, of his hardships, of all the bloodshed rose to the surface. Then all the rejections he'd gotten as he tried to start over. The suspicion about his motives, the teams of people trying to bring him down or chase him out.

He didn't know if he had it in him to try again. He didn't want to clutch hope and have it dissolve in his hands.

Then again, he *was* living a half-life. He didn't mind solitude, but it would be nice to have friends that didn't want something from him. People around him that weren't trying to get something. These people seemed to genuinely like being together, and they even got along well with the basajaunak. It was a community, even if a small one. He wanted that. He'd always wanted it. The chance to have it was ripped away early.

"Hey." A woman with spiky hair that almost looked green in the low light bobbed her upper body as she walked over. "Hi." She offered a wave, stopping in front of him. "You're the guy we came here to find, right?"

"Yes."

"Yeah, I thought so. They said you know your way around this wood."

"Yes."

"Cool. Are you into practical jokes?"

He paused, not having expected anything from the conversation, but still thrown for a loop. "What?"

"Practical jokes. Do you do them on people? Do you like that sort of thing?"

He frowned at her. He had no idea where this was going. "No?"

"Oh, good." She drew her hand across her forehead. "Phew." She pointed at the ground next to him. "Do you mind if I sit there?"

He looked at the spot as his mind tried to catch up. "No, go ahead."

"Thanks." She plopped down. "Woods freak me out. I always seem to get lost in them, and the basajunk like practical jokes. Did you know they can literally go invisible in the trees?"

She looked up at him, her eyebrows high and her eyes exaggeratedly rounded.

"Yes," he responded.

"Well, *I* didn't! I've never seen ours do that." She made a frustrated gesture with her hand. "Not *ours*, but the ones in our crew. You know what I mean. Anyway, one of them came to get me out of the car and lead me here. This was when you were talking to Austin and Jessie. I thought it was one from our crew, so I didn't think anything of it. Halfway here *it disappeared*!"

She looked up at him with that expression again. She seemed scandalized.

"For a moment I thought I was hallucinating, you know?" she went on. "Did I accidentally take some 'shrooms and not know it? That sort of thing." She pushed out a breath as she shook her head. "But no, I was there, in the woods, suddenly *by myself*. Worse, I'd turned around in confusion and didn't know which direction I'd come from. I didn't know where the car was! So, then I started running and calling for Jessie or Ulric or anyone to come save me."

"Why?" he asked in confusion.

"I don't know. I get a little crazy in the woods. They mess with my head. That's why I wanted to stay in the car. Well, finally one of the basajunk—"

"Are you saying basa*junk*?"

"Yeah. Basajunk. Isn't that what they're called?"

He wasn't into practical jokes, no, but that was too funny to correct. He nodded sagely.

"Well, one turned visible, and then a whole bunch of them did, and they were all laughing." She pulled up her knees and hugged her arms around them. "I gave a chuckle. You don't want practical jokers to know you hate practical jokes because then they do them to you all the time. So, I gave a chuckle, thought about telling Niamh to claim vengeance on my behalf, and they finally led me here. I'm hoping, since you don't like practical jokes, that maybe you can lead me to the next destination and not get lost until I can get out of this Godforsaken place."

Laughter bubbled up out of nowhere. He hadn't laughed in years. It overflowed until it consumed him, coming out in big body-shaking guffaws.

She chuckled without humor, and it was probably the same sort of laughter she'd given the basa*junk*.

He laughed harder. Everyone looked their way. Jessie had a lopsided grin on her face, probably wondering what the joke was.

Why was it so damn funny?

After some time when he was able to finally calm

down, he wiped his eyes and resumed staring off at the camp.

"So will you do it?" the woman asked, utterly serious.

That set him off again.

"Yes," he finally managed, re-wiping his eyes. "I will, yes. I'll make sure you don't get lost."

"You don't go invisible, right?"

"Ha-ha-ha, no," he wheezed. "I don't go invisible, no."

"Okay, good. I'm Fred, by the way."

"Fred?"

"Yeah. I'm a Dick."

That sobered him somewhat, trying to understand again. "Do you mean a Jane? A non-magical woman?"

"A non-magical woman, yes, but not a Jane, and I'll tell you why. While my pronouns *are* she, her and they, I have recently learned that there is a limit to my tolerance of a person's niceness. If they are too nice, I stop liking them. Like, I don't enjoy very sweet people who only want to do the best for me and wish me well. Which is not great. I know this. I've had to really look inward, and I've realized that I cannot call myself a Jane when I am so very obviously a dick."

That set him off again, and he still didn't know why. It really shouldn't be this funny. First that vampire and now her, two very different walks of life, and here they were. Misfits indeed.

"Hello, Fred-the-dick," he said. "I'm John."

"John? You don't look like a John."

"No? And what do I look like? A dick?"

She thought for a moment, ignoring the joke, looking up at him with squinted eyes. "Steve."

"Why Steve?"

She shrugged. "Steve just seems like a lion's name. You're the lion, right?"

"Yes. My uncle's name was Steve. He was a real asshole."

"Well, see? Steve. That goes with lion. Hmm." She squinted at him again. "Soren is nice. What about that? I think it means introspective. Or maybe it means stern." She rubbed her chin. "Either way, it would work."

"I'll think about it."

She didn't just bob her head, she bobbed her whole body, letting it go.

The night moved on, with several people coming over to chat with him or see if he needed anything. They'd be staying for the night, put up by the basajaunak, and for the first time, John was invited to stay with them, as well.

As the night was wrapping up, Jessie and Austin

stopped by. They were unmistakably the alphas, but they didn't act like it. Not traditionally, anyway. Austin had a quiet authority about him, expecting the most of everyone because he expected the most of himself, but not pushing his power or status around. He didn't act like the biggest player in the room. Didn't seem to care if he wasn't, actually. He certainly didn't care about John's power, past status, or think him a rival in any way. For Austin, the title of alpha didn't seem to hold any weight, it was the man that carried the mantle.

Then there was Jessie, who didn't act like she had any authority at all. She was kindness itself, asking if he needed anything because she was ready to provide it. Hoping John joined them, said with a genuine desire to help. She was in charge of the most power John had ever seen assembled and didn't give one shred of evidence that she knew it.

Neither of them had any ego. They weren't out to prove anything, not if they didn't have to. It was so damn refreshing.

They bid him goodnight. He walked Fred to her sleeping mat, chuckling most of the way, and then he sat by the fire, staring at the stars for a long time, thinking. Wondering if he'd take the risk. Wondering if he dared to hope in a life that so often let him down.

CHAPTER 25
ULRIC

"**B**RO, I'M NERVOUS." Jasper's wings fluttered as he and Ulric stood near the van. "I've never been to one of the top three cairns. Besides Gimerel, but that doesn't count because we raided and left."

"Me, neither. That's not why *I'm* nervous, though," Ulric replied. "My mom should've arrived over a week ago. She said she would go straight there, so she was probably only a few days late. She's had, like, *days* to get all up in everyone's business. I hope she hasn't pissed off the new cairn leader."

"Nah." Jasper waved it away. They watched Jessie climb out of her van. "Your mom will be fine. She's in her element. I'd worry more about Mr. Tom. He's been out of the gargoyle culture for…"

"No one knows. He never mentions it."

"Well…a long time. Long enough to be very strange. By gargoyle standards, at any rate. He won't help our image."

Jessie reached for her suitcase. The driver tried to hand it over, but Austin stepped in the way to retrieve it for her.

"Now, that really is going too far, sir." Mr. Tom intercepted and wrestled the suitcase away. "There is a time to be helpful, and there is a time to get out of the way. I would've assumed you'd know which was which at this point."

His wings fluttering, Mr. Tom grabbed Austin's suitcase as well before heading to the waiting private jet. Jessie put a hand on Austin's arm to stop him from reacting.

"He didn't seem to embarrass us at the connection request meetup," Ulric said slowly.

Jasper shook his head. "You didn't listen to much of the gossip about Jessie's setup, apparently."

No, Ulric had, he'd just tried to ignore most of it. He believed in this outfit and he knew Jessie would eventually win the day.

But Jasper was right. Going into an all-gargoyle establishment, one of the largest cairns… Well, Mr. Tom would not fit in.

Then again, would any of them? With all the various creatures in the convocation, it was necessary to compromise a great deal. That must've changed them.

They might be outcasts among their own kind.

"Hey, guys." Aurora stepped up to them as the group slowly moved toward the private jet. It was customary to give Mr. Tom about ten minutes to check out the plane and get things ready for Jessie. If they rushed him, he was a nightmare.

"Hey." Jasper put up his hand for a high-five, and she slapped his palm without hesitation. Even a few months ago, she wouldn't have done that. "Haven't seen much of you."

"Yeah." She glanced to the side, her gaze sticking to the new shifter. "Without a family pass, I'm not high enough in the pack to do much on these excursions."

"Well, then." Jasper lifted his eyebrows at her. "Get high enough. Word on the street is you've got alpha juice. You're plenty powerful enough."

"I'm going as fast as I can." She shoved him. "There are rules in a pack. I've climbed faster than anyone else but I have to stop for a moment at each level. It's how it's done."

"All due disrespect, my lady," Jasper said with a flourish, "this is not a pack, and our great alpha is making up rules as he goes. You've got the training. If you've also got the power, knock it out."

Her lips tweaked in a bud of a smile. Ulric pointed at it immediately. "She's human! Look Jasper, she's turning human. Our baby is emerging from her cyborg cocoon."

"Oh, shut up," Aurora said, her gaze drifting over to the new shifter again.

He had his hands shoved in his pockets and his body was slightly bowed, like he was trying not to be noticed. Even though he was moving in the general direction they all were, his body screamed wariness, and he looked ready to bolt.

Ulric dropped his voice to a whisper. "What's his deal, anyway? A bunch of the shifters seem to know who he is. They talk about him like he's some sort of god, but when I ask, everyone clams up."

Aurora grabbed their arms and moved them a little faster, putting distance between them and him.

"Uncle Auzzie told people not to talk about it," she murmured. "John wants to move on from his past, and Uncle Auzzie wants to let him. He might as well be a Dick for all he wants to do with packs and magic."

"I get that," Ulric whispered, "but you know my mom is going to try and sus out the details, not to mention Niamh. I need to know the deets so that I can buffer and keep them from pestering him."

"Stop saying things like *deets*," Jasper said. "You sound ridiculous."

"Comb your hair once in a while," Ulric retorted.

"You *look* ridiculous."

"Like you can talk," he snapped back.

"Okay, okay, fine. *Shh!*" Aurora shook their arms. "He's technically a generational alpha. His father was fourth generation of a huge and powerful pack. A very prosperous pack. His uncle, also a powerful lion, started his own pack, but it didn't work out. So, his uncle made a play for his father's pack. He challenged, but not to the death. Betas and enforcers were standing by to break them up. But the thing was, I guess, that they were very similar in power and fighting prowess. They were evenly matched. There wasn't a clear winner and so the betas let the fight continue, trying to decide when to step in. When they finally acted, it was too late."

"Who died?" Ulric asked.

"Both. First the uncle, and then the father bled out before they could save him."

"Oh, man, tough break," Jasper murmured. "It's strange, all this challenging that shifters do. What does one-on-one fighting have to do with being a good leader?"

Aurora ticked up a shoulder, her version of a shrug. A guy had to pay attention when she spoke, or he missed half the things she was trying to say.

"Yazanth—sorry, John, was only twelve at the time. He was big for his age, and already had a decent amount of power, but he was twelve. He was vulnerable."

"What about his mom?" Ulric asked.

"Died giving birth to triplets. His sisters were only four when all of this was going down. His grandma and grandpa stepped in to train him and help run the pack. That's probably the only thing that kept it together. But they had stepped down for a reason. They were older and couldn't withstand challenges."

"What about the enforcers?" Jasper asked.

"They were among the first to start challenging." Aurora bowed a little, sadness on John's behalf. "These were people John had known all his life. They'd probably helped raise him, were always around his father, and they turned on him. Tried to take him off the pedestal of alpha and claim it for themselves. They wanted money and power, and John had the keys to the castle." She paused. "Imagine if Uncle Auzzie tried to kill me to take my father's pack. It must've crushed him to field those challenges, because they *were* to the death." She shook her head. "He was only twelve, and I heard he nearly died with a great many challenges in those days, but miracle of miracles, he was able to survive."

"Wow." Jasper nodded with respect.

"When he got older, he got better, obviously," Aurora went on. "Meaner. Tougher. He still had the training from his grandparents, and not as many challenges, so he was flourishing as an alpha. And then his beta, who I hear was his longtime friend, tried to take him in the shadows. That means…" She tilted her head. "It wasn't a sanctioned challenge or even a public attack. It was when John's back was turned, and he was indisposed somehow."

"A sucker punch, but to kill." Jasper nodded. "Got it."

"Yeah. John had to kill his longtime friend and others, or so I hear. At that time, we were having our own family…issues, so I stopped hearing about it for a bit. But when he emerged from the fires, as it were, he was the undisputed power player in the alpha community. You did not mess with Yazanth. He had incredible sway, too. When he spoke, people listened. They dubbed him Golden Fang."

"So, what happened?" Ulric asked as they neared the plane.

"When his sisters came of age and had been solidly trained up and could hold their own, he shocked everyone by handing the pack over. To all three of them! Two co-leaders is rare and doesn't often work, but three is unheard of. That was about five years ago. Then he disappeared. I guess he took off in the middle of the night."

"Why?" Jasper asked.

She shook her head. "That's the mystery. Some say the sisters killed him. Others say—*he* said—he was exiled, but there's no real basis for that rumor. Why would they exile him? He *handed* them the pack. My dad thinks he needed to cut ties so people would follow the sisters' lead."

"Didn't Alpha Steele have something like that happen?" Ulric asked.

"Kinda. His situation was messier and more complicated."

"Well." Jasper slowed with the group in front of them. "I hope he's not a drinking man, or Niamh is going to sit next to him at the bar and start poking, you can guarantee it."

"She wouldn't want to poke very hard," Aurora murmured as the crowd parted. "He might rip her face off."

"Ulric." Jessie lifted her hand as the crowd parted further.

"She wants you." Aurora took her hand away from his arm.

"Yeah?" He hastened toward her. The stairs to the private jet waited just in front of her with a red carpet leading down. Attendants were stowing suitcases.

She met him halfway and lowered her voice. "Go back with John, would you? Be chipper and upbeat.

Maybe take Nessa, too. He doesn't seem very comfortable about all this. You guys are personable. Maybe grab Fred. She made him laugh."

"I think he was laughing at her and not with her, though." Jessie hesitated, and he shrugged. "We'll figure it out."

He made his way through the others before motioning for Nessa. "Come on, pretty girl. We've got work to do."

She beamed and jogged his way. She could always be counted on to act at a moment's notice with minimal questions.

John trailed behind the group now, the last of the line. He stared down at his feet, his hands still in his pockets. Every once in a while he would glance off toward the mountain he'd recently called home and the basajaunak that didn't much want him there.

He glanced up at Ulric and Nessa when they neared.

"Hey." Nessa fell in at his side. "We've been sent to corral you."

Ulric laughed. "Or help you escape, if that's the way the wind blows."

John grunted and looked back down at his feet. "She doesn't leave anyone behind, huh?"

"Who, Jessie?" Nessa stretched her arms wide. "Absolutely not. Edgar has asked to be retired, what?

Dozens of times?"

"Has to be over a hundred by now," Ulric said.

"Retired?" John studied Nessa's face with a blank expression.

She smiled at him disarmingly. She was very good at handling surly alphas. "Edgar is a vampire and already dead. Retired means *deader*. Like, retired from existence."

"He asks to be killed?"

"Whenever he does something wrong, yes." Nessa laughed. "And that's often. I'm glad she's got such a soft heart and doesn't listen. He's my battle buddy. He always seems to know how to skirt the worst of the danger and show up at the crucial moment. He helps me be a hero."

"He doesn't do much for your image any other time, though," Ulric said.

She laughed again. "What image? Death's angel? Evil villain mastermind and morally defunct mage torturer? Adding a senile vampire bestie really isn't taking me down a peg."

Ulric grimaced at her. "Are you sure about that?"

"Okay, we're here." Nessa looped her arm into John's. He stiffened, but if she noticed, she gave no sign. Or maybe she just didn't care. "Now, John, this is the moment of truth." She turned to face him in the line waiting to board the plane. The others were making their way up the stairs and finding seats. "Have you been on a plane before?"

A tiny line formed between his brows. Confusion? Bewilderment? Ulric couldn't tell. Shifters really needed to start using their faces more.

"Yes," he replied.

She ticked her head at him and Ulric wondered where she was going with this. "Have you been on a chartered plane with a prominent figure of authority where snacks were provided?"

His expression turned to stone. "Yes," he growled.

She held up her finger. "No, you haven't." Her smile was infectious. "Trust me. Okay, here we go. Don't worry about being trapped in a small space way up in the air with all these weirdoes. It doesn't seem so bad after the panic takes root. Hope you're hungry."

She let go of his arm at the exact moment there was room to progress and then stepped in front of him.

"Want me to go first?" Ulric said, pointing at Nessa. "I know shifters don't like people at their backs. Plus, this is your last chance to run. I can go before you, if you want?"

"Is it always like this?" John asked. Definitely bewildered.

Nessa stopped on the stairs to look back at him, her

brows raised.

"Is it always this…?" John didn't finish the sentence, probably not sure what words to put with it.

Ulric laughed and stepped in front of the powerful shifter. "Yup. It defies logic, but we are *incredibly* effective in battle."

Nessa winked before continuing up the stairs.

Ulric entered the doorway of the jet after Nessa and held his breath. Two steps, three, no one entered behind him. Jessie looked up from her seat, her brows lifted in question. Austin's face was blank, his alpha mask that hid his thoughts.

And then John appeared in the doorway, hands in his pockets, and stepped across the threshold.

They had him. If he hadn't run by now, he wouldn't. He'd be sucked in like they all were, a misfit recognizing a home when he saw it. A bunch of eccentric oddballs who somehow fit together.

It was incredibly humbling that Ulric was part of this oddity, but so was Tristan, and he was renowned in the gargoyle culture. That definitely softened the blow.

And then Ulric heard, "What in the hell is with all this food?"

Nessa turned back to John, laughing merrily. She leaned around Ulric to say, "Told you so!"

CHAPTER 26
ULRIC

AFTER A VERY quick flight that could've probably been a bus ride, the large private jet jolted as the wheels hit the runway. A plate of cheeses slid up the table in front of Ulric and nearly ended up in John's lap, who sat in the aisle, facing him. Aurora, sitting next to Ulric on the window seat, caught the plate and pulled it back into place.

John put his hand on the tray to keep it steady. "Why do I make you uncomfortable?" he asked, looking at her.

She pulled her hand back as though burned. "You don't. My father is Alpha Barazza, Austin Steele's brother. Dad shared news of the other packs with us as we went through our training. He used a lot of it as educational. I'm just…"

Her face flamed and Ulric grinned at her. It wasn't often she got flustered.

Jasper sat next to John, facing Aurora. "Processing?" he said, helpfully.

"I've heard a lot about you, is all," she murmured, looking out the window. "He thought you were a very good alpha."

John didn't look away. "Being good often comes at a great cost. At least it did in my case. You were the little girl who got in the way of your uncle fighting your father?"

She swallowed and turned to meet his gaze before dropping it respectfully. "Yes."

"You've joined your uncle's pack? You've forgiven him?"

Her eyes came up slowly, fire burning in their depths. She did not like being questioned about this, and the shifter subservience reserved for a formerly renowned alpha dissolved. "I forgave him the moment he approached Dad, apologized, and asked to be correctly trained," she said. "He hadn't been in his right mind. It took longer to forgive him for leaving, but now that I'm older, and having witnessed what it was like for him when he came home, I get it. He didn't have a lot of options, despite the rumors."

John held her gaze, something untamed moving behind his eyes. Something that made Ulric uncomfortable, like maybe he should switch seats with Tristan and let the big gargoyle handle things.

Aurora didn't look away, though. If anything, she leaned in. "Yes, I've joined his pack. There's more opportunity for me here. More of a challenge. More to learn. It's also the most important place a person can be when the mages strike next. It's the best way to help our kind."

They stared at each other for a long beat. Under the table, Ulric noticed Aurora curling her hands into fists, as though struggling to hang in there.

Finally, John dropped his gaze to the cheese. Taking a cube, he popped it into his mouth and looked out the window.

"I used to hate that rumor mill," he muttered, chewing. "I envied those who had time to sit by and gossip while keeping me in their sights."

"Then I guess you know how my uncle feels."

John's gaze snapped back to her before drifting away again. "I guess I do. What do they say about my sisters?"

"They don't have the clout and sway you did. They are a chorus rather than the preacher."

"Is that right?" John mumbled, and the air seemed to pressurize. "And why do you suppose that is, Miss Alpha-in-Training-Wheels?"

Ulric widened his eyes and Jasper grimaced. That

seemed like shots fired.

She didn't rise to the bait. "You know why."

"You sound like your uncle. Yes, I do. But do you?"

She hadn't looked back at him. "You left a big shadow over that pack, and you left in a strange way. After you put so much effort into earning your title, you handed it away before your time was through. While you're in your prime, I mean. Lastly, and what is probably the biggest reason—they are three people handling the territory of one. That has never been done before, not like this. Not after you bled to keep that territory whole and in the family. They are seen as a third of an alpha each, even though their individual power is rumored to be great."

Ulric couldn't pinpoint why, because John barely moved, but it seemed like he was impressed with Aurora's answer.

"They are each powerful in their own right, yes." John popped another piece of cheese into his mouth as the plane taxied down the runway. "Let me guess who leads the charge of these rumors." He paused. "Could it be Armendale?"

Aurora barely inclined her head in assent. "Dad said Armendale didn't hide his glee very well when you vanished. He stepped into the place you vacated and actively snubs your sisters whenever he can. Dad thinks he's trying to keep them from claiming your former clout. Some of the others follow his example."

"The others are sheep and fools." John rolled his shoulders and looked away.

The fire dwindled from Aurora's eyes as she studied him. "You weren't exiled, then. You left to give them a chance."

"After a certain point, stepping down had always been the plan. They knew that, even if the pack didn't. I was a guardian of the territory, nothing more. My grandparents and I spent long hours training them, equally. Each one showed just as much promise as the next. Leaving was for them, yes, and when it came time, they were working better together than any one alpha could work independently. The territory has expanded greatly, and they are managing perfectly. Every fitness report is glowing. But they don't boast about it. They don't throw it in everyone's faces. They are humble. They deserve to be the head of the alpha table, not ignored. Not pushed to the side."

Aurora lifted her shoulder a tick. "Part of being at the table is knowing when to toot your own horn."

"Does your uncle know how?"

The barest of a smile tweaked her lips. "Very well, yes. Better than my dad. I think the mages helped his swagger. When he wants to make an impression, he makes sure he is remembered."

John grunted, snacking on the cheese as the stairs were pulled over to the plane.

"Do you see them?" Aurora leaned back. "I ask because my uncle disappeared and cut off all ties. The only reason we knew he was still alive was because he was developing a wild reputation. I wished he would've visited."

"We meet in random towns, usually one at a time, sometimes two. Someone always stays back with the pack." He paused for a moment. "They hate that I live like this. It breaks their hearts. I really should stop meeting up, but...they're all I have." He cleared his throat. "This is very loose chatter for a couple of alphas in a plane full of snacks and strangers."

Ulric barked out a laugh. After John's initial "What in the hell?" upon boarding, he had barely spoken, only answering questions with one or two words, usually "yes, please" or "no, thank you," depending on what snack or drink he was offered.

"Is this...making an impression?" John asked, indicating the snacks.

"Yes, but not for you." Ulric laughed again and told the story about Mr. Tom not stocking the plane for Jessie and resorting to offering her chocolate covered laxatives.

By the time they'd deplaned, John was back to laughing like he had the night before. Thankfully it wasn't at Ulric, it was with him.

THE VANS, ALL provided by the cairn, climbed the last leg of the hill. The edge fell away on their right as they wound around a corner and then they were gazing at a vista of snow-dusted peaks and valleys. In front of them, a multi-level city sculpted from dark, weather stone rose and fell with the natural contours of the land. Gargoyles hunkered on spires and rooftops, watching the skies.

The main architectural style was gothic, with arched windows and buttresses, but there were other buildings that resembled a fortress with straight lines and sturdy walls. The jagged peaks of the mountains in the background created a gorgeous tableau that really needed to be rendered into a painting.

"Wow," Jasper murmured, gazing out the window at the city. "This is a lot bigger than I was expecting."

"This is the most impressive cairn, in my opinion," one of the other gargoyles in the van said. "Architecturally speaking. Gimerel used to be the most impressive in terms of Guardians, but I think that was due in large part to Tristan. They're nothing now. We rocked them."

"Guardians?" John asked Aurora.

"They're essentially enforcers," she answered, then

went on to explain how they practiced battle and what a raid was. As the vans toured the city, clearly giving Jessie and everyone an overview of the incredibly impressive layout and structures, she filled him in on how our raid against Gimerel had gone.

"We smashed them," one of the others said. "Absolutely *crushed* them. Some of my mates from my old cairn called me to say everyone was talking. It might not be official yet, but our status is through the roof. Just you watch."

Ulric took a deep breath. "We need to hope so. And hope this meeting goes well. We need more gargoyles in the convocation. We need fliers. They are essential as the first line of attack."

Everyone nodded and muttered their agreement.

"For the raids?" John asked in confusion.

The van fell quiet.

"No, not the raids," Aurora whispered. "You've been out of the news loop. I'll tell you about it later. The convocation will make a lot more sense, then."

✧　✧　✧

JOHN

HE TRIED TO keep his decorum as he looked at the beautiful architecture of this city in the clouds. He'd never seen anything like it, a forgotten place out of time, built with careful consideration and kept pristine by effort and diligence.

The vans stopped at a beautifully positioned house. Grand in scale, it cut into the cliff face at its back and was almost regal with its narrow, cathedral windows inlaid with stained glass and intricate designs. Tall spires rose into the sky amid steep slate roofs. A wide, stone staircase led to heavy double doors with arched stonework. From its position high in the hills, the residence overlooked the town, watchful and protective.

"*Someone* gets a gold star for their craftsmanship," Jasper murmured, and John had to agree. A master created this residence, and the city besides. Architecture was something of a passion of his, the older the better. He couldn't wait to get a better look.

The driver exited the van, but no one followed. Ulric put his hand on the door handle, bending to see out through the windows. He was watching the other vans. When the drivers of the various vans reached the rear doors, the passenger doors finally opened, and everyone exited in an orderly fashion. The large gargoyle—Tristan—cut an unhurried path to the right. Sue took his place opposite. Gargoyles and shifters formed a crisp line.

"I'm being pushed toward the gargoyles," Ulric said

when John got out. "You're going to go into the middle of our lines with Jessie's crew. Don't worry about lining up, they can't seem to manage it."

The gargoyles headed off to their lines. Aurora broke away to the back of the shifters. John was confused but kept his movements smooth, the product of many years of hiding any and all weaknesses.

And then the vampire randomly appeared at his side, and he flinched.

"Hello. Joining us?" Edgar asked. He didn't wait for an answer. "Come on. Just this way. The water is warm."

"Now ye're just tryin' to be unsettling," the puca told the vampire, waiting in the chaotic middle of the two crisp lines.

Edgar gave John a strange smile before he scooted into the throngs of people to stand behind a mousy sort of woman with unruly brown hair. The healer, if John wasn't mistaken, a very useful type of magic that John hadn't known existed.

He thought about slipping his hands into his pockets but straightened, years of muscle memory coming to the rescue. Shoulders and head high, he proceeded.

Austin walked with Jessie to the front of the procession, subtly submissive by being a step behind. He was giving her the floor, letting her handle things with her people as she'd let him handle things with John. Mostly, anyway. She had not liked Austin being in danger. Austin would probably be the same here, if not incredibly more volatile.

Sue's stance, like John and Tristan's, was bold, posturing. Alphas, all. Austin didn't react to either beta or to John when he glanced back. Clearly, he was comfortable leading alphas, secure in himself, his hierarchy, and his placement at the top.

For some reason, that tickled John. The little Barazza boy was all grown up and he wasn't any less headstrong. The difference now? He had focus, using his incredible might where he thought it mattered, and not bothering with the rest.

John was suddenly glad he'd chosen this path. If nothing else, it would be interesting seeing how differently this alpha managed his affairs, and whose feathers in the shifter community it ruffled. It would be refreshing to be on the outside looking in. All of this was none of his concern. Finally.

The front doors opened, and four large gargoyles came out, two by two. But while they looked muscular, especially in the shoulders and chest, and were tall, they couldn't match Tristan.

The gargoyles went to either side of the doorway, stood against the wall, and promptly disappeared. He let out a gush of breath in surprise.

"Yeah," Fred mumbled, pointing. "Did you know they did that? Magic is crazy, y'all. It is *cray*-zy. Thank god I can find my way in a city just fine or I'd worry one of them would lead me somewhere and then just disappear like that basajunk did last night. Remember me telling you about that? Nightmare."

Laughter bubbled up inside John as another gargoyle came through the door dressed in a rumpled navy button down shirt and black slacks. The laughter threatened to break free as he stepped to the side and another gargoyle similarly garbed stepped outside.

He squeezed his eyes shut and held his breath, tamping down on the guffaws that threatened. This woman was so odd it passed right by ridiculous and went straight into hilarious. He'd never had people like this around him as an alpha, and no one ever really talked to him afterwards.

"Austin Steele," the less-rumpled gargoyle said. He seemed younger than the others by about ten years, placing him at about thirty or so. A wave of dark brown hair fell to his ears and freckles adorned his face. His eyes crinkled. "Jessie Ironheart. Welcome. It's good to have you. I'm Evan Salsby. You can call me Evan, of course."

"Hello, Evan, lovely to meet you," Jessie said, no real

formality. "You can call me Jessie. Thank you for playing host, and I apologize about our lack of attire. We were treated to a basajaunak cook-out last night and slept in the woods. We didn't have the facilities to look more presentable."

"Not at all." Evan waved that away. "You're busy these days. Your right-hand woman, Patty, has no end of stories about what you've been up to."

In the gargoyle line, Ulric's wings shivered. John would have to start studying gargoyles to decipher what their various movements meant.

Evan turned to the side and held out his hand to the gargoyle in the rumpled shirt. "You know Gerard, of course."

Gerard held up his hand in greeting. "Hey! Fancy meeting you here."

"Hi, Gerard. It's great to see you again!" Jessie leaned forward a bit to convey her pleasure. "Your visit saved us from having to be late."

Gerard put out his hands. His demeanor was utterly blasé, like life was a surfboard and he was just waiting for a wave. "I do what I can."

Evan clasped his hands in front of him, not confident in his position right now. "I have refreshments ready while we get your people situated and then we'll let you get settled and freshened up. How would that be?"

"Sounds perfect, thanks." Jessie looked back at the gargoyle they called Mr. Tom. They never seemed to drop the mister from his name. "Can you get everyone sorted out?"

"Of course, miss. Shall I keep the miserable old woman confined to her room, as is proper, or will she be allowed to wander around the town and start trouble as usual?"

John went still, expecting Jessie or Austin to lash out at such flagrant disregard for propriety at a meeting. This gargoyle was embarrassing himself, his position, and whomever he was calling names.

"And ye think ye'd be able to stop me, like?" the puca said, ending John's confusion. Apparently she was the "miserable old woman" Mr. Tom was referring to. "Sure, these are gargoyles. They like a little color in their lives. Or don't ye remember because it's been so long since one of them identified ye as their kind?"

Tingles of warning worked up John's spine. He wanted to rush forward and put a hand on the two, stopping them from continuing. He didn't have to be the one to rip them to pieces to prove a point, but he still didn't want to witness it. He'd walked away from all that. He didn't want the memories of what Austin or Jessie would surely now be forced to do.

But even as he contemplated backing up, Aurora caught his eye. She subtly shook her head no, apparently warning him not to flee. Would that make things worse?

"I beg your pardon," Mr. Tom started, his wings shaking madly. "I'll have you know—"

"Stop." Jessie held up her hand, her eyes closed in a pained expression. Austin waited beside her patiently. "Please stop. Mr. Tom, Niamh knows better than to create trouble when she is a guest in another territory, right, Niamh?"

"Of course I do, what're ye on about?" she responded pompously, and there was more than a little bullshit to those words.

Jessie seemed untroubled by the woman's continued disrespect for her position. "Great. Mr. Tom, help everyone get settled, if you wouldn't mind. We'll be along later. Please iron my nice clothes for this evening if you can."

"Yes, miss, though you've surely forgotten the sort of sport the Irishwoman makes of gargoyles." Mr. Tom's wings fluttered again.

Jessie glanced over John's head at the basajaunak. "Phil, keep things in line, would you?"

"No, problem," he replied. "I'm very good at squishing fights."

Jessie held up a finger, and then swung it to Niamh. "No fights. If I hear of a fight, I will blame you two whether it is your fault or not—"

"It'll be their fault," Mr. Tom quipped.

"—and you will be flown home. Is that clear? We are guests. Do not rile them up just to see if you can. You deserved that beer glass to the back of the head in Drex's territory, Niamh. A gargoyle will probably do worse, and I will not heal you here, either."

"That glass was worth it," Niamh murmured. "I won a lot of money on that bet. I knew I could get that happy fecker to crack."

"Maybe you should use it to pay for charm school," Mr. Tom groused.

Jessie sighed and turned back to the cairn leaders with an apologetic smile. "Sorry about that. Gerard, you remember this crew."

"Yeah." He grinned. "What's this about a beer glass to the back of the head? That sounds like a fun outing. I need that story."

Evan gave her a comforting smile. "If your team is able to rile up my gargoyles, the gargoyles will get what they deserve."

"No, please." Jessie put up her hand in a stop motion. "Don't encourage them. Seriously."

Evan welcomed Jessie and Austin into the house,

followed by Gerard. Sue and Tristan stepped forward immediately, each leader seemingly getting two pack members—or whatever—to watch their backs. The doors closed, and then another gargoyle materialized that John had not previously noticed. He hadn't been a threat, but John would need to watch himself in this place of stone, where an enemy could hide in plain sight.

"Do not embarrass the miss," Mr. Tom told Niamh. "I know what you're planning."

"Do ya me arse," she responded. They bickered at each other like they'd been doing it for years. "Ye don't know yer head from yer foot."

"I will help you get situated," the resident gargoyle said as the ranks of shifters and gargoyles broke.

Aurora threaded through everyone to him. "Alph— John. Sorry. That'll take some getting used to. I thought maybe you'd want to hear about the trouble in the shifter world right now, the attack on my dad's pack, and maybe how Jessie tends to run things. I forgot how structured you had to be in your time. This must be quite a shock."

Structured. A nice way of saying brutal, culling trouble at a moment's notice so that it didn't grow and take him down. The early years had been nothing but, and in the later years he had to keep up pretenses or else people would think he'd gone soft and push harder.

He shook his head at the closed door. "Does that sort of thing happen all the time?"

Her eyes glittered with humor, but she didn't let it reach her expression. "You have no idea."

"And the alphas don't react at all? I realize most packs don't have to adhere to the level of structure I had to, but I've never heard of a pack so…" He shook his head, at a loss for words.

"Alpha Steele runs his people one way, and Jessie… Well, if you're willing, let's go get a coffee somewhere and I can explain."

He rubbed the back of his neck, his mind whirling. He was prepared for different, given all the creatures in this convocation, but not *this* different.

"Let's go to wherever that puca goes," he finally said. "I want to see if she starts a fight."

CHAPTER 27

JESSIE

"TRISTAN, GREAT TO see you again!" Gerard put his hand out for Tristan to shake with a big smile. "I heard about the raid on Gimerel. Wow! Talk about leveling up, huh? You put the heat on that cairn. They are still reeling. They're losing guardians left and right. You gotta show me some of that setup so we're prepared to fight with you next time."

Tristan smiled politely at him. "Of course. I've devised a pretty seamless system that can expand with more people or reduce to just a small team. It makes things safer, while being easy to integrate other guardians."

Gerard blew out a breath and ran his fingers through his hair. "Intense." He put his hand on Tristan's shoulder and faced Evan. "This gargoyle right here"—he pointed at Tristan—"is a genius. He's the best there is." He looked at me. "You got lucky to snap him up. I'm telling you."

"I think I'm the lucky one, actually," Tristan said humbly. "I didn't level up on my own. I followed Alpha Steele's exemplary leadership and pack structure, and I get to battle and train with a female gargoyle. She connects and organizes us all with magic, so I can much more easily do my job."

"Oh, yeah, I remember that connection." Gerard put his hands on his hips. "That was excellent. The battle was terrible, truly awful, but you can't help feeling alive during stuff like that."

"You are a battle species, after all," Austin said, his hand resting on the small of my back.

"Yeah, we definitely are." Gerard nodded.

"Thank you again for coming to visit." Evan smiled at me. "And thank you for the service you did for my family in helping my cousin. It showed what a caring person you really are."

"Don't believe any of those rumors from her first connection meet-up." Gerard shook his head at Evan. "They didn't even give her a chance at that meeting. It was over before it even began, and then the others had to lick their wounds. I mean…" He indicated Tristan. "Gimerel's best walked away from a cushy post and took a place in what he must've thought at the time was a risky venture. That's how well she showed, and they crapped all over her."

He did a raspberry and waved it away.

Evan smiled but didn't comment. He'd be making up his own mind. Hopefully, that mind would be open.

"Please." He stepped aside and gestured toward the house. "Come through. I have us setup in the drawing room."

The interior of the house was dimly lit and strangely hushed, like sound didn't travel very far. Colorful light bounced around the front room from the stained-glass windows. We walked into the main hall where a vaulted ceiling arched over us, supported by ribbed columns. In the center of the large space stood a round table with a polished black top. Showcased on the table was a sculpture I recognized from Ivy House. While very pretty and probably expensive, given the gold inlaid in the stone, it wasn't priceless, unlike some of the other pieces in that house. It hadn't made the cut into the art room that Mimi had set up. Clearly, Tristan thought it would be better used for this purpose.

Given it was on display in a prominent place in this gorgeous house, he'd been correct.

"You outdid me." Gerard paused at the sculpture, narrowing his eyes at me. "This is classy *and* expensive. I can never seem to get the two together."

"I beg to differ," Tristan said, following us with the

other guardians. "The Porsche you gave Jessie was expensive and very classy. I love that car."

Gerard shrugged. "I'll take it, though it definitely isn't classy like this."

Evan paused to admire the sculpture. "It's stunning. Every time I pass it, I'm riveted. The gold could be fake and the stone cheap, and I'd still stop and stare at it. The design, a flame in a breeze swirling with gold, is entrancing. The artistry is excellent." He shook himself out of his daze, his eyes shining as he looked at me. "It's perfect. You've pinpointed my love of art."

I opened my mouth to say that Tristan picked it out when I noticed the very subtle shake of his head, an action the gargoyles would surely miss. Training to read body language had its perks.

Instead, I said, "I have the bowl sculpture you sent on display, as well. Naomi, Austin's grandmother, is remodeling our home, and she had hoped it came from a new production cairn we'd acquired."

His smile was appreciative. He inclined his head in thanks. "That production cairn has yielded some great artistry. It is something of a risk, of course."

"Why is that?" Austin asked, following him as he moved on.

Light flickered from sconces on the walls, decorative bulbs made to look like small flames that resembled torches. He stopped in front of two wood paneled doors and his gargoyles stepped forward to push them open.

"Our kind typically look for practical items over those that are decorative." He led the way into the drawing room. "If they spend money, it's often on nice fabric for clothes or jewelry, or on furniture made to last. The glass coming out of that production cairn is mostly decorative. We can make wine and drinking glasses, bowls and plates, vases—but all of it will be higher priced than the usual fair. It's made to impress, not to exist. Then, of course, we make the sculptures, chandeliers, things like that. I'm not sure the gargoyle culture is going to buy on a large enough scale to earn real income. I'm coming up with ways to pivot if we need to."

I marveled at the study. It had the same gothic feel as the rest of the house, with a high ceiling and tall, mullioned windows. Heavy velvet curtains in a deep mustard color swept to either side, allowing in muted lighting. A large stone hearth on one wall with paintings caught Tristan's eye, and he went to investigate. Plush, burnt-red velvet sofas sat atop a patterned rug that somehow brought the room together. Lights made to look like candles glowed on the walls. It was absolutely gorgeous. Mimi couldn't have designed this room better.

"And why do you plan to only sell to your kind?" Austin asked, taking a seat on one of the sofas. After I sat next to him, he laid his arm across the back behind me. "Why do gargoyles keep all their products in-house?"

Evan sat facing us, and Gerard took the other couch. A tray housed snacks on the coffee table between us similar to those that had been offered on the plane, and a stand of drinks were kept on a rolling cart off to the side. The moment we were comfortable, a woman in a white coat and black slacks came in to fill our plates and offer us drinks.

"Because..." Evan blinked at him for a silent moment. "That's our market."

Gerard accepted a plate of cheeses and grapes before asking for a vodka soda with two limes. "Austin brought this up to me, too." He leaned against a pillow and threw an ankle over his knee, getting comfortable. "After I stuttered for a bit, I realized the answer was that we don't know how to sell to anyone else. We've cut ourselves off from Dicks and Janes, we don't do much with shifters, and mages are too dangerous. Who else are we going to sell to?"

Austin passed on the snacks, having eaten his fill on the plane, but accepted a glass of sparkling water. He didn't immediately comment.

Gerard went on, cheese stuffed in his cheek. "Even if we could sell to Dicks…" He pushed up a little more, swallowed and went on. "My cairn isn't setup to get large shipments of product to them, and we certainly aren't set up to ship direct to customer. We're not as removed as this cairn, but we're also high up in a mountain. Most of our production cairns are, as well. It isn't feasible."

Evan hadn't looked away from Austin. "What Gerard says is true of most cairns," he said. "We have the airstrip right there, though. Withor had his faults, but he did have a logistical mind. Regular shipments in private jets would be pricy, however. I doubt parcel carriers would come all the way out here. It wouldn't be worth their while. And then there is how to sell in the Dick world. I wouldn't have the first clue. Shifters, either."

"Then sell to me," Austin finally said. "Give me wholesale prices and I will give you sales in bulk. Not all your products, most likely, but I definitely want those glass products. We make money, you make money."

Evan ran his thumb along the top of his glass. "This is the carrot to join the convocation, I assume?"

"No," Austin replied. "This is business. Some of these cairns have excellent products, but they are wasted in the small amount of trade you do within the gargoyle community. I see an opportunity. Our production cairns are filling warehouses as we speak. We have salespeople already making deals. If you won't take this opportunity, I will be happy to."

I put my hand on Austin's thigh, pride welling up. He was one helluva businessman, as ambitious as he was tenacious.

He took a sip of his drink. "Food for thought."

"I'll say." Gerard scratched his chin.

"About this convocation," Evan said. His eyes sparkled with intelligence, and his gaze was focused. He was curious, and that was good. He didn't plan to shut us down right away. "Gerard has spoken a bit about it, and Patty has no end of information, it seems. I'm curious about your territory specifically, though, not the organization at large. Not yet. I wondered if you could field some questions?"

"Sure." I gestured him on.

His questions were direct and intelligent, and his follow-up questions were insightful. He wanted to know how much money Austin had pumped into it and how much it had grown. How much Ivy House did, and our plans for the future. Our goals of more housing and more production cairns widened his eyes, as did the current house prices, the rate at which businesses were being proposed to the city council, and how many people were currently a part of the territory.

Things started looking grim when he tried to break down our various duties, however. I could feel myself shrinking before his eyes. When it was all laid out, I didn't do much. Austin led the shifters, created their fighting plans, and protected the borders. Tristan managed the gargoyles. I looked after the Ivy House crew, which was only comprised of a dozen or less people and they didn't follow orders unless we were in a battle. I did magic, sure, but I didn't use it to protect the territory or in the day-to-day. I didn't even control the basajaunak, since Dave or his mom led them. Hell, Ivy House could handle her own grounds.

It finally boiled down to his needing clarification.

"And so, what is it that…" Evan squinted, choosing his words carefully. "What would you say is the chief item you bring to the table within your territory, Jessie?" He put out his hand. "I know you are an outstanding asset in battle. I saw the footage from the raid against Gimerel. As shaky as the camera people were on their phones, your prowess with magic is exemplary. You are a huge asset in battle, no question. But when it comes to daily life in a territory, what would you say—"

"She's the glue," Tristan said, cutting in from his place by the wall. "She's the backbone. She's the person who is deeply in touch with the well-being of the people."

"She's the heart," Sue said, anger lining his tone. He was feeling protective. "She's the reason Alpha Steele can push so hard, and demand so much. People go above and beyond *for her*. To protect her. To please her. Because they know she does it for them. She accomplishes the intangible part of being a leader, which is such a struggle for so many, and that is creating a community. Creating a family. She has bonded our territory better than any alpha or cairn leader I've seen. She's brought everyone together and keeps them unified."

Tristan cut in. "She's only been magical for a year or so. She's only been in this position for the same amount of time, and she has had no grace period, no time to get her bearings, like you are doing. She had no training, like Austin, Sue, and I have had. Suddenly, she must create and lead a territory, create and lead an army, learn magic and unite the magical world…all at the same time. While she does that, she buys businesses, learns how to run them, learns how to fly, and manages an obscene amount of power. I realize you are asking about stability, and so I say this to you—you come into this cairn after someone has set it all up for you. It's a prosperous cairn that is running smoothly, and you hope to take over and gradually make your mark. She has built her cairn from the ground up, and thankfully she has someone knowledgeable to help her do that, just like you've had someone knowledgeable help you. What makes you so different from her? Neither of you have any past experience leading. Why should you get handed status because of the cairn someone else setup, and she should not?"

Evan's eyebrows rose. My heart swelled to twice the normal size. I wiped away a tear at all their kind words.

"Food for thought." Austin pulled his arm from behind me and stood, reaching down for my hand. Tristan stepped forward at the same time as Sue, ready to go.

My first inclination was to hesitate and smooth this over, but I'd tried that the first time with gargoyle cairn leaders, and it didn't work out. It didn't help even a little. So, I took Austin's outstretched hand and gracefully stood, offering Evan a disarming smile.

"Thanks so much for the snacks. I look forward to dinner. Your home is beautiful. Truly a work of art."

Evan stood with us, and so did Gerard.

"Tristan does have a very solid point about stepping in and being handed status for someone else's work," Gerard mused, following us. "I hadn't thought about it like that—or at all, actually." He clapped. "Anyway, where did that puca go? I might be able to sneak in one or two before dinner."

AT THE FRONT of the house, and after Gerard gave us a wave and headed off in another direction, Tristan made a subtle movement I couldn't decipher.

"Sound proofing, Jess," Austin murmured.

I nodded when it was done, covering the four of us as we headed to the last remaining van at the front of the property. Gargoyles lurked against the stone house, invisible to everyone but gargoyles, but surely felt by Austin. Our shifters were well trained in detecting presences.

"He was trying to be delicate," Tristan said, his gaze scanning the surroundings. "He wasn't trying to offend you or say you weren't valuable in the daily life of the territory, but he's trying to figure out if it is wise to align with you. He has very little room for error when taking over a cairn this prestigious. Withor will be watching Evan's every move, wanting to step back into his role, and so Evan has to be smart. He's not sure you're a good play. I was simply...helping him think a little more realistically about the situation."

"They were good points." Austin reached the van first and pulled open the sliding black door, stepping back so Tristan and Sue could climb in first. "I wouldn't have thought of them."

"I've spent fifteen years studying gargoyles and cairn leaders," Tristan said. "I've had to manipulate a few from time-to-time. Evan is one of the easier situations because he's new, he's green, and his rise to cairn leader isn't usual. He probably thinks it was too easy. And it was, made so by you. He'll be easier to impress because he won't be inclined to stick to tradition. But he's still a gargoyle. He can't be pushed into it, and if we try, he'll dig in his heels, and it'll be months or years before he'll come around."

I climbed into the van, followed by Austin. He closed the door and the driver nodded, putting the van into drive.

"It was also a good speech by…Sue now, is it?" Tristan asked. "Are we officially switching all our names or what?"

Sue huffed. "Fred is working on John now, but yeah. I'm not lost, and I'm not broken. Not anymore. I hurt, that'll never go away, and I will always miss what I had, but…it's time to live again. My mate would've wanted me to keep living. Indigo has really helped me work through things, if I must be sappy about it."

"Oh, yes, that is incredibly sappy—*work through things*," Tristan said dryly. "I'm nearly bursting into tears here. Put all that emotion away, big guy."

"You sound like Niamh."

"Someone has to."

Sue huffed again. "Becoming Sue made me official in this crew, both because it was the first foray into danger with everyone, and because it is weird. Now it fits."

"It does fit the weird, that is true," Tristan murmured. "Anyway, Jessie, keep being you. Austin, you, too. I bet you got him thinking with that business proposal. He'll probably want more information, but he'd be a fool not to entertain it. I'll step in as I need to. I'm respected among the guardians again, ever since the raid. I have sway here. I'll use it to help steer."

Austin nodded, taking my hand and entwining our fingers.

"He's right, though." I chewed my lip. "I'm so often a passenger with all this stuff. I *don't* do all that much in the day-to-day."

Sue's hand covered my shoulder. "Did you not hear Tristan? You have an incredible amount on your plate. We don't need you walking around playing mayor, and your time is not well spent opening businesses and learning how to operate them. We need you learning your magic and training for battle. After the threat is extinguished, *then* you can be an entrepreneur. Not before."

"Not to mention I no longer have time to do those things, either," Austin said. "Mimi is stepping into the managerial role. She'll take over and that'll be that. Even if I wanted a say, I won't get one."

Tristan chuckled. "Exactly. This is something Gerard understands and no one else seems to. He saw the battle. He knows what we're up against. No one else does, and it is blinding them."

"How do you think we can enlighten them?" Sue asked, pulling his hand away. I appreciated the gesture. He didn't often use touch to connect with others.

"We're going to train," Tristan said, "and we're going to dazzle them with a female gargoyle and how natural it feels with her leading. We're going to make the gargoyles beg to be included in our reindeer games, and we're going to include the garhettes in our fun. Evan won't be able to stay practical for long. He's going to have to take a risk, and he probably already knows it. That is the only way forward in a changing world. We're going to push him to it. And right now, Niamh is very likely working on that."

I sighed and leaned into Austin. "All she seems to do is needle people anymore."

"She is prodding people who need it," Tristan said. "Aggressive types. They respond well to these tactics. Or so I'm inclined to believe because it's working."

"She hardly glanced at John." Sue shifted in his seat as the van pulled in front of a long two-story structure that lacked the architectural finesse of everywhere else. This seemed like a late addition to the city, and I guessed it was to accommodate more guests. Cheap and cheerful. "She stayed well away from him. She sized him up all right, but the moment he clued in that she was assessing him, she found somewhere else to be and something else to do. She knows what she's about, even if the way she goes about it can be horribly annoying."

Tristan barked laughter as we climbed from the van. "Very." He paused for a second as a gargoyle stepped forward from beside the door. "Why is that do you think? I've heard his story, and I know he's a legend in the shifter community—or was, back in the day—but why would Niamh avoid him?"

Austin put his hands on his hips and turned away from the building, his eyes going distant. "The guy is like a celebrity in the shifter world. The way he was able to hang onto his pack in the beginning is just shy of miraculous. The amount of times he was on death's doorstep would make your balls shrivel up. He ended up having to be an incredibly brutal alpha to maintain his position—*incredibly* brutal. Tristan turning people inside-out kind of brutal, but some of those people were his family and friends. His uncle's people and his dad's were all trying to pull the rug out from under him and assume control. That territory and all the family's holdings was—*is*—worth a fortune."

He paused for a second, the breeze ruffling his hair. The gargoyle who was clearly trying to lead us to our quarters waited in confusion a few feet away. He probably wondered why our lips were moving but he couldn't hear any sound.

"I really feel for that guy. I see what my life could've been if I was older and felt used up, and it's not a pretty realization. I had the same realization when a broken alpha gorilla asked if he could squat in my territory." Austin showed Sue a small grin. "If I had to guess, I bet Niamh knows how fragile John's situation is. How likely he is to spook. Needling Sue kept Sue focused on her and distracted from his past." He looked at Sue. "I assume you've figured that out by now?"

Sue grunted in acknowledge.

Austin nodded. "She clearly doesn't think she's what John needs."

"Needs for what?" I asked.

Austin pulled his lips to the side in thought. "I don't know, exactly. To hang around, maybe."

"Would he be helpful to your organization if he were to join?" Tristan asked.

Both Austin and Sue blew out breaths, Austin with a

sardonic grin.

"Without doubt," Austin said. "Coming back from perceived death would just make him *more* of a legend. I would love to see Armendale's face when he found out." He lost his humor. "But he's been through hell. I knew who he was when he burst out of those trees, but my offer stayed the same. He needs a community. He needs peace. We've built a safe harbor for people, and I will stand by that. Anything else is up to him."

Tristan nodded like a riddle had just been solved. "Niamh's giving you guys room to be altruistic until she can find an angle. Then she'll move in, just you watch."

CHAPTER 28
SEBASTIAN

SOMEONE RAPPED AT the door to Nessa and Sebastian's small room in the city's only hotel. The space had two single beds with night tables for each and two chairs, one on each side of the room. There was a bathroom shared by Jasper and Ulric in the adjoining room.

Sebastian glanced at Nessa, saw that she was just finishing organizing her suitcase, and moved to get the door.

Niamh stood in the hallway. Behind her, gargoyles and shifters passed by, heading for the stairs that would take them outside.

"Come on," she said without preamble.

"What?" he asked in surprise. He saw the cape in her hand, and surprise turned to panic. "Why?"

"Come on," she said again, jerking her head in the direction everyone was walking. "Let's go."

"No." He thought about shutting the door in her face. "I'm good. I'll stay here."

"Come on." She reached in, grabbed him by the shirt, and yanked him into the hall. "You need a drink."

Edgar skulked down the hall with a smile. He also had a cape on.

"No, I don't. Honest. I'm fine being this wound-up." Sebastian tried to backpedal. "Why in the world would you use capes in a gargoyle settlement? We're not hiding from mages. They are going to know these aren't wings."

"What's…" Ulric stepped out of his room next door with a growing smile. "What's going on here?"

"We need a conversation starter." Niamh held out the cape for Edgar to take before grabbing Sebastian by the shoulders with surprising strength for an old woman. Appearances were very deceiving here. "Put that cape on him," she told Edgar.

"No, no." Sebastian tried to weasel away from the vampire and his bright white canines. "It's okay. I'll do. I'll do it!"

"I'm coming," Ulric said as he made way for Jasper. "I want to see how this plays out."

"It won't play out well," Sebastian groused. "It never plays out well. For me, anyway."

"Nonsense. We always get what we're after, don't

we?" Niamh gestured him on. "Let's go. I've got the skinny on the roughest bar in the settlement. Granted, there are only three bars here, but it'll have to do. A few of the more powerful guardians always hang out there."

"Jessie said not to start a fight," Sebastian bleated, dragging his heels.

"We're not going to start a fight. We're going to create a little animosity so that when all the gargoyles train together, they'll make it personal and force Jessie to put them in their place. They'll respect her more for it. It's the gargoyle way, the stubborn donkeys."

Sebastian wilted as he followed her down the hall. Dang it, she was right, and it was a great idea. Ulric echoed his thoughts as he said, "Too true. Great idea."

"Yeah," Jasper said.

"Why does it have to be me, though?" Sebastian whined. Nessa jogged to catch up, wearing a big smile. "Why can't Nessa or one of the shifters do it? Or Fred. Fred is always down for one of your crazy ideas."

"Nessa has a way of charming people," Niamh said. "So does Fred. They'll make a cape seem normal. You do not have that gift. You'll make the cape seem awkward."

"*Everyone* would make a cape seem awkward," Sebastian grumbled as they pushed through the exit and walked down the stone path. He sent out magic to "see" the gargoyles standing by the stone, invisible. "Why do they do the invisibility thing when gargoyles can still see them?"

"It's customary for a guardian," Jasper said. "We can see them, but their appearance is slightly different when blending in than when they aren't. They are essentially denoting their rank when they do it."

"They're showing off that they are Guardians," Niamh said. "Don't bother looking at them. It'll rankle them that we don't care."

"Yes, it will," Ulric murmured with a grin.

"I cannot *wait* to fly with them all," Jasper whispered, keeping his voice low. "We have a new flight strategy now, so Gerard's gargoyles won't specifically know it, but we developed good aerial communication with his cairn. They'll catch on quickly. The others will feel totally out of place."

"They'll feel like novices," Ulric murmured. "And then add in how we work with Jessie and Cyra swooping and Hollace acting as an anchor—it'll be like their first day as Guardians. It'll punch holes in their egos."

"Which will make them lash out, especially with the animosity we're about to create." Niamh nodded. "Very predictable, gargoyles."

"You say that about shifters," Ulric said.

"Yeah, they are, too." Niamh pointed to the right,

around a corner. "That way."

"Is there anyone you don't find predictable?" Jasper asked.

"Momar." They traveled the sidewalk, sometimes nearly brushing up against the lurkers at the side, but not glancing their way. Cars and SUVs traveled slowly along the street, their occupants staring out the windows at Sebastian and his crew. Their gazes didn't miss the ill-fitting capes that Edgar and Sebastian wore.

Around a few more corners they found the bar in question. No one loitered outside for a smoke or a chat. Inside the dingy interior, however, the bar was half-filled with large gargoyles swilling beer and talking loudly. Pool balls clattered farther in the back and someone barked laughter.

At the very end of the bar, tucked in the corner where they could see the door and most of the room, sat Aurora and John.

"Oh. Look." Sebastian pointed at them and headed that way immediately.

Niamh slapped his hand out of the air and jostled him toward the end of the bar nearest the door.

"But—" he said.

"Leave them to it," Niamh murmured, nearly under her breath. "Let them come to us."

Sebastian frowned as Aurora noticed them. He gave

her a lame wave. She didn't move. Her expression stayed blank. John glanced up, and noticing him, said something to Aurora that elicited the barest of shrugs. He was probably asking about this stupid cape, Sebastian mused darkly.

"I look like an idiot," he groused.

"Nonsense." Niamh sat him down on a barstool and patted his shoulder. "You're grand."

"I think I look good." Edgar sat next to him and leaned too close. "Wings fit me."

The clasp of Edgar's cape pulled way to the right, draping loosely over one shoulder and leaving the other mostly bare. It didn't fit even a little.

Jasper and Ulric wandered down Aurora's way, all smiles and easy friendliness.

"Why do they get to go down there?" Sebastian once again whined. He felt like a child every time Niamh took him drinking.

Nessa leaned against the bar next to Edgar, not at all worried about the vampire's proximity, as Niamh sat down next to Sebastian.

The bartender glanced their way and did a double-take, his eyes narrowing as he spied the capes. Sebastian's guts churned in warning. He really didn't want to get in a bar fight. He'd use magic and it would create an issue, he just knew it.

The Guardians' voices reduced to a soft murmur as Ulric and Jasper threaded through them to the other side. The Guardians didn't step out of the way or even twist to create a little space. When they were new, they did that in O'Briens, too. Ulric and Jasper bumped shoulders and disturbed wings as they passed, not once offering an apology or even noticing the rudeness of either party.

The bartender approached Sebastian first before staring hard at Edgar. "What's with the capes?" he asked.

"Yer the last person who should be concerned with fashion, like," Niamh said, settling against the bar with her elbows on the worn wood. "Got any cider?"

The bartender glanced down at his brown shirt with the dark patch at the bottom that was some sort of stain. "Yeah."

Niamh lifted her eyebrows expectantly, but no more information came.

"How about a book? Bartending one-oh-one, heard of it?" she asked.

Sebastian slouched against the bar, hiding a grimace. She was coming out strong, and they'd only just gotten there. Usually, she went after a surly patron before working her way to the bartender.

"No." He waited.

"Grand. Shot of whiskey," she said. "Anything will do. Two more, for my superhero friends, and whatever the lady wants."

✧ ✧ ✧

ULRIC

AURORA AND JOHN leaned back a little as they reached them. That meant an invite to sit down.

"Hey," Jasper said as he took a seat next to John and Ulric plopped down next to Aurora.

"Hey," Aurora replied. "I just got done telling John about the battle at my Dad's."

"Yeah, you've probably missed a lot of what's gone down in the last couple years," Ulric told John, but he didn't keep up the conversation. He was tuned into Niamh's show at the other end of the bar. He told them what Niamh was doing and why.

"Smart," John murmured under his breath. "I wouldn't have thought of that."

"What kind of wine do you have?" they heard Nessa ask the bartender pleasantly. Her voice wasn't loud, but she was intentionally making it carry. She wanted the bar to notice.

"She's not what she seems," John said about Nessa. "She has a beautiful face and a gorgeous smile until she slips a knife into her enemy's ribs."

Jasper snorted. "She'd smile doing that, too. Then laugh after. She's cool, though. She's fun to have around. Very smart."

"Red or white," the bartender answered Nessa.

"Oh, good! I love when there are a lot of options." Nessa laughed. "White would be great, with ice cubes."

The bartender didn't move for a moment, staring her down and earning more wattage in her smile. His gaze slid to Edgar, who was strangely perched on the edge of his stool and leaning close to Sebastian, who was very obviously uncomfortable with the whole situation.

"He's the notorious mage?" John asked in confusion.

"Yeah," Aurora answered. "You see it when he's around other mages. It's a persona. You see his power and skill in battle. With us, he's just a big, magical nerd who gets pushed around by Niamh. A lot."

Ulric and Jasper laughed.

Once the bartender turned to get the drinks, Sebastian peered around Edgar to speak to Nessa. His words were lost to the murmuring of the Guardians, but his crinkled nose suggested he was questioning her choice.

Her voice rose above the din.

"He has two options of wine, and they are colors, not varietals," she replied. The Guardians quieted to hear. "We are at the top of a mountain, and they don't seem to trade with anyone but their own kind for some reason. The desire to be poor, maybe? Their trading partners are also very likely in high places that don't favor grape growing. The wine is probably shit. If you make it cold enough, you won't taste it as much. Hence the ice cubes."

"Jesus," Jasper said on a release of breath. "She understood the assignment."

She winked at Sebastian, who'd widened his eyes at her response. A few of the bigger Guardians stiffened. She did understand the assignment. She was helping Niamh create a problem and doing it with a smile.

"Jessie is going to be pissed if they actually start a fight, though," Aurora said.

"They won't," Ulric said with assurance. "Gargoyles like the buildup. We don't break and fight as easily as shifters. We like to get good and mad first. Niamh knows this. She's tested the limits on a great many gargoyles in O'Briens. She knows what she's doing."

"Hey, guys!" Fred walked in wearing a thick jacket and spikey green hair. She'd liked the humid heat in North Carolina. The crisp air of snowy mountains was not her jam. "Oh, cool capes!" She leaned against the bar. "I wish I'd known! I found a cape at a costume shop in Drex's city. I figured it would be a neat statement piece. I should've worn it. Next time!"

The bartender came back with an individual-sized bottle of white wine and a pint glass filled with ice. He was clearly trying to be obtuse on purpose.

"Fantastic." Nessa beamed. "Exactly what I was expecting in a place like this."

"Oh, man," Jasper said under his breath, shaking with silent laughter. "She's excellent. Look how uncomfortable Sebastian is." His laughter grew. "I wish I would've been there when Niamh took Sebastian to the shifter bar outside Kingsley's place."

The bartender slung up three empty shot glasses before pulling well whiskey from the alcohol trough below the bar. He poured the shots, spilling some on the bar as he did so, and dropped the bottle back where it belonged. He didn't bother distributing.

"And whatever the one at the end wants," Niamh finished.

"Hi! I'm Fred. What's your name?"

He didn't answer.

"Blank slate. I like it!" Fred replied, undaunted. "Do you have any fresh coffee?"

"No."

"No, huh? Hmm. You drive a hard bargain. What kind of bourbon do you have?"

John started to chuckle.

"The brown kind," the bartender answered, and a few of the eavesdropping Guardians snickered.

Fred looked at him in confusion, glanced at the wall of alcohol behind him, and surveyed the bar. "Is this some kind of practical joke or something? This is a real bar, right, not an integrated theater performance or something? I was a part of one of those in New York. It was pretty cool."

She wasn't joking, but because of her over-the-top nature, it came out like she was. Nessa spit out laughter and John laughed harder, clearly trying to be quiet about it. His face turned red.

The bartender tensed in anger.

"Get her the best bourbon you have," Niamh said, and even though she had to have been delighted with Fred's help, she didn't crack a smile.

The bartender pulled a shot glass over and reached down for the well alcohol again. He brought up the whiskey and poured it before pushing it toward Fred.

He moved away, stopping to refill a beer for one of the Guardians before bothering to help Ulric and Jasper, and Fred loudly whispered, "After meeting that guy, I don't feel like such a dick."

She clearly meant to keep it between them, but she didn't know how well supernaturals could hear. It reached all the way down to the end.

John's laughter boiled over. He covered his mouth, but his body shook with it. Guardians looked over, their eyebrows settling low. They knew their kind were getting made fun of.

"I assume those wings are real, if micro-sized?" the bartender asked as he reached Ulric.

"Like your dick, yeah," Ulric shot back. "A beer, in a bottle. Looks like you won't bother doing your job, so whatever kind you feel like grabbing."

"Same," Jasper said. "And maybe a smile to go with it."

The bartender leaned a hand heavily on the bar. "You guys holding a grudge after we took your female to task, huh?" He smirked. "Gimerel is falling apart, everyone knows that. We got a new leader, but we got the same Guardians. If I were you, I wouldn't rile them up. I'd let them take it easy on you."

"Says the guy who's never been a Guardian," Jasper responded.

"To the guy who's too small to be in any cairn but a female-driven start-up." The bartender smirked and moved on to get the beers.

"Ah," John said softly, his humor having dried up with the exchange. "I see. She's the underdog, then, in the gargoyle community?"

"Very much so," Aurora said.

"She's the only one of her kind. People haven't seen a female gargoyle in generations," Ulric said. "They were beginning to think female gargoyles were a myth."

"And she was a Jane who got her magic in a strange way." John nodded as the bartender put the beer down in front of them and walked away. It was anyone's guess who's tab it was going on. "She's no better off here than Austin is with the shifters. Maybe worse, right?"

Ulric took a swig of the watery beer. "And now you see the struggle."

A large Guardian headed toward Niamh's group at the bar.

"Here we go," Jasper murmured.

John tensed and started to stand.

"Leave it," Aurora said, putting out a hand. "That crew is more than capable. This is part of the plan. Let it play out."

John glanced at her, something unreadable in his eyes.

Aurora could clearly discern his body language in her peripheral vision. "You're not an alpha anymore, remember?" she said, not looking away from the Guardian strutting down to the others. "You're not even in the pack. You're a rogue. Taking a command will do you good."

"Miss Alpha-in-Training-Wheels, indeed," John

murmured, a little smirk playing across his lips. "My sisters would like you."

"What's with the capes?" the big guy asked Sebastian. Ulric could only see his back, his wings down to his knees. The shoulders said he was a strong flier, but without seeing the gargoyle form, Ulric couldn't tell anything else.

Sebastian hesitated, glancing at Niamh for help. The space in conversation allowed Edgar to answer.

"We are paying homage to the mighty gargoyle." Edgar put his spindly fingers on the bar. "I once created a shrine to honor your god."

"What is your god?" John asked quietly.

"One Edgar made up randomly and insists is real," Ulric replied.

"If I had a phone," Edgar said, "I would've taken a picture and could now show it to you. I don't have one, though. A phone, I mean. I've created a few shrines, many out of dead mage bodies, and it is assumed I am something of a liability." He chuckled silently. "I beg to differ. Art is art."

Nessa nodded sagely and looked at the gargoyle for a response.

"What?" the gargoyle said.

Granted, yes, that was a lot to unpack.

Sebastian realized he was getting no help from

Niamh and said in a rush, "We're experimenting with fashion. They look great on you, so we thought maybe we'd try them out?"

"They look great on us?" the gargoyle growled. His wings fluttered. "Are you trying to say our wings look like frumpy capes?"

"Well…" Fred blinked at him. "They do, right? Look." She pointed between his wings and the capes. "I mean, your wings aren't lopsided—most of you—but they *do* look like capes. That's what I thought they were when I first saw gargoyles." She tilted her head at them. "Haven't you spoken to non-gargoyles before? I'm sure everyone agrees—" She flinched and flung up her hands when he hit her with a wave of power. "Sorry, bro. I didn't know wings and their resemblance to capes was a sore subject. Our gargoyles aren't touchy about it. I apologize."

Ulric ran his hand down his face. "Niamh hadn't accounted for Fred in all this."

"Are you kidding?" Jasper wore a crooked smile. "She's *perfect* for this. *We* know she's utterly genuine and clueless, but they don't. They think she's talking crap on purpose."

"This is going to break out in a fight," John murmured with a warning in his tone.

"Here, relax." Niamh waved it away. Everyone in

the bar was now listening. "She's a Jane. What sort of Guardian gets riled up by a Jane? Do ye have any training at all in this cairn?"

More of the Guardians stiffened. Niamh glanced down at her lap. Her arm moved a fraction before she looked back up.

"She's texting," Aurora said.

"No wonder ye got a new leader, like," Niamh went on as more Guardians stepped away from the bar and headed for them. "The old one clearly didn't know what to do with ya if yer gettin' riled up like this."

"And what are *you* exactly?" the big Guardian asked.

"Mindin' me own business, that's what," she replied. "Yer ruinin' the taste of me cheap whiskey. Now that's a feat, that is. Bugger off down the bar, would ya?"

The other Guardians joined the first as a large shape ducked through the doorway. Phil walked in with a hardhat, a construction worker vest, and a kilt, his garb for blending into Dicks and Janes when he went to the bar. Ulric had no idea why he was wearing it now. He surveyed the scene before his hair puffed up and his gums pulled back from his teeth in a snarl.

He rushed toward the Guardians. Startled, John pushed to standing, the stool he was sitting on toppling over. Aurora reached out, fast as lightning to grab John and keep him put while Phil grabbed the large gargoyle at the other end and lifted him into the air.

"I am here to keep the peace," Phil growled in the gargoyle's face. "Mind your manners."

Phil turned, almost lazily, and tossed the large Guardian through the open door. The Guardian cursed as he flew through the air and then grunted when he landed outside. Tires squealed as a car veered to miss the tumbling gargoyle.

"Oops!" Ulric's mom walked in a moment later with her hair done in a tight curl, her nails painted pink to match her cloth pantsuit, and a smile on her face.

Ulric groaned.

"Hello, everyone!" she said. "Hello! I was just on the way to chat with your amazing new leader. Isn't he something?"

She took Phil's arm and led him closer to the bar.

"No, dear." She patted Edgar's shoulder. "No, no. You don't belong there. Everyone will lose their desire to drink. You're much better off being a wallflower, don't you agree?"

Edgar stood dutifully. "Yes, I've always thought so."

"Yes, there you go." She bustled him out of the way. "Now, here we are. That's lovely. There now." She helped Phil sit down. Sebastian leaned away from the basajaun.

"What are ye doing?" Niamh shoved Sebastian back. "Ye're after climbing into me lap."

"First Edgar and now Phil." Sebastian swallowed. "My bowels feel a little loose."

"Well, don't shite yerself right there," Niamh hollered. It was impossible to tell if she was serious or if she was putting on a show to better diffuse the situation. Probably the latter. "What, do ye need someone to wipe yer arse for ya? Feck off to the bathroom."

"Yes, that's a good idea." Patty practically yanked Sebastian to standing. "Go find the restroom. It's just there at the back. Hello, boys!" She shoved Sebastian out of the way and walked up to the Guardians. The one Phil had tossed out the door had not returned, presumably having decided it unwise to go up against a basajaun. "I don't think I got all your names." She didn't now, either, rushing on in a tumble of words. "Evan is so amazing, isn't he? He has all your interests in the forefront of his mind. That's what you really need after the last one, isn't it?" She ushered them back down to their drinks. "He's planning new play structures for the kids, raids for the Guardians—he's really got his finger on the pulse of the community."

Another large shape loomed in the doorway, and Tristan walked in with a swagger no one could match. His eyes glowed and his shoulders were rolled forward, as though he was ready for a brawl. His gaze scanned the bar, taking in the two groups, one in the back, and Niamh's crew at the front. Lastly, his gaze found Edgar, who had slipped behind a fake plant in a corner.

"Well, anyway, I better not dawdle." Patty tapped the arm of one of the Guardians. "I don't want to keep Evan waiting. Oh, Tristan, hello." She stepped away from the others and beamed at him. "Great to see you again! It feels like *ages*. Don't you worry, the gargoyles back home are training just as hard as ever. There were a few territory breaches from aggressive shifters, but they were handled, no problem. I need to give all the details to the alphas. Anyway, I must run."

She paused and leaned a little closer to him, lowering her voice. Given that no one else was speaking, having been shocked mute, every word could be heard.

"All any of the garhettees can talk about is you coming to stay. Word got out that you grabbed a garhette at the Gimerel raid—they think it was one of us and not Nessa. That was the only person you've ever snapped up, right? Well, now the rumor is circulating that you are finally looking to settle down. The unattainable bachelor is finally within reach. I thought I would warn you. You know how garhettes can get. Push-y." She winked before waving down to Ulric and the others. "Chat soon! Olly, I'll stop by later."

Tristan's hard gaze hit the Guardians, and they wilted slightly, quietly retaking their places at the bar. Phil had probably scared them, Patty had distracted them, and Tristan had ended the moment.

"What just happened?" John said on a release of breath, taking his seat again. He seemed a little shaky. Adrenaline probably.

Aurora grinned. "Jessie's crew happened. Organized chaos. I told you how well they work together, even when they don't really want to, like Sebastian in this instance."

A few women entered the bar, the only ones beside Ulric's crew, their gazes immediately finding Tristan. One of them turned red as they found a table. Leaning their heads together, they giggled. They were clearly here for him, just like Ulric's mom had said.

Sebastian stopped to speak, his face pale. "Did it work?" he whispered, the cape still hanging down his back. The Guardians kept glancing over at it, pissed but trying not to show it in front of Tristan. Clearly, they were wary of him. "Did we rile them up like she planned?"

"Oh, yeah." Jasper nodded adamantly. "The Guardian that got tossed out on his ass is going to be embarrassed he didn't fight back. He'll funnel that into rage. The others will feel similarly since they are letting

Tristan cow them. Tonight, when they are pounding beers and licking their wounds, they'll forget how much power Tristan and Phil have, and everything will start to boil. They'll want a battle."

"They definitely will." Ulric grinned. "Then you have those capes, and Fred comparing them to wings, which is a slap in the face for their egos. Nessa's rudeness—they're going to tell all the other Guardians. They're going to be itching to teach us a lesson for throwing our weight around in *their* cairn. It sounds like they think we beat Gimerel because of Gimerel's disorganization, not because we are that good."

"And in the end, it was all succinctly shut down without a fight." John shook his head. "You were right, Training Wheels. I didn't believe it, but you were right."

"Yeah." Sebastian let out a gush of air. "I think I'm going to sneak out the back."

"Actually…" Jasper grimaced. "I wouldn't go anywhere alone, if I were you. The cape, you know. You might get jumped."

CHAPTER 29
TRISTAN

THE TENSIONS IN the bar reduced to a simmer as Tristan ordered a cognac. He was given cheap whiskey in a shot glass.

"What is this?" he demanded of the bartender.

The bartender lifted his eyebrows indifferently in response.

Shadows swirled and rolled from Tristan's body in anger. He leaned aggressively over the bar.

"What. Is. This?" he enunciated.

The bartenders eyes widened minutely. Fear dulled his disdain. "Your order," he had the gall to say.

Tristan arched one eyebrow slowly, waiting. More shadows pooled out, leaking his nightmare magic. They polluted the air around the bartender, instilling fear. Pumping him with uncertainty the longer he resisted Tristan's expectant answer.

"Sorry, sir," the bartender said, trembling as he spun

for the bottles of alcohol on the shelf behind him. "Sorry. I meant no offense."

He grabbed the cognac with shaking hands and poured it into a snifter. He set it down in front of Tristan before backing away. "On the house. My apologies for the miscommunication. My fault."

Tristan kept his eyes on the man as he downed the contents of the glass with a lazy flip of his wrist. Fire spread through his middle. Straightening, he ran his gaze over the Guardians to his right, who suddenly became very interested in their drinks. He let his magic affect them for a beat, then turned away.

A woman glided up to him, making him pull up short. She flashed him a sultry smile with bright red lips. Long black lashes fluttered.

"Hi," she said, extending a dainty hand with long blue nails. "I'm Tammy."

Another woman joined her, posing in an enticing way, her bust mostly exposed. "I'm Rita."

Even as he stood there, two more women entered the bar.

He wasn't in the mood for this. He had important business in this cairn with things to accomplish. He couldn't do that with constant feminine roadblocks. Not to mention he wasn't interested in any of them.

"Charmed," he said, stepping gracefully around them.

He glanced at Natasha. She was sitting next to Phil, dressed in a hoodie and jeans and leaning over the bar chatting with Niamh. She seemed unconcerned about the women pursuing him, not at all possessive or territorial despite their growing interactions. Usually, that would be a good thing, something he looked for in a woman, but right now, he wanted the opposite from her.

"Hey," he said in a low tone, stopping by her side.

She turned to look up at him. The moment their eyes met, her pupils blew wide open, and her mouth parted. Energy swirled around him, mixing and merging with his nightmare shadows. He'd forgotten to pull it all back in, and now he was glad for it. She clearly liked it when he was at his most dangerous. She swayed toward him as though she couldn't help it. As though his darkness sucked her in.

"Will you do me a favor while we're in this cairn?" he murmured, looking at those plump lips. Even without makeup—*especially* without makeup—she was stunning, easily the most beautiful woman he'd ever seen. Always had been, since the very moment he'd set eyes on her.

"Sure," she said at once.

"Pretend to be my mate and scare away your competition."

He barely waited for her hesitant nod before he grabbed her ponytail and yanked her head back. Wrapping his hand around her throat, he bent to capture her lips and the world dropped away. His lips moved against hers, his tongue delving, her sweet smell stealing all his focus.

She clutched him like a lifejacket in stormy waters. He slowed, savoring the contact, delighting in her willingness to let him completely dominate. His tongue slid across her bottom lip before he sucked that lip between his own. She groaned softly, running her hands up his chest now and hooking them around his neck.

He thought about sliding her off the stool and backing her against the wall, craving more contact, craving *more*, but backed away instead. He had things to do. He'd only stopped by to help Niamh diffuse the situation.

"Stay with Niamh and the others," he murmured against her lips, still holding her hair and throat. She hadn't opened her eyes. "I'll come and get you after the dinner with the cairn leader and walk you home."

"Okay," she whispered.

And then he was gone, striding away from her and the bar before she could get her bearings. He felt the eyes of the women following him as he left. He glanced back at Natasha, disheveled and breathing heavily. She hadn't seduced him, *he'd* chosen *her*, and everyone in the bar knew it. He'd been in control. There would be no denying his affections and desires. He had a woman, and she'd captured his whole focus.

He'd kissed her out of necessity, but he had to admit it was a new and exciting facet of their game. With each new situation they spun closer together. Eventually, she would be unable to deny that she felt what he did. That she wanted more than physical intimacy.

Eventually, she would beg, and he would take it to the next level.

$\diamond \quad \diamond \quad \diamond$

JESSIE

"I CAN'T DECIDE what style to go for." I looked between a red satin dress with a plunging neckline and a navy power suit with a cream silk blouse to go underneath. "Where's Tristan?" I was addressing Mr. Tom, currently in the en suite bathroom organizing my makeup. "Or better yet, where's Patty?"

"Here!" Patty walked in with a smile, her lipstick matching the color of her pink clothes and nails. "Jessie! It's so good to see you again!" She stopped in front of me and gave me air kisses. "The red, definitely! Oh, how pretty. I just love it! Evan is going to be wearing a suit and a tie. Tristan is wearing something similar, as is Unfixable Sue."

I paused in picking up the dress. "Unfixable Sue?"

Patty laughed. "Sue went to check on the bar delegation. They'd switched to another one a few streets over and Sue wanted to make sure they weren't causing any problems. I was already on the job, and don't you worry, Jessie. They were conducting themselves like any gargoyles would. Not a problem. Except a little animosity, of course, but that's usual with Guardians. They always clash and then they take it out in the sky."

Patty wrestled the clothes off me so she could slip the dress over my head.

"Oh, Jessie, *yes*! That is perfect." Patty ushered me to the standing mirror. "Mr. Tom, we will be needing some very fancy jewelry for this. I hope you brought some."

"Of course I brought some, what do you take me for?" Mr. Tom sniffed.

"Well, Niamh and Sue did the thing they always do—one picks on the other and the other sends warning glances and visual threats. You know how it is. Niamh called him Unfixable Sue, and I thought that was hilarious. *Unfixable Sue!* You know, because he was Broken Sue, and he's finally finding his footing again, bless his heart. The poor dear has had a hard history.

But the *look* he gave her… Well, it was priceless. It'll probably stick, I'm warning you."

Mr. Tom brought over two jewelry boxes. Patty hesitated in taking them.

"Why do you carry them?" she asked.

"I *hide* them so that insufferable old woman won't steal them from the miss's bags or mine and wear them around town. She has no respect for the house jewels. She uses them to lure criminals, and thinks it is perfectly fine and legal to then kill those criminals. Then *I'm* left to do damage control so she won't be killed by the town alpha or go to Dick jail, and then I have to fetch the jewels from wherever she may have left them. It is a huge hassle."

"Ah. Yes, I see." And it seemed like she really did.

She opened each box, gushed, and chose a ruby and diamond necklace with a dripping spiderweb sort of design that was probably worth a fortune and had been in Ivy House for a great many years. It was absolutely gorgeous. I sincerely hoped it wouldn't lure those criminals Niamh was so fond of, because I'd be afraid of breaking it by accident while warding off an attack.

"How about a simple diamond stud for earrings?" Patty stepped back to survey me. "Big ones, though. Do you have big ones?"

Mr. Tom's annoyed look said that was a silly question.

"And a sparkly mage watch, I think." Patty patted her chin, assessing me. "We need Sebastian in his mage attire." She nodded in decision. "I'm going to ask Tristan if that could be arranged. We have Unfixable Sue and Austin as the shifter component, Phil threw a prominent Guardian out of a bar earlier, so they know what the basajaunak are about—"

"He did *what*?"

"We need the mage component." She snapped her fingers. "Yes! He needs to see mage culture and see that Gerard is comfortable with that culture. It'll further show that he doesn't have his footing in this new world."

She spun and headed for the door. Patty and Tristan were dancing around gargoyles politics.

I took a deep breath and headed for the bathroom and some makeup.

I hadn't been at it long when there was a soft knock at the bedroom door.

"In here," I called, finishing a smokey eye.

Sebastian filled the bathroom doorway. His hair was standing up all over, like he'd been repeatedly running his hands through it, his clothes were wrinkled and an ill-fitting, crooked cape hung off his right shoulder.

I slowly pulled the brush away from my eye. "What's with the cape?"

He sagged against the doorframe. "You would not believe how many times I have heard that exact phrase. It was Niamh's idea. The gargoyles are not amused. I'm pretty sure they're headed home to find brass knuckles and take the cape by force while they pound me. It doesn't help that Edgar is now showing everyone his cape and smiling as he says, 'Twinning!'"

I opened my mouth and closed it again, not sure what to say.

He waved. "It doesn't matter. Niamh says it'll be fine. Time will tell. Anyway, Patty said I was to join you for dinner tonight. I wanted to check to make sure that was correct? If it is, please let me take off this cape."

I dissolved into giggles. "Yes, lose the cape. And yes, I guess you should come to dinner. Wear Elliot Graves stuff with a very fancy watch. Also, does Nessa have a watch I can borrow? Mr. Tom only packed that Ivy House pocket watch you guys found in a drawer or whatever."

He hesitated, scanning my dress. "You look beautiful, by the way, and no, you don't need Nessa's. That pocket watch is perfect. I'll see if Mr. Tom has a sewing kit, and I'll make it work."

"No, Sebastian." I clucked my tongue in frustration. "I'm not going to do this weird mage pocket-watch-Cinderella thing you chose—"

He held up a finger. "Niamh said I needed to wear a cape to help you, and so I wore the cape because she knows about gargoyles, and I do not. We each know our jobs, and we need to trust each other. I know watches. I know which ones will work best when. We can talk about your persona in the mage world, but tonight, you wear that pocket watch."

I was ready to argue, remembering all the internal arguments I'd had about that mage dinner and him choosing what he *thought* was right for me. I'd looked ridiculous, and I wanted to choose what I wore instead.

But as I looked at him, I saw the Elliot Graves confidence shimmering in his eyes, along with his assurance that he knew what was best. I felt in my gut that he was right. We needed to trust each other. There were so many moving parts at this point and each one was important. We couldn't all be an expert on everything. We had to let everyone handle what they were best at.

"Okay." I deflated. "Just…please don't make me look as ridiculous as you do in that cape."

"Salt, meet wound," he mumbled, and I laughed again. "Give me the dress, please. Mr. Tom has the watch?"

"Yes." I slipped into a robe and let him take the dress away.

AFTER I'D FINISHED my makeup and hair, I found Sebastian in his full Elliot Graves garb waiting for me on Austin's and my bed.

"I swear," Mr. Tom said as he bustled around the room, tiding things that didn't need to be tidied. "The shambles that these gargoyles call guest rooms would make a lesser butler faint. Hardly anyone can fit in that excuse for a living room out there, and there isn't even a kitchenette! How do they except me to prepare snacks and breakfast, with a camping stove? They try to squeeze our betas into the only solitary rooms they provide besides this one suite, force everyone else to share, and *somehow* question our status and profitability?" He tsked as he straightened up and faced me, his wings rustling angrily. "It's absurd, all of this. You are the Ivy House heir! *They* should be begging to join *you*, not the other way around. *Begging!*" He made a disgruntled sound and went back to it. "Preposterous."

"*He's not wrong,*" Ivy House told me. "*These gargoyles have things backwards, and you need to show them.*"

I needed to do a lot of things.

Sebastian stood with a little grin and held out the dress. "It isn't perfect, but it should work."

He'd sewn a little black loop on the red sash at the waist. The watch would then tuck into the sash, secured with black material to make up a pocket. The chain would then dangle down.

Mr. Tom stopped to survey Sebastian's handiwork, his lips thinning. "It'll match the guest rooms, at least."

"I promise." Sebastian held the dress out to me.

How I presented myself to Evan was important. He'd be going out on a limb with someone who had no status and trusting that I boosted prosperity and convocation stability. Only recently, he'd taken over one of the largest cairns, and he was contemplating allying with a start-up, and an odd start-up at that.

Wearing an old pocket watch sewn into an evening gown…really didn't hit the right note, here.

Sebastian's eyes were pleading. He could see my hesitation.

"I promise," he whispered.

Trust. In the end, that's all we really had.

I nodded and took the dress. He let out a breath and withdrew to give me a moment to dress.

Mr. Tom didn't say a word as I slipped out of the robe and stepped into the luxurious material. He zipped me up in the back and went back to his task.

"What do you think would sway Evan our way?" I asked him, checking myself over in the mirror.

"You." He handed me a shawl. "In the end, miss, it is always you who bring people into the fold. You never do it the same way twice, and you are never calculating. You are just unequivocally *you*, and people realize there is nowhere safer or better than to be by your side."

I smiled at him, my eyes glistening with unshed tears.

He tsked. "There is no reason to get so emotional. It'll ruin your makeup, and then all that undeserving cairn leader will see is an old watch haphazardly sewn into—and ruining—a new dress. Let's keep the distraction to your face, shall we?"

"What's wrong with my face?" I asked, glancing in the mirror as I trailed after him.

"It's pretty. Unlike that horrendous watch. Here we go."

Two couches faced each other across a small coffee table. Austin and Sue sat on one, with Tristan in the other. The men held snifters of something or other. They wore tailored suits, dress shirts, and ties, each as dapper as the next. I would've totally fit in if not for the freaking watch.

Sebastian waited by the door, hunched. Despite the clothes, he hadn't yet donned his other persona. There was so much alpha power in this room, not to mention menacing muscle, it had probably squeezed out all his desire to be noticed.

Austin's eyes softened as he beheld me. "You look

gorgeous." He noticed the watch but didn't comment. Neither did the others. I could only assume that was because Sebastian or Mr. Tom had already filled them in.

He finished his drink and stood as I approached. His lips lightly touched mine, and then he paused for me to wipe away the lipstick left behind.

Tristan and Sue stood as well, finishing their drinks and readying to go.

"If their hired help is as shoddy as these horrible guest rooms," Mr. Tom said, "send for me. I would be happy to take over and show this cairn what is expected of someone with my prestigious job title."

"Thank you, Mr. Tom. I will," I lied. There was no way in hell. He'd probably come in a disguise or throw away all the food he didn't approve of, or some other embarrassing thing.

"He's laying it on a little thick," Sue said after we'd left the room and now walked down the hall.

"Actually, his attitude is perfect," Tristan replied. "He's responding to what we're all seeing. This cairn can't hold a candle to any part of our emerging convocation. Its territory is much smaller. Its wealth is insignificant. Its productions have no real outlet to make the sort of money Alpha Steele is thinking, and its people don't have even a fraction of the power. We are vastly superior in every way. The *only* thing holding us back is your lack of history—yours personally and the convocation's. That and the fact that Alpha Steele often presents as the alpha when they assume *you* should be the leader of the gargoyles."

"So then…all the things that grant the highest status." I took a deep breath as we emerged into the frosty evening air. My teeth chattered before I wrapped magic around myself to keep out the chill.

"The things that grant the highest status in gargoyle culture at present, yes," Tristan said. "But those things aren't the most important to gargoyles. They're just what gargoyles have fallen back to in times of extreme boredom resulting from peace. And he is only the most dominant when you can't be troubled to take control. Which, yes, is often. All they need to see is you handling trouble in the air."

Frustration started to rise. "Right but…we're not here to raid. How are they going to see that?"

"I've got it handled," Sebastian said from behind the others. "Trust me, that's all sorted, as Niamh would say. Ten times over."

I twisted around to look at him, but Tristan and Sue were in the way.

"How—" I cut off as I spied the first Guardian against the wall. Something told me this wasn't the conversation to have when others might overhear.

Austin threaded his fingers through mine as we walked along the sidewalk. We could've driven, but it wasn't far. Also, Tristan wanted us to be seen by more than just the cairn leader, although he hadn't said why. Thankfully, the darkness masked the presence of the pocket watch.

Evan's residence loomed in front of us.

"I wonder how much of the interior he inherited," I mused. "Did he redecorate like we're doing, or was that all Withor's doing?"

"He hasn't been here long enough to redecorate to that magnitude," Austin replied. "All the interior matches. He would've had to do the entire downstairs, and it's only been a couple months. You've seen from Ivy House what sort of undertaking all that is."

"So then..." I frowned at the beautiful architecture. "He's not that different from me, just like Tristan said. Why *does* he get status just for moving in?"

"It's for essentially taking over, either by force or by family," Tristan replied as we drew near. "The gargoyles assume someone had the power to take it over. For family, they have the training. The status passes that way."

"Ah. I didn't take anything over, and I don't have the family or training." I shrugged. "That makes sense."

"That's…not…" Tristan seemed at a loss for words.

But I did make it so Evan could take this cairn over. My maneuvering gave him the *in*.

We stopped in front of the door. It swung open before we could ring or knock. A man dressed in a white suit with a black tie and stuffy air about him greeted us. He looked about half Mr. Tom's age but just as pompous.

"Please, come through, Miss Ironheart, Mr. Steele." He stepped out of the way and gestured to the interior of the house.

Connections suddenly formed in my mind as I thought about the events leading up to this moment: how Evan had gotten here, and ultimately, my role in all this. I'd taken a backseat to so much recently—allowing Austin to lead because it was shifter politics and letting Tristan and Patty pave the way since they knew the details of cairn life—that I hadn't stepped up when I really needed to. But now, strangely helped by Sebastian's presence, suddenly I felt so much more in charge. Everything seemed so crystal clear.

"Cool," I said to no one in particular. I brushed my fingers over the Ivy House pocket watch, a relic out of time, like my incredible magic. Like the house I was mistress of, guarding its people.

I was a Guardian, as well. I was a cairn leader.

But I was also so much more.

It was time I remembered that. Evan was one of my people. They all were. That was the blessing and curse of a female gargoyle, so rare. We brought everyone together. We unified our army, through better or worse.

Evan could choose to ignore me, to cast me out, but I knew his people would want to join our convocation's purpose. They craved what Austin and I had to offer. The moment I extended a connection—and some of them already had it from when they visited us—was the moment they were mine. Not his, *mine*.

Gargoyle leaders could play hardball all they wanted, but if they didn't have the loyalty of their people, they had nothing. Just like in O'Briens, all I had to do was prove that status quo. In the end, as the shifters were learning with Austin, it came down to who could lead the best. And that was me. It was Austin. It was, without a doubt, the combined might of our team.

"I'm good." I nodded. My fingers brushed that watch again, and I remembered where I'd come from, why I'd chosen magic, and how I'd gotten here. "I got this."

"Exactly." Sebastian walked up to stand beside me, his shoulders back, his head high, ignoring the alphas entirely. He gave me a cocky grin. "We are enough in our own right, but sometimes we need to gloss things up to show everyone else what we are really capable of."

His gaze swept down my body, and I had no idea how I knew it, but he was adjusting the perception of my mage persona. His cunning gaze said it all. He'd adjusted my image based on what he was seeing now, based on me. I was finally connecting with who I was and what I'd become.

"Ready?" he asked me, and I knew he was asking himself, as well. We'd land this cairn and the rest would follow. Maybe not tonight, but eventually. This was trivial. The real battle was just beginning, and that was with the mages. Momar had recently proven he had his eye on us. Time to focus.

"Ready," I replied, thinking now of what we needed to combat Momar. Of how we could stack the odds—not in our favor—but at least somewhat more evenly.

A blast of magic rocketed out of me, shaking the air and making everyone flinch. It had been a while since that had happened. Austin knew exactly what it was.

"How bad?" he asked, probably wondering if I'd summoned another phoenix, or maybe something more terrible.

Whatever it was, he'd confront it. He'd put himself in front of me and wrestle the creature into submission. He wasn't the best because of Ivy House, his power or experience. He was the best because he *had* to be to protect me. He'd do it because I asked. Because I needed it. All of this, everything he did, was because of me.

I loved him so much it hurt.

But this wasn't his fight.

"Not bad," I said, knowing the sort of summons I'd sent. "For you, anyway."

I connected gazes with Sebastian—no, I connected gazes with Elliot Graves.

He knew without having to be asked. This was a summons he and I would handle. Mages, some nasty, some nice, all powerful. It was time to call in the next wave. It was time to finally combat the thing that was currently plaguing the magical world, and to do that, we had to put ourselves on the line.

"Come on." Elliot Graves gave me a playboy smile as he looped his arm through mine. His eyes were all Sebastian, though. Cunning, intelligent…loving and sentimental. "Let's have a wonderful dinner and help this leader realize that he didn't earn his status on his own, shall we? *Your* team cut the legs out from under Withor, and you were just about to put the nail in the coffin when Evan showed up. I think it's about time you stopped playing nice, don't you?"

A persona. Sometimes, to get the job done, you had to strap on your armor. And if you didn't have that, you had to strap on the confidence of a mediocre man looking for a raise in a job he didn't understand.

CHAPTER 30
TRISTAN

I T HADN'T BEEN a persona at all.

Tristan stopped at a darkened corner in the city and put his hand against the rough wall. He naturally blended into stone, like any gargoyle, but now his nightmare magic, as everyone thought of it, wrapped shadows around him. Even gargoyles would be hard pressed to notice him.

He smiled and thought about laughing.

Sebastian had told Jessie to put on a persona, like Elliot Graves. But that wasn't Jessie's style. She didn't have personas. What he'd given her was a shock of confidence. Was a reminder of her purpose.

More, though, he'd helped her connect the dots that Tristan himself should've put together. Ultimately, she'd gotten Evan this post. She deserved more status than him, because all he'd really done was show up.

She hadn't said that. She didn't even care about the

semantics. She had wanted him to understand why she'd stepped in at all. To realize that *she* had handled, in good faith, what other gargoyles should've done long before then. *She'd* paved the way, not because of the desire for the cairn or money or prestige, but to do what was right.

She hadn't gotten any recognition from the gargoyle community because she didn't boast about what she'd done, nor would she. It was clear she didn't care about the status issue or about having status at all. She'd do it again, and she'd do it the same way. It wasn't about her; it was about the people who needed her. This time, it had been that woman. Next time, maybe someone else. Maybe Evan.

Tristan had watched Evan's face—his entire body—gradually shift as that concept sank in. As he realized she was above him on the moral high ground, and she wouldn't, not ever, let her cairn suffer. She would give everything she had, without complaint, to ensure the happiness of her people.

Sebastian, of all people, pointed out that she'd gone out of her way for a total stranger. It had helped Evan, sure, but the main goal had been to help a faceless woman who never could've given Jessie a leg up. He'd solidified that Jessie had done it out of duty to her people. *Her* people—the gargoyles. And he'd said it in such an arrogant, flippant, dismissive way that it didn't seem like he was advocating for her; rather, that he pitied her soft nature and gargoyles in general.

It had worked like an absolute charm. Patty was a genius for including that weird mage, and that mage was a genius in a social setting. In his persona, at any rate—he really shouldn't be taken into public any other time.

Still suppressing his laughter, Tristan walked on. He'd been let free for the night. He had to pick up his mate, as promised.

Shivers worked through his body as he wound his way along the dark streets. Mate. Forever—a concept that had always terrified him.

Not anymore.

His homes had always been temporary. Always. It was safer that way. For him. His brand of nightmare didn't usually have a happy ending. He'd evaded death ten times over and expected it to catch up with him eventually.

Except…that's not how Jessie's team worked. It wasn't one person against many. It was one army against the world, and that army protected their own. Even Brochan/Sue had stopped caring where Tristan had come from. It was enough that Tristan wanted to do right by them, and that he was learning to trust them to have his back. Learning to trust at all, maybe.

The past didn't matter, not for any of them. Not even for the new shifter who clung to Aurora like driftwood out at sea and looked at all of them like strangely colorful and possibly poisonous bugs. What mattered was trusting each other. Was supporting each other. Was believing in each other.

He might never have a mate. Natasha could get tired of their game at any moment. She could have anyone in the world she wanted, and she might rightly decide he wasn't good enough. But he did have a forever, and it was with Jessie and Austin's team.

Laughter announced the bar before he'd turned the corner. Light spilled onto the street. Clouds covered the night sky, and a chill arrested the air. A couple cars parked along the main drag, but as with most cairns Tristan had been in, most of these gargoyles would fly home or walk. The ladies would get flown or they'd take the free taxi provided by the city. The taxi never had much to do.

He hadn't changed his clothes, wanting to get to Natasha as quickly as possible. He straightened his tie and his shoulders as he neared the glow of the open door. All the other businesses in the area were closed, shop faces as dark as the doorways.

The two people outside noticed him and paused in

their conversation, sucking on the end of a cigarette to pass the moment. He met their eyes and catalogued the hostility there. Niamh had done a good day's work. Today Jessie had unequivocally won over a cairn leader, and tomorrow she'd win over the whole cairn.

He peeled back his magic and ensured he postured like an alpha shifter, straight and broad and menacing. Shifters were great for their body mechanics. No words needed.

The gargoyles tensed and lowered their gazes. They didn't want his brand of trouble.

Pity.

Music blared from inside the establishment. Light covered all the surfaces. Three bartenders hustled behind the bar, slinging drinks and chatting up patrons. Bodies writhed on the dance floor, moved and jostled around tables, and pushed against the bar.

A small bubble opened around Tristan as he entered the space. Men frowned and tried to stand their ground but ultimately shrunk to the sides. Women preened and smiled or simply got out of the way. He shoved through, wondering if any of them would be brave enough to challenge him.

Ah, but these weren't shifters, and challenging wasn't the gargoyle way. Shoving through was a tough guy act and a way for women and men to rub up against each other.

He ignored them all, including the sickly feeling of strangers trailing their fingers against his wings. That was an intimate feeling, not meant for a situation like this. He only wanted one woman with that sort of access.

His crew sat in the corner, Niamh and Phil at the bar, and the rest of them at the tables behind them. John stood at the mouth of the little alcove where everyone hung out, a hostile expression on his face and his hand out in front of him. As Tristan neared, he saw Natasha sway and hit John's outstretched arm. His arm flexed, keeping her there until she swayed away. He didn't lower his hand. Apparently, he was her bumper.

Tristan nodded at him. "How goes it?"

John lowered his hand and stepped back, nonverbally letting Tristan take over the post.

Tristan furrowed his brow.

"You're doing the fake mating thing to ward away women, right?" John asked, as stoic as Austin would be in this setting. He did allow a little of his confusion to show in his expression, though. Or was it questioning? Either way, it wasn't Sue's or Aurora's level of blank.

Tristan apparently answered without realizing it.

John nodded. "She's had a lot of women interested in her. We've—well, Phil—has stopped the fights, and repeatedly disarmed Nessa, but the garhettes?" He read the affirmative again and nodded. "They've been a nuisance. You've made Nessa a target."

Tristan stepped closer as Natasha swayed again. He reached out to catch her, but Jasper grabbed her from the other side. The two of them nearly fell into the wall behind him.

"Garhettes almost never have weapons," Tristan said, grinning as Natasha threw her head back and laughed at something Jasper said. She was so carefree in her amusement. He loved it. "They don't train to fight. Or didn't, before Jessie. Natasha would kill them before they knew the danger."

"Yes. And despite Phil taking away a dozen weapons so far tonight, Nat…" John paused. "Nessa, right?"

"For you, yes."

John nodded as though that made perfect sense. And to a shifter, it did. Claims with them were sacrosanct.

"Nessa somehow keeps finding or stealing or…" He shrugged. "She seems unarmed until she suddenly has a weapon. Niamh is plying her with drinks." His disapproval was plain. "Nessa isn't safe for these garhettes. And while the garhettes are challenging and deserve the outcome, I've been repeatedly told that Nessa should not, in fact, kill them. For some reason."

Tristan grinned at the shifter, and then outright laughed.

"You're in for a real rough ride, alpha." He slipped by the man and grabbed a seat from the bar, pulling it back to sit next to John. "I don't know your story—"

John grabbed the last remaining empty bar chair. A gargoyle saw it moving and turned, ready to fight about it. John stared the gargoyle down.

Though half his age, bulkier, and taller, the gargoyle barely blinked before spinning and finding something else to occupy his focus. He did not want to mess with the crazy-eyed shifter.

That made two of them. Tristan loved to rile up shifters, and enjoyed getting challenged, though it so rarely happened, but John was one man he would mind his manners with. This shifter might just ring his bell. It was a humbling reality.

"I don't know your story," Tristan repeated when John had sat down. "I honestly don't really care. But I know you were trained as an alpha, and I am learning how very buttoned up those are. You are currently stepping into a reality where there are no rules. Not on Jessie's side of things. With her, you take things as they come, and you adapt. Trust me when I tell you that. On my very first detail as a beta, I was blindsided by a vampire and saved by Austin Steele. I repeatedly froze on the job. I was way beyond my comfort and expertise level. It was a hard reality to face at first. Maybe just a hard reality to face, full stop."

Tristan laughed, catching Natasha's attention. Her eyes were hazed with alcohol and face flushed. She was further gone than he'd ever seen her. Phil alone seemed to handle the nights out with Niamh.

"Hey," she said, drawing all his focus. She reached out for him, and then stumbled, falling into his side.

He grabbed her, helping her stand, and slid a hand along the small of her back. Pulling her close, he breathed in her intoxicating smell and felt her heat soak into his skin.

"Hey," he murmured, taking in her beauty.

She furrowed her brow and then slapped him across the face. Seeing him smile, she wrapped her arms around his neck and kissed him.

Arousal flared through him. Their tongues tangled before he backed off.

"Hi," he murmured against her lips. "Having fun, little mate?"

He didn't miss her full body shiver at his words. She liked the term.

She threaded in between his knees, her hands at the back of his neck now, her chest nearly pressed against his. "You set me up," she said loudly. She'd lost control of her volume. "Since when do you have entire territories trying to get in your pants?"

He ran his hands down her back, stopping just above the swell of her butt. He longed to keep going, to grab her athletic ass and pull her harder into him. He'd be taking advantage of her in the moment, though. She had zero inhibitions right now.

He settled for rubbing back up her sides and again along her back, enjoying the contact. Enjoying her eyes closed in pleasure.

"Since always, little angel," he answered arrogantly. Her eyes opened, her gaze now traveling his face. "You just never noticed because you had no interest."

"I still have no interest," she whispered, though more to herself. She swayed a little closer, as though a magnet, its other half tugging.

"No?"

"No. I have no desire for you at all." Her energy caressed every bit of him, exposing her lie. "I detest you most of the time."

"And when you don't detest me?"

Her resolve broke. "I want you so badly it's hard to think." Her lips crashed into his, needy and insistent. She chased his tongue with her own and her body pressed up against his sensuously.

"Okay, angel." He pulled away before he was lost to

the feeling of her. His groin pounded for release. "Let's take a second."

She snuggled into him, resting her head on his shoulder.

"I'm legless," she murmured. "That's what Niamh says. It means 'incredibly drunk'. But in fairness—" She pushed away from him so she could take a deep breath. If she wasn't already spinning, she would be soon. He needed to take her home. "I really did hold my own. I really did!" She breathed out heavily in alcoholic fumes, closed her eyes, and burrowed her face into him again. "I totally get what Jessie is always saying about a night out with Niamh. I thought—how bad can it be? Well. Let me tell you!" She yanked her upper body back. He held onto her to keep her from pitching backward. "It can be vera bad. Vera—ver-eee bad!"

"I'll take you home now—"

She slapped him again. Then her hands reached into his hair, clutched painfully, and she slammed her lips onto his again.

His arousal roared through him with the treatment. A tidal wave of passion threatened to take him away. Mustering all his strength, he wrapped his fingers around her upper arms and, as delicately as he could, pried her off.

"Wait, little angel," he said, breathing heavily.

"Wait, wait. We can't do this now."

"Take me home," she murmured, her forehead against his. "Fly me home. Apparently mates fly their women home. Fly me there and make love to me, Tristan. We both want it. I want it. I want you inside of me. I tasted you, now I want to feel you."

"Oh, God," he groaned, needing to push her farther away to get his bearings but not wanting her to take it as a rejection.

It was the last thought that sobered him.

"We need to go," he said, rubbing her outer arms. "I'll fly you home, but you need sleep."

"I'm good. I'm okay." She gave him a one-eyed thumbs up. "She has drunk two or three drinks to my one, did you know that?" She lifted her brows before attempting to turn and point at Niamh. "And *he*"—her finger vaguely waved in Phil's direction—"kept pace with her no problem. They don't even seem drunk. How is that possible?"

"It is not." Jasper took two wobbly steps closer, his hands on his hips and his hips trying to slide out of line with the rest of his body. "It is *not* possible. That is the synopsis."

"Synopsis?" Ulric asked from behind him, leaning heavily against the wall between two tables. He held a half empty drink against his chest, and there was a wet stain below it. "That is not the right word, dummy. How about…sum-der-ay. Wait, no."

"Go home, Larry, you're drunk," Aurora said from a table. She wheezed out laughter and bent over.

Fred sat on the other side of Aurora with her computer open and a coffee cup to the side. Without looking up, she reached forward and moved Aurora's mostly empty drink away, so Aurora didn't hit it with her face. Fred was apparently working while playing babysitter. She clearly knew better than to drink with Niamh and Phil.

"Whenever you're ready," Tristan tried again, "I will fly you back to the hotel and tuck you into your bed, okay?"

"*Your* bed," she stated.

He gritted his teeth. He wanted nothing more in the world, and maybe he would, but he wouldn't share that bed with her. He couldn't. He didn't trust himself to keep his hands to himself.

"Sure," he said noncommittally. "Whenever you're ready."

Her hazy eyes met his and stuck, vulnerability shining within them. "I have a lot of darkness inside of me, Tristan. I have done so many things I'm not proud of. That I had no choice in. But…to protect Sebastian, and Jala, I would do it again."

Jala was Sebastian's sister, Tristan remembered. She'd died years ago.

A tear slipped out of her eye. "I killed their uncle. Did I ever tell you that? I don't really tell people. He'd locked me in the closet again. He used to do that all the time when we were bad, which he thought was always. I'd get locked in the closet because I wasn't a blood relation and he didn't want to explain to my drug addled, dead-beat parents what had happened to me. He'd lock me in the closet, and he'd…" More tears fell.

"It's okay, we can—"

"He'd beat them bloody. I had to take Jala to the emergency room once. I used all my babysitting money to get a taxi. I had to leave Sebastian at home because I couldn't carry them both and Sebastian wasn't as badly off. We were just kids. I took Jala in and made up an excuse. She got jumped, I said. Because if they knew it was their uncle, Jala and Sabby would go into the system. They'd be separated and lose track of each other. They *insisted* I never tell. And so, I didn't. I just patched them up as best I could. But then one time, he locked me in the closet and it didn't latch all the way. I got out before the panic set in, and I saw him. He had a hammer. I knew this time, *this* time, he'd kill them. I just *knew* it. And so I went to the kitchen, and I got a knife…and I got to him before he got to them."

More tears slipped down. Jasper lost the fight to keep his body in a straight line and fell between the tables, distracting the others. John moved to help.

"There was so much blood." Her eyes held a haunted look. She cried softly. "*So* much blood. It was everywhere. All over the place. And then Jala had a vision." More tears fell. "There was no point in resisting her visions. You did what she saw or else it would happen the hard way but still end up the same." She cried harder. "We framed the neighbor. He would've gone to jail anyway. He had a warrant, I guess. We lived in a really bad place. We framed him to get us off. *Me* off. And then Sabby and Jala essentially hid in my house until we could steal enough to all run away. And that's what my life has become." Her cheeks glistened. "Killing and killing. Torturing. Stealing. Killing some more. And it's all my fault. It all started with me." She hiccupped. "Whatever I might say, I have no one else to blame b-but myself."

John passed by again, but he didn't take his seat. He faced the rest of the bar, his back to Tristan and Natasha, giving them a moment.

"You did what you had to do to save your family," he said gently, his heart aching for her. He tucked a stray piece of hair behind her ear. "You're doing that still. We all are. *I* have so much darkness within me, little angel, it would make you weep. It would scare you. You wouldn't want to share a bed with me or even stand this close. I have traveled the darkest parts of a world that isn't supposed to merge with this one. A plane of existence so vile, it is a wonder I didn't come out coated in evil. Or maybe I did."

"Tell me," she whispered, pleading. Wanting her own demons to get out of the way or maybe just have company.

He glanced at the bar where Niamh was sitting. "Another time. But I will, I promise, okay? I will trust you where I haven't trusted anyone else. Not now. Not when it could be used against me, or when you might not remember it anyway."

He wiped away the wetness on her cheeks.

"But you are wrong about one thing, Natasha," he said. "You *did* have a choice, back in the day. And you have a choice now. You have always had a choice. And you chose, and choose, to be a hero. You choose to do the dirty work and save the lives of the people you love. Not everyone has that ability. Not everyone has the courage.

"The point is, Natasha, the darkness doesn't define us. It doesn't erase the good parts of us. We are the best heroes, you and I, because we don't need to walk in the light to enact justice. We do it through any means possible. Jessie needs people like us. Like Niamh. Like Austin. She needs people who aren't afraid of the night. Who else will battle the creatures that exist there, but us?"

He ran his thumb along her jaw, and in a moment of absolute weakness, said words he'd never uttered to another living soul.

"I love you," he whispered, and realized with a jolt that they were true. Almost immediately, he wanted to take them back. To hide the truth. But they were out in the world, now. They no longer belonged to just him. Now they belonged to her as well.

Her eyes softened and filled with tears again. She leaned her forehead against his.

"I'm scared," she breathed, and he knew she was afraid to feel strongly for someone who wasn't family. Someone who could let you down and leave you, hurt you. A sentiment, until right this moment, he'd shared.

"I know," he replied. "Think nothing more of it. Say your goodbyes and then I'll fly you home."

She let out a shaky breath, nodded, and gingerly stepped away.

Ulric held out his hands, his drink on the table in front of him. "Brah. Where have you been? Jasper fell on his head."

She blinked at him stupidly for a moment, then at

Jasper still laughing on the floor, and started laughing herself. Just like that, her sunshine rushed back in. This time, it wasn't feigned.

John sat down next to Tristan and clasped his fingers together.

"I don't have to tell you that whatever you heard doesn't need to be repeated," Tristan growled. He might not win, but to protect her truth, he'd take on the beast next to him.

"I certainly know something about darkness and killing those who are trying to hurt your family," John murmured. "I came to it young, too. It scars you, and those scars never go away. I've got no interest in meddling with anyone else's affairs. I got plenty of shit on my own plate."

Didn't they all.

"You've gotten used to this situation, then?" John asked, gesturing at the Ivy House crew. Hopefully, they'd been cut off by the bartender.

Tristan took a deep breath. "No. I'm still reeling half the time, even tonight, when I thought I'd known everything. That's the thing about this cair—convocation. I've got cairn on the brain, sorry. But that's the thing about it—you think it can only go one way, or two ways, or five, and it ends up going in a completely different direction. When you roll with it, and trust your team, and work with them, then it works out. And only then."

"I don't want a job."

"I don't care. Doesn't change the situation as you sit here now, waiting for the next random thing to happen."

John studied him quietly. This guy was taking it all in, moment by moment. It must've been the way he was programmed.

Tristan let him. A woman separated from a cluster within the crowd and walked straight toward him wearing a smile that said she had devious things on her mind. Her hips swayed suggestively, and her slinky blue dress rode high on her thighs and low on her bust.

He looked away with a distasteful expression. Maybe she'd get the hint—

"Hello, Tristan," he heard. "I heard that—"

Light glittered along a blade, and energy coiled and churned around him as Nessa lurched forward. She grabbed the woman by the back of the neck, yanked her closer, and pressed a pocketknife against the woman's throat.

"Approach my man again," Nessa ground out, "and I will press this blade as deep as it can go. He is *mine*, do you hear me? I do not share. I have no problem with torture and less problem with unmarked graves." She grinned at the wide-eyed woman. "Hell, all I'd have to do is throw you and all your friends off the side of this mountain. Unlike my boss, the ladies here don't have wings. *Splat!*" She shoved the woman away. "Get gone while I still have my temper."

The woman didn't spare Tristan another glance. She and her companions hurried out of the bar.

"That last line didn't make any sense." Ulric scratched his head. "Right? Or am I missing something?"

"Oh, crap, Ulric, is that your mom?" Jasper pointed down the bar.

"Oh no! Tell her I went home. Call me when she's gone." Ulric ran for the back of the bar, knocking chairs out of the way.

Jasper bent forward in a wheeze. "Got him!"

Phil had turned from the bar to face Tristan. "I thought you were going to stop her from doing that! We're here to keep the peace."

"Nah. *You're* here to keep the peace. And you're not doing a great job of it from what I just saw. *I'm* here for a cognac. Niamh?"

Niamh shook with laughter. She put up her hand for the bartender.

"I will take that." Phil tsked as he grabbed Natasha's wrist and, with the other large hand, wrestled the blade away. "You are very sneaky, Miss Nessa. Where do you keep finding these weapons?"

"I'm seeing a completely different side to the basajaunak," John murmured. "*Completely* different."

"Better or worse?" Tristan asked.

"Better. Much. They're actually a joy to be around now. They used to be a nightmare."

That seemed like the summary of Jessie's whole crew.

"Training Wheels told me about the trouble shifters are having with mages," John said.

Tristan furrowed his brow. "Who?"

From the corner, he saw a hand go up and a finger point down. Aurora.

"Miss Alpha's Daughter, Alpha-in-Training, Training Wheels." She burped. "All right here."

A laugh escaped Tristan. "Good one."

"He certainly thinks so," Aurora groused, and even though shifters seemed to have a great tolerance, she was in an alcoholic haze. Niamh and Phil had really done a number on this crew.

"Nessa, before all the shots…" John paused as she staggered back over to Tristan, threaded her way between his legs and draped herself over him, tucking her face into the hollow between his neck and shoulder. "She filled me in about mages in general. Why would the gargoyles join a fight that doesn't belong to them?"

Tristan pulled Nessa in close, supporting her weight and feeling a delicious hum between their bodies. She moaned softly.

"Because gargoyles are made to battle. We *want* the fight. And we need a strong commander to lead us there. Give the gargoyles a cause and they will give you a favorable outcome. Why do you think Jessie and Austin are spending their time and effort trying to barge their way into a community that doesn't think they belong? We need them if we want to win, and we *have* to win. If we don't fight for each other, who will fight for us? Shifters are currently the targets, but if they fall, who is next? This isn't an individual sport, it's a team effort—for those who have the balls to play, at least. And Jessie and Austin have the biggest balls of them all."

"Lady balls, made of iron." Natasha tried to put up a fist but failed. "Did I win?"

"Did you win what?" Tristan asked her.

"Did I win the shot war?"

Jasper put up his hands. "I win! I got up so I win. I am still standing for the foreseeable future."

"You're leaning against the wall," Natasha said, her face still tucked into Tristan.

"Whatever. You're being held up. I win."

Ulric jogged out of the archway that led to the restrooms, clipped his toe on the corner, staggered, and sprawled across a table, bringing it crashing down.

John bounced up.

"You didn't win!" Ulric climbed to his feet as John righted the table. "You did not win!" Ulric put a fist into the air. "I am not done yet!"

"Atta boy," Niamh said, still without turning around.

"They're cut off," the bartender said, watching the melee.

"Ah, *schure*," Niamh said in a thick drawl, "they're just gettin' goin'. Leave 'em at it."

"No." The bartender shook his head. "No more for them."

"Yes, please," Aurora murmured from the corner. She groaned and thunked her head against the table. "Cut me off."

"Time to go." Tristan stood, cradling Natasha in his arms. She snuggled in close. "I just need to tuck her in, and then I can come back and see the others home."

"Nah." John stood and stuck out his hand.

Tristan balanced Natasha before shaking it.

"Thanks for not giving a shit about what I might do with my life." John grinned. "It's refreshing."

"Anytime." Tristan laughed and turned for the

door. Pausing, he stepped closer to Niamh. "Where do I put her? Her bed…or my bed with me in hers?"

"Easy," Niamh replied. "Yours. Your T-shirt on her, no bra, keep on her knickers and socks."

"Socks?" Phil asked.

"Yeah. She'll know he put her to bed, but that he didn't get a ride. She would've taken off her knickers and socks for that."

"But the bra is off?" Tristan affirmed quietly.

"That's for comfort," Niamh said.

"Put her in her bed," John growled before Tristan could turn for the door. "Don't play games when it comes to a woman feeling safe. Waking up in very little, in a man's bed, and not remembering what happened makes a lot of women panic, or so I've been told. Even if it is only for a moment, that is a moment too long, even for a woman who seems to find weapons like a normal person finds pennies—"

"She stole all those," Niamh interrupted. "For all yer starin', ye don't notice much of the details, do ya? She's the best pickpocket I ever saw."

John's eyebrows drew in. He hadn't noticed.

"She's clearly comfortable with you," he said after a moment, "so put her in fluffy pajamas, tuck her into her bed, and let her wake up in a comfortable setting knowing you took care of her. That'll go a lot further than whatever the puca is suggesting."

"Very uninspiring but I can see the merit," Phil said.

"The merit of calling me by my magical creature instead of my name to attempt to get my goat, or him throwing cold water on the fiery game they're playing?" Niamh asked.

"This just got too complicated," Phil muttered.

Tristan didn't wait for them to argue it out. He kissed Natasha's temple as he walked toward the door. Her head lolled and he snuggled her close before he set her down to strip. This was the crap part of flying her home in this state, but she'd asked for it, and it did set the right precedent.

Once in his gargoyle form, he tucked his clothes into her shirt to ensure they didn't drop in flight, then took her in his arms and pushed into the sky. He didn't waste any time, flying fast and straight toward the hotel. Once there, he barely hesitated before going to her room and knocking on the door.

Sebastian pulled it open, saw the situation, and got out of the way.

"Do you know which are her favorite pajamas?" Tristan asked, laying her on the bed. Her eyes fluttered but remained closed.

"Yes, but I don't think I'll tell you. You should pick out the ones you think she likes best. She'll like that you chose for her."

He glanced over his shoulder at her before looking down at her orderly suitcase. "Um…"

"It's okay if you mess up her things. In this, it really will be the thought that counts. I'll just go to the restroom."

It seemed like Sebastian was rooting for Tristan to make an impression here. The others were probably playing games or using logic, but Sebastian knew her best and cared about her the most. If he thought Tristan was a bad idea, or someone Natasha wouldn't want to handle her in this state, he'd get in the way. Instead, he was giving Tristan time alone to attend to someone he thought of as a sister.

Tristan blew out a breath, suddenly feeling unworthy. He'd never courted anyone, and Natasha was too good by far to mess with the likes of him. But he'd put himself out there earlier, even if she didn't remember. He put himself out there every time he was in her presence. While Niamh's idea would probably prolong this exquisite game they were playing, John was dead right. Even if this wasn't as much fun, making her feel safe, waking up with her brother, in her own space and fully clothed in her PJs, was better for her peace of mind. When it came to a woman's safety, that's all that mattered.

He got to work, dressing her with careful efficiency and desperately trying not to let his gaze linger on secret places. He was painfully hard by the time he slid her into bed, but he ignored it. He kissed her forehead, and then lightly kissed her lips, before excusing himself from the room.

He wondered how much she would remember.

He wondered when he'd have to make good and finally tell someone his murky and dangerous past.

CHAPTER 31

JOHN

FRIGID WIND WHIPPED by the cliff, swirling around him. After he'd seen everyone back to the hotel last night, he'd gone back out and sat on a park bench, looking out at the darkness and thinking. He'd tossed and turned when he did finally turn in, rising again early this morning.

Now he stood at the edge of the world, it felt like, looking out into the abyss as flying creatures gathered overhead to participate in a three-cairn—or whatever—training session led by a mysterious and intensely powerful creature that wasn't completely gargoyle. What else he was, nobody knew. They also didn't seem to care. Not about his past, and not about Nessa's, or Austin's or Jessie's or John's.

He felt the danger approaching from behind. His pack had learned never to do that. This convocation had no such qualms. Then again, he no longer attacked first, and asked questions later like in his youth.

The phoenix, a shorter woman of Asian descent, stopped beside him wearing a purple muumuu. He'd seen a great many of those this morning, all worn by the convocation and heckled by the resident gargoyles.

"You don't have wings." She looked at him expectedly.

He nearly checked to make sure he wasn't wearing a cape. "No."

"You are standing very close," she said, pointedly looking at the ground between his toes and the edge of the cliff. "If you fly off, you'll die."

The words sounded like a threat, but the tone didn't quite match.

He kept his face blank. "Yes, that is very likely."

"Unlike me, you don't come back to life."

Was it a threat? He didn't know if he could take a phoenix, but he'd certainly give it a go.

Remembering what Tristan had said the night before, he rolled with it. "This is true. Must be nice to have the assurance of not really dying."

"Oh, I die." She nodded adamantly. "It really hurts, most of the time. I hate doing it. But it's not forever, you know what I mean? Also, I have wings. I can shift mid-fall. You? A gust of wind would blow you off the edge. You'd flap your arms and flail, but eventually, you'd go *splat*. You wouldn't come back from that."

His eye was twitching. He still couldn't tell if it was a threat or not. The increased adrenaline was making his head spin. It wasn't as easy to *roll with it* as he'd originally thought.

"Correct," he said, feigning calm.

"Right. So maybe you should move back from the edge so you don't go splat." She put up her hands. "Hollace said you were a past alpha, and I shouldn't tell you what to do because you wouldn't listen, but this is just pointing out the obvious. Jessie would be awfully sad if you fell off the cliff, that's all. And Ulric said it might get windy. So."

Her eyes flicked to the edge and back to him again.

A grin pulled at his lips. It wasn't a threat, at all. The opposite, she was concerned for his safety. Moreover, she was worried about how his death might affect Jessie. He'd grossly misjudged her. Comically so.

The smile almost bubbled into laughter, and he took a large step back. "How's that?"

She judged the distance, about five feet, and then the wind howling past. She shrugged. "From there, you'd at least have a fighting chance."

"That's all we can hope for, in the end." He was joking, but she nodded solemnly.

The chuckles broke through.

"Why are you here, by the way?" he asked before she could step away. "Why are you signing on to help with this mage thing?"

She put her hands into the pockets of her muumuu and swished the garment around. "These are great for air flow, by the way. You should get one." She hesitated and then gave him a poignant look. "If you want."

His chuckles grew.

"I signed on to help Jessie," she continued. "She summoned me. I felt her need, and I answered. When I answered, she met the challenge—Austin Steele did, actually, but that counts—and gained my approval. I'm doing what I agreed to do."

"Help her."

"Yes."

"But not Austin?"

She pulled a hand free and used a finger to reach through her glasses, where there didn't seem to be a lens, to rub her eye. "Helping her *is* helping Austin Steele. Helping them is helping shifters and the magical world at large." She tilted her head and looked up at the sky. "Helping them is helping restore stability in the magical world. I'm not much of a philosopher, but that seems about right, doesn't it? One group—the mages— have too much power. That can't be allowed."

Thunder rolled across the sky.

"Oops." She gave him a sheepish smile. "I'm late. Tristan said I could blast the resident gargoyles if I didn't kill them or sever any limbs. Indigo said she'd help so that I could go a little wild. The Guardians deserve it, honestly. I better get to it."

She stripped off her muumuu, handed it to John, shifted, and launched into the sky. Her fire warmed his face as she took off, trailing after her.

A phoenix. He had just talked to a phoenix and was about to watch that legendary creature participate in a routine training. His sisters would not believe the turn his life had taken.

Another presence grabbed ahold of his awareness, this one not dangerous. Not at present, anyway.

Nessa walked up wearing a warm coat and fuzzy pants. Her hair, highlighted by the sun in golds and reds, was hanging down along her beautiful face. Her bloodshot eyes and the sluggish way she moved indicated she was feeling the effects of last night.

He remembered her confessions to Tristan, and the pain that had laced every word. The haunted way she had laid bare her past. It could've been him recounting some of the life he'd endured. Some of the experiences he hadn't created but had been forced to handle.

And you chose, and choose, to be a hero.

He hadn't felt like a hero at the time, but his sisters

would say he was. His pack.

"I came out to watch the training and saw you standing here on your own." She took a sip of something steaming in the mug she held between her gloved hands.

"How're you feeling?"

She scoffed. "Like I got run over by a truck. I didn't want to ask Jessie or Indigo to heal me before the battle."

"Battle?"

She did bunny ears with one hand. "*Training*. It'll probably get rough. Jessie seems very sweet, but then that gargoyle gets involved and she…isn't so sweet."

He slipped his hands into his pockets. A comfortable silence fell between them. The sound of wings rode the breeze, and then a beautiful, sparkly pinky-purple creature rose into the sky. Light trailed its movements.

"Is that…" He furrowed his brow, looking at the wings. They were almost dainty in comparison to the enormity of the gargoyles, especially as she got closer to the biggest of them all, Tristan.

"Jessie, yeah. Pretty, right?"

He nodded. Very. "Can't fly as fast, I take it?"

"No. Nor for as long. She has to get help. That's one of the things outside gargoyles look down on her for. Her team flies her around, essentially. You'll see. But it's a small price to pay for what she can do with magic."

The companionable silence drifted between them again. He let it lengthen as certain movements from Tristan's wings elicited sound. The gargoyles took shape in the sky, almost forming little pods within a larger web structure. John could immediately discern what Tristan was going for and marveled at the organizational dexterity.

"Have you ever seen gargoyles battle?" she asked him.

"No." Another wave of gargoyles came in, this faction clumsy by comparison.

"They're fun to watch, graceful when they soar and bank, but then they ram into each other, and it's so incredibly brutal." Her lips formed a smile against the edge of her mug. "It's cool."

Tristan's wings made different sounds, directing the newcomers, but these didn't seem to be getting the idea. Most of them were bigger than the convocation's gargoyles, and probably faster fliers, but they weren't as well trained. They didn't have the discipline.

"Tristan came from another cairn, right?" John asked.

"Yeah. We did a raid on them a month or so ago— it's like a mock battle with no casualties. Kinda like what this will probably become but they won't steal anything after. Jessie made a show of knocking them out of her way, and then Tristan and his team hammered them. *Hammered* them." Her smile was jubilant and her body language conveyed pride. "They made that cairn leader eat his words after all the crap he'd talked about Jessie and Tristan."

She explained that Tristan's mysterious past made him seem less reliable in gargoyle culture, which reduced his status. Jessie was the same.

"Except he had status with that other cairn leader, right?" John confirmed.

"Yes. And somehow didn't after he'd left." She rolled her eyes. "It's all bullshit, this status thing. I get the merits of stability within a cairn, or pack for that matter, but the politics are so obviously dragging Jessie down. She has to break through that glass ceiling."

"Austin does, too, but in a different way," John murmured. "Same sort of politics, there."

"Bullshit," she murmured again.

And they were doing all of this to help others. They were going through all this hassle, putting themselves out there time and again, getting talked about or laughed at, to create a safe place for magical people at large. It was noble. Selfless.

"I thought I knew all there was to know about the shifter world," he said. "My sisters never mentioned a mounting threat. I feel like I suddenly don't know anything at all."

A burst of magic rocked the sky. It cut through John and thrummed up his spine. It seemed to say *pay attention.*

He froze with the sheer power of will it took to resist that command.

"Was that Jessie?" he asked.

"Yeah. Tristan couldn't get Gerard's gargoyles in line so she's taking over."

More bursts of magic thrummed now, not as potent, all with directives.

The gargoyles finally started to integrate, not forming their own little clusters, but adding to those already established. They'd learn the ropes before forming their own. Smart. It's what John would've done.

He let out a breath. "I swore I would never be in a pack again."

"Then don't be."

"Except my sisters are in danger. Kingsley Barazza is a strong alpha leading a strong pack. Aurora told me what they were up against. My sisters have a larger pack, but it clearly isn't the size or even the force that is the issue. It's the mage magic. And they don't have any."

"But we do. That's the point. If they were in danger, we would help."

He huffed and studied his feet for a moment. "Shifters usually rely on family and pack friends for aid. We stick with what we know. We don't trust strangers."

"Yeah, I think Austin wanted to do that in the beginning. Or told Jessie it was his first inclination? Something like that. Obviously, he came to his senses."

"And you're saying I should come to my senses?" he growled.

She laughed in delight. "If the shoe fits, Mr. Island."

It was very hard to take oneself too seriously around her.

He continued to study his feet. "It floors me. Jessie, a Jane, and Austin, someone the alpha community ridicules, would drag their team and all manner of creatures—" He shook his head and looked at her. "*You* would go to a complete stranger's aid, putting your life in danger, at the drop of a hat?"

"Well…that is the point of the convocation. And in return, those shifters would hopefully help us if we needed it. Or others if *they* needed it. To beat the mages, it'll take a village. Surely you know the value of unity?"

He did, more than most. A unified pack was a strong pack. He wouldn't have been able to hold the line if his father hadn't been an impeccable alpha before him.

The problem was, it was hard to unify a lot of people and keep everyone content and peaceful. It was hard to keep a growing pack healthy and happy if that pack also had some powerful players, and enforcers had to be powerful. Only the best alphas managed. He'd been one. His sisters were. Kingsley Barazza.

He looked skyward at the gargoyles, their positions shifting and changing, synchronized despite the newcomers. They worked in their groups and helped the newcomers fit into the whole.

Wasn't that what Austin and Jessie had created with this convocation? They weren't asking everyone to be one pack or one cairn. They were asking the pack and cairn leaders to lead their people while fitting into the whole. Jessie and Austin were using their people as a hub to help the others integrate when needed.

John sniffed, shaking his head. The little Barazza boy had allowed a Jane and her magical house to open his mind, and in so doing, expand his horizons. He let her show him the way, having created her own hub, and he was attaching his people and hers to help fortify it. He had the training, and she had that special something that could not be taught. That John didn't himself have—he'd had to use violence to keep his people peaceful. The whole thing was so incredibly complex...and somehow seemed so simple.

"I'm not sure I've ever been humbled in my lifetime," he admitted, because even though Nessa probably didn't remember, she'd admitted a vulnerable truth in his presence. For her, at least. She'd done the right thing in protecting her family. So even though she probably wouldn't think this was a big deal, this was a vulnerability for him. It would make them even.

"I have always been the king of the mountain, but I feel utterly insignificant in this moment. Austin and Jessie have taken their setup to the next level. To a place I would never even *think* to go. It wouldn't make sense, all this, without seeing it. Maybe without my living in it. If still in my former position, I'm honestly not sure if I would've joined the convocation. I'd probably resist, like many others will. Or I'd try to take the lead, thinking I would be better."

He clenched his jaw and then laughed.

"I wouldn't be enough." He laughed again. "I must admit for the first time in my entire life that I would not be enough. If I took control of this thing, it would all come crashing down." He turned his head a little to glance at her out of the corner of his eye. "I've built a reputation on the opposite. I've upheld that image through some very rough times."

"I get it about building a reputation, upholding the image despite the warnings, and then needing a big alpha gargoyle to track you down in the middle of the night when you have your hands tied behind your back, and a bag over your head, to fly you to safety." She nodded at him, her eyes serious and laughing at the same time. "Yeah. That's what hanging on our laurels gets us in this new world."

She shrugged it away, so easy and light and carefree while also dangerous and cunning and intelligent. John could see why Tristan was in rapture.

"Look, Sir Ego, Austin couldn't do this on his own, either. Ask him. He'll tell you point blank. Jessie couldn't, and she wouldn't want to. As a team? Yes. Together, they make magic. Rather than comparing yourself, maybe ask why you care? And if it's for any decent reason, like the safety of your sisters, then maybe ask what *you* could bring to the table." She grinned without looking at him. "Sounds like you have a bunch of sway with that Ol' Image you've worked so hard for. Austin doesn't have that, and he probably needs it. Maybe that will take the bite out of the humble pie?"

He grinned, back to shaking his head. "You seem to have a talent for managing big personalities. If anyone had spoken to me like that back in the day…"

"And yet you're about to laugh."

"Somehow."

"Hmm," she answered noncommittally. "Sometimes it's nicer not to take things so horribly seriously."

Wasn't that the truth. He needed to go hang out with Fred again. Even when she *was* serious, it was hilarious.

He shoved all this from his mind. He didn't want to think about it anymore. He wanted to disappear again and walk away from the troubles and complexities of magical life. Same as Jessie wanted to do, really. That's what Ulric had said. Aurora had verified. Same as Austin, apparently.

Except they weren't doing that, were they? They were stepping up and shouldering the danger.

And you chose, and choose, to be a hero.

"Okay. Now they're rolling," Nessa said, thankfully pulling him from his swirling thoughts. She finished what was in her mug.

He watched her out of the corner of his eye, his curiosity getting the better of him. "You must've made it home all right last night."

Red infused her cheeks, and a shy little smile curled her lips. She half hid behind her mug, delighted with whatever had happened.

"I did, yes. Thank you for asking. Tristan had it covered."

He nodded, needing to let it go. There was no reason to get involved in her—or Tristan's—private life.

Yet...no one had mentioned which option Tristan

had chosen. John was too curious for his own good.

"You guys are mates, right?" he hazarded.

She tensed. "No. I just keep away the swarms of women that follow him around so he can focus on his job—helping Jessie and getting things done, you know."

"Ah. In other words, you woke up in your boots." He chuckled for show.

"That's not Tristan's style," she said softly, and her body turned languid with desire and something else he couldn't put his finger on. "He puts on the gruff, 'I'm an island' persona, but in the end, I think he's a caretaker. He put me in my fluffiest pajamas and tucked me into my bed, where I apparently snored so loudly that Sabby thought about smothering me in my sleep."

John huffed out a laugh. So, Tristan had chosen the girl over the games. Good man.

"You need a guy like that guarding someone like Jessie, it sounds like," he replied noncommittally. His curiosity had been sated. Time to move on.

She was silent, and he glanced at her. A sad expression flitted across her face and evaporated in a heartbeat as though it had never been there. She smiled at him, a disarming sort of expression to hide whatever she'd just been feeling.

"Jessie, yeah. She needs it."

He got the feeling she didn't want to talk about this

anymore. And also, that her heart was hurting. He remembered what she'd said last night.

I'm scared.

He swallowed, turning his face away again. But something kept trying to tug his focus back. He wanted to console her. Maybe comfort her. Hell, he wanted to help her. He just didn't know how.

Maybe he wanted to help himself, and didn't know how to do that, either. He hadn't been able to take a mate when he was fighting to keep his pack, and by the time he could've, he didn't have anything left to give. He had a feeling Nessa had some parallels, certainly the same scarring. She seemed to have the same fear that life would never get better and good things were just a mirage. An angel with a broken wing.

Before he could think what to do or say, or maybe just throw himself off the cliff to get away from the awkward situation he'd created, a shock of magic ripped his focus toward the sky.

"Now you will see what gargoyles can really do," Nessa said.

CHAPTER 32

JESSIE

WHAT IN THE bloody hell were these idiots doing? The resident cairn organized like they were ready to attack my and Gerard's forces. They clustered in a sort of horde over the city, a structure that hadn't done Gimerel any favors.

Gerard had only brought the bare minimum of his Guardians to save on travel expenses and to protect his cairn should another cairn think his absence was a good time to raid. Because of that, the resident cairn was on equal footing when it came to overall numbers.

When would these idiots learn that numbers were only part of the recipe, and they didn't have anything else going for them?

"Fine, you want to fight?"

"Wh-at?" Tristan asked, having only heard my collection of syllables. I'd given up trying to communicate with words in my gargoyle form.

Magic pulsed, a drum beat for my people and Gerard's. I sent it down to the city, as well, where Austin and the other shifters watched the training. They got the message immediately, stripping out of their regular clothing and shifting. Basajaunak came running to join the others.

A couple of Gerard's people didn't have a connection with me, and I extended it now. If they were confused what the new feeling was, they didn't show it. They joined our group bond immediately, suddenly on the grid and ready for action.

And action they would get.

Evan hadn't joined his Guardians for this, too new to the cairn to lead in the sky. The lead enforcer started forward, not giving us time to adjust.

Like we need it, I thought.

I sent a wave of magic up to Hollace, and he unleashed thunder into the sky. I started forward, and then Tristan was above me, grabbing me and flying me faster. The rest fell in behind as I felt Tristan's desires and blasted them out magically, keeping our people together for the moment. My drum beat of magic picked up the tempo, and my urgency let them know that I wanted this done as quickly as possible. Patty had better be getting this on camera, because this time, I *would* splash it all over the gargoyle community. I would not allow any more doubt about how explosive, dangerous, and effective my team was. Naysaying stopped *now*.

Another push of power, and Tristan's excellent strategy went into effect. Clusters of gargoyles spread out vertically, moving as a unit except for Gerard's additions. They didn't expect the change, didn't understand the directive because of it, and fell behind. Given most of them had flown with us before, it didn't take them long to figure it out and catch up.

I wiggled to be let go. Tristan threw me forward, ahead of the rest. I went straight at that lead enforcer, slower, clumsy in the air, but lethal. They could talk all the crap they wanted about my flying, but I'd make sure they never wanted to go up against me. I wouldn't kill him, but I would get damn close.

He put out his hands and claws gleefully. His body sang with it. His wings snapped as he darted at me.

I hit him with a magical spell that hurt like the blazes before blasting everyone around him as well. They all tilted and wobbled in the air and then I slammed into that lead enforcer, raking my claws down his front and peppering him with more spells. He yowled, a strange high-pitched sound I had never heard a gargoyle make.

Gargoyles didn't mess with each other's wings, and so I left those alone lest someone accuse me of foul play.

I magically drilled holes in his limbs. Scratched him to hell with my claws, bit into his neck and ripped out a chunk. He reciprocated but didn't get far because Sebastian had helped me concoct a spell to protect me from physical damage. And help it did, immensely.

I bit his face. Slashed his middle with magic, hammered him with blunt spells, and exploded him away from me.

His body went careening downward, his wings fine but he didn't have the presence of mind to use them.

"Damn it," I grit out. Or tried, anyway.

A plea for Tristan's help never materialized. He was there before I called, anticipating me.

"You did it!" I said without the smile I'd attempted.

He didn't bother saying, "What?" this time. He was learning there, too.

His rush of power and force sent us quickly after the lead enforcer. We neared, and I wiggled free, throwing a net under the falling gargoyle. Tristan let me go and headed back to the fight. I hovered in place, ripped away the net, put up another, and repeated the process until he was about ten feet from the ground. Then I let him fall. Good enough for him, the wanker.

My ascent was slow, but I didn't need to be close to do magic. Wind ripped part of their force to the side, and Cyra chased after them, sending jets of fire at their limbs. She enveloped a couple in weak flame, singeing their hair, and continued chasing when they tried to get away. Hollace, too, pursued, raining down lightning.

I sent more spells as our people worked through Tristan's battle design. Gargoyles up high dove downward, each group catching two or three of the larger Guardians and collectively ripping them apart. Those below came up, aiming for the soft bellies and ripping them open.

Anyone not targeted by the groups had to deal with me. I tried to chase, obviously couldn't keep up, and threw a wall of magic in front of them. They slammed against it, not knowing to claw or that it was there at all. Two knocked themselves out and fell. I caught them in nets and sent one of our Guardians to get Sebastian. He could keep people from falling to their doom.

A Guardian raced toward me from the side, apparently thinking I needed eyes to know where the enemy was. My magic alerted me, and a spell nearly took off his arm.

Oops. That one got away from me.

"*You should've killed him,*" Ivy House said. "*Pick one to make an example of.*"

We didn't need to bother.

The groups above and below went at an angle this time, all of them uniform, except for the few people of

Gerard's that were slow to catch on. They picked off the last of the strong Guardians and split in half, twice as many groups in the sky now. They started going for the smaller, weaker gargoyles in larger numbers, turning the sky into a washing machine of perfect synergy.

I hadn't seen the battle at Gimerel, and in trainings, I was always doing something. For a moment, I hovered in complete wonder. Good lord, Tristan had created something sensational. Our people pulled it off perfectly.

Below, the shifters and basajaunak showed that they had organization as well, running through the city in their own groups, growling and snarling and making sure they were seen. It wouldn't be a good look to randomly attack the onlookers, though the basajaunak did grab up a few people and carry them around by their ankles.

Back at the battle, I dazzled someone with light, distracting him before I rammed into his side. I scratched and clawed and peppered him with spells, as well, just to share the wealth. The lead enforcer would have someone to commiserate with.

Two enemy gargoyles came to help their guy. I turned to hit them with a spell, but Tristan came out of nowhere, barreling into the side of one, his weight and velocity continuing to the second. Jasper grabbed me, and Ulric took my place before two more gargoyles flew in to help Tristan.

Cyra squawked as she zipped by in a colorful plume of fire, hard on the trail of a wide-eyed gargoyle. Lightning struck another gargoyle in the back to the far left. The gargoyle froze, folded his wings, and fell.

Sebastian's ride flew him in, and the weird mage easily caught the plummeting gargoyle in a magical net before blasting another gargoyle to his right. Apparently, he hadn't gotten the note to simply keep people from dying, rather than helping take them down. Oh, well.

In less than an hour, it was over. We hadn't taken them all down, probably only about three-quarters, but the rest fled. With howls and yelps and every ounce of speed they clearly possessed, they took off for the city or the mountains.

I checked in with our people, healing those who'd gotten sliced up. Most only had scratches and bruises. Tristan's strategy had kept our people from the worst this cairn had to offer, despite some of the flying muscle they had. I then offered the connection to their people, because in the end, we did need them. We wanted them in the convocation, and the only way they could really experience being led by a female gargoyle was if they felt the differences I offered.

Tristan hovered in the air, beating his wings in victory. Gargoyles roared, many humming their wings along with him. Hollace let off waves of thunder, and Cyra turned and sent a stream of fire straight at me.

"Dang it, Cyra." I met the fire with water. It was easy because she wasn't putting much power behind her magic, and then I sent a blast of wind to knock her off-course. She went tumbling in a ball of flame, complete theatrics because I hadn't put that much power into my return fire. She was helping me show off.

I looked for Tristan because I didn't know what happened now. After training, we usually returned to base, me doing the equivalent of a new gym-goer limping out after their first session. That wouldn't look great here, though. I'd ruin the image.

He swooped down for me, and I turned to make it easy. His giant clawed hands grabbed me around the waist, and I tucked in my wings. He brought me in and banked before heading higher into the sky.

"Nowww," he said. "We tray-nn."

TWO HOURS LATER, yes, I did the flying equivalent of limping out of the gym. Tristan hadn't gone any easier on us here than he usually did at Ivy House. Maybe less so.

I landed on two feet and sank to my butt. I always worked on my flying stamina, but this time I'd pushed past my limits. I hadn't wanted to look so pitiful in front of Evan's cairn, but…well, here we were.

I turned to lie down on my face so my wings could stretch out.

My connections told me that Tristan had landed near me. My bonds told me Austin had come over and some of the shifters and gargoyles besides. I couldn't see any of this with grass obscuring my vision.

"Incredible," Evan said, and I heard skin slapping skin. High-five, forceful handshake—who knew? "I've never seen a cairn with that level of flying. Most of your Guardians are smaller in stature, slower in flight—didn't matter. You ruled the sky."

"It's not that it didn't matter," Tristan replied. "It's that working together in this way creates a stronger force. Add in more muscle and speed, and you get better results. The beauty of this structure is that, if we all practice it, we can easily integrate other cairns when we need to."

"And how does it relate to those…on…the…" Evan trailed away.

"Boys, *boys*! Austin, Tristan, I am surprised at you!" Patty's quick footsteps came my way. "Indigo, come here, dear. Jessie needs healing. No, no, leave that gargoyle as he is. If he can't go on with a couple scrapes, can he really call himself a Guardian?"

"His entrails almost fell out from a spell gone wrong," Indigo bleated.

Patty was not having it. "But they didn't, did they? No. Leave him there. Come here, you need to heal Jessie."

"I'm okay," I said, not bothering to lift my head. "I can heal myself in no time at all."

"Jessie is the most important asset we have in the sky," she went on as if I hadn't said anything. "I will not let her lay in the grass like discarded luggage while the boys talk amongst themselves. She is a leader. She should be treated like one!"

"It's fine, really," I said as I felt Indigo's hand brush a wing. Ah. I'd forgotten I didn't have a mouth that could easily form words.

Indigo's healing energy soaked into me. "Jessie," she said, and then tsked. "Jessie, you pushed way too hard. I told you not to overextend like this in training, remember? Tomorrow, you'll have to spend all day healing yourself because you'll be so sore."

Very likely.

"I apologize," Evan mumbled.

"She's fine missing the strategy part of flying," Austin said to Evan. "She's learning it now. She came later to it than most of the Guardians."

"That's my fault," Tristan said. "I wasted time trying

to learn *her* way of doing things, forgetting she'd never been trained. She'd learned by improvising in extreme situations, trying to keep herself and her people alive when she barely knew how her wings or magic worked. What she's teaching us is the logistics of combatting mages. Of using flight *and* magic, along with her team. In that, she is the pinnacle, and yes, as Patty said, our main asset. We revolve around her, or we all die."

"Exactly. Yes," Patty said. "Thank you, Tristan. That is correct."

"And how…" Evan paused indecisively. "This can wait until she's recovered, but how does this strategy alter when combating mages? Or someone on the ground?"

"The flight plan was devised with ground enemy in mind," Tristan said. "The diving is to do damage, where Jessie shields us from magical gun or mage fire, and then we pull out and make room for the next team. If we loiter, we give them more targets, and she has to do more work to protect us all. She is our chief asset, as we've said, and magic takes a lot of energy. We need to protect her at all costs, and that includes minimizing the work she does to keep us safe. That is just one piece of the battle plan that Alpha Steele and Jessie devised."

"For the rest, we should have Jessie and Sebastian available," Austin said. "Orchestrating our ground crew with the flight team is a dance, allowing for Jessie and Sebastian to move among us all and seek out the most dangerous threats. She uses her connection to the team to communicate with us all. It is incredibly complex, but she does it naturally."

"That is the wonder of the female gargoyle," Tristan said, a note of pride in his voice. "She is the glue, as we told you."

"Jessie!" Gerard's heavy footsteps crunched through the brittle grasses, almost sounding like a floppy puppy compared to Austin's. "What are you doing laying down there on your face?"

"*Finally*," Patty said. "*Someone* thinks about poor Jessie."

Gerard's knee hit the ground near me, clearly wanting to talk. Apparently, it was time to shift. Annoyance.

I fluttered my wings to back Indigo off and then sapped energy to change forms. I groaned and didn't bother trying to turn over. Indigo's palm touched down on the center of my back.

"She has a really nice butt," Indigo said. "I've always thought so."

"Thank you," I mumbled.

"Jess, do you want me to pick you up?" Austin asked, the closeness of his voice indicating he was bending over me. He'd apparently been waiting until I shifted to play my donkey and traipse me all around like he'd been doing lately.

"I'm good," I murmured. With effort I didn't want to expend, I rolled over and sat up.

"Here." Austin knelt beside me and draped a muumuu over my head.

Gerard sat down on the grass next to me, also wearing a purple muumuu. "Jessie! I am *impressed*! You're a master at this now. I hear you were really pulling the punches on the spells, too."

"Well, yeah." I stretched out my arms and twisted to loosen up my back. "If I didn't, I'd kill people."

"I hear you got into a scuffle recently." He tilted his head with his arms out. "Where was our call?"

I laughed and threaded my arms through the muumuu. "That was a surprise. We didn't even know mages were there. It was an easy one. You would've been bored."

Evan knelt in front of me, a kind smile on his face. "Sorry about excluding you a moment ago. I've just…" He shook his head. "I've never seen anything like this. Flying like this, I mean. The raid with Gimerel was over quickly, but this was shocking."

"And she was pulling her punches." Gerard nodded. "I told you, didn't I? I could tell you didn't want to believe me, but I *told* you. I missed a great session last night with Niamh to go over everything with you."

"It's hard to believe a battle of that magnitude when you haven't seen one." Evan plopped down onto his butt as well. "Even the shifters and basajaunak running through the town, snarling—even that was exceptional. Can you give me a day, Jessie? Austin? Can you guys give me until tomorrow to talk to my advisors and some of my Guardians and see what people are thinking?"

"Sure, yeah." I wasn't planning on going anywhere today, anyway.

"Fantastic." He pushed to standing. "And I'll fill you in on our best kept secret, something only leaders and top personnel get the benefit of experiencing."

"It's boring." Gerard patted me on the back before he got up. "I'd much rather drink with Niamh. I saw her spear someone with that horn, earlier. Right in the leg." He grimaced. "Had to hurt. Where'd she go?"

"There are three bars." I groaned as I got up. "She'll likely be in one of those."

"Good. I could use a libation after all that effort. This time, I intend to shirk all my duties. I deserve a day off!" He walked off.

Austin stepped close and wrapped an arm around my waist. He nuzzled my neck. "You looked sensational up there, baby. Everyone was in awe of you."

"Yes, they most certainly were." Patty beamed at

me. "This'll shut that ol' Nelson up for good, mark my words. I've got his number, now. He won't be able to weasel away from me." She nodded and trudged off across the grass toward the city.

"What shall we do now?" Austin asked. "Shower and rest?"

"Yes, please." I rubbed Indigo's arm. "Thank you for helping."

She nodded and slunk away without a word.

I took his hand, and we started the walk back. "And I guess we try not to worry about Evan's advisors finding ways to discount what we've shown them. Again."

CHAPTER 33

JESSIE

IT TURNED OUT, the secret was a hot spring kept at the bottom floor of Evan's house. The room smelled slightly of sulfur with the same design as was woven through the rest of the place. One side had a large window overlooking the distant mountains, dusted with snow, and nibbles had been laid out on a small table in the corner, including sparkling wine chilling in a silver ice bucket.

Austin slipped the silk robe from my shoulders and let it whisper down my skin to the stone floor. He trailed his lips along my shoulder and neck.

"What we're doing is very important," he said, taking my hand and leading me to the steaming waters. "But I wish we were on John's side of things. That the territory was established, profitable, and running smoothly, someone else was in charge, and we could get on with our lives. Travel, take in the sights, have a day off."

I laughed as he took three steps down and waited, still holding my hand, for me to follow. I did, sighing as the warmth crept up my legs to my belly. Benches of various heights were carved into the stone, and I sank down into the water to sit on one. Austin spread his arm around my shoulders and pulled me in as he settled beside me.

"I'd really love that," I said, gazing out the window at the beautiful tableau beyond. "But I do have to admit this is pretty spectacular. We're sitting in a hot spring carved from stone on the top of a mountain in a gargoyle's cairn. This isn't something I could have even imagined existed as a Jane. And I'm sharing this awesome experience with the love of my life."

He kissed my temple. "Very true. We do have the rest of the day off. Half is better than nothing."

"We do."

I turned my face toward his, my heart warming and my core suddenly aching for his touch. He bent and grazed his lips against mine before deepening the kiss. It wasn't hard or desperate, but a promise of forever. His fingers trailed lightly across my chest before gently rubbing a taut nipple.

I sucked in a breath as delicious sensations pooled low. He kissed my jaw and throat. His hand cupped my breast before trailing down lower and sliding between my thighs. My eyelids fluttered closed, and heat rose within me.

He rubbed in small circles, his kiss becoming more intense. I moved my hips, the pleasure increasing. I reached down and captured his length, sliding my palm against it.

He growled against my lips. His hand ran to the back of my thigh before taking hold and pulling it toward him, over his lap. I knelt on the stone, my knees on either side of his thighs. Lowering, I trapped his hardness between our bodies before I slid my hips forward.

Our lips moved against each other in growing urgency. His hand slid up to cup my breast again, and I rose up, dragging his tip against me. The dim lighting fell over his handsome face, golden and soft. His eyes connected with mine, full of love and devotion, and then pleasure as I slowly sank down on top of him.

"I love you, Jacinta," he murmured, his movements not hurried, cherishing the moment with me in this place. One thumb stroked softly over my nipple, and the other reached into the waters to restart the slow circles that drove me to distraction.

"I love you." I moved over him, taking him deep, losing myself in his eyes. Feeling our bond in my soul.

My hands roamed, tracing his muscles and running my touch along the expanse of his shoulders. Our breath increased, mingling in the heated space between our kisses. He worked me harder, and I jerked my hips over his, the pressure building. I groaned with the feel of it, wound tight. Striving for the finish.

The explosion felt like it turned me inside out, the pleasure sparkling through me. He moaned my name and released, shaking. I leaned harder into him, holding tightly, trembling in the aftershocks.

"I needed that." I smiled against his lips.

"When I'm around you, I always need that." His kiss turned languid before he sighed in relaxation. "It never gets old."

I pulled my leg away and settled in next to him again. One of his arms draped around my shoulders, pulling me in tightly, and the other sought my hand. He entwined his fingers with mine. We gazed out at the mountains in comfortable silence, enjoying each other in a rare moment of inactivity.

✦　✦　✦

NESSA

"ARE YOU GOING out this afternoon?" Sabby pulled his phone away to look over at her. He was resting after the skirmish, as everyone was calling it, and she was miserable with a hangover. She'd been too embarrassed to ask Indigo or Jessie to save her since they were fighting and exerting themselves, and Nessa was just living.

Today, it hurt to live.

"I don't know. I might just stay here and do some work."

He pulled the phone closer again. "You're not going to do any work. You need greasy food or the hair of the dog."

The idea of consuming more alcohol made her want to cry. But he was right, she definitely wouldn't be working. And without a TV in this room—or maybe anywhere in the city—she'd just be staring at the ceiling.

Then again, if she did go, she'd have to brave being sober with people who'd seen the absolute mess she'd been.

Hazy recollections of John catching her from falling trickled in. Of him pulling her off the wall, where it had felt like vines held her there, and then stabilizing her to keep her from falling back into the wall again. That was in the second bar. By the third, all she had were flashes of memories. Fever dreams, almost, accompanied by black holes.

Whose great idea was it to do a shot drinking contest?

Tristan had shown up, she remembered, tall, dark and insanely gorgeous in his perfectly fitting suit and flashing amber eyes. His body was cut from the mold of a Greek god, hard everywhere and perfectly sculpted.

And then the horror of that meeting bled through.

She groaned.

"I think I slapped Tristan." She threw her arm over her face, wanting to shrivel up and turn to dust. "I have no idea why, either. Was it a joke? Was he pissed, and I reacted?"

But if it was a joke, slapping someone was certainly going too far. If he hadn't been mad before, he surely must've been mad after. She would've been. *Anyone* would've.

Maybe he *had* been pissed. She'd been a mess when she was supposed to be acting like the mate of the most dashing gargoyle in the city, the beta to the queen of the gargoyles, the man every woman wanted. She should've been the model of decorum and grace, of beauty and elegance, to fit on his arm.

Instead, she'd thrown around obscenities like some sort of deranged sailor, cackled like a Halloween rendition of a witch, and kissed everyone in sight. With tongue!

Wait, did she kiss everyone?

She palmed her head as she willed her brain to

dredge out the fuzzy memories. Jasper? Ulric? Aurora? She'd hugged them, hung on Jasper before they both went tumbling into John's lap, but she couldn't remember kissing them. *John?* No, not him. She hadn't even hugged him.

"Oh, god," she groaned. "I think I kissed Tristan, too."

"Well, that's only fair. He kissed you the other day. In the kitchen in Drex's territory, remember?"

"Yeah but…that—"

Was sexy, she finished silently. Last night would've been…

She didn't even want to think about it. She'd probably tasted like stale whiskey. *Cheap* stale whiskey, at that. Not to mention she'd probably slobbered all over him. Hell, she might've licked his face for all she remembered. He'd been sober, too. She remembered that, because it had made her feel drunker.

She had to have made him angry, even though he'd never gotten mad at her before.

She thought back to sober times, wondering if that were true. But no, regardless of all the stupid things she'd done and said, he'd never raised his voice at her. He'd never called her a nasty name or threatened her in a way that didn't tighten her core and make her think of begging him to take it further. He'd teased, he'd sauntered around full of infuriating but sexy arrogance, but he'd never turned anything she did against her.

And she'd slapped him.

More memories, distorted, of something painful. Something sweet. Something sad. She couldn't remember any details, just that…

"I think I cried at one point."

"Everyone needs a good cry," he said noncommittally.

"Sure. And I have good cries—alone, in my bedroom with the door locked. Not in a *bar*."

"I heard everyone in your crew was blind drunk. Jasper couldn't stand straight, and Ulric upended a table and got you all cut off. They think it's funny."

"They didn't slap Tristan, then stick their tongue down his throat, then cry all over him."

"They probably would've if you'd dared them."

He wasn't helping. "I threatened a half a dozen people with stolen weapons." She flopped her arm back onto the bed. "*What* was I *thinking*?"

Someone knocked at the door. Sebastian swiped out of the game he'd been playing and tossed his phone onto the bed.

"You were letting your hair down, Nessa, that's all. Niamh and Phil were there. They would've stopped you if things went too far."

She looked at the ceiling incredulously. "Niamh once wrestled Phil through a fire. She's not the person who is going to tell anyone to stop."

Sebastian opened the door before turning for his suitcase. "Which means she is not the person who will judge. It's fine."

"Hey." Jasper came in with a jovial grin. He sat on the edge of Nessa's bed and looked down at her. "You look like I felt this morning. You gotta get healed, babydoll."

"I gotta get some brakes," she grumbled.

"Nessa is worried she made an ass of herself last night, especially with Tristan," Sebastian said, pulling out a black button-up shirt.

Jasper laughed. "Lady, we *all* made asses of ourselves last night. Aurora passed out on the table. John had to carry her home. And we're going to do it again tonight because Gerard is ready to tie one on. Remember at Kingsley's when he got so drunk he flew into a building?" He nodded with a grin. "Yeah. He's reserved a VIP section for us. Not for his people—us! He's pissed he missed us having a blast last night. He'll make up for it tonight, I bet."

"No," she moaned. "I am not doing that again tonight. I've embarrassed myself enough for a lifetime."

"Nah. Come on." Jasper grabbed her hands and

hauled her to sitting. "You didn't do anything crazy. You're fine. You'll feel better once you have Indigo lay the healing mitts on you. Or you get a Bloody Mary, whichever comes first."

"No," she said again, faux crying as he pulled her to standing.

"If Aurora can face everyone, being as buttoned up as she was trained to be, you certainly can. You didn't even fall down! I don't think. There are some very blurry sections in my memory."

"I tried to stab someone, Jasper." She let him lead her to her suitcase.

"You didn't so much try as you threatened. Which was what Tristan said to do. You were following orders. Not your fault."

"Oh, yeah, Tristan, the guy I slapped."

"What's going on?" Ulric popped his head through the door. "What is taking—oh man." He came in wearing a huge smile. "Look at *you*! You look like I felt this morning."

"That's what I told her." Jasper rifled through her suitcase, disturbing the order. "She's embarrassed because she slapped Tristan."

"He's a gargoyle," Ulric said. "He liked it. That's a garhette's version of courtship, right there. Which was probably why he couldn't keep his hands off you. Wear something sexy. All will be forgiven, trust me."

Her face heated, as did certain parts of her body. "I also cried. You don't cry at a bar."

Jasper pulled out a slinky dress that was much too fancy for an evening swilling suds. He laid it on the bed before grabbing some high-heeled shoes to go with it. "I'm pretty sure I cried at one point."

"Yeah, you did." Ulric put his hands on his hips. "You were telling John about Nathanial, remember?"

Jasper blinked at Ulric. "No."

"Oh." Ulric started to chuckle. "John started to awkwardly pat you on the back, since shifter pack people aren't touchy-feely, and Niamh made a wise-crack that John was afraid because everything he touched turned to gold." Ulric laughed harder. "It was only funny because it really rankled John and none of us could understand why. Like, turning things to gold is good. He should be proud. But he seemed really taken aback and pissed off, while trying not to show it, and Niamh just did her normal unimpressed thing, which wound him up more—"

"I think you had to be there," Jasper said, and that made Nessa laugh silently.

She didn't remember any of that, and clearly neither did Jasper.

Jasper leaned in to smell her. "You have alcohol

seeping out of your pores. Jump in the shower real quick. Ulric, go get Mr. Tom to help her get ready. He needs something to do or he'll try and find Jessie. She's with Austin somewhere and probably wants to be left alone."

"That guy needs a hobby," Ulric said, heading for the door.

"He has one. Jessie."

"No, I can do it, honestly—"

Jasper ushered her toward the bathroom. "You are in no mood to try at your appearance, and tonight we need to show up looking like the most prestigious of the cairns. We widened a lot of eyes today. Everyone is watching. You can usually do super-hot in your sleep but hungover is a hurdle you aren't used to, apparently. It's fine. Mr. Tom needs something to do. Let's go."

He slapped her butt to get her moving, and she laughed and did as she was instructed. Afterwards, as promised, Mr. Tom met her in her room. Sebastian sat in the chair on his side of the room. He was wearing a slightly dressed-down watch, slacks, the button up he'd pulled out earlier, and dress shoes. His hair hadn't been done yet, since she'd been steaming up the bathroom.

"Tie?" she asked him as Mr. Tom waited at the end of the bed.

Sebastian looked up from his phone. "No. I don't follow the same rules as everyone else, not as Elliot

Graves. They probably won't even realize I was the idiot in the cape yesterday. Popped collar, a couple buttons undone, and no time for anyone. I just need to do my hair and spritz on a little cologne and I'm good."

"Is everyone waiting for me?"

"Ulric and Jasper are waiting for you. They want to make sure you dress the part. Also, that you tag along and face your demons. They see no reason why you should be embarrassed for last night, and showing up today will put you straight. Their words, obviously. *I* am waiting for you because I'm hoping you'll provide a buffer between me and Niamh, who sees through this persona, and is liable to make me nervous enough to drop the act and do whatever harebrained scheme she is up to today."

"A simple *no* would work wonders for you," Mr. Tom told him.

"One would think. And yet, it never does. I might as well discuss the philosophy of flowers with Edgar."

Nessa paused as she looked down on a different dress than Jasper had picked out. Her suitcase had been set to rights with crisp folds and put in a different order that fit better.

"I took the liberty of properly packing your suit-case," Mr. Tom said, "since it seems you lack the ability."

"Thanks…"

"Yes. And that dress will work better if you plan to dazzle the gargoyles, though in your current state of *wilt*, we'll have to work harder at your makeup to reduce the puffy state of your eyes. Maybe if you look good, it will hide the fact that you clearly do not feel good. You should've had someone heal you. Or, I don't know, maybe not tried to drown yourself in a whiskey bottle." He sighed. "Into the bathroom. We'll do your face first, and while you dress, I'll run over and grab some jewelry."

"What about Jessie?" Nessa asked. "Won't she be needing the jewelry?"

"Not that her whereabouts are any of your concern, but she is indisposed with the alpha and will relish in her freedom for the evening. She gets so few days off. She won't be needing jewelry, and if she did, I have brought plenty for the pair of you. Just don't let the Irishwoman get ahold of it, or she'll make sure the whole place erupts in chaos."

He shooed her into the bathroom and then tisked at her appearance. "Must I constantly need to fix up people who find enjoyment by guzzling down the contents of a bottle? Well." He sighed. "At least I have experience. Take a seat, come on. We haven't got all day."

CHAPTER 34
TRISTAN

A HUSH FELL over the bar, the same establishment they'd been to the night before. Instead of the small area tucked into the corner, though, this time they had a section blocked off on one side. Two signs were posted at the entrance of the area, and a waitress occasionally walked around to get orders. It was a far cry from the VIP section in Los Angeles over Christmas. They weren't in a Dick world anymore, and it showed.

Gerard had invited anyone of high status, which included the leaders, betas, lead enforcers…and anyone from Jessie's crew who wanted to come. He'd known that Jessie and Austin planned to stay in tonight, and Evan and his lead enforcer would be busy hashing out details, but he'd made his invitations for them clear.

Most people thought he was making a statement, putting Jessie's entire crew on level with the best and the brightest. And part of that was likely true. Tristan knew, though, that in reality, Gerard wanted to party, and he knew the Ivy House gang was a damn good time.

Previously loud chatter and barks of laughter reduced to a murmur. Shoes slid against the floor, people shifting and jostling each other to change position. It reminded him of when Jessie entered the bar in O'Briens, and her gargoyle forced everyone to simmer down and step aside so she could greet her mate.

"She decided to show," John said in a low voice, seated next to Tristan on a high stool with his back to the wall.

Tristan's heart picked up its pace. The crowd parted to let the newcomers through, not usual for gargoyles. Tristan got his first glimpse, and his breath caught.

Natasha walked slightly in front of Sebastian clad in a stunning, form-fitting evening gown. The nude tone of the dress was overlaid with vertical lines of silver sequins and beading that caught the light and created an elegant shimmer. The plunging neckline was framed by a slight scallop over her breasts, adding drama and polish. A thigh-high slit ran to the floor, and her long hair cascaded past her shoulders in a wave. A diamond and sapphire necklace adorned her neck, as extravagant as something Jessie might wear to an important dinner, and instead of a watch, she wore a matching cuff bracelet that must've cost a fortune.

Her hips swayed suggestively as she moved through the room, catching everyone's eye, male and female alike. She held her shoulders back, arrogance and confidence, while her energy flirted with everyone she passed, adding a flare of sexy sophistication. Dark makeup outlined her eyes and a pop of color drew attention to her lips, pulled into a smile as though she were just about to laugh.

He watched, transfixed, not able to tear his eyes away from her, not caring who walked in behind them.

John moved to give her the seat next to Tristan.

"No," he said. "Stay there. Just move a little away if you would. Not far."

John didn't ask questions. He followed the directions to the letter.

Natasha paused in her progress to say hi to Gerard and thank him for the invitation. His lead enforcer stepped closer eagerly, looking for an introduction. She'd already stepped away, finding Hollace. Cyra drifted closer, and Fred met them there, Natasha drawing people like bears to honey.

"Not to stick my nose into your business," John said, his voice still low, "but it was a good move, taking her to her bed last night. I spoke to her this morning. She seemed to like it."

"She probably thought I had an ulterior motive."

"Actually, she mentioned that you seem like a caregiver."

Tristan's focus snapped John's way. "She was probably being sarcastic," he said carefully.

"No." He hesitated. "I don't think she had the capacity for sarcasm this morning. She wasn't feeling the best, given the crap whiskey they'd been drinking all night."

"And the quantity."

"That, too. If I had to guess, she seemed pleased. Like she might like that sort of thing." He shrugged. "But that's just a guess. I never devoted much time to understanding women. I just made sure the scorned ones weren't at my back."

It didn't seem like a guess at all. It seemed like a hint from a guy who didn't want to get involved but couldn't help himself. The former alpha was peeking through.

Tristan smirked, turning away. "Noted—"

He jolted when he realized Natasha had been looking at him. Her gaze zipped away quickly, as though she hadn't wanted him to notice.

"She mention anything else about last night?" he asked, keeping his voice low. She didn't have the hearing of a shifter, but just in case...

"Are you kidding? I had to come up with a creative

way to get that much. I'd wondered if you'd chosen the girl or the games, that's why I asked."

When he put it like that, Tristan was glad he'd made the choice he had.

"The guys, Jasper and Ulric, don't remember much from that time period, though," John went on. "Aurora doesn't remember anything past the first shot in this one. Doesn't seem like she got out much as an alpha's daughter."

"She kept things respectable in her territory. It sounded like she had to. Austin Steele allows her plenty of freedom. She's trying to figure out a new normal."

He could see John nod out of the corner of his eye. "I thought as much. A lot of alphas can be suffocating with their children, especially in generational packs. Uncles often are, too."

"You're going to hear this a lot if you insist on comparing normal shifter life to this convocation, but Austin is not like most alphas."

"And one day, it might just sink in."

"Dare to dream."

Natasha was chatting with Aurora now, the two of them laughing and then grabbing their heads or each other's hands, clearly sharing their embarrassment from the night before. Tristan watched Natasha's every move, riveted. Spell-struck. To meet her anew, he'd think the same thing as the first time. He'd assume some sprite was showing him his greatest desire to lure him away, drain all that he was, and kill him for his folly. The difference was, with Natasha, he wouldn't regret a single moment of it.

The others didn't remember much from last night. He wondered how much Natasha did. If she knew she'd confided in him with something so horribly personal, the root of the trauma that kept building from there. And also, the root of her terror of small, dark places. He'd seen an episode of that when he'd first met her.

He wondered if she remembered his heartfelt admission, or if it got to go back in the vault, unsaid. He couldn't decide if he hoped so or not.

He would stick to his word, though. He'd tell her about his past, and he'd give her another chance to be open about hers. He'd give her a safe space and an opportunity to maybe heal a little. To at least share the burden.

Finally, her gaze had no choice but to turn Tristan's way. She'd run out of people to talk to. Her hand brushed her hair over her shoulder and her heeled shoes clicked against the hardwood, though she was in no hurry. When she'd nearly reached him, she noticed John, and a little tension drained away from her shoulders.

"Hey." She smiled, an expression that could light up even the darkest of places. "Sorry about last night. I got a little too much into the party spirit."

"No need to be sorry." John inclined his head gruffly. "We've all been there. I'm happy you gave me something to do, or I might've been the one to finally go too far and start a fight. The way gargoyles stand in my way gets under my skin."

She laughed. "It does with most shifters. If Jessie is around, stand behind her. She forces people to move with her magic. It's much easier."

She fidgeted, clearly looking for something else to say before the inevitable.

A wave of butterflies filled Tristan's middle. Maybe she did remember.

"It worked, though," she said, and cleared her throat, the nervousness getting to her. "Niamh's plan worked. We got them all riled up, and they tried to stage their version of a battle."

She swallowed and adjusted her weight. The hip closest to Tristan popped out as she marginally leaned his way. A steadying breath, and her eyes slowly, grudgingly followed.

Their gazes met, and his body went loose and tight at the same time. His legs spread a little, a silent invitation for her to thread between his knees like she had last night. To drape herself against him.

Her energy exploded around her and reached for him immediately, sliding against his skin and taking root deep in his middle, sucking him closer. He very nearly got off his chair and closed the distance like she so obviously wanted. Like her magic was trying to unconsciously force.

He resisted and let his nightmare magic out to play, dancing with hers, licking at her. Her pupils dilated, the only person in the world who had ever been positively affected by his magic. She liked the danger, because she knew, for her, he was safe. His danger would be used to protect her, not hurt her.

"Your leadership in the battle was incredible," she purred, taking a halting step toward him, as though she hadn't had a choice in the action. He hadn't succumbed to her magic, and so it was yanking her toward the object of her desire.

"Is tonight the night you beg, little deathwatch angel?" he asked her in a rough voice soaked with desire.

John got off his chair and walked away, giving them space.

He reached out a hand to her, leaving it in the air until she slipped her palm against his. He gently pulled her closer.

"Mates aren't this nervous to be around each other,

Natasha." When she was close enough, he dropped her hand to his thigh before moving his to her wrist. He stroked her upper arm before curling his hand around to her back. He applied pressure, coaxing her closer. "Tell me more about how amazing I am."

Her nose crinkled, and her eyes glittered with a smile. Her lips twisted to the side, though. Her expression said his company was wanting.

"I would, but I can't think of a single other thing that might fit."

"Hmm." His other hand braced on her hip, bringing her closer still. "I don't think that is true at all. I think you want to compliment me. To tell me how good I feel, and that you want me to go harder. Deeper."

A breath tumbled from her parted lips. "Those aren't compliments, those are demands."

"Then let's play the game of demands. Run your hand up my inner thigh and over my hard cock."

Her chest rose and fell against her dress, pushing her cleavage out of the confining top. He could see her pulse thumping like a frightened rabbit. Her eyes were focused on his mouth as she leaned forward. Her hand inched up, its pressure firm. His hard length was stretched down onto his thigh, trapped within the material. Her fingers brushed the tip, continuing to move. They flowed over his trouser-covered shaft and up until her thumb could stroke across the tip.

He fisted her hair and dragged her closer. She let out a tiny whimper of desire. Their lips crashed together. Her taste exploded into his world, and he growled with the rising tide of passion.

Her hand went to his zipper.

"Undo my pants," he commanded.

The air heated between their lips. She licked out, running her tongue along his bottom lip.

He bent forward for more of her kiss. More of her taste.

"Nah," she said, and her energy turned taunting. "I don't think I will. I'm not the one who's owned. Or didn't you get that bracelet I sent you, *Daddy*?"

She leaned back, her eyes on fire. A sensuous little smirk twisted those plump lips.

"I think it is *you* who will beg tonight," she said mischievously. "Too bad I'm not a real mate. At least then, I might have pity on you."

Her fingers applied more pressure as her hand ran back down his cock. Pleasure coursed through him. She ran her palms back down his inner thighs before bracing on his knees. She was still leaned in, her gaze stamping his lips, and her mischievous smile grew.

"And you can't even look to another to ease your suffering, or they will know you are open to their advances. With you looking like sex itself—dirty, twisted, filthy sex—you won't be able to go anywhere without them hounding you."

She pulled back, and this time he did succumb to her. He couldn't help it. He leaned forward to stay within her heat.

She winked. "I need a drink. I feel like absolute shit, and it seems the hair of the dog is my only choice."

With that, she gracefully turned around and sauntered out of their section, her hips swaying methodically and his cock pounding so hard he wasn't sure there was any blood left in his entire body.

"I get it now." John resumed his seat. "The games, thing. I still think it was wise to choose the girl. When the games get old, she'll know you weren't playing for fun, you were playing for keeps."

Tristan groaned and bent over, bracing his hands on his knees. "I don't think I'm going to last that long before I combust."

"No, probably not."

CHAPTER 35
NESSA

HER BODY WAS so hot it felt like literal flames poured out through her skin. It was probably pushing out all the remaining alcohol from last night. Her core pounded, and her panties were soaked through.

She would've begged. This time, she would've *pleaded* for that big gargoyle to throw her down and take her. To own her. To dominate her in a way that only he could. He would've finally broken her this time…except that if she'd kept going, she would've thrown up all over him. Then fainted. She was *really* regretting her choices from the night before.

"Hello, hello." Jasper caught her as she headed out of the VIP area, looping his arm within hers. "You do not look great. Are you going to yack?"

"I am very seriously thinking about it. Blood flow was hampered a moment ago. It was all down around my Lady Land. I feel faint, and the butterflies are making my stomach dodgy."

"Been there." Jasper nodded in commiseration. "I have definitely been there."

They stopped halfway to the bar. Jasper looked right. Down the way was the sign for the restrooms.

"I'm good." She took her arm from his. "Any word from Indigo?"

The guys hadn't been able to reach her earlier. She was probably off with Edgar somewhere, looking at flowers. His lips twisted, and he shook his head.

"Okay." She steeled herself. She needed to stay in the headspace of the Captain. It helped prop her up. "It's fine. I'll stay a little longer, hope the hair of the dog helps, and then I'll slip out the backdoor."

Niamh and Phil sat in the same place they had yesterday, Nessa remembered that much. Once Niamh found a spot she liked, she didn't usually deviate. Gerard would probably find his way over later when he was done playing host.

She stopped in front of an open stool beside Niamh, the only one vacant in the whole place.

"Is someone here?" She pointed at the empty space.

"No," Phil said. "Niamh keeps scaring everyone away. It's funny."

"It's so easy, like." Niamh took a sip of her cider.

"They're all rattled from the skirmish today. I think they think I'm the phoenix. I'm leaning into it."

Nessa plopped down. "Sorry if I was—"

"Not at all," Niamh interrupted her.

Phil's hair puffed up in a warning. "We don't say sorry for having fun," he growled. "We have it, we pay for the damage, and we move on."

Said the creature who killed anyone that gave him offense.

"Okay." She sagged against the bar. It was easier to just agree.

"Besides, you all provided great entertainment," Phil went on.

"Not to mention you did a great job stirring the pot." Niamh nodded. "Sure, yis were probably responsible for that raid-style push-back up there today. Before that, they just seemed like they might cause a ruckus. This was a full-scale battle. In their opinion, anyway. This was much better. All the taunting you gave was spot on."

"Much." Phil nodded sagely. "It was worth the hassle of changing bars to spread the taunting."

Memories flooded back to her. She'd called out insults, made random judgements, and talked loud and long about the convocation's superiority. Niamh had often started it, and Nessa had run with it, dragging everyone else with her.

"Oh, god," she murmured, putting her head on the bar.

"She drunk again?" The bartender stopped in front of her.

"No." She picked up her head, her gaze momentarily swimming. "I haven't had a drink yet. I'm debating if I really should."

"Probably not," the bartender replied. She didn't remember, because she'd never ordered her own drinks, but it was probably the same guy from last night.

"If we want yer opinion, we'll give it to ya," Niamh told him. "Can't ye see the girl needs the cure? Get her top shelf whiskey with an ice cube, a lemon zest, and a Coke back."

Nessa groaned.

"Make it a couple ice cubes," Niamh amended.

"Did I do anything I will regret when I hear about it?" Nessa asked.

"Probably," Phil said as Niamh said, "Nah."

Nessa groaned again, bracing her head on her forearms. "Do I want to know?"

"Definitely not," Phil replied. "Listen, regret is only for the things you *didn't* do. Last night, you did it all. There's no point in regretting that."

Nessa winced. "All of what?"

"All of nothing, that's what." Niamh took the drink from the bartender. "Here, start with the cola. Get a little sugar in ya."

She sat up and did as instructed. It couldn't hurt.

"Ye stole a few weapons, threatened a few women, and passed out on that gargoyle-monster." Niamh passed over the whiskey once Nessa was done. "All in a day's work. Anyone who says different is lying. Now, go back over to Tristan. Pretend like ya like him. It's good for business."

She didn't know what that meant, and she greatly suspected Niamh was glossing over things, but she didn't have the ability to care right now.

"Okay," she said, shakily standing from the bar and making her way back. Halfway there she would've normally flicked her hair over her shoulder and smiled at the group of guys looking her way. It was the easiest way to make connections that she might need for information down the road. Thankfully, there was no need for that here. She didn't have the ability for it, anyway.

As she neared their section, Gerard's lead enforcer stepped in front of her, blocking her way. "You're Nessa, correct?" he said, looking at her with heated eyes. "Did I remember that correctly?"

From two seconds ago when he must've heard

Gerard use it?

She worked up a smile. "Yes, hello. And you are?"

"Sam, the lead enforcer for Khaavalor."

He said it like that might matter to her.

"Great." She started to edge around him. "You did great today."

He stepped in her way. "Yes, thank you." He put a warm hand on her upper arm. "At first we didn't know—"

Tristan's hand shot out, his body moving from behind her. She hadn't heard him approach! His fingers tightened as he gripped Sam's throat. With a show of strength that widened her eyes, he lifted the lead enforcer into the air with unspeakable menace and zero effort. Sam's face turned red, and his eyes tightened in fear as Tristan leaned in.

"If you touch her again," Tristan said, his nightmare magic soaking the air around him, "I will rip that arm off. Do I make myself clear? She has a claim on her. It belongs to *me*."

He waited for a second while the other gargoyle sputtered and tugged on Tristan's arm. His feet kicked. He dipped his head in an urgent nod.

Tristan flung him away as though he were nothing. The lead enforcer hit the ground and slid past the section's barriers. Nessa's heart pounded in time with the pulse in her core. Holy hell, he was hot when he was possessive and incensed. She saw now why Jessie liked it when Austin got like that.

Tristan slipped his arm around Nessa's shoulders. Electricity danced within the touch, and she leaned in gratefully.

Gerard watched the whole thing with interest, then resumed his conversation with Ulric. He wasn't worried about Tristan manhandling his Guardian.

"Sit." Tristan stopped at his chair.

"It's fine, I can—"

His voice turned deep and rough and commanding. "Sit," he said again.

Damn that heat racing through her. She turned and let him help her into the bar-height seat. He stood beside her, his arm over the back of her chair and his chest partially pointed at her. He leaned in slightly, like a shifter advertising a claim on his mate.

She sighed and relaxed her shoulder against his chest.

"You put on a good show," he murmured, "but you look like you don't feel well."

"I feel much worse than that."

He didn't laugh at her jest. "Do you need me to go find Indigo?"

"They couldn't reach her. It's fine—"

"So help me god, Natasha, if you say it is fine one more time, I will spill red wine on your dress."

She laughed silently as her heart swelled. "I feel like death warmed over, but I just had a Coke, I have what Niamh thinks is the cure, and the second Gerard's back is turned, I am going to sneak out of here. I will be—"

He put up a finger, a warning in his glowing eyes.

She smiled at him. "I will be okay."

"What does Niamh think—" He noticed her untouched drink. "Ah, right. The hair of the dog."

He took the glass and pressed his full lips to the rim. She watched the brown liquid crawl toward his mouth, and then his Adam's apple as it bobbed with his swallow. He nodded, probably to himself.

"Good quality. It might help."

She couldn't bring herself to want that kind of help.

He clearly saw that and kept the drink. He'd finish it.

"You look handsome," she admitted, because he'd made her feel pretty earlier when he couldn't help staring, and because he made her feel cherished now, watching over her and offering to go get help despite being the most important person in the room. "You look equally handsome when you're all battle stained and shirtless."

"I don't smell as good then, though."

She laughed, letting her head fall against him. His arm constricted, wrapping around her shoulders now. His thumb stroked her bare flesh.

"You are a vision," he murmured. "You are equally a vision when you wake up in the morning, all sleepy and groggy, not sure if you're in a good mood or angry that you're awake, wearing a little grin and then a pout."

A memory stirred from last night that she couldn't quite grasp, hazy and blurred. She tilted her head back to look him in the face. His eyes dipped to hers, still glowing brightly, so open. In that quiet, unguarded moment, something deep and raw moved within his gaze, answered by a warmth pulsating in her middle.

"Do you want me to close my eyes?" he murmured, his lips curled at the corners. "You don't seem well enough to go running just now."

"When have you seen me in the morning?"

His gaze traced her features as though he were memorizing every line. "Just the once, and I will remember it always."

She reached up to run two fingers against his raven stubble, drawing them along the underside of his chin.

"Yes, close your eyes," she whispered.

He drank her in for another moment, giving her his entire focus, before doing as she said.

She trailed her fingers to the other side of his jaw

before applying pressure. His face turned slightly and then he bent as she reached up for him. Their lips touched softly at first, electricity running between them, and then more firmly, moving together.

A wave of dizziness overcame her, forcing her to pull back. "I am *really* hungover." She kissed him softly one more time before letting him straighten so she could lean against him again. "I don't remember the last time I was this hungover."

"It's the cheap booze. Mass quantities certainly don't help, but the quality makes everything ten times worse."

He took a sip of her drink—his drink now.

"I can't not know—did I slap you last night?" she blurted.

His lips curled even more. "Twice. Don't talk about it, though, or I'll get hard again—too late."

"Are you super mad and just too nice to say anything?"

"I am super turned on, just like you were when you slapped me. Twice. And when you kissed me soundly." He took another sip of his drink, watching the people in the bar. "Probably not so much when you passed out on me."

She slouched even more. "It really wasn't my finest hour."

He chuckled. "I don't know, I was pretty entertained."

"That's what Phil said." She paused. "And crying. Did I cry?"

"Yes, and you had good reason."

"Which was?"

"Ulric's singing. He sounds like a bullfrog getting choked."

She barked out a laugh before covering her mouth. "That's mean."

"But it's true."

"Yes, it is true, but it is still mean." She slipped an arm around his waist.

He stepped more toward the side of the chair so she could turn toward him and lay her head fully on his chest. His fingers curled a strand of her hair.

She liked this, pretending. There were no strings, no fears, no worry that he'd turn into the monster he claimed to be and hurt her or leave her. She got all the benefits without any of the drawbacks. If only she felt even a tiny bit better, she'd use the mate excuse and let him take her to his room. She'd finally relent and give in to her desires. As it was, she'd perform horribly, probably throw up, and that was not how she wanted to be remembered.

"My timing has always been incredibly bad, did you

know that?" she asked as Aurora walked toward them with zero giddy-up in her step.

"I did not know that. And what should I do with that fascinating information?"

"Put it in your pipe and smoke it."

"Hey." Aurora's attempt at a smile didn't work. She looked like she'd just seen something horrific. "How are you faring?"

"Probably about how I look." Nessa grimaced at her.

Aurora's brows pinched together. "You look amazing, like you're just about to let Tristan fly you out of here. Why do you look so amazing when you feel like I do?"

"Firstly, you also look amazing—"

"Except for the dark circles under your eyes," Tristan said, "and the violence you're promising whenever someone says something you don't like. Like I just did. Didn't you get Jessie to heal you?"

"Jessie had important things to do earlier today, and I was *supposed* to just stand around and watch. I was prepared to handle it. I did *not* know that we'd have to run through the city and act menacing, nor did I know I would throw up in my beast form. I learned a lot of things this morning. None of them were pleasant. By the time it was over, Jessie was too tired to ask, and Indigo had stuff to do."

"We thank you for your service," Tristan said. "As messy as it sometimes is. Someone needs to call your dad and tell him you're having too much fun."

Aurora rolled her eyes, turning to face the bar. She did a bad job of hiding the smirk.

"Second, if I look amazing, it is because of Mr. Tom," Nessa finished. "He was in charge of makeup and picking out the dress. When I tried to take over and do my own makeup, he told me that my time would be better spent taking notes."

"Note to self, Mr. Tom will make you look great but feel rotten." Aurora laughed, so rare that she should do so. "Anyway, I was going to—ah crap." She turned back to us, her eyes squeezed tightly. "Damn it."

Gerard walked toward the newcomer with his arms outstretched. "Unbreakable Sue, you made it!"

Nessa felt laughter bubble up. "Unbreakable Sue—good one."

Sue stopped walking to chat with Gerard.

John, seated beside Nessa, had been silent and minding his own business all this time. "What's the problem?" he finally asked.

Aurora didn't get a chance to answer, and then she didn't need to. Sue walked up to their cluster. Stopping beside Aurora, he looked down at her.

"Susan," she said by way of greeting, straightening.

She lifted her drink to her lips but didn't take a sip, lowering it again. In a flat voice, she said, "Nice to see you."

"I see you've crawled out of your hidey-hole," he replied evenly.

Her lips tightened.

"What's this now?" Tristan asked.

Sue looked at her expectantly.

Her chest barely rose with her inhale. "After the third time I threw up, I figured it would be better for the pack image if I just crawled into a hedge and stayed there until it was over."

Tristan laughed, and John looked away to hide his grin. Sue's stare did not waver, but Nessa didn't miss the twinkle of mirth in his eyes. He'd loosened up a lot in her absence, no longer needing Nessa as a lifeguard. No longer needing her at all, really.

And strangely, for how much she'd wanted him at one time, she hadn't thought about him like that since she'd left. Not in any real way. They were too different, and they both knew it. She was only a sunny day to make him smile. That wasn't the real her. She existed in the shadows by trade and the darkness by necessity. And maybe also by choice.

A hazy memory drifted to the surface from last night. Of Tristan's heartfelt speech, splashes and chops of words cobbled together.

You have always had a choice. You chose to be a hero. To do the dirty work. Not everyone has the courage. The darkness doesn't define us. It doesn't erase the good parts of us. We are the best heroes because we don't need to walk in the light to enact justice. Jessie needs people who aren't afraid of the night. Who else will battle the creatures that exist there but us?

She looked up at Tristan, drawing his notice, her eyes shining with feeling. How much of that was an actual memory and how much she'd implanted because she'd needed to hear it, she couldn't say. But the root, the sentiment, had been his, said to her. *That* she remembered.

"Did I cry because you called me a hero?" she whispered.

His eyes softened. "You *are* a hero, little deathwatch angel. You've proven it many times over."

"And so has Edgar," Aurora cut in, raising her brows. "Edgar is a hero, and I crawl into bushes to throw up in peace. Okay? Now we all know where we stand."

John started chuckling helplessly, his face still turned away to hide his smile. Sue didn't join in, though. He was looking at Nessa, his eyes intense. His gaze zipped to Tristan's thumb, roaming over her bare shoulder, and took in her position, snugged against Tristan's chest. When they connected eyes again, she barely caught his subtle, approving nod. They'd always been best as friends, and despite not trusting Tristan in the beginning, now he approved of the big gargoyle-monster. Another little piece of her resistance melted away.

"Yes, it is good to be a hero, some of the time."

Everyone jumped, and John damn near fell off his stool.

Edgar stepped from the shadows nearby. Not one person had realized he was there. He held a little blue pouch in his spindly fingers, tucked in at his stomach. His suit was made for a shorter lady, judging by the ample room in the breast and lack of room in the groin.

"And sometimes, to be a hero, you should start by throwing up in a bush." He smiled at Aurora. "So, you see? You're on your way."

"Somehow that doesn't help at all," Aurora murmured.

"Here you go, Al-Joe." He held out the little blue pouch. There was a picture of a crocheted whale on the front. "You sit there with your mind working and your hands idle. Many hands make a devil's playground, as they say."

"Almost got that one." Nessa giggled. "Where'd you

get the suit?"

Edgar looked down at himself, still holding the pouch. "Oh, Cyra let me borrow it on account of her creating the problem that ruined mine. Mine had holes cut into it with garden shears. Gnome accident, you know. She tried to hogtie them with the clothesline to keep them put while she rounded up the others, and one got free. It freed the others, as they do. My suit, which was hanging on the clothesline, was collated drainage, she said."

"Collateral damage," Nessa supplied for the others.

All of them were staring at Edgar with bewildered expressions.

"And this was on Ivy House soil, I hope?" Nessa lifted an eyebrow.

"Oh, yes, don't worry. I sometimes know better than to bring gnomes in my luggage. Before I left, I put a flower next to one of the gnome nests. With any luck, the flower will greatly reduce the population."

"And if our luck runs out?" she asked.

"The gnomes might befriend the flower and convince it to turn on us." Edgar smiled with crimson-stained canines. "I have high hopes the flowers don't fall for their tricks."

"Well." Nessa beamed. "That explains that. What've you got there?"

Edgar held the pouch a little higher. "I thought Al-Joe might like to hone his craft."

"Al-Joe?" Nessa prompted.

"Yes." He passed the pouch to a very unimpressed former alpha shifter. "If you get good enough, I might let you in on the secret of the doily."

He skulked back into the shadows.

"What is it?" Aurora asked, turning to make sure Edgar was really gone.

"It's a crochet kit for beginners. It's a little whale." John put it under his chair. "I have nieces. I thought one of them might like it."

"Practice makes perfect," Edgar said, his voice drifting out of the shadows.

"He's going to give me nightmares." John shivered. "I saw it in a store and thought I might try it to pass the time. I regret that now."

Phil would probably be fine with that use of regret.

"Al-Joe?" John asked.

Aurora snapped her fingers. "I've got it. I—and Susan, too, who really should know better given he is a beta—keep catching ourselves when we address you as alpha. Then we say your name. Edgar didn't grab the right name." Her face lost color. She put two fingers to her temple. "I'm understanding that vampire. That can't be good. It's time for bed. I'm going to sneak out the back."

Nessa straightened and climbed off the chair with Tristan's help. "Thank God. I thought I'd be the first to duck out."

"I'd go out the front." Sue took a sip of his drink. "Gerard just went to sit with Niamh at the back."

"Good point." Nessa turned to say goodbye to Tristan, but he was finishing the drink.

He stepped forward. "Natasha, I'll fly you home. Sue, I'll be back. There's a couple things we should go over for tomorrow. They might try to play hard ball, and I have some ideas on subtle ways to counter."

Sue nodded and said goodnight to Aurora and Nessa.

Once outside in the refreshing chill, Aurora stopped Nessa and Tristan. "Can you guys take my clothes? I want to shift and run home."

They did and stepped away from the door so Tristan could undress. The moonlight bathed his broad chest and defined muscles. He folded everything and handed them to Nessa.

He shifted and towered over her before he scooped her up. Pressure dragged at her as he blasted into the sky, power and might.

She snuggled closer to him as the frigid wind rushed by. It was pleasant, playing his mate. She liked the dangerous security of it. She wondered if she'd ever come around to someone who didn't like playing games and wanted something for real.

Meanwhile, she needed to come up with more new names for the-shifter-formally-known-as-Brochan.

CHAPTER 36

JESSIE

"WHATEVER HE SAYS, take it in stride," Tristan coached as we headed out the hotel door toward the waiting vans to take us to Evan's house. "He wants to be *in*, that is fairly obvious, but he is new, and none of his people were actually picked by him. They might have bad blood from the previous meetings or from Withor talking bad about you. Hell, they might be pissed you essentially chucked Withor out of here."

I nodded and put a sound-proof bubble around us as Tristan and Sue climbed in first. I sat in next, and Austin took the seat beside me.

"Even if Evan is ecstatic and leaping at the chance to join, take it in stride," Tristan advised. "There might be some negotiations and contracts down the line, and for that, you don't want to appear too eager."

That I already knew. Nothing like dealing with salesmen working on commission to quell any sort of showy excitement when one was trying to haggle.

"If they *do* have bad news," Tristan said, "then it goes like this… If Evan is direct and open and speaks respectfully to you and Alpha Steele, then answer and engage in kind. If he is vague or his people are talking, it opens the floor for my input. I'll jump in. There are a great many ways experienced cairn leaders give subtle digs and soft warnings, and Nelson was great at it. I know the tricks. I can teach you eventually but time is short. As you know."

Austin threaded his fingers through mine, and calm flooded through our bonds. He was confident.

"If they pass us up, don't worry," Tristan went on. "Patty is working incredibly hard behind the scenes. The battle from yesterday is everywhere. Her contacts are firing hard. She's spreading rumors of what you pay Guardians and all the perks, which I've told you, are substantial. She is making us look very good, and the pictures coming from the battle and celebratory bar scene last night are making us look better. Smaller and mid-sized cairns are very interested. A 'no' here is not the end of the world. We have ten times the options than before we showed up. Whatever happens in this meeting, we are solid. We've cemented ourselves as a force to be reckoned with, okay? This trip was essential, and whatever answer we get, we've still pulled it off."

I didn't need the pep talk this time. I didn't need the Ivy House watch, even though it was currently tucked into the pocket of my pantsuit. After our first meeting and the battle yesterday, I knew our worth. I knew how my team stacked up against ordinary gargoyles.

In short, we were exceptional. Our team was the best there was. I would no longer suffer anyone to question that.

"I'd say it's about time," Ivy House drawled, *"but haven't we been here before?"*

Honestly, I had no idea. Probably. This job seemed to have milestone after milestone. We'd conquer one thing, and another challenge would present itself. Each would get harder and harder.

That was necessary, I supposed. If things stayed the same, we'd never grow in magic or as a team. Silver lining.

As before, the door opened when we reached it. The butler stepped away, revealing Evan standing nearby in a suit. His face was grim.

I took a deep breath, remembering the assurances I'd *just* been thinking. We were amazing. They were lucky to know us. They were fools to say, 'no'," etcetera, etcetera.

"Jessie. Austin." He offered us a slight bow, which was odd for him. "Please. Come this way."

He led us past the sculpture as before but didn't head to the den. Instead, he took us to a room at the back of the house. One entire wall was glass, offering a breathtaking view of the mountains beyond.

"Sit. Please." He indicated a couch that faced the view and took a chair on our right. "Tristan." He pointed at the chair opposite the coffee table from him. "Suuue." He elongated the vowel, as though not quite confident that was the right name.

I felt Tristan's confusion through our connection.

"You'll notice that I don't have my Guardians present." Evan braced his elbows on the arms of the chair and steepled his fingers. "I'm not standing on ceremony for this meeting. I'm going to get right to it, is that okay with you?"

Austin didn't move a muscle. I nodded for the both of us. I'd been trained to be polite all my life. Some things were hard to uproot.

"*Try*," Ivy House said.

I barely stopped from rolling my eyes.

"What you two are doing with the convocation is unprecedented in the gargoyle culture," Evan went on. "The older members among my advisors don't trust it. More than that, they don't like it. It is too much change for them. Too much instability." He paused, his eyes delving into mine. "Too much risk. They worry about aligning with a situation like yours, we'll say. Ultimately, they worry about losing status."

He crossed an ankle over his knee.

"When I read those letters you sent to my cousin, Jessie, I had a feeling about you. I had a very strong gut reaction. When I got that sculpture, the feeling grew. And when you walked in yesterday, carrying a pocket watch out of time—thank you for allowing me to see that, by the way—my heart started racing. *You* are unprecedented, Jessie. A female gargoyle feels like something out of time, like that sculpture, and the watch you carry. To me, they feel symbolic. *You* feel symbolic."

He entwined his fingers in his lap.

"A female gargoyle is supposed to unite her kind," he continued. "So many take this to mean uniting the gargoyles. Uniting our Guardians, more specifically." He shook his head. "You are uniting *all* of us. Guardians, yes, but also the garhettes, like the barista at the coffee shop who chats to your green haired Jane. The non-Guardian gargoyles, like the bartender who now respects shifters and basajaunak and even the puca because they kept the drunks in line. The people on the sidelines yesterday, who are usually left out, but felt like part of the action because the ground force chased them around. Who saw a man being flown through the air by a gargoyle so he could help protect his people. This kind of thing speaks to us, Jessie. Austin. It's inclusive of not just our fighters, but of our community. It is *that* which makes me feel the power of your position and your role. It solidifies that I was right, they were wrong, nah-nah-nah-nah-nah."

I felt my brows draw together with that last bit, surprised that such a serious and heartfelt speech had taken a comical turn.

"I have ten advisors. Five are all in. Two are on the fence. Three threatened to quit if I entertained this folly. They've been fired." He shrugged. "Honestly, it was a pleasure. They've pushed back on everything I've done since the beginning, including sending Withor away."

I felt my eyebrows lift. No one in the room moved.

Evan nodded. "We're in. My people want to be part of something bigger, and I feel the rightness in this. We've sequestered ourselves onto lonely mountains, as your people like to say, and isolated ourselves from the rest of the world. From each other, even. We *need* to be united. We need to step back into the world of the living." His gaze swung to Austin. "I want to talk more about the production cairns and selling to a larger market. Before we do that, I want to see your operations. If you are half as good as you say you are, I'll want to discuss terms, logistics, and how to get my blown glass into every house in America."

Austin pulled his hand from my thigh where it had been resting and placed it along the back of the couch. He liked Evan's ambitiousness. It spoke to his own.

"That can be arranged," he said simply.

Evan nodded, focused on me now. "I would like to offer you my sincerest apologies for some of the questions I asked you in our first meeting. I was trying to…" He tightened his lips, clearly searching for the words. "My former advisors wanted certain guarantees from you personally, not grasping how co-leadership worked. And maybe I didn't grasp it, either. It does you credit that your…betas threw it back in my face and identified your importance in a way that my former advisors will probably never understand. Which is fine. They were due to retire, anyway. Their time would be better spent in front of a fire with their feet up, or at their grandkid's flying lessons."

I waved it away. "They were fair questions."

He shook his head. "No, they weren't. They were ignorant questions, asked by someone not accustomed to actual battle and certainly not understanding the very real war. We only play at fighting, something you made all too evident yesterday. Your leadership will never be called into question in this cairn again, nor in my presence, without my speaking up on your behalf. I wanted you to know that."

"Thank you." I smiled at him. "That's really nice of you to say."

He twiddled his thumbs, and this time he looked at Tristan.

"Nelson is the biggest fool I have ever heard of for letting you go. I don't care where you came from, you will *always* have a friend in this cairn, and a standing job offer." He leaned toward Tristan marginally. "Did you hear me about the standing job offer?"

Tristan grinned. "Nelson letting me go was the best outcome possible. And no, I'm good where I am. I leveled up because I have shifters around me who are impeccable in their battle acumen."

"You don't have to use big words to impress me." He smiled as he glanced at Austin and Sue. "That stands to reason, though. Flying in uniform is one thing—we can see each other to correct positioning. But you guys had perfect formation while running around buildings and converging seemingly at random. That is a level I don't think most gargoyles realize. I'm still a little baffled by it, honestly."

"They have exemplary training," Tristan said.

"They must." Evan nodded. "There are many impressive facets to your visit, Jessie, Austin. My cairn noticed the most spectacular of them." His eyes narrowed, a grin pulling at his lips. "But it's the little details that I am most impressed with. Your team has learned gargoyle culture so well that they use that culture against us."

I frowned at him and glanced at Tristan. What was Evan talking about?

Evan grinned at Tristan. "I heard about the capes, and about the disrespect towards my gargoyles. I couldn't, for the life of me, figure out why your gargoyles would stand for it. You weren't just pissing on us. Your team was pissing on their own. I wondered if there was dissension in the ranks, so to speak."

I released a breath and leaned into Austin's side. Niamh had visited after the skirmish yesterday to explain what they'd been doing. Honestly, it was a great idea, and I understood why it was kept from me beforehand. Had I known we'd started the discourse, I would've tried to calm it down or at least take it easy on them. We wouldn't have impressed them to the level we had.

Evan shook his head, his gaze still on Tristan. "Very clever, sir. Now, about that job opening..."

"Wasn't me." Tristan leaned back and entwined his fingers on his stomach. "That would be our puca. She has a knack for finding pressure points, and she is good at poking those points to get a reaction."

"The puca?" Evan put his foot back down on the floor. "I'll be damned. Well, she's done her homework. Nice touch to show that your people can hang like ours, drunken violence and all, and that in your crew, different creatures can get along and have fun together."

"I've settled the bill for the table, by the way," I murmured. "Sorry."

"All's fair with debauchery, didn't you know?" Evan laughed, waving that away. "Another little detail is Patty. Where do I get such a marketing expert? She didn't want a job, either."

I laughed. "Ulric sold her as someone with a lot of connections."

"And she's made a lot more here, it seems. I knew she was buttering me up on your behalf, but I didn't realize she was farming me for information that she'd then feed back to me to prove a point. Or post on social media to crowdsource various reactions to attempt to sway me."

"Did it work?" Tristan asked.

Evan smiled. "Not with me, but I will say that I'm surprised I didn't have to fire a few more advisors."

"And why are you so open-minded about so much change?" Austin asked. "You could lose status for this. Your people might want this now, but what about down the road? This isn't a slam dunk for you."

"A what?" Evan asked. Apparently they didn't have basketball. We'd already realized they didn't have TVs.

"This isn't a home run—"Austin cut off. Evan probably wouldn't know that one, either.

"It's not a guarantee," Sue helped. I pointed at Sue, nodding.

Evan put out his hands. "Gerard hasn't lost an iota of status from joining your convocation. He's actually *gained* Guardians and garhettes. No one talks about the garhettes, but they are essential to keep a community thriving. If they are happy, we are all happy. If they aren't happy, life is a living hell I wouldn't wish on anyone."

He and Tristan both laughed. Apparently it was funny because it was true.

"His cairn is thriving and expanding," Evan went on, "which means he'll be able to pick up another production cairn or two and bring in more money. My advisors didn't see the correlation."

"They didn't want to see it," Tristan said. "Nelson in Gimerel has similar advisors, and they *definitely* do not like change."

"And they will get left behind because of it. In answer to your question, Austin, I *do* think this is a slam run." He'd gotten close. "I think we'll grow. I think we'll stop caring so much about status in a stagnant community and start caring more about stepping into the twenty-first century. I mean to escort us into the future. Ambitious, I know. Pompous even. But I trust in my gut, and that is what it's saying."

He'd chosen the side of winners, and he wasn't looking back. Excitement and pride in my people filled me. Austin lowered his arm from the back of the couch to my shoulders, feeling it through the bonds.

Evan looked between us, drumming his fingers on his thighs. "Are you sufficiently bolstered? Because this is the part where I ask for the world."

"You're either going to be really well liked in the gargoyle community," Tristan said, "or torn from your position and made an outcast."

"Well liked, obviously. I can't make such grand claims as I just did and not think the world of myself." Evan laughed. "In order for this to work, we need to be able to easily integrate into your fliers at a moment's notice. Gerard said you had ample time to train for the last battle. For the next battle, we might not have any time at all. We will need to show up and know how to work together."

I nodded, because that was entirely true. Evan was proving to be incredibly intelligent and forward think-ing, with his eyes on the future.

"I would like to send my lead enforcer and another

couple of my best Guardians to train with you. I ask that you teach them how to integrate into your team, and that you instruct them on how to teach others. We have good fighters, but not necessarily good teachers."

"Done," Austin said, "with the condition that they answer to our authority. They will not be equal to Tristan or Jess. They will be led by them. In town, they will follow the rules or answer to Sue or myself. They shouldn't bother turning up unless this is understood. We'll make them suffer for it and send them back."

"Absolutely." Evan nodded. "The other *humble* request is that you don't take all my Guardians and garhettes. Tristan, I'm sure, has told you that our community rob personnel from each other. Gimerel has been torn to shreds with the amount of people leaving."

I glanced at Austin. Patty had mentioned an influx of new people into our territory, but said we'd go over details after we were done here. Obviously, the influx she was referring to were gargoyles and garhettes. It was starting to feel like we'd been away too long.

"Obviously, if people really want to go, I will not stop them," Evan went on. "I just ask that you don't actively recruit."

"We won't," I assured him.

"Shifters look down on that practice," Austin said. "It's nothing to extend the courtesy here. Get to something I want to say no to."

Evan laughed and twisted a little button on the lamp beside him on an end table. "Don't worry, that'll come when we talk about the business of the production cairns."

"There's one issue, though." I paused as someone came in with a pitcher of water and a tray of fruit. Apparently, we'd covered the hard-hitting stuff and were getting into the more relaxed portion of the meeting. "We will be on the road for the discernible future. Austin needs to—"

Austin reached over with his free hand and braced it against my thigh to stop me. "I was going to tell you this when we were getting ready to leave as a surprise. There's been a change of plans. I'm not going to continue the shifter tour like some sort of door-to-door salesman. Like someone begging them to join a cause that will save their lives."

"What are you suggesting?" Tristan asked, but I already knew from the arrogant sparkle in Austin's eyes.

"You're going to go full peacock, aren't you." I smirked at him.

He shook his head at me, warmth now competing with the arrogance. "Not me, *us*. You're going to dazzle them with the riches and history of Ivy House, while I strut my posh businesses and fancy toys in front of them. Then together, we are going to create a spectacle of power and ferociousness that will widen their eyes and make them check their boxers. I will not beg for their time. Not anymore. I will force them to beg for mine, and I'll do it without mercy."

"An Alpha Conclave," Sue murmured. "There hasn't been one of those in…"

"Over a hundred years," Austin said with a nod. "Mimi was at the last one. The way she tells it, it devolved into chaos. Too many big egos and far too much power and need to dominate."

"There's a reason it hasn't been put on since," Sue said.

"Yes." Austin got a little more comfortable. "Most of the alpha network wants to see me fail, and some of them, especially those jealous of Kingsley and my family, want to see me fail in a huge way. They won't resist the invitation because they'll want to see it in person. They'll want the stories from this. It's the one way to get them *all* to come to me. I'm going to invite every powerful alpha to one place, and I'm going to harness Jess's and my team's power to control it."

Goosebumps rose along my flesh. "Not just shifters, though." It felt as if Fate lodged a heavy weight in my middle. Talk about gut feelings. "All the alphas. The gargoyles, basajaunak—invite them all. Let's show the shifters they're not the biggest and baddest creatures that walk this earth. And then, when we dominate, we'll go after the mages once and for all."

CHAPTER 37
JOHN

THE JET HIT the landing strip, sending the plates and trays sliding forward as the plane braked. Austin caught a tray headed for Jessie's lap, but another slid onto the floor, scattering truffles.

Tristan bent and scooped up the truffles trying to roll down the aisle. "Five second rule." He popped one into his mouth and dropped the rest into his empty pocket. The other pocket was already filled with a different kind of chocolate. The guy was like Willy Wonka.

A glass fell over in the back. Other trays were grabbed and John—who everyone was now calling Aljoe because they thought Edgar's logic was hilarious—looked at all the snacks in utter bewilderment.

Why would anyone think all this food, littering every square inch of available space, was a good idea? Past mistakes or no, this was beyond rationality.

Then again, wasn't that the very nature of Jessie's crew? No rules. No logic. It was just pure chaos. No pack would ever survive run like this.

The mind-boggling thing was that it worked. And honestly, it worked really well. John was pure astonishment.

"I really do need to tell Mr. Tom that this is all way too much," Jessie whispered to Austin. John assumed Mr. Tom couldn't hear. The butler was sitting a few seats back without a table to monitor. That couldn't have been by coincidence.

Ulric leaned across the aisle. "Yes, you do. It's one thing being covered in a mountain of cheese and another eating the stale leftovers from these flights. One I can tolerate. The rest I guilt-eat so as not to waste, and I am not a fan."

"Would you have the miss go hungry?" Mr. Tom asked Ulric with a sniff, who'd been too loud by far.

Ulric's eyebrows pinched together, and he centered himself back in his seat.

John, sitting across from him, grinned. The whole group was honestly hilarious. He couldn't remember ever laughing so much in his life. Or seeing such powerful shifters being so expressive.

Mind-boggling, all of this. He felt like he'd stepped through into a different realm where everything was upside-down.

They disembarked from the plane and headed toward passenger and cargo vans, not unlike what Evan had sent for them in the cairn. The land here was much different, though, tucked into the Sierra foothills in California. The air was dry, the sun warm, and a few puffy white clouds scudded through the blue sky. Green trees crept up the mountains in the distance, the height far less than John had grown used to.

Unlike when heading to the cairn, here no one dallied. Everyone helped the attendants grab luggage, and they walked briskly to the transportation. Everyone was happy to be home.

A wave of nervousness rolled through John as he followed. He kept his unease at being in a new place and possibly his new home tucked in tight.

"Hey." Aurora drifted in beside him. Trust her to read him when no one else could. Except for maybe Miss-Nothing Sue. "I meant to ask you. How did Edgar come to have that little whale you're making?"

Ulric and Jasper weren't long in joining them, always ready for a laugh and to make him feel comfortable. They really were a close-knit group. Battle would do that, and given the sort of cohesive fighting both the air and land crews exhibited in that cairn, they were well versed in fighting and working together. That had been a level of harmony John had never seen before, and he'd thought his pack was one of the best. Talk about humble pie.

"It was on my nightstand in the cairn," John replied as they loaded into a van.

"He was your roommate?" Ulric asked, aghast.

"No."

"Ah." Ulric started shaking with laughter. "And I assume your room automatically locked like everyone else's?"

"Yes."

Ulric shook harder. "And I also assume you didn't confront him about it because you really didn't want to know the particulars of why that vampire was poking around your room without a key to get in?"

"I was trying not to think about it at all, actually."

The laughter spilled over, joined by Jasper and Aurora.

"What's so funny?" Nessa asked, poking her head into the van with a bright smile. They'd stayed in the cairn one additional day for the leaders to hash out a few things, and now today, Nessa was back to normal. She was a beautiful solar flare masking the magma that caused it, radiant and dangerous at the same time. Tristan was a lucky man.

"Aljoe is learning to ignore Edgar." Ulric filled her

in about the whale.

"Ah." She nodded and scooted over as Sebastian filed in after her, the two never far from each other. "He's just checking things out, making sure Aljoe isn't dangerous or a threat to Jessie or anyone else. Don't mind him. When he clears you, he'll go back to being his normal weird."

"His normal weird isn't much better," Sebastian muttered as Sue sat into the front passenger seat. Sebastian closed the door and the van got underway.

Nessa turned in her seat to look back at John. "Did you get that whale done, though?"

John looked out the window. "No. I've been watching you guys, deciding if this is a good fit for me. I'm still not sure."

Nessa shrugged, turning to face forward again. "You need to settle wherever you feel comfortable. I regret to inform you, however, that you do fit here. With us, I mean. It's a shock to realize you're the type of person who would ignore an addled vampire who goes through your things and then brings you a bit of arts and crafts to finish while in a bar having drinks, but here you are. Welcome. Sorry for your loss of sanity. It's all downhill from here."

Everyone started laughing, except for Sebastian.

"It's true, though," Sebastian muttered. "When you

start having meaningful discussions with that vampire, you're on your way out. After that, you just hold on and hope for the best."

Aurora put her hand on her face and leaned forward with a groan. "I'm blaming it on the hangover. I'm never drinking again."

Everyone laughed again, and it was a wonder Edgar himself didn't pop up from the back and invite John into the madness.

Or maybe he didn't need to, John decided. He was already there.

SOMETIME LATER, THE van turned onto a street with a sign that said NO OUTLET. Houses lined the quiet street. At the end, set back on a large lot and cloaked in a strange shadow despite the sun and clear sky, sprawled a massive gothic structure, three stories high with spires and a pitched roof. There was so much to focus on that John couldn't focus much at all. At the top of the house, a single light glowed in what must be an attic.

"Home again, home again." Nessa bent to look out the windshield. "Hello, Ivy House."

"I hope it doesn't hold a grudge," Sebastian murmured. "I have a lot of work to do. I don't need it killing me the second I get into the crystal room."

"Something you should note," Sue said to John, "the

house is sentient. Once you step on its grounds, it knows where you are, it hears you, and it has numerous ways to kill you. Also, the people connected with the house—most of Jessie's crew—also know where you are. The gnomes are dangerous, though we're still not sure if they're deadly. They will, however, hack off something. The dolls will only kill you if you wrong Jessie or Ivy House in some way. Those aren't the only horrors of that house. Mind yourself."

John felt his jaw go slack. "*What?*"

✧ ✧ ✧

JESSIE

JOHN LOOKED SHELLSHOCKED, standing stock-still as everyone bustled around him, exiting vans and grabbing luggage and calling for rides to come get them. After months of being away, everyone was happy to be home. Except for John, who didn't have one.

"You okay?" I asked him.

"I gave him a quick rundown about the house," Sue said with a little grimace. "I should've probably broken it to him gently."

Ah.

"It's fine." Nessa patted John's arm. It was sweet how welcoming everyone had been, trying to help him find a place to settle. His camp in the woods had been more than a little dismal. "You'll get used to it. It's not as weird as it sounds. Really."

Sebastian gave her a funny look.

"What?" she asked him. "You're the one looking forward to working in the crystal room again."

"That doesn't mean the house isn't as weird as it sounds. It is *exactly* as weird as it sounds, and ten times more dangerous."

I put my hand on John's arm to bring his focus back to me. "Would you like something to eat or some coffee? Mr. Tom is headed in now to figure something out, though I'm sure he'll have to go to the store. You're welcome to come in and relax. We have a lot of quiet sitting rooms. You're also welcome to take a room here until you find a place to settle, if you'd like."

"Take the room," Ulric said, and Jasper threw John a thumbs-up as he moved toward the house. "Mr. Tom is always making food and doing laundry and cleaning and all the things you won't want to do yourself. It's great."

"Here. I'll show you around." I tugged John's arm to get him moving as Austin got on the phone to check in with the shifters in town. We had a lot to catch up on.

The grass was still vibrantly green, though wild and in desperate need of mowing.

"We can't hire normal gardeners," I told John. "Ivy House doesn't like strangers. She runs them off."

"I'll get to it post-waste," Edgar told me as he hurried by. "Don't you worry, Jessie. I'll have this handled in no time."

The tall grasses rose along the path leading to the front door. I squeezed John's arm.

"What's the matter?" he asked, clueing in to my nervousness immediately.

"Nothing. If you see garden shears poke out of the grass, though, run."

As I said it, the grass up the way wiggled in an unnatural way.

"That better be a flower," I mumbled, urging John on. "It's fine. We'll make it."

A gnome's head popped out with a wide smile and little white teeth. A gardening trowel pushed through the grass, aimed in our direction in a threatening manner.

I stopped in my tracks.

"I got it!" Cyra knocked me into John as she ran by. "I got you, you little devil!" She blasted fire at it.

It issued a high-pitched scream and ducked back into the grass. Fire blazed a path after it.

"You better run!" Cyra sprinted into the grass after it, spreading fire as she went.

"What in the—"

I yanked John forward. "Don't talk, *act*!"

He didn't delay, running after me to the front door. Before we got there, another gnome popped out, holding a weeder pike like a sword, and charged.

"Oh, crap!" I blasted it with a spell. The spell bounced off somehow and ricocheted back. "Watch out!"

I barely put up a shield in time to cover me and John. The force of the spell knocked me into him. He was off-balance, and we tumbled into the grasses at the other side.

"Go, go, go!" I scrambled to my feet.

"Hurry!" Nessa was there, yanking me to standing. "Get out of there. They're ambushing us!"

Of all the times for Patty to have taken the long way home to visit friends. She was the only one, besides Cyra and her fire, who could make these little suckers run.

Garden shears chopped at the grass next to John's leg. He received a nick and jerked away. Leaping to his feet, he moved so fast his limbs practically blurred.

He grabbed me and Nessa around the waist and took off running. Clearly, this alpha had some serious protective instincts, and the gnomes had just put him into survival mode.

"I got it!" Cyra erupted through burning grasses to fire-bomb the place we'd just vacated. "C'mere, you little bastards."

We reached the porch at a sprint. John half-dropped Nessa, making her stagger to the side, so he could grab the door handle. He turned and pushed to run inside. The door acted like it was unlocked, but did not open, and he slammed into the hard surface. Ivy House was messing with him.

I overrode her, feeling her laughter, and made the door swing open. Fire raged behind me, and I let it. Ivy House could handle that. She's the one that kept hiding the gnomes from my detection. I needed to find a way to override that, too.

The cool interior greeted me like a long-lost friend. I sighed in relief, but the moment was short-lived.

"Damn it, Ivy House!"

Dolls teetered down the steps wearing horrible plastic smiles. "Mama," one repeated, over and over.

"What in all that is holy—?" John uttered behind me.

The mural on the arch changed to a lion running through the countryside, chased by an army of gnomes and dolls.

"That's not funny." I frowned at it and directed John to the large sitting room on the right. "She's just messing with you."

"She?"

"The house. Don't show a reaction, and she'll get bored."

"*Probably not*," Ivy House said.

I rolled my eyes. "We can get you a room at the hotel or try to find a room someone is renting in town. We're low on housing right now, unfortunately, but there's bound to be something. We're working on the housing issue, too. But we have plenty of space here."

Fred walked in, ashen-faced and wearing a lopsided smile. "I don't know what was scarier, the gnome attack or the fire." She plopped down next to John on the couch. "We made it, though." She smiled at John. "Cool house, right? There is so much cool stuff in here. Ivy House lets me wander around because I'm helping all of you. Come on, I'll show you some stuff. I saw you checking out the buildings in that cairn. You'll love this. Come on."

She plucked at his arm, and surprisingly, he slowly rose and followed her like a lost lamb.

CHAPTER 38
AUSTIN

THE SMALL SITTING room at the back of the house felt like a welcome relief after all the traveling and tension from the road. He sank into the couch with a tired sigh.

"There you are, sir." Mr. Tom came in with a plate holding two sandwiches and a bag of chips. "This'll tide you over for now. We'll have a big roast tonight with all the fixings now that I have a proper kitchen with space and appliances that actually work." He eyed the scotch. "Do you need me to bring you the bottle?"

Usually, Austin hated when the gargoyle waited on him, but right now, he welcomed it.

"It's fine, Mr. Tom, I can manage. Thanks."

Mr. Tom closed the door behind him with a click. Silence surrounded him as he took a sip of his drink and breathed out another sigh, this time one of relief. He'd been slow to adjust to Ivy House, only moving in when it was renovated and more to his tastes. But now, it felt distinctly like home, especially because he could feel Jess upstairs taking a shower, safe in the confines of the house.

Two fast knocks and the door opened again, admitting Mr. Tom, who was clearly irritated. "Apparently former alphas don't know that *retiring* means people are no longer at their beck and call," he said, his wings fluttering. "Aljoe is *insisting* on seeing you, sir. Shall I tell him you have more important things to do than coddle a grown man old enough to look after himself?"

"No, Mr. Tom, thank you. Let him come in."

Mr. Tom narrowed his eyes at Austin before sweeping his gaze to the drink and food and then around the area. "You see, sir, what happens when you don't consume so much sugar? No wild mood swings and unexplained tempers. Now do you see why I limit you?" He sniffed and turned for the door.

Home, sweet home.

John walked in a moment later, glancing back down the hall at a retreating Mr. Tom.

"Before being in your company"—John closed the door behind him—"I would never believe an alpha would allow someone to speak to him like that gargoyle just did. I would never believe *I* would allow someone to speak to me as he so often does, or that I would ignore a vampire letting himself into my room to wander around, or let the mate of a powerful alpha comfort me by touching my arm."

He surveyed the room with interest, obviously wanting to look around, but instead walked to the loveseat facing Austin. He noticed the food.

"I apologize," he said. "I won't take much of your time."

"Not at all. You'll forgive my casualness. This is a room Jess and I wind down in."

"Of course." He leaned back, easing himself into relaxing. "I appreciate what you are trying to do for me. There isn't another alpha in the world who would. They might offer me a place to reside, but they'd ask something from me to get it. Advice on running a territory, maybe, or training."

He paused. It sounded like he'd decided not to stay. Austin waited for him to go on.

"You haven't asked," he said. "Neither has Jessie. I can tell you won't."

"Correct. I sought out a rogue, looking to offer help. Nothing has changed."

John nodded in agreement. "I swore I would never join a pack again, not even one run by my sisters."

Austin continued to wait, no energy to feel much at all.

"The thing is…" John fell silent as the door opened again, and Mr. Tom entered, carrying another scotch.

"If you insist on hanging around, you might as well *try* to relax a little," he said. "We can't have you making the whole house jumpy. We've got that horrible Irishwoman for that."

He handed John the drink, fluttered his wings, and left again.

John stared at it blankly for a moment and then started chuckling. "This is actually just the thing." He took a sip and relaxed a little more. "Austin, I'm going to be frank. I ran my pack like I did, and stuck with it as long as I did, out of duty. My life was about protecting my sisters' futures. And now I find myself in a world where they are in jeopardy again. If someone can nearly take down a pack like Kingsley's, there's nothing to stop them."

"Except us."

"Right." John ran his fingers through his shaggy hair. "Except us. I have a duty to my sisters, as I said, and to the magical world at large, as do you. As do we all. I cannot, in good conscience, turn a blind eye when I am able to help."

Austin felt his confusion show on his face.

John smirked, allowing himself to be just as expressive. "Thought I was about to say thanks, but no thanks, huh?"

"Yes, as a matter of fact."

"The last test, I guess. I just had to make sure, because I don't really want to be saying this, but I feel I have no choice." He took a deep breath. "I can help you sway the shifters. I still have pull."

"I'd imagine you still have a lot of pull, but won't that be a sticky situation for your former pack? Don't they think you are exiled or dead?"

John's lips tweaked into a smile. "Is there no end to your honor? I could greatly help you and you're more worried about the people of a pack you have no ties with."

"I'm an alpha. Taking care of others is my job. It doesn't matter if they are my people or not, they don't deserve to have their lives ripped apart by having to choose—allegiance to you and this convocation, or to their pack and your sisters."

John nodded slowly. His gaze was hyper-focused on Austin, reading him. "True. You're shaping up to be a very good man, Austin Steele, an alpha worthy of the king of the mountain status. Quite the change from the little Barazza boy who terrorized his pack."

"In some ways, yes."

"In many ways. I've been watching." He took another sip of his drink. "I've spoken to my sisters and then chastised them for not telling me how serious this mage problem is. They didn't want to worry me, apparently. They want me to get on with my life. They've had mage visits. Many, it seems, in groups and once in a crowd. So far, they've been able to run those mages away. This was before the attack on Kingsley. The visits have totally stopped since that battle. They get the feeling the mages are regrouping."

A shock of adrenaline coursed through Austin that made him tense. Niamh would want that information.

John gave a tiny nod, reading Austin's thought. "My sisters are highly intelligent and excellent at their jobs. But they are shifters. Rather than reaching out to Kingsley to compare notes or contact you—both strangers—they collected their pack friends. They thought more numbers than Kingsley had would be enough."

"And they'd be annihilated."

John took a deep breath. "I've realized that. My sisters are going to talk to our pack and explain why I really left. I'm sure most of them suspect. Once that is smoothed over, I will use what pull I still have to help you. On a few conditions."

Austin kept from widening his eyes. Having Golden Fang as a backer would be huge. *Huge.* It would push this thing in leaps and bounds. Unlike that cairn leader, Austin was prepared to offer him the absolute world.

"Which are?" he said evenly, not giving anything away.

The other man took a sip. "I will not join your pack. If I tried to fit myself into your hierarchy, inevitably I'd have to pit myself against Sue."

That was true. John had ten times more experience, and he was raised to be in a leadership role. He didn't come to it late, like Sue had. He'd fall into the role without thinking, and eventually people would turn to him rather than Sue. Eventually, they'd have to battle for dominance, and John would win.

"Sue is exceptional in his place," John went on. "He's a better fit for this convocation. He understands it, and he wants it. I don't want to get in the way of that, even if I wanted to be in a pack at all."

It spoke highly of John's sense of responsibility and overall regard for the people that he recognized that and had acted upon it. It was clear what had made him such a good leader.

"But I do want to be in the convocation," John went on. "Just like that cairn leader, and everyone in your crew, I believe in it. I can bolster it. I can add power and might and fit within the chaos. The stint in the bar told me that."

"Except you can't fly. You'd have to be in the ground crew. Don't get me wrong, John, I want your help. Only an idiot wouldn't. But you'd still be able to undermine Broc—Sue."

"And that's my next condition. To have a place, I ask that you give me a specialized force. Find me more rogues. Give me the wild shifters that have a hard time existing in a civilized pack. Send me the lost causes. You and Sue will be busy managing the bulk of the shifters. You won't have time for the troublemakers. Give them to me. Let me shape them into your overall battle image. And let me work under Jessie and with her people. You can call me a special unit, part of the convocation. I can work with the basajaunak, also a ground crew. I know you might worry that I'd use that force to—"

Austin held up his hand, knowing where John was going with that. "I told you before, I'm not worried about you taking over this pack. My relationship with Jess, and how my life has been shaped, makes me uniquely suited to handle my role here. You wouldn't be able to. No one would. Trust me, you wouldn't want to."

John laughed and took another sip. "Fair enough and true. Very true. People who try to challenge you for this pack are mad."

"As to the special force, that's a good idea, and I might just claim it."

John laughed again. "Fair enough," he repeated.

"Give me a week to check in with efforts here and make sure things are running smoothly—"

"I'd like to shadow you, if I could. No one needs to know who I am, yet."

Austin hesitated. This guy was really on board. He wasn't just helping, he was re-emerging. He was stepping back into the world of the shifters, and he was doing it under Jess and Austin's umbrella. Holy hell. The little Barazza black sheep, the kid who would never amount to anything, was currently having a meeting as an equal with Yazanth Golden Fang.

Was this real life?

"Fine," Austin said, playing it cool "We'll go with the special force and say you need to be brought up to speed. It's true, after all. Your power and posturing will make that a no-brainer. You can tell people who you are in your own time."

"At the Alpha Conclave," John said in a firm voice. "Armendale is going to be gunning for you. He won't like the power you are amassing. He won't like someone trying to take his place as the king of the mountain, a position he only has because no one is contesting him."

"My brother doesn't have the power."

"No, your brother doesn't have the wildness to attempt it, and in so doing, upset the status quo. No one does. Except me. And now you. My time is done. It's your turn to knock that jackass down a peg. But it won't be just brawn. It'll be political. He's going to amass his followers and throw his weight around."

"He was always going to do that. I never thought he'd join, but I have always intended to shove my power in his face and give people a new voice to listen to."

John nodded, his eyes twinkling. "I can help. I will step forward as part of the convocation and Jessie's team. My sisters and former pack will step forward with me, and by then, so will their pack friends. I'm going to fly one of them out to meet the team and give them some talking points. You'll have me, my old pack, and their network. Plus, what you've already amassed. We'll give Armendale a little shock and some much-needed opposition."

"And I assume you'll get even for how he's treating your sisters."

John laughed. "If we can't be petty, what even is the point?" He sobered up. "But I will caution you—an Alpha Conclave will be incredibly dangerous. Chaotic. It might be mayhem with all that power. There'll be deaths, and you might end up worse than you started, if you make it out at all."

Austin huffed out a laugh. "It'll be more than that because we're not just inviting shifters. And we'll manage it because we must. We have no choice but to succeed. Failure is not an option."

John was quiet for a long time, studying Austin as he sipped his drink. Austin let him, knowing the other man was sizing him up.

"In this, as with the convocation, I think you and Jessie are uniquely suited to see it through," he finally said, shaking his head. "You deal with chaos and danger on the regular. Sue took me through the town on the way here. You're primed, and you already seem to handle a *lot* of power." He blew out a breath. "Well, I'm on hand to help, as I've said." He held up a finger. "I'm not going back on my word. I'm not joining a pack. I am joining the Ivy House crew and corresponding convocation."

"It's the details," Austin said with a grin. It slipped away slowly. "I'm sure you know that this is…beyond helpful. This'll push us forward an incredible amount. Your help is a blessing I never would've dreamed of. This is all highly unexpected."

"For myself, included. Yours and Tristan's teams are inspiring. You've done incredible things with them. But Jessie's team is special. Odd. Horribly so. But very special. I find that I fit in there, and I've been told it's the beginning of the end for me because of it."

Austin laughed. "Very likely."

"I'll independently talk to Jessie about all this, of

course, but I know she'll say yes. She's gone out of her way to help me. I see now why Sue and Tristan think she is the glue. Because she is."

"Yes. I couldn't do any of this without her."

"No, you couldn't. What is it Jessie keeps saying as a mantra? If we *can* help, we *should*. She's right. And this time I don't have to do it on my own. It'll be nice to join a team rather than create and lead one for once, I'm not going to lie. I would like to ask a favor, though."

Austin sipped his drink and waited, still prepared to offer the world.

"My sisters are too…humble, apparently. I hear you know your way around being a showy bastard. They might need your help. I was always more focused on being a scary bastard. I never really worried about flaunting my money and looking like a peacock. My sisters didn't get any training on that front."

"I know something about that, definitely." He laughed. "I was the black sheep younger brother, after all. Nessa and Sebastian are also excellent. Tristan. We have a few divas in this outfit."

John smirked. "I'd appreciate it." He nodded and started to rise but hesitated. He clearly didn't want to, finding himself just as relaxed as Austin was.

"Please." Austin gestured at the plate. "Have a sandwich. Mr. Tom would be all too happy to give you abuse about it while he brings in another couple."

John laughed gratefully. "I'll take you up on that, thanks. Despite the house's antics this place is comfortable. I might take Jessie up on staying here for a while. There's obviously plenty of room."

"Plenty, yes. She'd be happy to have you. She likes to make sure people are fitting in."

"The glue," John murmured with a little smile.

LATER THAT NIGHT, with Jess sleeping soundly and the darkness laying heavy across the backyard of Ivy House, Austin sat at the little table in their room and called his brother.

"This better be urgent," Kingsley answered in a sleepy voice.

"You will never believe who has just moved into Ivy House." He was going to let John declare himself on his own terms, but some things you had to share with family just to make them real. "You're sworn to secrecy."

He heard the shuffle of the phone as Kingsley moved around.

"Who I shared a meal with in the little study," Austin continued. "Who I talked about pack politics with and who I am bringing into our crew as a specialized unit."

"Who?" Kingsley asked. "It better be someone good after all this build-up."

He paused for a moment. Butterflies filled his stomach. "Yazanth Golden Fang."

The silence stretched. And stretched.

"Fuck off," Kingsley finally said. "No way. No *way*! Are you serious? It's really him?"

"The legend in the flesh."

"I studied everything that guy did. I owe a lot of my early enforcer strategy to him. And you shared a meal with him?" The breath went out of Kingsley. "Unreal. How did this all come about? I heard he was exiled, though that didn't make much sense. That he was dead, too, but no body ever turned up, obviously, so that was highly suspect."

"I heard of a rogue, went to offer him a place to live, and that ferocious beast came bursting out of the trees. Jesus, Kingsley, the stories don't do him justice. I had a moment of panic before I got my senses together. He has a…*way* about him. People gravitate to him."

"Power?"

"A little less than mine. I could take him, but it would be a knock-down, bloody, ear-detaching sort of fight. He'd give me a run for my money. He is what we've always heard."

"And he's with you?"

Austin shook his head, looking out at the grounds. "Yes. I can hardly believe it myself. He's going to smooth things out with his former pack before he declares himself. He wants to help. He's in it for the same reasons you tried to start this thing. For the reasons I am doing this. He's legit."

Kingsley swore. "That is great for the cause, and I am also unreasonably jealous."

Austin laughed quietly, hearing the respect and teasing in his brother's voice. "Don't be. It wasn't me that swayed him. It was Jess and her crew. He wants to be slotted within her team."

He told his brother the particulars.

"That's a good idea," Kingsley affirmed. "Maybe he'll bring a little order to that motley crew."

"I'm not taking bets on it." Austin grinned.

"Well, it'll at least give her clout in the shifter world. That's what she sorely needs. It's really the best place he could've gone."

"That's what I was thinking. After I'd fallen over myself accepting his help, obviously."

"Obviously," Kingsley said, and laughed.

"Also—and I won't announce this yet either—I'm going to put on an Alpha Conclave. That's where he's going to announce himself and that his sisters are joining the convocation."

Austin laid out his plan, summarizing most of it. When he was done, the pause was longer this time.

"No," Kingsley said. "That's too far, Austin. Don't let having Golden Fang join your crew go to your head. With that much power amassed, a conclave is suicide."

"I decided before him, and it's happening. Clear your schedule, because you're going to help us plan it."

Kingsley let out a string of curses, a prayer, and then acceptance. Austin's brother would always be there for him.

And now they had a secret weapon, but it wasn't Golden Fang. These shifters liked to show off? Then Austin would make sure their efforts paled in comparison to the wonder that was Ivy House and its mistress.

ABOUT THE AUTHOR

K.F. Breene is a Wall Street Journal, USA Today, Washington Post, Amazon Most Sold Charts and #1 Kindle Store bestselling author of paranormal romance, urban fantasy and fantasy novels. With millions of books sold, when she's not penning stories about magic and what goes bump in the night, she's sipping wine and planning shenanigans. She lives in Northern California with her husband, two children, and out of work treadmill.

Sign up for her newsletter to hear about the latest news and receive free bonus content.

www.kfbreene.com